AT BUFFALO

The Invention of a New
American Poetry

T0164521

Edited by
Sean Pears

First published 2020 by Lake Forest College Press.

Carnegie Hall
Lake Forest College
555 N. Sheridan Road
Lake Forest, IL 60045

lakeforest.edu

Lake Forest College Press publishes in the broad
spaces of Chicago studies. Our imprint, &NOW
Books, publishes innovative and conceptual
literature and serves as the publishing arm of the
&NOW writers' conference and organization.

ISBN: 978-1-941423-06-6

Library of Congress:

Book Design by Emma O'Hagan

Printed in the United States

LAKE FOREST
COLLEGE
PRESS

CONTENTS

Form, Politics, and Pedagogy:
A Long History of Poetics at the University at Buffalo

Sean Pears 1

FROM THE POETRY COLLECTION
TO THE SUNY ENGLISH DEPARTMENT 11

Origins to 1978:
The University at Buffalo's Poetry Collection

Michael Basinski 13

When Buffalo Became Buffalo

Michael Anania 21

Olson's Buffalo

Michael Boughn 33

Charles Olson: Recollections

Albert Glover 47

Buffalo English: Literary Glory Days at UB

Bruce Jackson 57

Vernacular Pedagogy: Buffalo in the late 1960s

Michael Davidson 63

FRONTIER CITY 71

Some Poetic Debts to Buffalo

Carl Dennis 73

Buffalo's Outriders Poetry Project

Max Wickert 79

Excerpt from the Introduction to Just in Time: Poems 1984-1994

Robert Creeley 89

Excerpt from "Robert and Books [on Creeley's Library]"

Penelope Creeley 95

I Have Forgotten All Human Relations, But Not Poetry

Debora Ott 101

Editing, Not A Democracy: Working (or my small press mentorship)
with Robert Creeley on the Black Mountain II Review
Stephanie Weisman 105

Poetry on the Moon: Buffalo 1977
Peter Middleton 111

Across the Frontier: Buffalo's Border Poetic Communities
Steve McCaffery 123

FOUNDING THE POETICS PROGRAM 127

Poetics Program Flyer 128

Excerpt from "A Blow Is Like an Instrument:
The Poetic Imaginary and Curricular Practices"
Charles Bernstein 131

Some Questions and Answers for Raymond Federman
Charles Bernstein & Raymond Federman 141

"There Are Not Leaves Enough to Crown to Cover to Crown to Cover"
Susan Howe 145

Zwischen den Linden:
The Electronic Poetry Center & the Technologies of Imagination
Loss Pequeño Glazier 149

Buffalo Symphysis: A Growing Together of Site and Small Press Poetry
Geoffrey Gatza 159

Gender Trouble
Juliana Spahr 163

Toward a Telling: Notes in Memory of Dennis Tedlock
Rosa Alcalá 169

POETICS FOR THE MILLENNIUM 173

Excerpt from "Ear Turned Toward the Emergent"
Myung Mi Kim 175

"Once we leave a place is it there": Radical Pedagogy
Andrew Rippeon 185

Routes in "This Ecstatic Nation":
The ABCs of Growing as a Poet-Translator-Critic in Buffalo

Eun-Gwi Chung 191

The Poetics Program and the Poetry Collection,
2001 to Present (A Personal History)

James Maynard 201

Once and Future Buffalo Poetics:
(The Next) 25 Years Conference

Evelyn Reilly 207

APPENDIX A:
TIMELINE OF THE UNIVERSITY AT BUFFALO
POETRY AND POETICS 213

APPENDIX B:
CHECKLIST OF THE PUBLICATIONS OF
FRONTIER PRESS, 1965-1972

Michael Boughn 217

APPENDIX C:
CHECKLIST OF THE PUBLICATIONS OF THE
INSTITUTE OF FURTHER STUDIES, 1969-1997

Michael Boughn 225

APPENDIX D:
POETRY IN THE MAKING: A BIBLIOGRAPHY OF
PUBLICATIONS BY GRADUATE STUDENTS IN THE POETICS
PROGRAM, UNIVERSITY AT BUFFALO, 1991-2016

James Maynard 229

CONTRIBUTORS 251

FORM, POLITICS, AND PEDAGOGY: A LONG HISTORY OF POETICS AT THE UNIVERSITY AT BUFFALO

Sean Pears

The University at Buffalo has for decades been associated with innovations in American poetry and poetics. In general, *poetics* refers to how a piece of literature was made or produces its effects, and so the term can be found in the titles of books across every sub-specialization in literary studies. But at Buffalo, it has a unique history. *Poetics* has often referred, at least in part, to a particular theory of academic pedagogy: that people who consider themselves primarily poets can be well-suited to teach graduate-level courses on literature, even if they lack the academic credentials that are traditionally prerequisite (i.e., a doctorate and/or substantial scholarly publication). It offers the chance to bring scholarship closer to the scene of composition, the unstable space of generation. The teaching of literature by poets without traditional credentials is not, however, unique to the University at Buffalo. Evan Kindley's recent study of the development of "poet-critics" argues that they were the product of the Great Depression: modernist poets turned to the shelter of the university after the market crash depleted the wealth of private patrons. In his article "How Poets Learned to Stop Worrying and Love the Academy," Kindley identifies John Crowe Ransom's work at Kenyon College as significant in the establishment of the role of the university "poet-critic." But few people, now or ever, associate Ransom's work with Buffalo, or *poetics*.

Poetics at Buffalo is perhaps centrally associated with the Poetics Program, founded in 1991. The founders of the Poetics Program intentionally left its core concept amorphously defined. James Maynard writes in his introduction to his 2016 bibliography of Poetics Program publications that "the defining vision of the program is based on an anti-foundational understanding of poetry—i.e. the processural activity of *poiesis*—as a liminal field always evolving out of its multiform past in response to the overlapping aesthetic, social, and political needs of the present" (see Appendix D). Put simply, *poetics* at Buffalo is the site of its own constant redefinition. As this collection shows, the founding of the Poetics Program inaugurated a radically new set of institutions and practices, while also representing the culmination of a long history of anti-foundational, processural, multiform engagement with poetry that extends back at least to the work of Charles Olson in the early 1960s, and indeed even farther. Through sketches, firsthand accounts, and interpretive essays from students and faculty who spent time at the University at Buffalo—some for decades, some for a few days—this collection offers a history of that development, primarily at the university, and secondarily in some of the waves sent out across the city and around the world.

This collection is not a comprehensive or focused study on the founding of the Poetics Program; when such a study is produced, it will be an invaluable complement to this work. This collection tells a longer history of the institutional and intellectual origins of the study of poetry at the University at Buffalo, beginning in the 1920s, and using the term *poetics* to trace a constellation of activities and engagement. The university's faculty of renowned poet-critics—Charles Olson, Robert Creeley, Charles Bernstein, Susan Howe, Dennis Tedlock, Steve McCaffery, Myung Mi Kim, and Judith Goldman—are central to this history. Many of these faculty members were or are "Core Faculty" in the Poetics Program. But the broader institution of the university, and various non-academic institutions in the city, are mutually constitutive agents in the development of this legacy. Poetics is larger than the Buffalo English department, and the Buffalo English department is larger than Poetics. This is even more true for the city of Buffalo. The essays that comprise this collection are heterogeneous in their form and content. They are written primarily by students who studied poetry at the university, though there are also essays by and interviews with faculty members, as well as their colleagues, friends and family. As a whole, it most closely resembles an oral history, but it is an oral history in which the majority of the contributors are trained scholars, specialized in analyzing the formation and development of communities of poets and writers. Naturally, in many cases they apply some of the analytic strategies and vocabularies of their field to reflect on their own experiences. This is both unusual (for an oral history) and uniquely illuminating, but readers should question the guise of disinterested investigation that is sometimes produced. A common maxim: never trust poets writing about their own work. That holds here. In certain cases, key figures chose to avoid this odd rhetorical situation altogether, and are represented by excerpts from interviews or previously published essays. In some cases, Charles Bernstein—one of the main founders and architects of the Poetics Program—kindly provided editorial introductions for these excerpts. The pieces reveal a history of intense collaboration within tightly-knit communities. They also reveal a history of intense conflict: with and within the larger world of literature and politics, the city that hosts the university, the university that hosts the department, and the department itself. This collection attempts to provide an expansive view of those communities and those conflicts.

In 1962, the private University of Buffalo merged with the State University of New York system and saw an influx of money and institutional support; Albert Cook, who had just been appointed Chair of the English Department, decided the following year to hire poet Charles Olson as a visiting professor to teach classes on Modern Poetry and Myth and Literature. If Olson's arrival is a foundational event in the legacy of Buffalo poetry and poetics, the preparations for that moment began at least a generation earlier (before anyone had heard of the "poet-critic") with the initial establishment of the Poetry Collection as part of the university's libraries. The Poetry Collection is perhaps the longest lasting and the most significant symbol of the institutional support that the University at Buffalo has given to the study of poetry. Today the Poetry Collection is, as Michael Basinski writes in his essay on its history, "one of the world's most significant institutional libraries for the study of twentieth century poetry and twenty-first century poetry, a destination library, and a capitol in the geography that is the realm of the poem" (see his essay in this volume). The Poetry Collection began in the early 1930s, after bibliophile and lover of modernist poetry Charles Abbott founded the archive in the newly-constructed Lockwood Memorial Library. Abbott's unique idea was to write letters to contemporary poets asking them for their drafts and worksheets, the parts of the poem that typically ended up in the wastebasket. This interest in the material processes of poem-making was uncommon in the 1930s, but wound up anticipating much of the guiding ethos of poetry and poetics at Buffalo, as well as a broader interest in genetic scholarship in literary studies as a whole, which increased over the century.

Michael Anania speculates in his essay that the Poetry Collection was instrumental in drawing Charles Olson to Buffalo. He also shows that the Poetry Collection was one of many cultural institutions (including for innovative dance, theater, and art) funded by the city's industrial past. Anania, Michael Boughn, and Albert Glover all present perspectives on the fomentation of intellectual and creative energy around poetry that Olson's presence contributed to this moment. Given the brevity of his tenure at Buffalo, Olson's influence is remarkable. One gets a strong sense of the force of his personality—his theater of gruff masculinity, both inside and outside the classroom—described in Anania's essay in this volume as "pure politics, LBJ or Tip O'Neill rounding up votes." Embodied performance (his height and physical presence, his mannerisms) was crucial not only to Olson's interpersonal relations, but to his understanding of poetry, literature, and pedagogy. These essays give a detailed portrait of how the poet who wrote "Projective Verse" translated an emphasis on embodied reading, listening, and writing into the university classroom. It is easy to imagine that this voluminous personality could have been at once deeply intoxicating and deeply alienating, depending on whether one was inside or outside of its circle. Critics of that circle, as Boughn explains, often describe it in religious terms: Olson is the "High Priest," his former students the "disciples," or "acolytes." Given the mysticism imbricated in Olson's own theories of literature (or, for that matter, in the messianic parables that comprise Glover's essay), such terms may not be altogether inappropriate. Boughn suggests, however, that Olson himself conceived of "community" as a space for the mutual constitution of individual subjectivity in ways that complicate notions of hierarchy, genius, and individual power, anticipating Post-Structuralist theorist Jean-Luc Nancy's notion of "being singular plural."

One can see this emphasis on rethinking conventional modes of hierarchy and community, at least on the level of literary form, in the publication projects of that period. In 1965, poets Jack Clark, Fred Wah, George Butterick, Boughn and Glover began printing *The Magazine of Further Studies* in an attempt to disrupt traditional, "showcase model," publishing practices that presented poems as decontextualized, hermetic art objects. Instead, their journal aimed to publish, "fragments, challenges, responses, broken utterances that provoked other broken, incomplete utterances, so that by the final issue, the magazine has become a kind of clamor, a convocation of a conversation, in action" (see Boughn's essay in this volume). Part of the point of this fragmentary aesthetic was to decenter the role of the single author as proprietor of the text. In the impulse to reconsider and reimagine institutional publishing practices, especially using the small press as a vehicle, *The Magazine of Further Studies* inaugurates part of what will come to define Buffalo poetry and poetics. So too, this period was characterized by an interest in unsettling and loosening the narrow specialization of advanced literary studies, and broadening its disciplinary scope. As Anania writes in this volume, Olson's lectures—ranging across "neurology, geology, linguistics, history, music, dance, perception, proprioception, myth and early politics"—anticipated attitudes toward disciplinary boundaries taken up by the Poetics Program in the 1990s. As Charles Bernstein writes at the opening of the excerpt of his essay: "There are no core subjects, no core texts in the humanities, and this is the grand democratic vista of our mutual endeavor in arts and letters…" Olson's legacy at Buffalo is today a source of controversy, but it is incontrovertible.

Even in Olson's tenure at Buffalo, he was, however, only one poet and one scholar among many. The intellectual and political energies fueled by the Civil Rights movement and opposition to the Vietnam War, coupled with a generous English department budget that enabled expansive hiring of prestigious faculty, generated an atmosphere at the University at Buffalo in the mid- to late 1960s that Bruce Jackson dubs the "literary glory days." Robert Creeley, Leslie Fiedler, John Logan, Lionel Abe, John Barth, Donald Barthelme, Irving Feldman, William Sylvester, Robert Hass, John Coetzee, Raymond Federman, René Girard, Michel Foucault, Hélène Cixous, John Sullivan, is a short-list of renowned writers and scholars who came to Buffalo in that period, either to teach or to visit. Michael Davidson recalls as well the investment in innovative art outside of the university, embodied in the 1968 Buffalo Festival of the Arts, which featured performances, concerts, and readings by John Cage, Morton Feldman, Iannis Xenakis, Luicano Berio, Louis Zukofsky, Robin Blaser, and Allen Ginsberg. He recalls too that this same period was the beginning of rapid de-industrialization that devastated Buffalo's working-class population; part of what allowed artists and academics to purchase turn-of-the-century mansions in the city was massive labor outsourcing in the 1960s and 1970s that drove down property value. The cultural vibrancy of the surrounding city (even as its industry was exported), and the ephemeral and impromptu learning environments that it offered, provides the background for a pre-institutional poetics program described by Davidson.

Given this vital linkage between poets and the city's institutions in the 1960s, the university's decision to move its central operations—including the English department—to a new campus fifteen miles outside of downtown (in Amherst, a municipality in the northern suburbs) fundamentally re-shaped *poetics* at Buffalo. Mark Goldman writes in his history of Buffalo, *City on the Edge* (2007), about the pressure from various community activists and politicians who lobbied for an alternate downtown waterfront plot for the new campus. But the SUNY trustees were resolute in their selection of Amherst. According to Goldman, endless speculation continues to surround that decision, including theories that the university trustees had a financial stake in the Amherst property, that downtown business leaders were averse to students' political radicalism, or that the downtown plot was simply deemed too small for the university's ambitious growth plans. Whatever lay behind the move to Amherst, it is reflected in the essays from the 1970s and '80s, perhaps most poignantly in Peter Middleton's account of arriving as a graduate student in

1977. Compare the intimacy and ephemerality of Davidson's "pre-institutional poetics program" to Middleton's account in his essay in this volume: "SUNY Buffalo as a whole felt vast and as confident as a skyscraper corporation." As the University at Buffalo transformed into a massive corporate-style state commuter school, intellectual and creative energies around poetry (both in the city and on campus) never went away, but their contours and qualities changed significantly.

One major change was the establishment of new institutions that would supplant the university as a cultural center for the promotion of poetry and the literary arts in Buffalo. Most significant was the founding in 1975 of The Just Buffalo Literary Center by Debora Ott, one of Robert Creeley's former students, turned colleague and friend. Part of Ott's explicit purpose with Just Buffalo was to appeal to a broad and diverse community of Buffalonians in their selection of poets and writers, including inviting poets who might engage the city's large African American population. Though neither is often invoked in relation to Buffalo *poetics*, two of the most influential African American poets of the 20th century have a deep connection to the city: Lucille Clifton was born and raised in Buffalo; Ishmael Reed moved to the city as a young child, and attended the University at Buffalo as an undergraduate. Another important institution for the promotion of poetry in the city was the Outriders project, run by Max Wickert, a professor in the Buffalo English department for most of his long career. What one sees in the essays from this period, including in that by poet Carl Dennis (who also taught in the English department for decades) is a commitment to engage the local: to participate in local politics, to promote local poetry, to engage local audiences. Behind this commitment seems to be the suggestion that such engagement had been made difficult, perhaps not only by the university's relocation but also by its shifting aesthetic and intellectual preoccupations. This era saw the rise of French Post-structuralism and Deconstruction in the American academy, along with the emergence of "Language poetry," another heavily contested term that would come to be strongly associated with Buffalo after the foundation of the Poetics Program. The emphasis on difficulty and opacity that these movements share may have further contributed to the perceived rift between the English department and the city's literary arts.

It is tempting to see the increasing obscurity of academic discourse around poetry and the transplantation of the English department into the wealthy northern suburbs as related, if only in some cosmic sense. Certainly, both have profoundly shaped the Poetics Program as it exists today. But does one find in the essays collected here a development toward exclusion and elitism, or simply an epochal shift that makes room for new perspectives, while marginalizing others? Was Charles Olson, for example, writing "accessible" poetry? Even more to the point, the one figure whose presence and influence in Buffalo bridges the long period from the late '60s through the foundation of the Poetics Program is Robert Creeley, whose poetry was widely read and appreciated, and who was famous for his love for and cultivation of his "company," an expansive network of poet-friends. Creeley's charm, indefatigability, and commitment to poetry made him an institution unto himself. If his presence is monumental, it is a monument to intimacy; as he says in his interview with Charles Bernstein reprinted here, he wanted poetry readings to generate the feeling of a story told among friends in the living room. Indeed, many in Buffalo still recall today the actual living room that he and his partner Penelope Creeley maintained as a site for the appreciation of poetry. In Penelope's portrait of Robert's care and attention to his books, and in Stephanie Weisman's account of his editorial mentorship, we can trace the contours of a personality characterized by a deep and infectious commitment to poetry. As we can see from Max Wickert's strange, quasi-gothic tale of being trapped in a room with him, Creeley's presence, while more oriented toward the domestic, was no less masculine and intimidating than Olson's. If Olson was Ahab, perhaps Creeley was closer to Ishmael.

The prevailing sense in Peter Middleton's expansive essay on Buffalo in the late 1970s is, however, that Creeley—and perhaps poetry in the Buffalo English department more generally—was caught in a "lunar eclipse," with a "widespread sense of needing to relocate its happenstance." A decade later, a new vision and organizational coherence would arrive with tremendous force with the hiring of Susan Howe and Charles Bernstein, and the establishment of the Poetics Program in 1991. The program flyer that is reprinted on page 107 provides the most succinct overview of the Poetics Program's vision, which is in many ways a reflection of the eclectic group of "Core Faculty" that it lists: Robert Creeley's innovation's in lyric poetry, awakening the beauty in the syntax of everyday language; Charles Bernstein's work editing $L=A=N=G=U=A=G=E$, one of the focal points in a movement of re-conceptualizing poetic expression and the terms between writer and reader; Raymond Federman's development of "surfiction," blending realist fiction and Surrealism; Susan Howe's use of visual arts praxis in poetry, combined with her feminist revisionist scholarship; Dennis Tedlock's application of contemporary poetics to cultural anthropology in his work on Mayan and Native American poetry. Part of why it is difficult to define *poetics* at Buffalo is that it was originally conceived as a highly interdisciplinary and inter-generic field of study. These writers share a radical stance toward the literary hegemony of the day, both in relation to its methodology and its canon. In the excerpts from interviews with and essays by the Poetics Program's original Core Faculty, one can also identify a commitment to reinventing the ways that history is captured by language. As Susan Howe writes in her introduction to *Europe of Trusts*, excerpted here, "time and again, questions of assigning *the cause* of history dictate the sound of what is thought."

One common misconception (perhaps only increasingly prevalent as PhDs in Creative Writing become more numerous), is that the Poetics Program is a creative writing degree. At its beginning, its founders decided to house the program within the English department, and so its graduate students are beholden to the department's course requirements, and write traditional dissertations. The department does, however, offer an unusually high proportion of courses on twentieth- and twenty-first-century poetry and poetics, focusing especially on modernism, avant-garde movements, radical feminist writing, and various formally innovative post-war and contemporary poetries. It has also produced a remarkable number of successful poet-critics, including Carla Billiterri, Ben Friedlander, and Juliana Spahr, whose essay on gender and politics during her tenure as a graduate student in the early 1990s begins on page 135. In addition to the success of its faculty and students, the program's influence and recognition can be accounted for in part by the work of Loss Pequeño Glazier in establishing the Electronic Poetry Center (EPC). According to Glazier in his essay in this volume, this massive online archive of innovative poetry, when it launched in 1994, was for a few seconds "not just the largest poetry site in the world but the largest site of any type in the world." The EPC was a natural complement to the Poetry Collection, and also a radically new format for poetry and poetics, with its own limitations and possibilities that have only begun to receive more serious critical attention. The early embrace of the digital helped publicize the Poetic Program's work and vision to an audience far outside of the Buffalo area.

The Poetics Program as it exists today is largely shaped by a turn-over in faculty in the mid-2000s. In 2003 alone, Charles Bernstein left for the University of Pennsylvania, Robert Creeley left for Brown University, and Myung Mi Kim was hired as a new faculty in Poetics. The following year, Steve McCaffery—a poet with a long relationship to Buffalo—was appointed to the David Gray endowed chair previously occupied by Creeley. In 2006, Susan Howe retired. While many of the institutions and the intellectual preoccupations of the Poetics Program were retained, the new faculty recalibrated the primary disciplinary focus, particularly in the direction of translation and translatability. This same period also saw broader shifts in literary studies toward an interest in postcolonial studies, transnationalism, and borders, as well as developments in queer and gender theory, critical race theory, and the emergence of disability studies. One finds in the interview with Myung Mi Kim reprinted here, as well as the essay written by graduate student Eun-Gwi Chung, a distinct interest in the failures or gaps or impossibilities that surround the project of translation, a committed attention to things that cannot be said or articulated, or have been repressed somehow from expression or representation. So too, McCaffery's essay focuses on cross-cultural and transnational borders and boundaries as sites for the productive transfer of creative energy. He shows that—in part purely as a result of geography—Buffalo has for decades been a hub for cross-fertilization between Canadian and American innovative writers.

While the university continues to grow its student body each year, the population of the city of Buffalo has continued to steadily fall from its height in the 1950s. For a city of its size, there are a startling number of poetry readings each year. Many of the most high-profile and well-attended readings are organized by the Just Buffalo Literary Center, now under the direction of Barbara Cole (who also received her PhD in the Poetics Program). A literary map of Buffalo, produced by poet and Poetics student Joe Hall shows the contemporary constellation of poetic happenings in the city. The Poetry Collection at the university continues to be a vibrant hub, under the curatorial guidance of another Poetics PhD, James Maynard. Maynard writes of the almost overwhelming publishing activity among Poetics students, fueled in part by funding from the program's endowed chairs. These publications are one space in which contestations over poetic form and contemporary politics continue to be fiercely waged. In 2010, Poetics students Holly Melgard, Chris Sylvester, Joey Yearous-Algozin, and Divya Victor started Troll Thread, publishing books online and through on-demand printing services. In an interview with Tan Lin on the Poetry Foundation website, Sylvester describes the tumblr page that eventually became Troll Thread as "a platform for other work or work by others that is as pointless, sloppy, or unwieldy as my own." The notion that poetry should troll—provoke, harass, or even wound—its reader (or at least its reader's sensibilities) perhaps reflects a more widespread sentiment. Another current graduate publication is titled Hostile Books.

These "hostile" publications perhaps reflect a broader shift in *poetics* at Buffalo, and in literary studies as a field, from the post-war optimism of the 1960s to a discourse characterized more generally by pessimism and negative critique. This is eminently palpable in the essay written by Evelyn Reilly on the "Poetics: (The Next) 25 Years Conference," a conference held in Buffalo in April 2016 to commemorate the 25th anniversary of the founding of the Poetics Program, organized by Myung Mi Kim, graduate student Allison Cardon, poetry scholar and then department chair Cristanne Miller, and Judith Goldman, a poet-critic hired to the poetics "Core Faculty" in 2012. Reilly, in her essay in this volume, "Once and Future Buffalo Poetics," describes the millenarian tone of the conference, "the usual side references to impending catastrophe, nervous acknowledgements of the frailty of our current circumstances, including our poetic endeavors, which were in this case heightened by the almost quaint hopefulness represented by the carefully tended archives of the Poetry Collection." The hope for the next twenty-five years of poetics expressed in Reilly's incisive essay is highly qualified, an expression of hope that foregrounds cultural and political divisions, as well as anxiety over the existential threats facing the planet and the human race. Commingling with these broader anxieties are those around more acute threats to the existence of *poetics* at Buffalo, as undergraduate English enrollment continues to fall and the university continues to divest from the humanities. At the time of the writing of this essay, university administrators maintain a freeze on hiring to replace Dennis Tedlock, who died in June 2016.

Though it is at this point probably eminently clear, Reilly's essay also addresses a fact that ought to be explicitly noted: the history of *poetics* at Buffalo was for a long time dominated—in its culture, faculty, and canon—by white men. Considering the broader context of American poetry and literary studies over this period, this is not altogether remarkable. What is perhaps more remarkable is the extent to which this legacy remains. Despite having a more diverse core faculty, and far more diversity in the poets and writers who are invited to read and who appear on course syllabi, graduate students in the Poetics Program are still overwhelming white and overwhelmingly male. And even while the Poetics Program faculty becomes more diverse, the faculty across the university as a whole is becoming *less* diverse: African-Americans represent less than two percent of tenure-track faculty, and the number is falling. As one former graduate student (who forcefully declined my solicitation for an essay on their experience at Buffalo) pointed out, this fact cannot be changed by simply making a more diverse table of contents. My efforts to complicate the legacy of Buffalo *poetics* along the lines of race and gender in this collection largely failed, and perhaps that makes it, unfortunately, representative. A more comprehensive history of poetry and poetics *outside* of the university, in the surrounding city and region, would perhaps yield a more diverse set of figures. It would certainly include the decades-long work of *Earth's Daughters*, a feminist collective formed in 1970s by Judith Kerman, as well as that of *White Pine Press*, an independent publisher of world literature, or *Slipstream Press*, an annual anthology of small press poetry located in Niagara Falls, just north of Buffalo. Such a history of poetics in the city, when it comes, will be a felicitous complement to this study of poetics at the university.

I want to extend a deep note of appreciation to all of the people who made this book project possible. The current faculty in the Buffalo English department, especially Cristanne Miller, Stacey Hubbard, Bruce Jackson, Myung Mi Kim, Judith Goldman, and Steve McCaffery for taking time to be interviewed on Buffalo history and for their thoughts and guidance on the project. James Maynard, Curator of the Poetry Collection, for his frequent and indispensable assistance and encouragement throughout, along with Alison Fraser in the Poetry Collection. Penelope Creeley for guidance, stories, and great conversation. George Life for his deep knowledge of, and love for, Buffalo's poetry history, and also for assistance in communicating with faculty. Charles Bernstein and Michael Anania for useful guidance on the table of contents and the shaping of the history. Fred Wah for sharing his remarkable photographs from the 1960s. A special thanks to my friends and family, for their conversation, love, and support.

FROM THE POETRY COLLECTION TO THE SUNY ENGLISH DEPARTMENT

ORIGINS TO 1978: THE UNIVERSITY AT BUFFALO'S POETRY COLLECTION

Michael Basinski

A rolling designation: The Poetry Collection of the University Libraries, University at Buffalo, State University of New York began as a simple, yet expansive idea in the imagination of Charles David Abbott while he was a student at New College, Oxford in the early 1920s. Growing from Abbott's inspired notion to one of the world's greatest libraries of modern poetry took decades. That development was fostered by a constellation of pioneering and passionate individuals dedicated to the evolving history of literature, books, poetry, the creative process, experimental progressive university education and university administration, legacy, and philanthropy. It also involved a leap of faith that a unique and focused research library dedicated to poetry would be of significant scholarly and creative use more than half a century after the first book was shelved. These optimistic, hardworking pioneers formed an affinity that established the Poetry Collection of the University Libraries as one of the world's most significant institutional libraries for the study of twentieth century poetry and twenty-first century poetry, a destination library, and a capitol in the geography that is the realm of the poem.

In October 1935, Charles Abbott, using book dealer lists, placed his first orders for books by T.S. Eliot, Robert Frost, Edith Sitwell, Elinor Wylie, and W. B. Yeats. This culminating instance that allowed Abbott to begin collecting books of poetry began a decade and a half earlier with the inauguration of Samuel Capen as the first salaried, full-time chancellor at the University at Buffalo. In 1920 Walter P. Cooke, a Buffalo lawyer, banker, and Chair of the University at Buffalo Council, organized a city-wide financial campaign to create a UB Endowment Fund that would enable UB to hire a full-time chancellor to unite the university and to begin a new educational era in Buffalo. Samuel Capen had previously refused an offer to become a college president. But when Cooke approached him about the newly-created chancellor position, he was lured by complete academic freedom and the challenge of building his imagined progressive and liberal university, one that was absolutely unique among all other American universities. Part of that work was hiring faculty, and important to poetry in Buffalo was his hiring Charles D. Abbott and Oscar A. Silverman to UB's expanding Department of English.

When Capen began his mission of reshaping the University at Buffalo into an elite institution, the university still lacked a library building. But in 1929, just weeks before the market crash, Walter Cooke announced that Thomas and Marion Lockwood had pledged $500,000 to build a library. Lockwood was a cultural philanthropist and book-collector who was born in Buffalo in 1873. After law school, he had run for Governor of New York and narrowly lost, seemingly to the benefit of Buffalo, book collecting, and poetry. After the death of his father, he retreated from actively practicing law to manage his family fortune and to become an active philanthropist. In 1904, he married his second wife, Marion Birge, the daughter of Carrie Humphrey Birge and George K. Birge, president of the M. H. Birge & Sons Company AKA the

Birge Wallpaper Company. Lockwood had begun collecting books while he was a student at Yale but in 1910 he began passionately to build a collection. In 1918 Thomas and Marion Lockwood moved to 844 Delaware Avenue, a house that provided a 40 by 75 foot bookshelf lined library for Lockwood's growing book collection. Adjacent to his library was his private office, which offered a door that lead down a winding staircase to a large, furnished, and private basement room, and also a secure safe-room. Lockwood's collecting followed the Grolier Club's list of *One Hundred Famous Books in English Literature* (1902), and he acquired books via book agents, dealers and at auction. Among his collecting peers in Buffalo was Robert B. Adam, founding partner of the Adam, Meldrum & Anderson Company (AM&A's), a chain of department stores based in Buffalo. Adam maintained the world's largest collection of works by Samuel Johnson. Another book collector was Lockwood's neighbor John Clawson, who maintained a prestigious collection of American and British first additions.

Lockwood's collection of more than 3,000 titles included Shakespeare's four seventeenth century folios, a first edition of Milton's *Paradise Lost* (in ten books), Edmund Spenser's *The Fairy Queen*, the collected works of Ben Jonson (1616, 1640), *The Comedies and Tragedies* of Francis Beaumont and John Fletcher, Samuel Johnson's *Dictionary of the English Language*, Wordsworth's *Lyrical Ballads*, and Percy B. Shelley's *Prometheus Unbound*. Among his American first editions were Melville's *Moby-Dick*, *The Scarlet Letter*, signed by Hawthorne in scarlet ink, and Whitman's *Leaves of Grass*, and first editions of Thoreau and Emerson, as well as many other nineteenth century authors. Among Lockwood's finest books were those designed and printed by private presses like William Morris' Kelmscott Press and T. J. Cobden Sanderson's Doves Press. Lockwood owned a Kelmscott *Chaucer* on vellum (one of thirteen) and the Doves Press *Bible*, which was a retree copy on vellum assembled from extra production sheets used in the printing of the only two other known copies. Lockwood's private library also featured a Whitman manuscript, a Harriet Beecher Stowe manuscript, and letters from Charles Dickens, Charles Lamb, and for instance, a letter by Charles Darwin tipped into a first edition of *On the Origin of Species*.

The new library at the University of Buffalo would be named the Lockwood Memorial Library, and it was built in memory and as homage to their fathers, Daniel Lockwood and George Birge. Construction began on Lockwood Memorial Library in September 1933 and in preparation of the spring 1935 dedication, Lockwood emptied 2,500 of his books and deposited them in "his" library. It was a joyous moment in Buffalo's cultural life. While the library system was in the capable hands of Buffalo native and University Librarian Ruth Bartholomew, both Capen and Lockwood wished a unique person to head the new Lockwood Memorial Library and to steward Lockwood's books. They chose Charles Abbott. After falling in love with the expansive Bodleian Library at Oxford, Abbott arrived in Buffalo in September 1927 with his wife Anna Pratt Abbott. Between 1927 and 1930, Abbott was first Instructor of English and then Assistant Professor of English in the UB Department of English. The Buffalo climate did not suite Anna Abbott and this precipitated a move to Boulder, Colorado where in 1930 Abbott first became Assistant Professor of English and then Associate Professor at the University of Colorado. Mrs. Abbott died in Boulder, which freed Abbott to return to Buffalo in 1934. Less than a year later he founded and directed what was then called the Poetry Project.

Abbott was summoned to the poem prior to his years at Oxford but it was at Oxford that the essence for a twentieth century poetry library began to germinate. Abbott records this early period of his life in a diary that he began in June 1926 and ended a month before he returned to Buffalo in April 1934. The diary is penned in diminutive, nearly unreadable script. In 1926 Abbott was reading Thomas Love Peacock and exploring the legal proceedings of Thomas Gray and William Mason. The diary begins with his detailing his exuberance at spending his day at the Bodleian reading *Notes and Queries*. The pedantic Abbott was quite critical of his fellow students, commenting often that they assume their college time should be one given over to immature, trivial activities, and socializing. Dull is a word he often uses to describe various interactions with his fellows. The portrait of Abbott that emerges from his diary is of a man who is most happy with his nose deep in a library book. At one point he writes that he wishes to simply be at home on his sofa reviewing his book catalogs.

For Abbott a library was not simply a gathering of books but a collection of rarified art objects. At Oxford he began to build his own library of books by twentieth century British poets. He scoured London bookshops for books of contemporary poetry unavailable in the Bodleian. He enlisted his colleague to do the same. A library of nothing but books of poetry became a small but tangible reality. To books of poetry and magazines of poetry, Abbott added the dream of collecting the manuscripts of twentieth century living poets. In his introductory remarks to the opening exhibition of the Poetry Collection's Robert Graves Collection in 1960, Abbott spoke about the significance of Robert Graves on his imagination of a poetry library. At Oxford Abbott read and fell under the spell of *Poetic Unreason* a book of mostly imaginary criticism by Graves, and his earlier book *On English Poetry*, which was rich with flights of fancy. The books suggested that literary scholarship would be enhanced if a library held the beginnings of poems, the rough drafts, and records of all changes of mind. Abbott imagined that this fancy could be fact, and he held that thought.

Once at the helm of Lockwood Library, Abbott began to collect British and American first edition fiction and poetry to augment Lockwood's books. Initially, Abbott collected retrospectively using money from a Friend's Fund, which was a pool of money used to buy items that were already out of print or collectable. New books for the growing Lockwood Library collection were purchased through a general acquisition fund. Fiction and other unique books fell quickly to the wayside as Abbott ranked poetry first and foremost in his collecting agenda and he did this with fierce and determined pursuits. Following his Oxford pattern he bought from British dealers and dealer lists. Receiving a Carnegie grant, he journeyed to New York and to London in 1938 and these trips allowed him to collect and supply want lists to book ferrets.

In the late 1930s, Abbott began a letter writing campaign asking poets to donate their work sheets. Outside of occasional literary letters, these materials in the 1930s had little if any market value and poets simply threw them away. Most poets responded to Abbott's request by sending a portfolio of worksheets from a single poem or group of poems in progress. In 1938, he petitioned his inspiration Robert Graves for a donation of work sheets. Laura Riding, Graves' companion, responded that none were available. Nevertheless, Abbott persevered by continuingly writing poets and begging gifts for his library of poetry and in the face of very limited library funds, he and took great pride in the manuscripts the poets generously provided.

In Buffalo, Abbott married Teresa Gratwick, who was from an affluent Buffalo family that amassed a fortune in the lumber processing trade along the Erie Canal in Tonawanda, New York. The Gratwick family owned a summer house on a 350 acre "farm," sometimes called Gratwick Highlands, along the Genesee River valley outside of Pavilion, New York in Livingston County, 50 miles east of Buffalo. To settle a sibling dispute with her brother, Teresa and Charles were granted a five-acre parcel, the caretaker's house, a garage with an apartment, and a barn on the Gratwick property. This was their home for the rest of their lives. Abbott made the 50-mile drive to UB where he often literary lived in the library four days a week returning only to Gratwick Highlands for long weekends. There his three-story house was spacious and provided a third floor library attic for Abbott's own books, which spilled out into nearly every room in the house and numbered thousands upon thousands of volumes.

Completely surrounded by poetry books, poetry magazines, and poetry manuscripts at work and at home, Abbott began to invite poets to visit and stay at the country retreat, which featured among other things a one-acre enclosed garden, an in-ground pool, tennis courts, an Italian garden, a miniature village for children, and William Gratwick III's tree peony garden. Among those poets who visited and stayed at the Abbott household were Wyndham Lewis, W. H. Auden, who claimed he felt more at home at Gratwick than any other place in America, of course, eventually, Robert Graves, and Williams Carlos Williams who with Flossie Williams visited or stayed for extended visits throughout the 1940s and 1950s. During one visit Williams was crowned King of Peonies. Williams' poems "The Yellow Tree Peony" and "The Italian Garden" were among the poems he wrote inspired by life at Gratwick.

Believing whole-heartedly in the power of the poem, poetry, and poets, Abbott was a workaholic, hyperactive, cerebral, expansive, and practical. He built his one-stop scholar shop for poetry with extremely limited funds. Nevertheless, the Poetry Collection grew, expanded via the magic of his focused and committed vision. It was Abbott's rule that manuscripts were *not* to be purchased by the Poetry Collection, a rule that was easy to follow since no money was available. The rule was, of course, circumvented. The first purchased, major author collections to come to UB was a Dylan Thomas collection composed chiefly of Dylan Thomas's early notebooks from which the majority of his poems were harvested. Bertram Rota, British book dealer, made Abbott an offer and for roughly $150.00 UB owned a unique Dylan Thomas Collection, thanks to the generosity of Thomas Lockwood who paid the bill. Eventually, the manuscripts of Robert Graves came to Buffalo. Mildred Lockwood Lacy, Thomas Lockwood's third wife, made the Graves purchase for the Poetry Collection to celebrate the twenty-fifth anniversary of the opening of Lockwood Memorial Library in 1960. Miraculously the manuscripts of more than 1,000 poems appeared when a monetary offer was presented to Graves. Turning his trash to treasure, Graves was the poet who noted that he pulled his worksheets from the waste paper basket and placed them in the library. When Graves attend the twenty-fifth anniversary event and gave a poetry reading in Lockwood Library, he mused that the Poetry Collection was the grave of Graves.

The Poetry Collection was quickly becoming a specialty library for the genetic study of poetry, for bibliographers, and for editors. There were rich and extensive collections by poets like William Carlos Williams and W.H. Auden, and there was an extensive collection of Wyndham Lewis manuscripts. The correspondence and papers of poetry anthology editor Louis Untermeyer were in the Poetry Collection and the book and magazine collections were enormous. All of this was spectacular. But one collection, a crown jewel would forever fix the Poetry Collection among the world's greatest research libraries and that collection was the James Joyce Collection, a collection that would not exist without Oscar Silverman. Silverman was born of a modest background in 1903 in a steel manufacturing and coal mining city in industrial western Pennsylvania, but wound up receiving his Ph.D. at Yale in 1941, and was recruited by UB English Department Chair Henry Ten Ech Perry. Demanding the most competent faculty available, Chancellor Capen ignored the era's bias against Jews as faculty and invited Oscar Silverman to his liberal and burgeoning university. Silverman arrived in Buffalo in 1926, and met Abbott, who was teaching similar courses. A friendship grew, organized around their intense passion for books and the power of literature to shape culture.

Silverman believed that the world's problems could be resolved via engaging with classic books, and he believed whole heartedly in learning and teaching and did both with exuberance. Silverman became full professor in 1943 and chair of the Department of English in 1956, holding the position until 1963 when he resigned, making way for the hiring of Albert Cook and a wave of UB English Department hires. New SUNY rules forbid faculty from holding more than one administrative post. Chancellor Furnas offered Silverman the option of English Department Chair or Director of the Library. Silverman had assumed the directorship in 1960 when his friend Charles Abbott was forced to retire citing deteriorating health. Silverman decided to remain director, being the first Director of the Library after UB joined the SUNY system. He remained director until in 1968, and during his eight years as director he added 750,000 books to the UB library. He continued teaching until 1972. Outgoing, full of charm, playfulness, and wit, Silverman was the definition of the town and gown intellectual and was always in great demand in Buffalo's socially orthodox cultural circles of the late 1940s and 1950s. Truly, he was UB's ambassador to the city of Buffalo.

While on sabbatical in Paris in 1949 Oscar Silverman went to see an exhibition of the archives of James Joyce at the Libraire La Hune bookshop.

It was still post-war Europe and the Joyce family was attempting to sell Joyce's books, family portraits, photographs, and manuscripts to raise funds. Silverman immediately recognized the importance of the archive. The collection fit perfectly into Abbott's vision of a research library for the genetic study of literary works. Returning to Buffalo, Silverman immediately urged Charles Abbott to acquire the Joyce Collection. Of course, the library had no money for such an endeavor. However, fate intervened. Mr. Philip Wickser, a prominent Buffalo lawyer, unfortunately died, and his wife Margaretta Wickser donated $10,000 to Lockwood Library for the purchase of something as a memorial to Mr. Wickser. With this donation Silverman and Abbott were able to outbid all other institutions in a closed auction. The first consignment of Joyce material arrived at UB in 1950.

A decade later when Sylvia Beach, Joyce's publisher, was about to retire, she recalled Oscar Silverman and approached him with the idea of purchasing her Joyce material. Silverman was able to engineer the purchase with the generous assistance of Constance and Walter Stafford. Sylvia Beach was awarded an honorary UB Doctorate in Buffalo. With the Beach material the Poetry Collection became the largest and most prestigious James Joyce library in the world with more than 10,000 pages of James Joyce manuscripts, including all 66 known surviving notebooks that Joyce used in his composition of *Finnegans Wake* and notebooks, corrected typescripts and proofs from his novel *Ulysses*. There were also thousands of letters, businesses documents, photographs, portraits and three of Joyce's walking sticks as well as his glasses. The Poetry Collection had reached the rarified and lofty rank as one of the world's greatest libraries.

Both Charles Abbott and Oscar Silverman were extraordinary stewards of the Poetry Collection but their primary concerns and responsibilities were to the greater library and the university. As part of the Poetry Collection's maturation from fancy to premier research library, the Collection needed a curator, a steward of poetry. A curator is a hybrid person that is part administrator, collection content specialist, and above all that person that shapes the content of the primary research collections. The Poetry Collection's collection policy to collect all first editions of Anglophone poetry published meant that the Collection's curator had to be immersed in the ever-changing world of poetry and to gather all forms of poetry, sacred and profane, without prejudice.

The first curator that Abbott hired was poet and translator Mary Barnard. Barnard was part of the evolving world of progressive poetry, publishing in *Poetry* and a winner of *Poetry's* distinguished Levinson Award. She had a literary relationship with Ezra Pound (which she defined as an apprentice to the master) and was a colleague of William Carlos Williams. She arrived in Buffalo from New York in 1939. Taking every chance to berate Buffalo's weather, she was much involved in not only the life of the Collection on the UB campus but also in the social aspects of Buffalo poetry life. Living on Winspear Avenue, adjacent to the original Buffalo UB campus, she left Buffalo in 1943 as a result of dwindling library funds. Her literary autobiography, *Assault on Mount Helicon* details some of her life in the Poetry Collection.

For the next four years there was no curator and Ivah R. Sweeney, a Buffalo native, assisted Abbott with his voluminous correspondence and daily Poetry Collection chores. Between 1947 and 1955 Eugene Magner was curator. He was a librarian, poet, and editor of *Glass Hill*, an early mimeo, little literary magazine. After Magner left for a library position at another university, there was a two-year period when the official curator post was vacant. Between 1955 and 1957 librarian Anna Russell conducted the business of the Poetry Collection as acting curator. Between 1957 and 1960, poet and English Department Assistant Professor David Louis Posner was acting curator. In 1960, with Abbott's declining health and absence, he became curator of the Poetry Collection, holding the post between 1960 and 1967. Born in New York City in 1924, Posner was a graduate of Kenyon College and Harvard and attended the Sorbonne and Wadham College, Oxford. The author of a half dozen books of poetry including *The Deserted Altar, and Other Poems* for which he won the Newdigate prize for English Verse, Posner was a collector of china, British drawings and caricatures, and Victorian novels.

Karl Gay became curator of the Poetry Collection under Oscar Silverman, probably at the suggestion of Scottish poet and translator Alastair Reid. Reid was part of the Robert Graves inner circle on Majorca. As such he would have known Gay who as personal secretary worked with Graves for 30 years, typing his manuscripts, and proof reading his novels, commentary, and poems. Born in Germany, Gay left in 1933 with rise of Hitler and met Graves and Laura Riding on Majorca. During WWII, he served in the British Army and Royal Navy. Born Karl Goldschmidt and a Jew he altered his name to Gay during the war fearing immediate death if he was captured by the Nazis. During the 1960s Graves's reputation was at its popular culture peak. He wrote for *Life, Playboy*, for example, and appeared on the cover of the *Atlantic*, proposed using psychedelics, lived on an exotic Mediterranean island, and proclaimed himself as Goddess worshiper. And UB held the majority of his manuscripts. An obvious choice, Silverman brought Gay to Buffalo in 1965. At first, he was a bibliographer, a subject specialist in German and Spanish. In 1967, he became the fourth curator of the Poetry Collection.

In the mid-1970s UB expanded into its North or Amherst Campus. The English Department moved from its long-time, temporary housing in Annex A and Annex B to Clemens Hall, Lockwood Library also moved to a much larger building on the North Campus, and the Poetry Collection found a new home in Capen Hall. In 1976 Albert Cook, the architect of U. B.'s famed English Department, left for Brown University. In 1977 Oscar Silverman died after serving UB for 43 years. In 1978 Karl Gay retired. Within the space of a few dozen months the last of the individuals and their affinities for each other, books, and particularly poetry that built and sustained the Poetry Collection were gone. The University evolved, grew, and expanded. The intimacy between the city of Buffalo and UB waned as a result of time and distance and focus. An era ended.

WHEN BUFFALO BECAME *BUFFALO*

Michael Anania

There are several issues embedded in my title, I suppose, not only *when* Buffalo, the private University (after 1962 the State University of New York at Buffalo), became *Buffalo* but *how* and *why* Buffalo became a center, perhaps the center, of American poetry. For me, "when" is easy. Buffalo became *Buffalo* on August 5, 1963. That afternoon, the poet David Posner, then the Director of the Lockwood Library Poetry Collection, gave a party in his apartment on Main Street, just across from the old campus, one floor above the Chicken Delight take-out shop, for the incoming chair of the Buffalo English Department, Albert S. Cook. Posner was a collector, and his shotgun-style apartment, with windows on Main Street at one end and above the rear alley at the other, was a dense clutter of camelback couches, old, velvet-seated chairs and a soft, forest-floor matting of oriental rugs. The effect was a kind of worn luridness, aged Persian reds and Victorian blues. Books were stuffed into glass-fronted oak cases, and there were paintings and prints, mostly 19th century English landscapes, though above the weighty dining room table, there was a small Derain, nude dancers in a circle.

I don't remember everyone at the party. Al Cook was there, of course, so were Mac Hammond, who had followed Cook from Western Reserve in Cleveland, Aaron Rosen, who had been on the Buffalo English faculty for some time, the poet Saul Touster, who taught in the law school, Charles Doria, Irving Feldman perhaps, and towering above everyone, Charles Olson. Al introduced me. "Michael is writing on William Carlos Williams." Charles took my hand, pulled me toward him and draped his left arm over my shoulder. "Bill Williams," he said in what started out and ended as a rumbling kind of laugh. "He got us part way there. We'll manage the rest." *Us. We'll.* A part of Olson's genius was pure politics, LBJ or Tip O'Neill rounding up votes. Held close, with that great round face bending down toward mine it was clear that I was, we all were, eventually, in his company. Poetry was for Olson a project we would manage together. That was the underlying assumption, never quite stated, but always clear, of his seminars, which were not workshops in any sense but rather shared, speculative endeavors, to use his word, *projections*, toward a significant poetics.

I had met Al Cook for the first time, just minutes before he introduced me to Olson, in the archway leading to the table of wine and snacks in Posner's back room. That he knew that I was writing on Williams was surprising then. Later, it would seem just ordinary Cook, who never went into any situation, academic or social, without researching all the players. His descriptions of the backgrounds and relationships of any meeting, panel or a publishing venture were at times dizzying and always Byzantine. By 1963 Cook had been at Harvard, Berkeley and Western Reserve and had already published *The Dark Voyage and the Golden Mean*, an effort at creating a philosophy of comedy from Aristophanes to *Finnegan's Wake*, a book on "meaning" in fiction, a casebook on Oedipus that accompanied his own translation and a book of poetry. In 1963, he was at work on *The Classic Line*, a book on the epic. He read Greek, Latin, Italian, German, French and

Spanish. For a book on the Old Testament, he acquired Hebrew. A month or so into a semester-long stay in Russia he had enough Russian to write to me at length about the language in Yevtushenko and Voznesensky. His level of energy was extraordinary. Olson called him "the muscle," flattering in an Olsonesque way. At any moment, while he was recruiting faculty and reshaping the department, he had a stack of book projects underway in his study plus a vertical file of Manila envelopes into which he would deposit scraps of paper with ideas for as yet unnamed, future work. He stayed at home one day a week to write and famously told Virginia, his secretary, that she could call him if the building was on fire but only after she had called the fire department. He could be harsh, especially in dealing with unearned privilege, but his enthusiasms were boundless.

Perhaps because his own career had so many strange angles to it, Cook had a fine sense of the grievances and academic injuries he found scattered around him. In that early fall, I was at lunch with Ralph Maud, for a short time my dissertation advisor. Though he had published the best early book on Dylan Thomas, had a number of well-placed articles and was at work on a book on Thomas' manuscripts, Maud had been, at least from the time I arrived in Buffalo, out of favor with the English department. I never knew the source of the problem, but the effects were obvious. Despite his accomplishments, he wasn't given advanced classes in modern poetry, didn't teach graduate students and was pretty much excluded from the department's social life. Al Cook and three or four companions were behind us in the cafeteria line. Ralph and I found a table. Al and his group took a place across the room. Al put his lunch tray down and walked over to us. "Ralph," he said in a fairly public voice, "I just finished your new essay. It's wonderfully argued. . . and I really admire the grace of that opening paragraph." The Cook era was still new enough and I suppose scary enough that everyone paid close attention to who he went to lunch with and what he said, something he was completely aware of, so his dramatic and public gesture toward Ralph was significant, a deliberate effort at repair and restoration. Ralph, whose complexion was extremely fair, almost translucent, flushed with some mixture of surprise, gratitude and embarrassment.

In an introduction, I once called Cook, "an egalitarian elitist." He was happy with the notion. What I had in mind was his sense that if you managed to present an idea or point of view he hadn't already considered, you joined his circle as an equal. More impressive, though, was that he never forgot your insight and always attributed it to you. At the 1963 MLA in Chicago, he took me to dinner with Northrop Frye and Benjamin DeMott and spent part of our time over State Street pepper steaks praising an analogy I had made between science and poetry in an earlier conversation. Browse Cook's indexes, and you'll find entries for ideas and texts by former students. A single Cook essay in that period, say "Diffusion as a Technique of Composition in Modern Poetry," would include references to Yeats, Pound, Hopkins, Valery, Rilke, Benn, Dickinson, Baudelaire, Reverdy, Perse, Whitman, Mallarmé, Williams and Montale. It was obvious that the graduate school world of narrow, cautiously defined areas of specialization was about to change, and the first public signal of that change, and in many ways its most enduring marker, was Charles Olson.

Olson's first reading in Buffalo was held in the Baird Music Hall recital auditorium early in the fall term. The building was modern, faced with black glass and walled inside and out with exposed grey concrete. The auditorium walls were bare, the fixed seats cushy velvet and the sloped ceiling scaled with dark, acoustic baffles. One corner of the front of the hall was taken up by a concert organ with graded pipes in brushed aluminum. The stage was raised and large enough for a chamber orchestra.

The reading began with a fuss over a portable tape recorder that had been set up on a small table next to the podium. Olson and a student checked and rechecked the machine. The student withdrew and Olson began. He was dressed, as almost always that year, in dark pants, a blue work shirt with a wool tie. I'm not sure how he began or whether there was an introduction, and I'm not sure what he read or the order of the poems. I was in his seminar then, where he sometimes read poems or played tapes, so though I can still hear him reading a number of poems, I can't be sure of what he began with or in what way the poems followed each other. I am certain, though, that he began laughing. At Olson's wake, Allen Ginsburg talked about Olson's round face, how it came down and blessed you. In larger gatherings, his laugh had the same effect, a kind of general blessing that settled on the crowd.

In the course of the hour, he read from *The Distances* and *The Maximus Poems*. From uncollected work, he read "The Gulf of Maine," which had appeared in the anniversary issue of *Poetry*. He was fond of it and of its ending, "and mostly well-dressed persons frequent it," an example, for him, of how a poem could simply exhaust its occasion and its speech with a single breath. At one point, he announced that he would read "The Death of Europe/for Rainer Gerhardt." And he began reading it, out of *The Distances*. He managed a few lines, stopped, then started again. He explained that he was not reading it well, and gave us the sense in successive starts and stops that his voice was trying to catch up with a pace that was moving in his mind, moving even in his tapping foot, like a dancer trying to catch the music, which somehow, in its first moves, the body had irretrievably failed. Setting the book aside, he said that he had read the poem well that summer in Vancouver and that he would, rather than read it badly, play a tape of that reading, so the tape recorder was turned on, and Olson pulled a chair up next to it and with us sat listening to "The Death of Europe." He was so tall that when he sat in the chair, his legs rose in long angles up from the seat. He smoked a cigarette and leaned forward, his elbows on his knees, and tapped his foot to the rhythm of his recorded voice reading his poem. In the center of all those angles of arms and legs, his great round face smiled and nodded. Somehow, it didn't occur to me until later that something very strange had happened. While it was going on, I was too focused to notice that Olson had turned the whole ritual of the poetry reading upside down, that the familiar drama of those occasions had been at once radically altered and marvelously parodied. I had just begun to know him so I was just becoming accustomed to the way he would, without apparent effort, move things into another order of occurrence. The voice on the tape recorder read the poem brilliantly. Olson listened, and we listened and watched him listening, tapping our feet with his, as though it were the most natural thing in the world.

I have tried for more than fifty years, never very successfully, to characterize that first Olson seminar at Buffalo. It is difficult, in part, I think, because the seminar evolved as it went along. On the first day he wrote his name, Duncan's, Creeley's and Ginsberg's on the board and said, "These are the old guys," the poets we were meant to succeed. He asked a few of us to read. Boer read one of the *Odes*. Doria read a poem from a sequence, called "The Versions." I read one of the Missouri River poems. Olson listened intently but didn't comment. Instead, he read "The Gulf of Maine" ("They were in a pinnace off Monhegan...") rumbling through its opening historical details as though they were shimmering particulars in that very moment. Perhaps, that first day was just a getting-to-know-you exercise, but the readings, ours and his, put us in an equal literary space, a flattering and empowering gesture. Charles Boer and I discussed that first day for years. His memory had a different focus (see *Charles Olson in Connecticut*). He has Olson stalking around the seminar tables, pausing behind Boer with his coat draped over Boer's head. Boer's laughter began their long friendship and was, according to both Boer and Olson, the opening note of the class. It wasn't my head or my laughter, which is probably why I don't remember it except in Boer's wonderful, always laughter-filled retelling. That class included Boer, Charles Doria, William Moebius, Charles Brover, Henry Lesnick, Mary Griffin and Joe Keogh. There were three or four linguistics graduate students from the University of Toronto and as the year went on visitors— Robert Duncan who conducted one session, John Weiners, Jonas Mekas and Grayson Ruethven, a poet and titled Earl from London, who lived for a time in a Chicken Delight apartment above Posner's.

For most of my student life, I was an obsessive note taker. I have piles of spiral notebooks from all sorts of subjects, graduate and undergraduate, but I don't have single notebook from that year with Olson, not because there was nothing to save but because the class moved with such speed that writing down one idea might mean that you would miss the transition to the next. The subject was Olson's concerns, modified and amplified by our interactions with them. He liked, even invited, contentiousness. He would lean into your remarks. "I hear you," he would say emphatically, then lead you back to the central question. The notion has been around for some time that Olson was in search of followers, a subset of younger Black Mountaineers. He attracted followers, certainly, but that was never the goal of the seminar. Most of the poets in the class had already written a good bit and published. There was no effort to shape our poems. The goal, when it came up, was to give us permission to be more ambitious and inclusive. No time was spent on positions he had already taken; that is, he didn't reprise projective verse, his view of Melville or the Elaine Feinstein letter. He assumed, correctly in most cases, that we knew those texts. He was particularly taken that fall by the idea from J.A. Noutopolis of parataxis, that sense that there was a poetic in Homer that was determined by the order of perception and not by an over-arching syntax. Eric Havelock's

Preface to Plato was another recurrent focus of attention, the notion that there was a pre-Socratic, pre-Aristotelian discourse to be recovered, a unity of body, speech and perception that existed before the alienations inherent in rhetoric. Etymology was seen as a route (*root*, Duncan would add) into that past and the conviction that sounding, speaking, as well taking the word's etymological depth, as a sailor sounds a harbor or a whale sounds plunging downward into the sea, could give the contemporary poet access to that past, but the topics also ranged to neurology, geology, linguistics, history, music, dance, perception, proprioception, myth and early politics. I'm not doing justice, I'm afraid, to the excitement involved in these discussions. Olson was inviting us into his thought process—brilliant, angular, unpredictable, often initially wholly puzzling—as companions, sometimes merely as oarsman, sometimes at the helm. Poetry and poetics were, for Olson, collaborative ventures.

Each afternoon's progress was in the best sense improvisational, inventions at once scholarly and transgressive. The best measure of Olson's seriousness about these excursions and their originality is that he would stay after class and copy down what he had written and drawn on the blackboard. The board was the register for what emerged from the discussion. He would move around the room, sit sometimes, but always go back to the board where words and figures were connected by arrows, spirals and brackets. After he saw the Emilio Grossi photo of himself at that blackboard, which eventually became the cover of the first issue of the *Niagara Frontier Review*, he assigned a student to photograph the board at the end of each class. That Grossi photograph, showing only about a third of the board, is for me a kind of shard, something that represents that occasion but certainly doesn't explain it. "Embodiment." "Enharmonic." "Gesture." Three words in a kind of column, capitalized. *Gesture* has an arrow heading off the page. There's an essay lurking there, tempting—*embodiment* as an essential fact of myth, *enharmonic*, that is, the continuity of the musical scale, each sharp sharing the succeeding flat, hence the continuity of song, and gesture, art's and the poem's business, the appropriate outcome of the previous two. Perhaps? Or merely guesswork across a chalky haze of time.

The seminar didn't have a syllabus or a reading list, and no papers were required. Instead, Olson asked that we write him letters on the weekend that he could incorporate into the next Thursday's class. There were only a few letters. I wrote one on appearance and reality, Bradley, Pierce and Whitman. He brought it to the next meeting and set out to use it to open the discussion. He read a sentence or two, stopped, then pushed it across the table to me. "You read it," he said, "I can't." I took it initially as a kind of rebuke, but as we went on it was clear that he wanted me to occupy my argument. His reading—and he didn't care for my rather rank and file prose—would have, as he forced his way through it, taken the text from me and displaced him. Olson had a deep faith in the efficacy of reading, occupying, as I said, the text in speech and breath. It was more than a question of performing something well, the issue at the Baird Hall event, but an essential interpretive act. At the first of Cook's famous English Department colloquia, David Landrey, then a graduate student, read a paper on *Benito Cereno*. Olson was there to give the faculty response. David's was a well-crafted, closely argued essay. When he finished, Olson, sitting in the front row, leaned forward and said, with apparent affection, "David, you've got it all wrong." No one knew what to do. Olson said, "Do you have the book?" Landrey pulled it out of his bag and gave it to him. Without additional commentary, Olson read the first three or four paragraphs aloud, gave the book back and said, "See what I mean?" A critical reading of Melville was less important than a literal reading—the body in breath and speech, first.

Olson's presence, even though he lived more than an hour away in Wyoming, New York and was on campus just one or two times a week, was felt everywhere, as was Al Cook's. Cook's vision for the department was based in his view that poets were, at their best, scholars. It was a personal issue for him. Despite the range of his scholarship and its depth, he always thought of himself first as a poet, and like Olson, he viewed those of us who were also poets, however young, as companions. In his first year at Buffalo, Cook brought Mac Hammond, Bill Sylvester, Jack Clarke and Irving Feldman onto the faculty. More would follow. At Olson's suggestion Cook filled the 1964 summer session with poets. Ed Dorn, Robert Kelly, Amiri Baraka (then, LeRoi Jones), Gregory Corso and Diane Wakoski were there for the summer. George Starbuck, back from two years in Rome, was working in the library. Galway Kinnell had a privately funded research project in the Poetry Collection and taught a Williams class to undergraduates. Hugh Kenner was there teaching a graduate seminar in the *Cantos*. In the middle of the summer session, Leslie Fiedler, poet, novelist, essayist and provocateur, arrived from Montana and with his station wagon as yet unpacked, joined a panel discussion in the basement of the Student Bookshop on Main Street with Dorn, Kelly and Baraka. There were readings, always off-campus at the Greensleeves coffee shop downtown, and very briefly an English Department baseball team with me, Starbuck, Dorn, Baraka, Harry Keyishan and others. Olson, who had set this all in motion, was back in Gloucester for the summer.

In early 1964 Olson called a meeting at Cole's restaurant near Buffalo State University to discuss a new literary magazine. Charles Boer, Saul Touster, Charles Doria and I were there. I think he included me and Doria because he thought we might fold *Audit/Poetry* into this new venture. *Audit, a magazine of poetry and opinion*, was started in 1960 by Ralph Maud. David Galloway, a Buffalo graduate student, had a parallel magazine, *Audit/Fiction*. When Maud abandoned his *Audit*, Galloway joined his magazine with Ralph's and created *Audit, a quarterly*. I was poetry editor. When Galloway took a job in England, I inherited the magazine and created *Audit/Poetry*. I went to Cook to ask for some support. He agreed to help, gave me offices in a house on Winspear and suggested Doria, a former student of his from Western Reserve, as a co-editor. At the time of the Cole's meeting the Frank O'Hara issue of *Audit/Poetry*, the first project under the new title, was near publication, and we had solicited the poetry for the next number, a portmanteau issue. I had also mapped out the Duncan issue with Robert the day after his visit to the Olson seminar. We were, to Olson's distress, out of play. He was also less than pleased with our choice of O'Hara, who he called O'Haha. That lasted until they met later that year at Mac Hammond's house. After dinner, they insisted on walking back to the University, the two Worcester poets coming to terms.

Most of the lunch, like all magazine first meetings, was given over to deciding on its name. Boer suggested—I never knew how seriously—"Geo-Bio" or "On the Geo-Bio" and sang a version of "On the Bayou" as part of his proposal. A city bus stopped just outside of Cole's window. The logo on the side was "Niagara Frontier Transit Authority." Olson said, "That's it. The Niagara Frontier Review." The first issue appeared in the summer of 1964 with Olson, Brover, Boer, Lesnick and Harvey Brown as editors. The Frontier Press, directed by Harvey and active from 1964 to 1972, was also born in that moment. Within a year Olson would refer to the Niagara Frontier as the nexus for a new alignment of culture, poetry and politics, a suitably Olsonesque grand gesture, but the amount of literary activity in 1964 was amazing—*Audit/ Poetry*, *The Niagara Frontier Review*, *Manuscripts* (an independent student magazine), *Fubbalo* (published by Ed Budowski at the Student Bookstore, a serious sort of send up) and the first of the Frontier Press imprints, Dorn's *Rites of Passage* and Ed Sanders' *Peace Eye*.

Despite all of this fervor and Olson's obvious success at creating a new literary center, 1963-64 was a difficult year for him. He had been one of John Kennedy's tutors at Harvard, so took the assassination more personally than the rest of us. Then, in March, his wife Betty was killed in an automobile accident outside Wyoming, NY. In the fall of 1964 he left his son, Charles Peter, in Gloucester and returned for his second year at Buffalo. He didn't go back to Wyoming but lived in the University Motel. I was teaching so attended that second year's seminar intermittently. Andrew Crozier, Albert Glover, George Butterick, Fred Wah, David Landrey, Stephen Rodefer, Charles Molesworth and Harvey Brown joined Boer, Doria, Lesnick, Brover. In that year the class would often be extended through dinner and at the motel well into the night. Talk filled the space left behind by his family. In 1965 Olson took a leave of absence from the University but never returned. He had taken just two years to fashion a new poetic center and turn the established order on its ear.

Why Buffalo is another matter. Of course, it's possible that Cook, Olson et al. might have produced the same revolution elsewhere, but the University of Buffalo had become, well before 1963, a unique poetic space. Charles D. Abbott, Lockwood Memorial Library's first director, founded the Poetry Collection when the Library opened in 1935. When Abbott's book, *Poets at Work*, was published in 1948, the collection had 10,000 books, 350 files of literary magazines, 3000 sets of worksheets and 2500 letters. *Poets at Work* brought me to Buffalo in 1961. By then the Collection was several times larger and complete enough to be considered documentary in its holdings in 20th century poetry and literary magazines. The manuscript and worksheet files, though eventually emulated by other libraries, were—still are—unique. The Collection became essential for critics and biographers working in the field. It was also a stopping off place for poets, and poetry readings were regularly held in the large lecture room across the atrium.

Using the Poetry Collection's as his base, Abbott created a number of local organizations to support his interests. The Friends of the Lockwood Memorial Library had sponsored poetry readings for years. Between 1961 and 1963, before the poetic sea change, e.e. cummings, Robert Graves, W.H. Auden, John Berryman. Louis Simpson. Gregory Corso, Adrienne Rich. John Nims, Thom Gunn, Phillip Hobsbaum, John Fuller, Edward Lucie-Smith, George MacBeth, and Anne Sexton all read there. Robert Bly and James Dickey came to read after '63 but still under the Friends' auspices. For a time, there was a fund that brought a British poet in residence. In my first year, Peter Redgrove was there with his wife and family. John Fuller came the next year. Despite all of this, the English Department remained steadfastly traditional. No graduate seminars were offered in modern poetry, though Buffalo's national reputation was tied to the Poetry Collection. There was, however, a general enthusiasm for poets, an effect of the Library probably and of years of poetry readings and the dinners and parties that followed them. The structural linguist, Henry Lee Smith, came to me and Redgrove and asked that we act as informants, in the anthropological sense, for his seminar in Middle English morphemics. Smith thought that as poets we would have a special ability to read poetic texts, even in Middle English, and that somewhere between Peter's BBC inflected South London accent and my Midwestern American speech he could approximate the phonemes of the Gawain poet. It was slightly mad but exciting to watch the lines we had just read transposed linguistically onto the chalkboard, and neither of us missed a session. In one sense, what Al Cook did with the financial support of the University's President was to turn the English Department in the direction of Lockwood's resources and the active poetry scene that had grown up around it.

Unrelated to what was happening at the University but companionable and indirectly supportive was a period of artistic change in the city. The Albright Knox Art Gallery mounted a series of challenging exhibitions. Abstract expressionist painters were shown in spacious galleries. Clyfford Still was interviewed in *Audit* while he was there in 1963 to hang his own massively jagged paintings. The two shows that had the greatest impact were a masterfully curated exhibit of found art—masterful because the objects shown were pristinely set out in museum fashion, a rusted reel lawn mower on a white pedestal with an artist's card that said "Lawnmower II, 1960"—and a year later, an exhibit of kinetic and optic art that included mobiles, certainly, but also some computer driven, interactive sculptures that would react to your shadow passing over their light sensors in one way and to your speech in another. The optic portion of the show played with the capacity and limitation of sight, colors and patterns that would change as you moved past them and disconcert the otherwise reliable aspects of vision. Also, in 1963, Josef Krips, the very traditional Austrian conductor of the Buffalo Philharmonic, left and was replaced by the young, modernist American composer, Lukas Foss. Foss had a commitment to contemporary music and experimentation and brought John Cage, Karlheinz Stockhausen and others to Buffalo. The shock of the new in the Buffalo music community was not as great as you might think. In addition to annual residencies by the Budapest Quartet and Ralph Kirkpatrick, the Baird Music School had a program that brought contemporary composers to campus, among them Aaron Copland, Virgil Thompson and Ned Rorem.

So Buffalo became *Buffalo* as a result of the energies of Cook, Olson, Fiedler, Hammond, Sylvester, John Clarke, Irving Massey and a cadre of graduate students, mostly poets and translators, they recruited or in Olson's case, merely attracted, and because a poetry and literary scene, however inchoate, already existed. In the 60s there was a small swimming pool nuclear reactor on campus that glowed with a strange blue latency—energy awaiting energy. And Buffalo became *Buffalo* because its industrial past had left behind arts institutions, libraries and endowments, and its subsequent industrial failure made it an inexpensive place to live. Until the high cost of heating oil drove them to the suburbs, professors lived in three story houses with music rooms, servants' quarters and carriage houses. The infusion of state money and an administration eager to create a new, notable University out of an old, established one supported a period of hiring so intense that the city's best French restaurant survived almost entirely on dinners given for hiring committees and job candidates. And Buffalo became *Buffalo* because it was "a second city," so conspicuously not New York that it brimmed with a kind of cultural urgency—poetry, music, ballet, master classes, exhibitions, artists' residencies of all sorts. If you missed a recital, people called to see if you had come down with something, or if you changed seats at the symphony, they would ask why. If you were in the arts, loyalty and comradery were required.

Bruce Jackson has called the period following 1965, the "glory years at Buffalo." Cook brought more poets and writers— Robert Creeley, John Logan and Robert Hass, John Barth and Donald Barthelme—and gave the experimental poet and novelist, Raymond Federman, who had been hired by the French Department as a Beckett scholar, a joint appointment in English. Lionel Abel, Charles Altieri, Irving Massey, Norman Holland and C.L Barber came, so did René Girard and Eugenio Donato. Unlike departments that sustained themselves by filling slots with appropriately slot-oriented specialists, Cook aimed for intellectual quality, breadth and energy without being overly concerned with credentials or curriculum, a department, you might say, made in his own image, or better, perhaps, made to suit the topography of his enthusiasms. Here's Robert Creeley, who had been an undergraduate Latin student with Cook at Harvard and after Olson, was Cook's most affecting appointment, in "For Al":

> What we got on
> kept happening, happening—
>
> ....
> All that you got done
> was earned, was earned—
>
> ....
> Now they see
> the ampleness of it all
> was for free, for free.

"The ampleness of it all." Despite eventual, less sympathetic administrations and the erosion of State funding, a certain ampleness and freedom survives. Buffalo was a giant step ahead of the changes "theory" and "studies" brought to literature departments. It championed early on digressive poetics, experimental fiction and a kind of speculative scholarship—polymorphous, and provocative. Consider a just a few titles—*The Children's Hour, Freaks, Enactment, Surfiction, My Emily Dickinson* and *Get Your Ass in the Water and Swim Like Me.* The Poetics Program, founded in 1991 by Creeley and Susan Howe survives, and though it has often lacked the grace and acceptance of its own past, it is an outcome of what was started by Olson and Cook in the 1960s. Institutionalizing innovation is problematic always. All the habits of universities, departments and schools tend to ossify what they contain. Aesthetic change, "the de-definition of art," is meant to be disconcerting, even disruptive, to use O'Hara's term, "raffish." Housing change, sheltering it, more often than not requires a bulwark of explanations—theories, manifestos, defenses of all sorts— lengthy and frequently overbearing, a shell of "poetics" around poetry. But the impulse toward innovation remains at Buffalo, perhaps because to some extent that is what Buffalo came to stand for, "continuous revolution." Fifty years is a long time to be on the battlements. Adjustment is over time the necessary companion of commitment.

If, as I have suggested, the literary changes that occurred at the University, first in poetry, then in fiction and in literary studies in general, were aided both by Lockwood's collections and by a long-standing enthusiasm for art and artistic change in the city, the intense poetic activity at the University has had, in turn, a lasting effect on the city. In his years at Buffalo, Creeley was involved with and supported public poetry programs in schools and community centers. And Buffalo remains an active literary center. There are poetry readings almost nightly around town, several flourishing small presses, a poetry café, independent book stores with readings and a small press book fair with readings and workshops. Hallwalls, the contemporary art space founded by Cindy Sherman and Robert Longo in the 70s, is still going with exhibitions, music programs and poetry readings.

Afterword

The 1964-65 academic year had another, deeply troubling side. In April of 1964 the House Un-American Activities Committee came to Buffalo to conduct hearings into what they called "Communism in Buffalo." Although they spent some time on post-war left-wing organizations among local unions, the center of their attention and the longest testimony involved Paul Sporn, a doctoral student and an instructor in English at the University. Sporn was extremely quiet, soft spoken and a wonderfully sympathetic teacher. It's hard to imagine him rousing any rabble at all, but he was deeply committed politically. The committee heard testimony from a paid informant, who had been associated with the Party, that Sporn was literature director for the Communist Party in Buffalo, that he picked up copies of *The Daily Worker* and had been seen carrying printing equipment (a typewriter) and paper into his apartment. What came of this—and of course all of HUAC's work—was pointless alarm and a great number of newspaper stories. Why Sporn? Well, clearly his past had been caught in the FBI surveillance net. The Committee produced, among other things, his high school and college records, even a copy of the application he had filled out for a factory job in Buffalo. It seemed clear then, that HUAC had been aimed at Buffalo and Sporn by the state legislature, as a means of reigning in the University, which had become a state institution just two years earlier. Their unease, at least from their point of view, was understandable. The University of Buffalo had been private and behaved as though it still were. In 1962 Barry Goldwater was invited to speak and filled the gymnasium. Posner, for reasons I've never understood, invited the British fascist, Sir Oswald Moesby, to campus. We—that is, the Graduate Student Association—invited Bayard Rustin and Malcom X.

The principle effect of HUAC's successful public association of the University with Communism was a new earnestness about enforcing the Feinberg Law, which required all employees of the State of New York to sign a loyalty oath. Sporn, who according to some reports had signed, was fired. A number of others refused to sign and left the University, among them Harry Keyishian, John Silver, George Starbuck and Ralph Maud. Gregory Corso, who had been given a class to teach in the night school, also refused. The case went to the Supreme Court as "Keyishian, et al. vs The Board of Regents. In 1967, the Court ruled that the loyalty oath was unconstitutional. None of the people who were fired ever returned, and there was an unspoken guilt among those who had, either willingly or out of sheer inattentiveness, signed, which may have been in part responsible for the broad faculty involvement in the Buffalo anti-war protests a few years later.

OLSON'S BUFFALO

Michael Boughn

> When wallflowerism becomes sufficiently established to control history
> then we have a hell of time believing what is said (of what is said)—the
> Herodotean Way—over what we suspect (& we are suspicious, no?)
> & therefore speculate as to, what went on, like REALLY. It's the urge
> toward the MONO—...
>
> John Clarke to Tom Clark, 1/20/87

When Charles Olson first came to Buffalo in 1963, it had been 18
years since he'd turned from politics to writing as the work which would
center and drive his life (although, in another sense, as the Berkeley reading
demonstrated, he never left politics).[i] He came to Buffalo with a significant
body of work already accomplished. *Call Me Ishmael, Y & X, The Mayan
Letters, In Cold Hell, In Thicket, The Maximus Poems*, and *The Distances* had
all been published, as well as "As the Dead Prey Upon Us," "The Kingfishers,"
"The Lordly and Isolate Satyrs," not to mention the important philosophico-
poetics essay "Projective Verse." *Maximus IV, V, VI*, though unpublished, was
already written. He'd been to Yucatan and led the wild, intellectual free-for-
all at Black Mountain. Crucially important for many of those who came to
Buffalo to work with Olson was the tremendous push he had made to rethink
the epic as a way around the lyric impasse much contemporary poetry was
then locked in and which went on to breed malignantly in the Creative Writing
Industry that developed after his death. How, that is, to rethink this crucial
mode of discourse and move it past the limits it had been taken to by Pound
and Williams? He was thus what Albert Glover recalls as "a living connection
to an 'old' tradition rather than simply an isolated lyrical voice which was
pretty much all there was otherwise." Though Donald Allen's anthology, *The
New American Poetry 1945-1960*, had opened people's eyes to a wider range of
writing than Glover's comment might suggest, his point about the dominance
of the lyric mode largely holds true even today.

All this work was implicated in a move away from what we think
of as the "literary," finally claiming for poetry an altogether other range of
importance. What Olson founded in Buffalo, what followed from his arrival
there, begins with that. "Literary" in the context of both Olson's work and the
work he engendered in Buffalo has to do with two different but related issues.
It refers both to the conventions, modes, and procedures of writing that mark,
however broadly and ambiguously, what is proposed at any given moment
as "literature," and also with the "life worlds" such practices are implicated
with, something loosely called, say, the "literary life," complete with all its
competitions, prizes, career paths, disciplinary bodies, canonical aspirations,
and so on. The literary, then, as an institution and as institutionalized practices.
Crucial to Olson's sense of a move beyond or around the literary was his
drive to reconnect with or recover energies that pre-exist their historical
institutionalization into a specific, fixed grammar of social practices. And even
more importantly, that to do that, to push one's self toward that connection, is
to disrupt or alter that grammar, a profoundly political act.

Such a move involves two crucial linked concepts—the ordinary and the archaic—and depends on an understanding of how they might be seen—or revealed—as converging in a new world. The ordinary is just that—where we are, what we do, here, today, that laundry waiting attention in the dryer, those dirty dishes on the counter from last night, *this* which is arrayed around us. It is the same ordinary Emerson pointed to – *the meal in the firkin, the milk in the pan, the ballad in the street* – that Americans can't quite grasp, what Olson called "the secular that loses nothing of the divine" this common immanence. Olson's crucial move was to understand that the ordinary, as such, is archaic, has always been, so that what we are in fact estranged from, as Heraclitus and Wittgenstein had it, is so familiar because it has always been there. In this sense, Olson's proposal is not so much anti-literary (a move which paradoxically is locked in an economy with the literary—the fate of the oppositional and the non-ordering) as pre-literary, an antithetical decentering in whose prolific and devouring wake the unprecedented is recovered.

What Olson called the *projective* accompanies this convergence. Like form and content in the famous proposal that emerged from the Olson/Creeley correspondence, they are really a Janus-faced energy. To take up the archaic/ordinary invokes the projective that is its method, the way forward. And to take up the projective invokes the archaic/ordinary, which is its ground.

One more term is crucial to this antithetical practice—community, which Olson famously had as *polis*. Of all the terms raised so far, this is in some ways, given our current condition, the most troubled and difficult to come to terms with, if only because of the ubiquitous nostalgia for it. Jean-Luc Nancy proposes community as what "*happens to us*—question, waiting, even imperative—*in the wake of* society."[ii] It is "neither a work to be produced, nor a lost communion, but rather as space itself, and the spacing of the experience of the outside, of the outside-of-self."[iii] There's no need to dwell here on the way Olson's sense of America as *space* foreshadows Nancy's proposal. One of the ways Olson's poetics as enacted in the Berkeley reading was antithetical to the literary (in both the senses given here) was in his insistence that such a discharge of energies arises from the circulation and generation of those energies within just such a space as Nancy identifies, and that that process is the act in which community reveals itself to itself.

Such a proposal undermines not so much the concept of *genius* (there's still room for the extraordinary within the space of the ordinary) as the promotion of individual production and the specific product, even in its current generic, non-author specific forms. It holds that work to the responsibility of an ordering intervention. Genius, as the Romantics knew it, is really just an especially intense receptivity to those circulating energies mentioned before. But the community orders (as in ordinary) itself out of the exchange—the call and response—that arises in the projective practice of the ordinary. Whatever else such a community may be, it's a "place" where hierarchical/anti-hierarchical orderings are dissolved in a synergistic circulation of authorities (authoritative finitudes, Nancy might say) that egg each other on toward their further possibilities—which are the further possibilities of the self-revelation of the community as well.

The critics of the community Olson engendered in Buffalo have from the beginning proposed its defining relation as one of dominance and submission, with Olson positioned as what's been called the High Priest. Typically, those around him then become identified as disciples, acolytes, or some other usually religious term meant to signify a loss of autonomy or individual authority. Within the community invoked here, however, such traditional vocabularies (mostly directly derived from Enlightenment polemics against the *ancien régime*) having to do with static hierarchical relations of power—equality, autonomy, derivative, original, subservient—as well as the accompanying package of anti-religious/pro-Reason pejorative labels like *cult, church, disciple,* etc., are drained of meaning and become inoperative, along with the cosmology that generates them. This is not to say specific persons who still passively identified themselves in that old cosmology didn't enter into such relations. But they weren't part of "the community" which actively proposed itself. In any case, as we've known for some time now, that old cosmology (the cosmology of critical modernity)[iv] is in acute, probably terminal crisis. One of Olson's great contributions here was, as Ralph Maud has pointed out, to link the resolution of that crisis to the emergence of the archaic/ordinary, to propose that what he called after Toynbee the post-modern is identical with the archaic/ordinary.

This exercise in clarifying vocabularies is not intended as an encompassing picture, some theory that can include Olson's work and what it engendered in Buffalo in a neat package. It is a provocation and the challenge to the hidden assumptions that found the dominant critical discourse, an attempt to open the further space within which Olson's Buffalo emerged. It's a call to which Olson's Buffalo is a response, a further opening. It equally moves the other way. Each call elicits a response, but each response in turn becomes a call. That is the circulation of authoritative finitudes. How else understand what happens with Frontier Press or in the *Magazine of Further Studies*, for instance, unless you simply want to give up the game and resort to literary judgments, which in the final case can only say what isn't ("this isn't literature," "it is out of bounds") not what is? Each instance in this circulation remains its own splendid and irreducible finitude.

The earliest appearance of community in this sense occurred around Harvey Brown's Frontier Press. Harvey Brown came to Buffalo in the fall of 1964. Like many of the others then flocking to the city, he came from Cleveland, Ohio via the Al Cook connection. Cook, who had been teaching at Case Western University, was hired as Chair of the English Department at the new State University of New York, and given tremendous resources to build the Department. Many of those he had worked with and taught at Case Western were hired to teach at Buffalo, or followed others there as students. Unlike most others, however, Brown was a millionaire, a designation that still meant something of consequence in 1964. His grandfather had invented a crane that facilitated the off-loading of materials from river barges, and the money he accumulated from his invention propelled his family into the upper echelons of Ohio society.

By the time Harvey Brown got to Buffalo, he had rejected both his social position, preferring the company of jazz musicians to debutantes, and his financial position. His relation to the money he inherited was based on the understanding that it embodied two contradictory energies or powers: accumulation and circulation. Call them angels. Brown felt that to capitulate to the angel of accumulation was to give power over your life to money, to allow it to rule your spirit. To give that power over to the angel of circulation, on the other hand, was to subjugate money to spirit. That was the path he chose, and Olson became one of the main instruments he used to realize it.

Harvey Brown's connection with Charles Olson was immediate and intense. In so far as they shared a sense of political priorities, Olson fit into Brown's plans to use his money to further certain specific ends. Brown, through his connections with jazz musicians in New York and Cleveland, had started a recording company to further the work of struggling artists such as Don Cherry, Ornette Coleman, Clifford Brown, and Clifford Jordan. Brown understood the work of these artists to constitute the ground of a new American republic, the visionary incarnation of the Jaguar World of pre-Columbian America. It was an eccentric community whose importance was both in its antithetical message, and in the method it had pioneered: improvisation based on the call and response of traditional African-American music (see Brown's fascicle "Jazz Playing" in *The Curriculum of the Soul*). That method for Brown resonated precisely with Olson's sense of the projective, and that correspondence provided the basis for Brown's ongoing support for both the recording project, and for Frontier Press.

His first act was to fund *Niagara Frontier Review*. After he arrived in Buffalo during the fall semester of 1964, he took over active editorship of the magazine. The *Niagara Frontier Review* eventually ran to three issues between 1964 and 1966, and became one of the centers for the diverse writers represented in Donald Allen's anthology, *The New American Poetry 1945-1960*. In addition to Charles Olson, Edward Dorn, John Weiners, Ray Bremser, Robert Duncan, Gary Snyder, and LeRoi Jone (Amiri Baraka), the magazine also carried work by John Temple, Diane DiPrima, Albert Glover, Fred Wah, the jazz musician Don Cherry, Stephen Rodefer, Herbert Huncke, Charles Boer, and Andrew Crozier. The third issue also carried Cantos CX and 116 by Ezra Pound. It was a site of profound and radiating imaginative tumult.

Olson's interest, however, extended beyond the magazine, and largely through his instigation, Harvey Brown expanded Frontier Press into book publishing. The initial idea was to publish books central to Olson's current thinking but otherwise out of print. The project soon expanded far beyond that, however, with the "editorial" participation of Ed and Jenny Dorn, and Ron Caplan, a book designer from Pittsburgh, so that the list eventually emerged out of a kind of uncentered collectivity. Deeply interested in the new poetries then emerging, Caplan first met Olson in 1963 when he'd visited the poet in Gloucester. As the book-publishing venture took shape, Olson suggested to Brown that Caplan, who had a small design business in his native Pittsburgh, be involved in designing the books. Given their shared interest, Caplan's involvement soon extended beyond design to participation in the selection of books for the press's list. The Dorns had been in Buffalo that summer when Ed

Dorn taught in the first Buffalo Summer Program in Modern Literature. The process was so open, that it is almost impossible at this point to know who was responsible for which books. Ron Caplan writes, it was "eccentric but with a strange unity."

> I know there were books I loved that I wished were in print—the Haniel Long stuff in particular, and Spring and All. I think Mid-American Chants was something we both had in waiting. Lenz is Harvey. I THINK I remember it being something Dorn wanted.
> . . . I think Olson was the main person to please in choosing the books. Then Dorn. Then? Perhaps me . . ..ᵛ

Between 1967 and 1971, Frontier Press published 25 books and pamphlets. There is no other list quite like it (see Appendix B for a checklist of the publications). For all of its eclectic mix, however, certain unifying features stand out.

Above all else the list is political, though the definition of politics here needs to be pushed beyond its institutional sense toward a kind of visionary activism (see Charles Olson's 1968 Berkeley lecture). During the time the press was active, the U.S. war against Vietnam was in full swing, and the discord it bred in the U.S. was reaching crisis proportions. More and more Americans actively opposed a government that, in turn, was trying desperately to repress them, using increasingly violent tactics that culminated in the slaughter of unarmed students at Jackson State University and Kent State University in May of 1970. All those involved in Frontier Press shared a sense of the extremity of the Constitutional crisis and an understanding that it was first and foremost a visionary crisis. To move ahead (to finally discover America) necessitated the nurturing of an eccentric, antithetical community that might provide the ground of an American conversion, as Emerson would have it. Call it a recovery of what had been lost to the usurpation of America by the Angel of Accumulation.

The politics of the Frontier Press list proliferate in unpredictable and often surprising directions. The core books suggested by Charles Olson—Brooks Adams' *The New Empire*, W. E. Woodward's *Years of Madness*—characteristically propose a reading of American history that is antithetical to the authoritative history that founds the current regime of power. Adams proposes a history that explains the advent of an American Empire whose origins he locates in European pre-history. Woodward radically rereads the U.S Civil War calling into question the proposal it was waged to end slavery. Other books supplement that reopening of American history.

The poetry equally reflects a visionary, antithetical politics. One of the great contributions of Frontier Press was to reprint William Carlos Williams' *Spring and All*, which had been out of print for almost 50 years. H.D.'s *Hermetic Definition* had never been in print. It had been copied by hand by poets visiting the Beinecke Library, and circulated around the U.S. Norman Holmes Pearson, H.D.'s literary executor, claimed that he was unable to place it with a publisher of sufficient standing and proposed that Brown was trying to make a profit off the pirated edition. Both Brown and Caplan felt that Pearson was holding back the book for reasons of his own, and that the only way to force his hand was to go ahead and get it in print. In any case, there was a great clamor among poets to have the poems made available so that they could work with them. From the point of view of many poets, the prestige of the publisher was less important than having the poems to work with, and that was the position that Brown took. He illicitly published the text, beautifully designed by Ron Caplan, in 1971, and continued to distribute it free until he died. Within a year of the Frontier publications of *Spring and All* and *Hermetic Definition*, both books had been copyrighted and published by New Directions in trade editions and have been in print ever since.

Frontier Press was also well known for publishing contemporary poetry and fiction in beautiful editions designed by Graham Macintosh, Ron Caplan, and Philip Trussell. The writing was diverse, including work by Edward Dorn, Edward Sanders, Michael McClure, Stan Brakhage, Albert Glover, and Robert Kelly. As different as all of those writers are, most of them had been in Buffalo during this period, and had participated in its energetic exchanges. Not that they constituted in that sense a unity, or held some common "theory." Only that the energies unleashed arose out of a common provocation, and are, in that very general sense, part of a community, both the more general community that the Allen anthology registers, as well as the community specific to Buffalo at that moment.

Some of the work—Sanders' *Peace Eye*, for instance—is specifically political in its address. But even the work that isn't—Dorn's love poems, McClure's mammalian cosmological body poem, Kelly's visionary investigations—are radical departures from the then (and largely still) dominant notion of the well-made poem as literary construct. That departure for parts unknown to the "literary" imagination constitutes, even more than any explicit content otherwise would, the nature of the "political" as it in turn constituted this antithetical community.

But Frontier Press had it limitations, and not everyone was happy with the high quality of the production standards which interfered with, or slowed down, the circulation of the work. Not that Brown's work wasn't deeply admired. But as Fred Wah said, "Some of us wanted to move more quickly than Harvey."[vi] Wah had come to Buffalo from Vancouver via Robert Creeley and New Mexico, drawn by Al Cook's active solicitation of poets to join the new program at Buffalo. He had become involved on the editorial board of *Niagara Frontier Review* at Olson's suggestion. At the time, he was a graduate student in linguistics taking Olson's seminars. Sharing Wah's desire for more speed were John Clarke, a new Assistant Professor in the English Department, and Albert Glover, a graduate student in Olson's seminars.

Clarke had met Olson in the spring of 1964. Al Cook had directed Clarke's dissertation on William Blake and was trying to hire him away from the University of Illinois, Champagne-Urbana. Clarke came to the interview knowing nothing of Olson, and with several reservations about the possible move to Buffalo. After the interview, there was a party at Cook's house. Clarke recalls:

> Later that night Charles came down to the party. I was sitting on
> a straight chair by the fireplace and he sat down on the couch, like

so ———— ⚹ and the connection was instaneous—maybe that's a new word, I meant instantaneous, but like that one better, it accents the sta etymon . . .. Olson's report of the meeting, as someone later told me, was that he dug my pants, the material they were made of, and the way I was sitting with my legs crossed. Upshot of course was that all other considerations were blown away: I was coming to Buffalo.[vii]

Al Glover had come to Buffalo in the fall of 1964 from McGill University, following his teacher, Irving Massey, who Cook had also hired. Knowing nothing of Olson, but being deeply interested in contemporary poetry (Glover had won a prestigious poetry prize at McGill the year after Leonard Cohen had won it), Glover enrolled in Olson's two graduate seminars (Poetry and Myth and Contemporary Poetry). The fourth person involved in the move toward more speed was George Butterick, later to be Olson's editor and literary executor.

The issue these four addressed with their collective desire for more speed was the "projective" and the community founded on it. The projective method relies on speed—speed of production and speed of circulation—in order to reach a kind of escape velocity needed to break free from the inertial pull of the "literary" and reaching a vital knowing, a transformative gnosis, only accessible through poetry. Before Olson left Buffalo in the fall of 1965, he proposed founding an Institute along the lines of the Princeton Institute of Advanced Studies, with which he'd been connected through Black Mountain College. When he left, and Al Cook was unsuccessful in getting the new University at Buffalo to support the project, Clarke, Wah, Glover, and Butterick decided to go ahead on their own.

They immediately began publishing *The Magazine of Further Studies*, the first issue of which appeared in the fall of 1965. "I think it was Glover's IBM Selectric we used," Fred Wah writes. "And we got a big roll of corrugated stuff for covers . . . and us and our wives wld set up in one of our basements and cut covers and paint chicken blood (George wanted the thing to decay in the readers' hands) and glue fur." Butterick's desire for decay emphasized the projective nature of the magazine, the fact that as you held it, it disintegrated, leaving you with nothing to hold to but what was further. Butterick was successful in that the various objects and substances applied to the covers of the magazine have by and large either faded over time or fallen off.

Between 1965 and 1969 IFS published 6 issues (see appendix C, item 8). The magazine was unique for a couple of reasons, both of which had to do with the rejection of the showcase model of the poetry magazine, already prevalent even then among small press magazines. The showcase magazine typically presents poems completely isolated and decontextualized. They appear as beautiful (or ugly) objects on the page. This mode of presentation reinforces the culture of the literary by stripping the poem from the intellectual matrix it is part of, and then emphasizing its object status as a pure literary event.

The Magazine of Further Studies refused, first of all, to isolate the poem. It included, in the body of the magazine, letters, prose exchanges, and bibliographies (most from the Poetry/Myth class John Clarke took over when

Olson left), so that the poems that were also presented there were clearly proposed as simply one kind of event in a larger discourse that included many different kinds of events. They were not proposed as products with implicit value in and of themselves. On the contrary, the larger discourse was emphasized.

As the magazine developed, it increasingly embodied an active conversation, further undermining the product-status of the "poetry" it included. Rather than including poems intended as finished and self-sufficient literary products, the magazine increasingly published fragments, challenges, responses, broken utterances that provoked other broken, incomplete utterances, so that by the final issue, the magazine has become a kind of clamor, a convocation of a conversation, in action. There is nothing to hold on to, not even a poem, which can be proposed as "literature." There is rather an event that is constantly pushing beyond itself.

The Institute of Further Studies went on to publish a number of items that recapitulate this antithetical dynamic. In 1968, there was a burst of small publications, designed as "letters." The goal, according to Al Glover, "was to be fastest, and Charles did, in fact, love the speed."[viii] Olson would send poems he'd just written from Gloucester and they'd be printed and distributed within a week (see Appendix C, items 3,4,5,7), moving the poem into the realm of discourse, communication, provocation, thinking, and conversation, and away from the object-status that turned it into a commodity and founded the culture of the "literary."

Other publications evidence the same goal. John Clarke pushed the Institute to publish plate 25 from William Blake's *Milton*. His plan, though it wasn't finally realized, was to mail the "letter" to the delegates to the Democratic Party convention in Chicago. The Olson note, item 4, was another provocation printed as a postcard for immediate dissemination. Poetry, which is the news, could then be the news rather than a memory of the news.

Perhaps the most lasting accomplishment of the Institute of Further Studies has been the ongoing publication of *The Curriculum of the Soul*. Olson's "poem," "A Plan for the Curriculum of the Soul," first appeared in *The Magazine of Further Studies 5*. After Olson's death, the Institute decided to break up the curriculum into discrete topics and get different writers to take them on. 29 fascicles (including one numbered 0—Charles Olson's "Pleistocene Man"), initially imagined as akin to the Cambridge Ancient History Project, were assigned to various poets with relationships to Olson's work. Al Glover has called it both "a collaborative epic,"[ix] and "a bouquet on the grave:"[x]

> Original "vision" was of a large book written by "Olson"— and I would still, someday, hope to publish it as such. It is that sense of "Homer" and would make only the second one (this one, of course, somewhat different in its concept of "history" and "narrative") in "the tradition." You see it in "The Mushroom" ("as if we were all one voice / of various sounds"— since revised: "we are all one voice / of various sounds").[xi]

The reference to "Homer" here is to Milman Perry's famous proposal that in fact, rather than being an individual, Homer was the name given to a bunch of bards who had invented and assembled the *Iliad* and the *Odyssey* over hundreds of years. The notion of "epic" as it is deployed here, and as it always was used by Olson, is not what is now proposed as a monomaniacal drive toward a singular representation of the world. Olson always saw epic in that sense as a late, literary derivation, something he hated.[xii] The pre-literary "epic," as he proposed it, was a communal invention of culturally shared narrative meanings, the invention of a cohesion of diversities within the otherness of language. The problem for Olson was how get to a procedure, a method that would make possible a similar mode of knowing/speaking as/for community.

The *Curriculum of the Soul* addresses that issue in its own way. Whether it is truly an epic is in a sense beside the point. Perhaps more important is its conscious invocation of a specific notion of community. The community revealed here in relation to Olson's provocation and the call and response of the participants is anything but uniform, anything then but a communion with and within, say, a "theory," the unobstructed visibility of what John Clarke called the MONO. It is rather a register of the immensity and incommensurability of the relations of authoritative finitudes circulating within and beyond the space of the thought Olson's work provokes.

Both this sense of community and of epic are central to understanding the work of John Clarke which always moved, as he proposed in his seminal work on poetics, *From Feathers to Iron*, "to [constellate] the epiphany in a communal place."[xiii] Perhaps more than anyone else to emerge from "Olson's Buffalo," Clarke worked with unwavering dedication to further the understanding of the complex implications of the notions that haunt this essay, and to realize them in his life and work. Never given to the kinds of self-promotion required for literary success, he was largely unknown outside a small group of dedicated readers when he died in 1992. "I personally enjoy the ultimate freedom of being unknown," he wrote to his friend, Albert Glover.[xiv]

Clarke's work culminated in three interrelated efforts: the editing of *intent.: letter of talk thinking & document*, *From Feathers to Iron: A Concourse of World Poetics*, and *In the Analogy*. Clarke's *intent.: letter of talk thinking & document* provided an alternative to the showcase model of publishing that presented poems as literary productions. In a letter to Tom Clark, for instance, he discussed using the poems Clark sent as reviews, situating them a larger discussion of films that themselves are embedded in the thematic discourse of each specific issue of the newsletter. Clarke's insistence that all submissions, including poems, adhere to the particular theme of a given issue was a way of establishing each issue, not as a showcase, but as a space within which a community was revealed at work in language.[xv]

Each issue embodied that community in conversation by including a wide range of work that was transgenerational and trans-genre-ational. The lead article always came from the ancestors, establishing the continuity of the conversation. Charles Olson, Robert Duncan, Eric Gill, Dora Marsden, Robert McAlmon, Simone Weil, and H.D. were featured in various issues. Art work, poems, reviews, essays, and letters were collected from sources as diverse as the *Fugger Newsletter*, contemporary writers, both known and relatively unknown, musicians, and children of various ages, some as young as 7 or 8.

The operative center of each issue was "The Mail," an encapsulation of the enormous correspondence Clarke carried out with myriad writers around the world, as well as what he came to call "The Editor's Quotron." The Quotron was a collection of quotes from diverse sources relevant to the particular theme at hand. It extended the conversation taking place in the newsletter beyond the bounds of the particular moment, or perhaps more accurately, situated that moment in its further complexity. This use of quotation as a way of locating the work in a world of thinking and talk became crucial to the practice of the epic that Clarke developed in his own poetry.

The two places where, in his final years, he worked that out were *From Feathers to Iron* and *In the Analogy*. These two books embody the theory and practice of Clarke's projective art—though the distinction finally won't hold up. *Feathers*, the book of "poetics," is not only a "poetic" text—a text where language is constantly pushed toward what Roman Jackobson called the "poetic function"—it literally incorporates poetry in its body. Clarke's earlier book of poems, *The End of This Side*, is reprinted within the text as part of an elaborate complicating counterstructure of footnotes that amplify, develop, and sometimes overtake the thinking of the text. In the same way, *In the Analogy* develops a complex argument within the structure of the sonnet sequences, while also incorporating chunks of "theoretical" thinking in the numerous quotations which precede each of the sonnets. Clarke confronts and demolishes the still dominant Platonic notion that poetry and thought are distinct, even at odds with one another. He creates an interdependence of texts that enacts a complex passionate thinking.

This work was not meant to demolish or escape genre. Rather it calls our attention to the inadequacies of our thinking of it, and comes out of Clarke's reading of Romanticism as an unfinished project. Blake, Friedrich Schlegel, Novalis, and Coleridge were all active in his thinking. At the heart of the writing is Clarke's ongoing struggle to further Olson's work with the epic. As Clarke thinks the issue through in *Feathers*, it becomes evident that the issue is not a literary problem. If anything, it might be called a political problem, as long as politics is kept located within the visionary. His push is always toward the reconstitution, or re-cognition, of the *elsewhere* here, something he argues we lost with the collapse of Minoan civilization. This is one of the ways in which he continued to address Olson's proposal about the archaic/ordinary. *From Feathers to Iron*, a complex and difficult book that defies summary, proposes the problem as a loss of order and sees the epic as the form of what it calls the strengthening method of world completion. Within this framework, poetry plays a role that has nothing to do with the literary.

By the late 1980's, Clarke had been writing sonnets for a number of years. More than 1,000 of them remain unpublished in his notebooks. For someone so thoroughly focused on the importance of the epic, it was always curious to him that he had been given to write so extensively in what was the quintessential lyric form. During the last five years of his life he came to see how he could ride that form beyond its limits toward the scope necessary for the epic. The result was an enormous outpouring of work that he called *In the Analogy*.[xvi] *In the Analogy* consists of 6 completed books and a fragmentary seventh. Clarke's plan, as Cass Clarke has transcribed it in the opening pages of *In the Analogy*, was to write twelve books, the classic epic form. The fact that it remains fragmentary itself is significant, a post-Romantic gesture of the impossibility of completion.

As Shao John Thorpe pointed out in the introduction to *From Feathers to Iron*, "Clarke doesn't envision the epic as a literary genre so much as an inherent human narrative comprehension, wherever there's an interplay of story with its telling." In *In the Analogy*, Clarke made that archaic comprehension a continuing projective event of community, the voice not of a single person (or even mythic persona), but of a world, itself revealed in a clamor of relations.

One of the ways he accomplished this was to embed each sonnet, as well as each sequence of sonnets, deeply within a world of thought by preceding each poem and each sequence of poems with a number of quotations. The quotes are myriad and diverse, and they provide a universe within which the poems are actively located in conversation. Some quotes mirror the poem, others contradict it, some seem to be its inspiration, while others raise questions about the issues it addresses, and still others develop thinking tangential to it. The overall result is to push the reader into the world of thought out of which the poems arise. The very notion, "Clarke's poems," is called actively into question at every moment, even as the poems proceed to address the questions crucial to the epic impulse as it asserts itself here, now.[xvii] This is what Clarke calls a non-central position, as opposed to a non-ordering intervention. That this epic finally is fragmentary is a fact itself as rich and full of complexity as every other aspect of this truly extraordinary work.

The influence of Olson's Buffalo—and finally it must be seen as that collectivity, that *strange* being in common—is not easy to measure because of the resistance to the literary central to its thinking of itself. Movements come and go. Theories are hot one day and cold the next, commodities in the dynamics of the consumer culture that gives rise to them and the controlling conceit of "modernization" that has seized hold of "reality" in this century.

But the sense of "work" that this community of circulating, authoritative finitudes consistently embodied continues to percolate quietly and invisibly in diverse corners of the mental world, far outside the official ("mainstream" and "avant-garde") precincts of literature. What it will give rise to, what it has already given rise to, is a *remains* that will be seen. Donald Byrd has proposed that the work "of Olson and Clarke demand our attention as few others because they occasionally find means to make and to think at once. That is, they bring evidence that there are means of preoccupation with life that is sufficient to life."[xviii] *To make and to think at once*. What's at stake in such a gesture will always exceed itself as it pushes to shake off the stupor of the literary and realize poetry's necessary vocation.

Special thanks to Albert Glover, Ron Caplan, and Fred Wah for their invaluable assistance in putting this history together. All errors and inaccuracies are my own. Also, thanks to B. Cass Clarke for generously allowing me access to John Clarke's papers.

---

[i]   Daniel Belgrad, in *The Culture of Spontaneity* (Chicago: U of Chicago P, 1998) usefully locates Olson in this regard within a community of writers, artists and musicians, arguing that Olson's poetics are inherently political, having largely been formulated in response to his experience of the liberal/corporate takeover of the Office of War Information and the Office of Facts and Figures (which had been led by Archibald MacLeish) in 1942 and 1943. As a result of the takeover advertising techniques and content replaced reasoned argument for democratic principles.

[ii]   Jean-Luc Nancy, *The Inoperative Community*. Minneapolis, U of Minnesota P, 1991. 11.

[iii]   Nancy, 19.

[iv]   Writing of the modern critical passion, Octavio Paz says: "In love with itself and at war with itself, it cannot affirm anything permanent or take any principle as base, its sole principle being the negation of all principles, perpetual change." *Children of the Mire*, Cambridge: Harvard UP, 1974. 5.

[v]   Caplan to Boughn, July 15, 1998.

[vi]   Wah to Boughn, August 7, 1998.

[vii]   Clarke to Clark, October 23, 1986.

[viii]   Glover to Boughn, May 22, 1998.

[ix]   Albert Glover, review of *In the Analogy*, Poetry Project Newsletter, 1998.

[x]   Glover to Boughn, August 28, 1998.

[xi]   Glover to Boughn, September 2, 1998.

[xii]   "WHY I HATE | Greeks & Italians | [The Vatican since | Dante | [Grecian since | the earliest Renaissance | —including in fact Thomas Aquinas at least] | is | the *Classical — Representational*, either one | THE STATE———COLORED TELEVISION". *Pleistocene Man*. Canton, NY: IFS, 1968. 17.

[xiii]   John Clarke, *From Feathers to Iron: A Concourse of World Poetics*, (Bolinas: Timbouctou, 1987): 152. Octavio Paz, Clarke points out, calls this the "convocation and gravitation of the world in a magnetic here."

[xiv]   Quoted by Glover in his review of *In the Analogy*.

[xv]   Themes included Plants & Animals, For the Sexes, Alphabetics, UFOs, Heaven, Trust, and Embryons.

[xvi]   *In the Analogy*, (Buffalo/Toronto: shuffaloff press, 1997).

[ixvii]   Here is Clarke, for instance, on the issue of the hero:

Devil's Triangle

"How should the hero now speak? Who is after all—a vision?"
—Nietzsche, The Birth of Tragedy

"Texas has a lot on its head."
—Edward Dorn, "The Degeneration of the Greeks"

"Power can stage its own murder to rediscover the glimmer of existence and legitimacy."
—Baudrillard, "Precession of the Simulacra"

"Happiness is not based on oneself, it does not consist of a small home, of taking and getting. Happiness is taking part in the struggle, where there is no borderline between one's own personal world, and the world in general."
—Lee Harvey Oswald, Letter to his brother

If we are the seminal fluidity, then we contain already, as Whitman knew, *everything*, "diddling" (Poe) as well as the Good, however forced sometimes the dilation as seen from old heroic organization before the shit rolled like termite droppings into the load-bearing bridges for everyone to cross into Dealy Plaza, Dallas "takes us" November 22, 1963, and not only Oswald and Ruby, but Guy Bannister, Shaw, Ferrie, Bloomfield and Permindex, now Roscoe White and more aliens up from the South, Watergate's Sturgis, Union survivors up North, all those insane in Honolulu since the birth of the Nation/Hail to the Chief shot American Transcendentalism out of the feudal individual and delivered into the hands of Walt's "unprecedented average," thank you Abe, thanks Jack, now it's up to us.

[xviii] Byrd to an informal internet discussion group, April 14, 1997.

CHARLES OLSON: RECOLLECTIONS

Albert Glover

He was like an angel on earth. It struck me that deeply: 'this is not just an ordinary person.' And I'm enough of a believer to think very seriously about that. I've been touched in some way by something greater than life.

Elvin Jones recalling John Coltrane

I first saw Charles Olson when I enrolled in his course on myth at SUNY, Buffalo, in the fall semester, 1964. Irving Massey, who had been my freshman English teacher at McGill in 1960, had encouraged me to apply for a graduate fellowship at Buffalo; he had joined the English department and knew that fellowships were available for young poets. Since I had graduated from McGill with a first honors in English and the annual Peterson Prize for Poetry, Dr. Massey thought I might fit into the state of New York's plan to build a graduate school to rival the state of California's. That was the rumor. He also suggested I sign up for a class with Olson since there was so much talk about him. Even though I had always spent summers in Provincetown and was dimly aware of Black Mountain College from conversations there, I had not heard of Olson and had no expectations whatsoever as I entered that first class in the basement of one of the gray stone buildings at the "old campus" on Main street. During high school in Needham, MA, my poet models had changed from Whittier, Longfellow, Dickinson, and Frost to Kerouac and "the Beats" made available in Ferlinghetti's marvelous little books which we used to smuggle around in our pockets. One could be suspended for carrying *Howl*, a punishment that increased our admiration for the work enormously. In my 16th summer I wore dark glasses, tried to grow a beard, and hung out around a number of older poets from NYC and Washington, DC, most notably Bill Ward, who was editing *The Provincetown Review*, Dick Dabney, and Bill Walker. Dabney took me along to interview Tennessee Williams one morning at The Crown and Anchor. Williams, someone told me, had once been a bus boy at the Lobster Pot restaurant, a job I had taken that summer. One night at the "head of the meadow" beach, I witnessed for the first (and only) time a truly Dionysian orgy of poetry while, to the sound of flutes and drums and the shapes of topless women dancing, Bill Walker, out of his mind and unable to stand, was passed around the fire shouting inspired, spontaneous poems. I was too young to drink at The Old Colony Tap, but I could attend the Sunday afternoon jams and poetry readings held in the back room there. One Sunday somebody got upset at Walker for using the word "nigger" in a poem, and he responded by displaying a scar on his neck inflicted by the KKK who had tried to lynch him. Poetry readings could be intense in 1958.

I didn't know any of the other graduate students on my first day of Olson's class, but I sat beside another new kid, George Butterick, who seemed almost as disoriented as I was. Later I would discover that George had written an undergraduate thesis on Olson and had some idea of what he was getting into. The class was scheduled from 3 to 5, and on that first day Olson entered the room a bit late. He was rumpled in appearance, as if he had just gotten out of bed and had slept in his clothes: a pair of khaki chinos, a shirt, and a heavy white sweater that he wore over his shoulders, the sleeves tied around his neck. He brought with him a square, quart bottle of orange juice from which he would take occasional swigs. He didn't say anything for a bit but shuffled around in front of us, rubbing his balding head, rummaging in his tote for books or papers. Next he lit a Camel which he consumed in enormous breaths as if he were smoking a joint. I had never encountered a "professor" like him, of course, and felt immediately drawn into the drama. In the second semester and then the third, I would recognize and appreciate this first day routine which was designed to drive away as many students as possible. The basement room quickly filled with smoke, but he would not let anyone open a window. And when he did begin to talk he made himself offensive, aggressive, obscure, even belligerent. "That *fucking* Albright! You *hear* me? Huh?" Rubbing his unshaved chin, shuffling around at the blackboard, making the chalk screech or breaking it in half under the pressure of his writing. "*Jeezus*! I still don't know, like, that *begrunden*, we need to get that, you know, **sta*, which is really, like, *stlocus* or some shit." A few of the students who had been with him during the previous year knew what was going on, but the rest of us were left to fend for ourselves. My education to this point had trained me to "understand" whatever the "teacher" said, but I couldn't begin to understand Olson. He started talking about subjects I'd never encountered: Sumerian poetry, Phoenician studies, Hesiod's *Theogony* – though even then I might have grasped something if his intent had been to make these subjects understandable. On the contrary, he seemed to assume a knowledge that I didn't have. What was he to do with "educated" people who hadn't read Pritchard's *Ancient Near Eastern Texts* or Jane Harrison's *Themis* or Hans Jonas' *The Gnostic Religion*? Having been one of the "smartest kids" in English since I could remember, the situation was interesting. Later Jack Clarke told me about jazz musicians of the time who might initiate young players by calling a familiar number in an unusual key at a lightning tempo; no way to think your way through it. You either played or sat down. Olson played *unfamiliar* numbers like that.

After an hour or so, I was in pain. The atmosphere, in all senses, was too much. But Olson went on as if oblivious to whatever discomfort he might be causing. After ninety minutes, he was just getting started. The pace quickened; the shifts from subject to subject with no apparent logical connection increased. We might go from Sanchuniathon to John Wieners to "the space cadets" to Shakespeare to Mnemosyne and "the nous of Zeus" to Cyrus Gordon in a few minutes. His speed was fabulous. And while it was incomprehensible to me, it was the most brilliant talk I had ever heard. The sheer energy of the discourse (the "high energy construct" he called it in his "Projective Verse Essay") as Charles summoned his power was awesome. I was one who decided to return, but many were not so taken. In fact, I was surprised to learn that some students and faculty thought Olson was a "charlatan" or "guru" or some other disreputable thing. That hostility would later be shifted to his students, the "Olsonites", as if we had somehow improperly encouraged him at a time when he was overwhelmed by grief. Not that I considered any of that or what the implications of this meeting would be for me as I left the first class. I knew that something had happened, but I had no idea what. I'd never really thought about angels. And what was an Ismaeli anyway? *The Gilgamesh Epic?* It all struck me as esoteric.

Because I had been trained as a scholar, my response to Olson's dizzying array of reference was research. I found a copy of *The Maximus Poems*, then in a Jargon/Corinth paperback edition, thinking they would help explain the talk. But, to my surprise, I couldn't understand his poems any more than I could understand his lectures. *The Maximus Poems* were the first poems I had encountered which I could not read with at least some degree of understanding. But then my education, being canonical, had left out a great deal of poetry. I recognized the words; I tracked down the references; I felt the obvious energy of the work. Nevertheless, I couldn't begin to translate the poems into a familiar meaning. It was as if Olson's 'letters" were written in another language. Nor could I find anyone in class who was able to help me. I asked Fred Wah what it all meant (he seemed to be "in the know") but all he could offer by way of explanation was that whatever this was had started in 1963 in Vancouver. No help. I decided I needed further study. And since I was also in a course with Ralph Maud working on a bibliography of critical responses to Dylan Thomas (published as *Dylan Thomas in Print. A Bibliographical History* by University of Pittsburgh Press in 1970) I decided to look for Olson materials while going through periodicals with Ralph. This work began to bear fruit. I started finding early poems in magazines such as *Harper's Bazaar*! I also began collecting publications from booksellers, a collection I later sold to Simon Fraser University as the basis of their Olson collection. This work would result in the first Olson bibliography (1967) with George Butterick published by Robert Wilson in his Phoenix Bibliographies series. But during that fall semester it was simply my way of trying to get a grip on things, to make Charles Olson "understandable."

But "understanding," truly, was not the point. If any "thought" began to solidify, Olson would demolish it. Knowledge was "'what you did with it," he said. So the real work was, in fact, just to be there. It wasn't easy. Exhaustion was almost immediate if I tried to "keep up with" or "understand" anything he said. My 'unlearning" had to be extensive – not the unlearning of whatever information I'd managed to gather in my sixteen years of education (Charles valued facts and I found I had surprisingly few of them); rather, I had to unlearn habits of student behavior and facile "understanding" which school had so rigorously taught me. Few of those habits served this situation though they came in handy for my other courses. There was nothing "to hold on to," nothing "familiar," no place to rest other than in the immediate presence of oneself and others. After an hour, my head would ache with the effort. And then Olson might prowl the room like a Jesuit demanding that I "wake up." There was no escape from him. Yet he was not mean or cruel; after his initial tactics had purged the group of the "non-serious," Olson was an extraordinarily generous teacher. In fact, I soon thought of him as a *"real* teacher" like those I had read about studying zen Buddhism or Gurdjieff's *Meetings with Remarkable Men*. After one of the early classes I nervously approached him. "Are you Gurdjieff? I asked timidly. He bent over, drew me in with his arm, put his face in my face and said: "What, are you on some kind of self-improvement program?"

Olson's presence may well be indescribable; I have never met anyone who could generate the sort of high energy that came from him. Allen Ginsberg, shortly after he'd been crowned King of the May, one night at a party at Leslie Fiedler's house, had the same quality as he danced drunkenly past me in the hall displaying the objects he found in his pockets, most notably "keys" which he intoned so that the word echoed with significance. "Charisma" the popular media used to call it at the time. To be in Olson's "field" was to be at the center of a vortex, a magic *nebel* from which everything originated. Everything was *happening*, to use the language of that time. I don't know how that sounds to anyone who has not had the experience. Michael Castro's poem "The Man Who Looked into Coltrane's Horn" tries to capture the sort of excitement I mean. Olson knew more, had read more, had met Yeats and Pound, could make history present. I have now lived in a world in which such men seem everywhere denied. Is it they are dangerous to themselves and others? I really don't know. What I do know is that Olson was "out there" existing in a dimension that for me was absolutely inspiring. Some of that condition comes through in his writing, but his living presence was, to me, of more importance than all the poems no matter how much I read and value them. The poems, I believe, are what is left after Olson had done what he was doing. They record an event which produced them. These things have value as the residue ("residue as residence" Jack Clarke once wrote) of the "*time*" in which the event actually took place. Charles used Whitehead's *Process and Reality*, he once told me, to justify what he knew from his own experience: that novelty occurs when there is an intersection of the self and universe. What he was making was a world, a cosmos; the poem issued from this world, not the other way 'round as I had thought. Thus, I came to understand, the making happened in the writing which was itself an "event."

Because he was the "unacknowledged legislator," other poets made the trip to Buffalo to visit Olson. That was another benefit of his class. One afternoon Gregory Corso appeared. He was "out" in the way Bill Walker had been. Intense, drunken, "burning for the ancient heavenly connection to the starry dynamo," Corso confronted us, wanted us to match him in lines by Shelley. He would recite a line and wait for our response. Everyone was silent; I wanted to hide for shame. So, unable to play with the students, he turned to Charles. "We're all on death row," he began to chant. (I learned later that Gregory had been educated, in part, at Dannemora.) "We're all dying!" The lament grew in intensity; he began to weep and wail. "Aren't I Captain Poetry, Charles? Aren't I *Captain Poetry*?" "Yes," says Olson, calmly. "Then what should I do?" And without missing a beat, Olson says: "Report for duty."

I kept on with my Maud-guided research finding all sorts of things. Nobody that I knew of had done any serious research on Olson as of 1964, so the field was pristine. I could buy rare items cheap. Early essays like "This is Yeats Speaking" in *The Partisan Review* (Winter, 1946) opened up Olson's relationship with Ezra Pound, and it wasn't too long before I found Pound's letter saying "Olson saved my life." Pound scholars had identified "Olson" as a doctor. (Later, when I sent a copy of the letter to Olson, who had never seen it, he was gratified.) I decided to gather a "Collected Poems" and made copies of everything I discovered from the 1940s and 1950s. I also began to meet my remarkable classmates: George Butterick, Harvey Brown, John Wieners, Jack Clarke, Fred Wah, Charles Boer, Andrew Crozier, John Temple and others. I never considered the paucity of women in the group, though later I became aware that some women were angry about Olson's work as a poet and teacher. Denise Levertov is one example. I had lunch with her on the occasion of her honorary degree from St. Lawrence University in 1984, and I told her about a conversation I'd had with Charles at 28 Fort Square. He'd asked me what I wanted to be (when I grew up, I suppose) and I told him I wanted to be a poet. "Don't *ever* want to be a poet!" he had responded with some ferocity. Denise, who made it clear she did not approve of Olson as a teacher, found in this story an instance of negative dominance; he should have encouraged me and nurtured me, she thought. I, on the other hand, still believe it was necessary advice. You either are or you aren't, and "wanting to be" puts one in a bad situation, to say the least. It also gave me fair warning about how this country treats poets. Then there is a letter from Elizabeth Bishop to Robert Lowell dated May 5th, [1959] in which she writes: "There are three or four people in this world I really hate – Richman, Charles Olson, and a man named Lord Glenavy, who is probably dead of drink by now...." As graduate students, in any case, we were a sort of fraternity, the brothers of Phi Nu Theta (*phusis, nous, and theos*). Olson liked trinities: "*topos, typos, tropos*" was another one at that time. Marjorie Perloff would later call us "the Olson cult," the "last all-male group gathered around a particular poet." But in 1964 I hadn't thought in such terms.

In the spring semester, 1965, I enrolled in both of Olson's courses: "Myth" and "Poetry." The first met on Tuesday afternoon at 3 and would go on until 5. After some post-class milling around, which might go on for another half hour, some of us would join Olson at Onetto's, a roadhouse across Main St. where we would drink and have dinner, often at Olson's expense. It was the banquet where we analyzed what had been said during class in keeping with the notion of a double experience, the "theoretical" and the "applied." While anyone was free to speak, Olson usually held the table in thrall. He would go over issues raised in class, remark upon somebody's response to something said (there was constant evaluation), laugh loudly, drink, slam the table to underscore important ideas, and generally carry on in high spirits. One night John Temple (a marvelous young English poet in whom Charles found a resemblance to Keats) had listened long enough. Standing, he cut through Olson's monologue with an aggressive "Be quiet, Charles. It's my turn to talk." Everyone froze as in a scene from Ed Dorn's *The Gunslinger*. But John had nothing to say; the sudden silence overwhelmed him. He sat down. Olson beamed, laughed, and got right back to talking as if nothing had happened which, of course, was the case. These feasts at Onetto's usually lasted until closing at 2 a.m., though I never lasted that long. Then a few would move on to Olson's motel room or some other place where the conversation would continue, sometimes until the next class, which met at 3 on Wednesday. Then the same routine followed until

Onetto's closed, about a thirty-two hour "run." Jack Clarke, who had some training as a jazz player, had the best nocturnal endurance of anyone in the group. He also had a deep knowledge of William Blake to offer. John Wieners and Harvey Brown also had some staying power. I had a wife and child waiting for me in Cheektowaga. I noticed in his "A Plan for a Curriculum of the Soul" one of the entries is "training in exhaustion and completion."

During one of these nights at Onetto's, Jack Clarke convinced me to show Olson the "Collected Poems" which I had been gathering. Since one was supposed to bring something to table and I rarely had much to say, Olson was surprised and delighted that I had showed up with something perhaps useful. He began asking me about other early work and we had a somewhat private interview on his personal history. A few nights later he called at 3 a.m. Only half awake I lifted the phone to hear: "Glover? Olson." He asked me if I wanted to edit his letters to Cid Corman as my doctoral dissertation. The only stipulation was that I couldn't include Corman's letters to him. I agreed without hesitation. The conversation lasted about three minutes. But from that moment forward my relationship with Charles changed considerably.

There were some marvelous scenes in Buffalo during the spring of 1965. The city was full of poets. Robert Graves came to read at the Albright Knox gallery, for instance, and there was a large turnout. After the reading Olson approached him, embraced him, and said: "You're just like a loaf of fresh-baked bread; I'm going to eat you all up!" Olson laughed, but Graves looked shaken. Poets were conspicuous and public, like movie stars. When we gathered at public tables, people came over to get autographs. One night in a restaurant on Elmwood, Charles and John Wieners and Harvey Brown began smoking a joint and passing it around the table; nobody said or did anything about it. The revolution was underway and the poets were political leaders. Olson was to be president of the "Nation of Nothing but Poetry." Later, during the summer when he returned from seeing Ezra Pound in Spoleto and tried to make the Berkeley Poetry Conference into a political convention, some, including a few of his closest friends, did not return to the hall after intermission. That, really, was the end of that. When he returned to Buffalo (we had already heard the tape of his lecture) Olson raged about the event at Onetto's; I had never seen him in agony before. He had been *wrong*, he thought. But then his conviction would return and he'd curse his false friends for deserting him. As a result of Intelligence Agency action or not, by the end of 1969 all living revolutionary leadership was dead or in hiding. Rock music had met its limit at Altamont and Ed Sanders would soon investigate the "Manson Family" murders.

But in the spring of 1965 something else was happening. One Sunday morning David Posner, the custodian of the Lockwood Library poetry collection, invited the Olsonites to a brunch honoring the visit of Stephen Spender who happened to be in town. It was a stiff affair for the most part. Spender had Charles Olson confused with Elder Olson, for starters, and the conversation remained polite. After an hour or so David had to go somewhere, and he surrendered the apartment on Main St. to Olson, Clarke, Brown, and some others who had nothing else to do. It was a glorious day when the green is more gold than green, an observation Olson made about one of Frost's lines: "'nature's first green is gold'...Jeeezus I wish I'd written that," he told me. So we decided to have a picnic. Jack and Harvey went in one direction to get whatever, and Charles and I headed across Main to a liquor store for wine. We had to travel only 500 yards or so, but the trip was dizzying. I quickly realized that try as I might I could not stay beside Olson. He'd go and stop and turn and move again, perhaps backward, in an unpredictable dance. I was on his right and became determined to stay at his side; I put all my attention on that. As soon as I managed to stay with him for a few minutes, he stopped, took me by the shoulders, and turned me 90 degrees to the left. In front of us was a rural roadway full of flowering trees, songbirds and wildflowers. It was paradise. We walked about ten yards into it as if we were walking into a movie when Olson stopped, bent over, and plucked a flower which he then tucked into a buttonhole of my shirt. "This is wild myrtle, sacred to Aphrodite," he told me. Then he turned me around and we were back on Main St. with pavement and cars and all the rest. I returned to the place the next day but couldn't find any trace of it.

The picnic turned out to be a great adventure. Olson led the way in his Chevy wagon. (Earlier that year I'd had my first ride in that Chevy as Charles drove Butterick and me down Main St. for some reason. The back of the wagon, which had no reverse gear, was full of manuscripts, and with the windows open or when the door opened pages swirled into the street. George was horrified, but Charles, smoking, talking and laughing all at the same time, couldn't have cared less. I thought of those ancient Chinese poets who, in legend, scattered their poems upon streams. How thrilling it felt to meet one.) He led us to a convent run by the Sisters of St. Francis where we encamped in a large, open field under a somewhat scrawny tree. As we started to settle in, Olson keeping up a brilliant monologue, we saw a State Trooper walking across the field toward us. Apparently the sisters didn't want us having a picnic on their property. It was the first (and only) time I had seen Olson confronted by "authorities." He simply stayed himself, expressed some surprise and disappointment that we were not welcome, and announced he knew an even better place to go. We followed him and the troopers (there was another one in the car) followed us. We were going to "Melissa's place," wherever that was. And, in fact, after a short ride we came to a large estate; Olson turned into the impressive driveway. The troopers pulled over to see what would ensue. At the end of the long driveway Olson parked, got out, went to the door and rang the bell. A woman opened the door and spoke to him. Then Olson returned with a big smile and led us to a lovely lawn on the grounds which had a lively brook running through it. Here we spread our stuff on a blanket and continued as if there had been no interruption. Unlike many political people at the time, Olson expressed no animosity or paranoia toward the sisters or the troopers. No complaints. Everywhere was paradise.

Another extraordinary event took place at Melissa and Charles Banta's pastoral estate, one which (like the myrtle flower) made an enormous impression on me. Olson was telling us Civil War stories. At some point, Union troops were waiting along the edge of a brook very much like the one near which we were sitting. Upstream, another contingent of soldiers had encountered Confederate forces, and the men downstream could hear the sound of a ferocious battle. "Suddenly," Charles said swinging his arm dramatically over our view of the brook, "the water turned red with blood." I swear at that moment the water in front of me turned red! I thought at the time I was the only one who saw it, but later when I asked Clarke if he had witnessed that, he nodded. Was the power of Olson's imagination so enormous that he could create that sort of hallucination? In his wonderful book *Charles Olson in Connecticut*, Charles Boer tells similar stories. At that point in his life, at least, Olson seemed to enjoy "entertaining Indians." He had certainly entertained at Timothy Leary's Newton house a few years earlier. Timothy Leary gives an account of his psilocybin session with Arthur Koestler in *High Priest*: "To put on a good mushroom ritual, I had wired up to Charles Olson, our father who art in Gloucester." Lately I've been thinking of Terence McKenna's "You See What I Mean."

Meanwhile the semester went on in the usual way. There were many chores spread among the excitement. *The Niagara Frontier Review* appeared and Frontier Press began publishing books. I typed the sheets for Ed Dorn's *Rites of Passage* (later reissued as *By the Sound*) on a used varitype machine that Harvey Brown had purchased somewhere. Olson became caught up by Ed Sanders and *Fuck You. A Magazine of the Arts*. Butterick, Wah, and I had moved our young families into a public housing project on Kensington Ave. where we began collaborating in modest ways. As a TA ($2,400 a year and tuition waived) and Ph.D. candidate, I could not devote myself entirely to the poetry scene. My research paper for Olson's "Myth" class was on the cave at Dicte in Crete, and in it I argued that the broken tablet excavated there reads "Melissa" rather than "Wanassa." Olson disagreed, though I had some satisfaction when he announced to his audience at Berkeley he had recently read at Melissa's theater in Spoleto. While the poets had gathered in Berkeley for the great conference, I sat on the steps of the housing project in Buffalo and listened to the gunfire going off not many blocks away; the sky was red with fire. The riots were on.

In the fall of '65 I enrolled again in Olson's courses. He did the opening number, familiar to me by now, but after a few weeks he disappeared. He'd gone back to Gloucester we were told. It had never occurred to me that a "Professor" could simply leave; I took it as a great lesson. But, now, what were we going to do? Jack Clarke, who was an Assistant Professor and the only faculty member who had actually studied with Olson, agreed to take over the course in myth. He wrote to Olson for instructions and led us through a semester on the basis of that correspondence and his own research. Olson had wanted to create an Institute patterned on the Princeton Institute of Advanced Studies but had been unable to obtain funding for the project. So I proposed we start something called "The Institute of Further Studies" (IFS playing with Leary's IFIF, Institute for Internal Freedom) and George Butterick, Fred Wah, and Jack Clarke liked the idea. We named Jack "the Director" since he was a member of the faculty. In the semesters to follow we produced six issues of *The Magazine of Further Studies*, held poetry readings and lectures, and tried generally to keep Olson's presence alive. During the same time Charles had asked me to act as his "secretary." He would send me new poems which I would put in files "for publication" or "not for publication." Then he might direct editors looking for work from him to me. That arrangement didn't work well. A bit later he asked me to come to Gloucester with a truck and take all his boxes of stuff to start an archive somewhere. "I honestly believe you are my archivist" he wrote. But I refused that request because I knew George was far more disciplined than me and should be the one to do the job.

I visited Olson's Fort Square rooms once during the summer of 1966. My wife Pat and I drove up from Provincetown. We didn't get past the kitchen, but Olson stayed up talking late into the night. He displayed a jar of mushrooms "laced with strychnine" that someone had sent to him from California. Perhaps I would like to try one? I declined. At one point, he read to us about Buddhism from his favorite dictionary, *Webster's Second Edition*. The Four Noble Truths. As the evening went on I became sleepy as usual, but Olson would shake me if I started to sleep. He seemed to be having a good time with Pat who challenged him with her spiritual ferocity: "Say it in three words or less!" He'd slap the table, laugh, and set off on another twenty-minute solo. Then he'd look at her for approval, and she'd do it again. There was a Jackson Pollock drawing on the fridge, put up there like a child's homework by an admiring parent.

When we moved to northern New York in 1968, I brought The Institute of Further Studies with me. Issue #6 of *The Magazine of Further Studies* which contains Olson's "A Plan for a Curriculum of the Soul" was edited at Stan and Mary Holberg's house across the street from the pine plantation where I'd come upon my first *amanita muscaria* mushroom. In the months preceding the publication of Gordon Wasson's expensive *Soma, The Divine Mushroom*, Charles and I had been discussing this mushroom which appears in *The Maximus Poems* briefly: "while on / Obadiah Bruen's Island, the Algonquins / steeped fly agaric in whortleberry juice, / to drink to see." I wanted to try it. We had both also been reading *The Teachings of Don Juan*. As my research deepened and I grew nearer to eating these mushrooms which I had gathered and dried, Charles wrote to me on one of his wonderful postcards that he didn't know from experience if "whortleberry juice" did, in fact, "cut" fly agaric. He let me know that the risk I might take was *mine* alone. I've written about some of this foolishness in *The Mushroom*, my contribution to *A Curriculum of the Soul*. And it is true that the "vision" for the project which has kept me busy for many years came from the mushroom shortly after Olson's death and the arrival of Wasson's beautiful book purchased for me by students at St. Lawrence University. I would publish an epic tribute to Olson, a work with many voices, all of them "one voice." Jack Clarke took the "Plan" and made the assignments. The fascicles would go out in various colors and together construct a "rainbow bridge." The Ford Foundation via St. Lawrence University purchased the publishing tools I requested. My colleague and friend in Fine Arts, Guy Berard, helped me with book design and printing. After the "proof copies" (about 400 of each) had been made, I would edit the whole into a volume as lavish in production as *Soma* itself. The last fascicle (*one's own Language* by Lisa Jarnot) came out in 2002 and the lush limited edition of 51 copies was ready for the Charles Olson centennial in Vancouver, 2010. Finally, a trade edition in 2 volumes appeared from Spuyten Duyvil in 2016.

The last words I heard from Olson came by messenger, a phone call from Linda Parker. *Letters for Origin* had been published by Jonathan Cape early in 1970, and Charles wanted me to know that he liked the book. "But the words at the back" (an editor's note I had made in lieu of a scholarly preface) "top it." He was ever generous with me. And the last time I *saw* Olson was at the "Olson Conference" in Iowa City, 1976. George Butterick, who was on his way to becoming "the Dean of Olson Studies" (as a distinguished panelist would announce a few years later at an MLA conference) had prepared the event with Sherman Paul who was promoting his new book *Olson's Push. Origin, Black Mountain, and Recent American Poetry*. Though I had not been officially invited, George had become embarrassed by what he called the "loose Visigothic horde" of Olsonites and was determined to make Charles a respectable literary figure through his work at the Olson archives at the University of Connecticut. Ironically, the University of California would become Olson's posthumous publisher! Nevertheless, my efforts on Olson's behalf made it hard for George to keep me out when I pressed. Eventually it was arranged that I would introduce George and thus have something to do, i.e., I could have a room at The Rebel Motel in Iowa City and apply for travel money from my home institution. Still, as a reader of "Letter for Melville, 1951" I felt both guilt and anger about the Conference and the agenda that came with it, scratching "each other's backs with a dead man's hand." Regardless, George and I went to lunch together after one of the morning sessions and whom should we see in the school cafeteria but Charles! We both recognized him immediately, though the occurrence did stretch our credulity. I thought George was going to drop his tray, but he only turned white and held on. We didn't want to stare as we made our way to a vacant table. Seated, I said "It's him. He's here!" George nodded. Charles came over toward us, but we made no sign of recognition; on the contrary, we both pretended we didn't see him. So he sat at the table directly behind me, his back toward mine. And then, more amazing still, he pushed himself back in his chair so that his shoulders were actually touching mine. I continued with difficulty to act as if nothing were happening as my body filled with an incredible warm, golden light which seemed to flow out of him where we touched. Then he got up and disappeared. George and I never talked about it and the story sounds gaga to me as I write it down more than forty years later. And though I have had occasional dreams of him, Olson has never again appeared to me in the flesh since that day.

BUFFALO ENGLISH: LITERARY GLORY DAYS AT UB

Bruce Jackson

Originally published in 1999 in Buffalo Beat; *used by permission of the author.*

A thin man sat quite still at a grey metal desk, staring down at a lined yellow pad. I asked him where the main office was. He turned, looked at me for a moment, then erupted. "I'm not here to answer questions!" he screamed. "Why do all you people ask me questions? Why don't you all just leave me alone?" He slammed the door shut with his foot.

It was September 1967, my first day in the UB English department.

A man about my age came down the hall carrying a huge stack of books. I asked him the same question. He pointed through a corridor connecting the two long sheds on Bailey avenue that were the English department's home in those days. (The sheds were named Annex A and Annex B. No one knew what they were annexes of.) I thanked him and then asked him about the thin screaming man.

"Oh, that's John Wieners. You shouldn't talk to him. He just goes off if you talk to him."

"What does he teach?"

"Teach? Nothing. He's a poet. He's not a member of the department."

"What's he doing here? In a faculty office, I mean."

"Writing poems, I guess."

The hot center and the cutting edge

For at least a decade, the UB English department was the most interesting English department in the country. Other universities had the best English departments for history or criticism or philology or whatever. But UB was the only place where it all went on at once: hot-center and cutting-edge scholarship and creative writing, literary and film criticism, poem and play and novel writing, deep history and magazine journalism. There was a constant flow of fabulous visitors, some here for a day or week, some for a semester or year. The department was like a small college: seventy-five full-time faculty teaching literature and philosophy and film and art and folklore, writing about stuff and making stuff. Looking back on it from the end of the century, knowing what I now know about other English departments in other universities in those years, I can say there was not a better place to be.

It's not like that now. For a long time UB has drawn on its bragging rights to the Department but abandoned the responsibility of nourishing it. Faculty are down by a third and the infrastructure has all but vanished. Riding on reputation is like driving cross-country without putting oil in the crankcase: you can get away with it for a while, then you hear bad noises.

What Al Cook did

The UB English department was built by a man named Al Cook. My image of him is of a man in constant motion, forever talking or reading or writing. Al left Buffalo in the mid-seventies and went to Brown, but right up to when he died last year people talked about him as if he'd been part of the department until a few months ago. He was a presence, Al Cook was. I saw him over the years at academic meetings or when he came here for special events, like Fiedlerfest at UB in 1994. He never seemed to change. Other people got older, paunchier, balder, slower, but Al Cook was always Al Cook. He transcended the physical. He was medium height, big in the chest, always scheming. Al was always my idea of what Odysseus looked like.

They must have had hiring committees and meetings during the three years of Al's chairmanship, but he seemed to make connections and hire people at will. I met him at a dinner in my next-to-last year at Harvard. Al said, "You're going to be looking for a job next year. Call me and maybe we can work out something for you at Buffalo." I suppose the look my face was one that Al had seen before. Academic jobs were plentiful in those days, I was at Harvard, and Buffalo was, well, Buffalo.

"We've hired Charles Olson, Dorothy van Ghent, Leslie Fiedler, Stanley Edgar Hyman, and John Logan," Al said. "Buffalo is more interesting than you think. Give me a call when you're ready, come and visit, we'll talk. Right?" I nodded.

I didn't. When the job cycle began the next year, I got job offers from University Pennsylvania, UCLA and MIT. I forgot about Buffalo entirely. Al Cook called. "Have you taken a job yet?" I said I hadn't. He said, "Since I talked to you we hired C.L. Barber. John Logan. Lionel Abel. John Barth. Robert Creeley."

I don't know how these names resonate for you in the spring of 1999. I can tell you that in the mid-sixties the list was breath-taking. Fiedler was the author of the most important book on American literature of the decade, *Love and Death in the American Novel*. It was written in such lucid English that you found it on the shelves of non-specialists as well. Cesare Lombardi Barber (Joe to everyone who knew him) had written only one book in his academic career, *Shakespeare's Festive Comedy*, but it was one of the most respected books on Shakespeare. John Logan had written *Cycle for Mother Cabrini* and *Ghosts of the Heart*. Lionel Abel had written the key book on midcentury drama: *Metatheatre*. John Barth, author of *End of the Road, The Sot-Weed Factor* and *The Floating Opera*, was like Bellow and Malamud: someone whose work we all read as soon as it came out. Just about everyone I knew in college and grad school owned a well-worn copy of Robert Creeley's *For Love*, and half the aspiring poets I knew spent their nights trying to mime his spare lines and never getting close.

Charles Olson was the magister—a poet and scholar who had followers. I knew him from *Call me Ishmael* and *The Maximus Poems*. People had described him as a huge figure of a man, six-foot-six and big on the frame, a man who filled a room. I'd heard Olson stories the whole time I'd been at Harvard.

Olson was mythic before I got here and so he remained. I never set eyes on him. When I came for my interview he was on leave, "But he'll be back next year," they said. I got a fourth year on my grant at Harvard so the next year I only visited Buffalo once on a house-hunting expedition. Olson was still away at his place north of Boston they said, "But he'll be back next year." Then he died.

His friend Jack Clarke, another UB English department poet and visionary, told me, "But he knew it was coming for a year. He finished what he could, filed what he wanted to, got rid of the loose ends." Someone else told me that Jack was with Olson at the end and that Olson came out of a deep sleep or a coma, sat up, pointed with his right index finger, said, "So THAT'S it!" And died. I always meant to ask Jack if that was really what happened but I didn't and now it's too late because Jack died too.

Even before Al Cook got around to talking about the money (more than all the other offers), the job conditions (I could teach whatever I wanted), the perks (many), I was ready to sign anything he put in front of me. There just wasn't a better place to be.

Being here

The names I've told you are just part of it. There were other writers and critics here, and more who came soon after, some to stay and some to visit: the critic Dwight MacDonald, the story-writer Donald Barthelme, the scholar Angus Fletcher, the poets Jerome Mazzarro and Irving Feldman and William Sylvester and Robert Hass, the novelist John Coetzee, the critic David Bazelon. And there were writers and artists and thinkers in other departments who were part of our community of words and ideas: Raymond Federman (who eventually shifted from French into English), René Girard, Michel Foucault, Olga Bernal, Eugenio Donato, Lucas Foss, Hélène Cixous, Warren Bennis, John Sullivan.

By the time I moved to Buffalo, Al Cook had finished his three years as chair and had been succeeded by Norman Holland, a psychoanalytic critic who also had a law degree and who had done his undergraduate work in engineering. I'd met Norman when I'd interviewed at MIT. After the conversation, the man who'd taken me around said, "Don't worry, when you're here you won't have to talk to him." During that extra year at Harvard I got a letter from Norman saying he'd taken a job as chair of the UB English department, so we'd be colleagues after all.

Al had promised that I'd be promoted after I was here a year. Norman fulfilled Al's promise, but gave me no raise with the promotion; it was just a change in my rank from assistant to associate professor. I fronted him in the hallway about it. He said, "You said you wanted a promotion, you didn't say anything about a raise." I said some truly awful things, very loudly, after which Norman said, "I can see you're angry about this." Norman could say things like that. He was, as psychologists say, a man nearly without affect, which drove a lot of people quite crazy, not just me.

One time Norman asked if I'd photograph him for the dust jacket of his new book. I went to his house and shot two rolls of film. Norman picked out a few he liked on the contact sheets and I made him several eight-by-ten prints. Some months later he came to my office and said "I have a present for you." He handed me the dust jacket of his new book, with my photograph on the back or on the flap. "I hear you have a new book coming out soon. Maybe when you get it we can exchange copies of our books." This time I couldn't even froth; I was just speechless.

Not long after, someone who knew him really well and who heard me ranting about the dry promotion and empty dust jacket said, "It wasn't deliberate. Norman is very wealthy and he doesn't want people to know it so he never confronts what he thinks are money issues. That's why he only serves Kool-Aid at those afternoon departmental parties at his pool."

Before that year was out there was a departmental revolt because nothing was coming out of the chairman's office. A troika was appointed to run the department. Norman was still nominally chairman, but everything was managed by a man named Joe Riddle and two other people.

I thought the whole enterprise was falling apart: junior faculty were doing all the business and this rich guy with no affect sat in the chairman's office and smiled and did nothing. Warren Bennis, who was what we then called "provost" and what we now call "dean" of the School of Social Science and Administration told me to calm down. "As long as somebody's signing the papers, who's signing them and who sits in what office doesn't matter to you. Not in that department. Not with all that talent."

Lionel Abel's toothpicks

The thing I most remember about department meetings in those years was Lionel Abel talking with a thick red toothpick hanging from his mouth. Lionel's toothpicks were called Stim-u-dents and I always assumed he chewed on them to deal with a former cigarette habit, though he may just have had a jones for Stim-u-dents. The meetings were vigorous and engaged. I loved every one of them. A regular feature of nearly every meeting was Leslie Fielder waiting until the end of an argument by everyone else to say something eminently sensible, whereupon Lionel would say, his New York accent coming from way back in his palate and halfway up his nasal passage, "Lessssslee, that's the STOOOPedest thing I've ever hearrrrd." His Stim-u-dent would wiggle up and down.

The Vietnam war

The key thing about those years was the war in Southeast Asia. It touched nearly everything we did: how we taught our classes, the lives of our students, our conversations. You can't imagine now the antipathy between town and gown. For a time, hundreds of Buffalo policemen in riot gear occupied the Main Street campus. Forty-five faculty were arrested for demonstrating against the war in the administration building one Sunday morning when the building was empty of anyone save them. Tear-gas canisters were fired into stairwells of the old Norton Union (now part of the School of Dental Medicine) so they would enter the circulating air system of the entire building. A Buffalo police official went on one of television news programs and denied firing any tear gas anywhere on campus. Warren Bennis and I looked out the windows of the old WBFO studio on the second floor of Norton Union and watched them fire into a women's dormitory across the street while that interview was on the air; we followed it with a report on what we were seeing a hundred yards away. I have a photograph of the window over the front door of the Union riddled with holes from the blast of a police shotgun. A police official said the blast couldn't have been done by the police because the police on campus hadn't been issued shotguns, all they had were their sidearms and the teargas launchers. He didn't note that the teargas launchers were twelve-gauge pump shotguns, one of which was in every squadcar.

Faculty argued on both sides of the war issue for years. I didn't realize it then, but that argument made us a community as nothing else has since. Even in arguing against one another, we met people we would not otherwise have met, engaged in conversations we would not otherwise have had, dealt with ethical issues that transcended the ordinary politics of the campus.

Things we know for sure

In *Godfather 2* Michael Corleone tells one of his henchmen, "If anything in this life is certain, if history has taught us one thing, it is that you can kill anyone." More important things are also certain. The sun will rise. The sun will set. And nothing lasts. Nothing.

Joe Barber went to UC Santa Cruz and died a few years later. Eugenio Donato went to UC Riverside and killed himself a few years later. Bob Hass moved to Berkeley and later won a MacArthur and was named Poet Laureate of the United States. Jack Barth got so famous Johns Hopkins hired him to teach in the Writing Seminars and he went back to his beloved Maryland to sail and write more novels. Bill Sylvester and Lionel Abel retired. John Logan and Dwight MacDonald retired and died. Donald Barthelme died young. Al Cook died. John Coetzee went home to South Africa, wrote novels, won the Booker Prize. Jerry Mazzarro found the English department too grumpy, moved to Italian, and retired. David Bazelon retired. (David and I squabbled and groused at one another for years; not long ago, we met at a Guggenheim Foundation party in New York and spent much of the evening drinking the Foundation's booze and telling good-old-days-in-Buffalo stories). Ray Federman is retiring. René Girard went to Stanford and Angus Fletcher went to CUNY. Olga Bernal abandoned literature entirely, moved back to France and became a highly-acclaimed sculptor. Irving Feldman is still in the English department, he won a MacArthur, and I've never been able to have a conversation with him. Lucas Foss went to conduct symphonies elsewhere. Warren Bennis went to Cincinnati as president for a few years, then settled in as distinguished professor at USC. Bob Creeley is still here; he won the Bollingen Prize this year, the best poetry prize in America. And Leslie Fiedler is still here too, not giving classes any more, but still working with students, still writing all the time, still able to cut through the fog.

Martin Meyerson gave Al Cook a blank check and Al built a grand department with it, a department that was deservedly world-famous, one that was fun to grow up in. No college president nowadays could give anyone a blank check. In the Meyerson-Cook years, the state was still building SUNY and Rockefeller was pouring money into the system. There was money for research, students, promotions, hires, secretaries, hardware, travel, assistants, money for anything you could think of spending money on. I came here in the middle of that and I thought that was the way colleges were. I didn't know that

UB in the 1960s and 1970s was anomalous, abnormal, freaky. Glorious and brilliant, but nonetheless anomalous, abnormal, freaky.

VERNACULAR PEDAGOGY: BUFFALO
IN THE LATE 1960S

Michael Davidson

When I arrived in Buffalo in 1967 it was the best of times; it was the worst of times. The best of times was embodied by the 1968 Buffalo Festival of the Arts which featured the Merce Cunningham Dance Company performing *Rainforest* with sets by Andy Warhol, designed by Jasper Johns, music by David Tudor and John Cage. In the audience were Robert Rauschenberg, Jasper Johns, Taylor Mead, John Cage and, miraculously, Marcel Duchamp. During that week, there were concerts by Morton Feldman, Iannis Xenakis, Luicano Berio, a lecture by Buckminster Fuller and one by Cage, appearances by Cecil Taylor and the Ayler Brothers, with poetry readings by Louis Zukofsky, Robert Creeley, Robin Blaser and Allen Ginsberg. The entire festival was filmed by Richard Leacock and D.A. Pennebaker. For an incoming graduate student from the suburbs, this was pretty exciting stuff.

But it was the worst of times, manifested by the expansion of the Vietnam War following the Tet Offensive and invasion of Cambodia. Race riots in Newark, Chicago and other major cities—including Buffalo--transformed Civil Rights activism into more militant, confrontational movement. It was also a moment of transition from a domestic industrial economy to neoliberal globalization. Buffalo was particularly hard hit by the "great sucking sound" of labor being outsourced to other parts of the world that led to the decline of US manufacturing in the late 1960s and 1970s. Bethlehem Steel, Buffalo's major employer, began to lay off workers in the late 1960s and by 1982 the vast Lackawanna Pant was closed for good. As a result, the town of Lackawanna lost 70% of its tax base. Republic Steel, Westinghouse, Trico, General Electric, U.S. Electrical Motor Company all left, contributing to an extended industrial archipelago of decaying factory towns throughout the Midwest.

My experience at what was then called the State University of New York at Buffalo (in those days on Main Street) was framed by both of these factors: a vibrant arts and poetry scene and escalating domestic and global crisis reflected in student activism on and off campus. In solidarity with the latter, 45 faculty members sat in and were arrested in President Regan's office after he allowed police on campus to confront student demonstrators. Strikes, sit-ins and demonstrations were an almost weekly occurrence making teaching and attending classes a challenge. Poetry readings on campus were invariably related to anti-war activities, and we made regular trips across the Canadian/US border to Toronto to visit American expatriates fleeing the draft. Major poems of the period—Robert Duncan's "Up-Rising," Allen Ginsberg's "Wichita Vortex Sutra," Ed Dorn's, *North Atlantic Turbine*, Denise Levertov's *To Stay Alive*, work by Robert Bly, Amiri Baraka, W.S. Merwin, Muriel Rukeyser, George Oppen—became models for an energized political poetry.

At that time, there was no formal poetics program, but poetry was central to the curriculum. At a present moment when narrative dominates cultural studies, it is hard to remember a time when poetry was the central discourse of literary study. At Buffalo poetry and poetics were amply represented in the curriculum, as evidenced by some of the seminars I attended: Leslie Fiedler's course in Dante, Fred Plotkin's seminar on seventeenth-century poets (through phenomenology), Stuart Schneiderman's seminar in Blake (through Lacan), Bill Sylvester's seminar on Spenser, Robert Creeley's seminar on Crane, Gerald O'Grady's seminar on Langland (through new media and cybernetics), C.L. Barber's seminar in Shakespeare's sonnets. Such ample coverage of individual poets would be an anomaly at my university today and I suspect elsewhere as well.

My new critical training in literature, with its emphasis on the organic, autotelic poem and close reading of texts was profoundly challenged by several factors at Buffalo. The first and most important was the wake left by Charles Olson, who stopped teaching at Buffalo in 1965 but whose impact was still very much in evidence. Many of us had come to Buffalo to study at "Black Mountain West," and that fact was apparent in the occasional visits of former Black Mountain students (John Wieners, Fielding Dawson, Ed Dorn) and faculty (Robert Duncan) and fellow travelers (LeRoi Jones, Robert Kelly and Gregory Corso, each of whom taught briefly at the university). The Olson legacy was characterized by an emphasis on process rather than product, methodology rather than result. Poetry could not be separated from history or ethnography or geology, and to become a poet was to become an "archaeologist of morning," digging beneath the surface of received opinion and canonical history. His reading list was eccentric, including in addition to literary figures like Shakespeare, Blake and Melville, philosophers (the Pre-Socratics but not Plato or Aristotle, Henri Corbin on Avicenna, Whitehead) historians (Heraclitus, Brooks Adams, Frederick Merk), anthropologists, linguists and naturalists (Benjamin Lee Whorf, Carl Sauer, Edgar Anderson) and scientists (Norbert Wiener). Not everyone teaching poetry at Buffalo was an Olson adherent, nor was his reading list by any means the standard for instruction. In fact, there was a good deal of grumbling among some professors over what they took to be the bombastic and incoherent qualities of Olson's teaching. But among student poets, Olson was definitely a primary source.[i]

A second influence, at least for me, was the emergence of critical theory into the curriculum. Structuralism, Russian formalism, semiotics, Lacanian psychoanalysis and phenomenology were very much in evidence in seminars for which poetics was a litmus test of linguistic indecidability and indeterminacy. Michel Foucault was in residence for two semesters (he brought Borges to give a reading) as was Roland Barthes in 1972. This continental strain of poetics was brought by Eugenio Donato who with Richard Macksey had just edited *The Structuralist Controversy: The Languages of Criticism and the Sciences of Man* from Johns Hopkins University Press, an anthology of essays that served as an inaugural English language introduction to critical theory. Donato's presence was experienced as a threat by some in the English department, a fact vividly illustrated by the unannounced appearance of theater critic and dramatist Lionel Abel who crashed one of Donato's seminars, openly attacking him for leading students astray. "Cultural Stalinism," Donato muttered as he cancelled class and walked out. The appearance of critical theory and continental philosophy into the poetics discussion was symptomatic of a shift in academic culture that was a bellwether for things to come.

If there is a link between these rather disparate influences it is a focus on the materiality of language, whether through Olson's emphasis on voice and page in the poem or his critique of entrepreneurial rhetoric ("the musickracket of all ownership"), Creeley's stress on the physical materials of writing, and Structuralism/Semiotics' emphasis on language as signifying system. This aspect of the "linguistic turn" marks a significant shift from the expressivism of much 1950s and 1960s poetry, and becomes central to the later Poetics Program. The Subject, capital 'S,' that underwrote so much postwar poetry was itself subject to erasure by being regarded now as the product, not the source, of discursive protocols and idiolects. Or as Creeley says in "The Pattern," "As soon as / I speak, I / speaks. It // wants to / be free but / impassive lies // in the direction / of its /words."[ii]

"take the way of / the lowest"[iii]

These lines from Charles Olson's "Songs of Maximus" epitomize the theory of pedagogy that I experienced as a graduate student at Buffalo. There was a sense that knowledge should not be spoon fed but had to be earned by hard work and self-motivation, not by formal instruction. I was never given a bibliography or study guide, never told about the MLA bibliography or other data bases, never instructed in how to prepare for a job interview. Such excrescences of what we would now call "professionalism" were frowned upon—at least in my circle—and we were told, as Olson said, to "take the way of / the lowest/ including your legs" which meant following a hunch through whatever rhizomatic circuits and avoid, at all costs, the conventional routes to knowledge. To some extent the model here was Olson's advice to Ed Dorn— that to understand THE WEST he had to know everything about barbed wire and pemmican.[iv] But Olson's cryptic notes required an interpretive gift that I didn't possess, and the clerics who were on hand were no more helpful. Jack Clarke's seminars on Blake and mythology were inspiring and confusing in equal parts. He would put cryptic diagrams on the board referring to various mythological or Blakean systems that everyone else in the class seemed to have mastered. The presumption was that we had already mastered Blake's prophecies or Heraclitus or Pound's *Cantos* and all that was necessary was to provide a metonymic trigger for specific issues in those texts. I remember reading poems from Robert Duncan's *The Opening of the Field* and asking Jack to recommend some books or articles on George MacDonald. His response was "go ask Duncan." At the time, I thought this was pretty stingy on his part, but it did lead me, eventually, to ask Duncan about MacDonald and many other authors, the result of which was a dissertation on the San Francisco poet. In a sense, a good deal of what I have written since leaving Buffalo is indebted to what I did *not* learn or what I had to find out for myself.

This parsimonious, work-ethic pedagogy was extended to my experience of teaching. There was no formal research seminar or tutorial on pedagogical method (Peter Middleton informs me that this had changed by the time he arrived in 1977). I arrived as a first-year graduate student, asked to make a reading list and thrust into a classroom without any training. I had to invent teaching from the ground up, and since my only pedagogical models were my professors I tried, in vain, to imitate them. I cringe to think of what I passed off as information in my years as a graduate teacher, and it was only much later that I learned to calibrate what I brought to the classroom to what students needed to learn. On the other hand, those years were so broken-up by strikes and protests that the chaos of my classroom reflected, in various ways, the chaos in the U.S. in the late 1960s.

If pedagogy was a mystery, using the Lockwood Library's Rare Books collection of modern and contemporary literature was a grail quest. The Rare Books collection was presided over by Karl Gay who had a proprietary sense of the archive he guarded. Manuscripts and rare books were often inaccessible, subject to Gay's whims of the moment. Much of the small press poetry I wanted to read was dispensed in small doses, and copying from them was severely restricted. When I wanted to copy Jack Spicer's *Heads of the Town Up to the Aether*, I was told that I could only copy three pages a day with a library attendant looking over my shoulder at the Xerox machine. I managed to copy the entire book over a period of many weeks, a task that I imagine would have amused Spicer.

Creeley represents the bridge between my period at Buffalo and the establishment of the Poetics Program, and was an enormously helpful and generous figure. He cared deeply about his students and would spend long hours in office sessions or at one of the local bars. His seminar on Hart Crane typified his teaching method. He would come into the classroom, light up a thin cigar and start free associating, depending on his mood. Bobbie (then) Creeley observed that if he was in a good mood, he'd remove his overcoat, but if he was preoccupied or depressed, he'd leave it on during class, the ash on his cigar becoming longer and longer until it fell on the floor of its own weight. Occasionally he would open a book and turn at random to a page, read a few lines and then continue free-associating or call on a student to respond. Many of his remarks were anecdotal, based on his experiences of meeting Williams (being shown the older poet's typewriter) or Zukofsky, corresponding with Olson, living in Mallorca, working as a pigeon farmer, listening to Sarah Vaughn or Charlie Parker, editing *The Black Mountain Review*. His desultory monologues were often anchored by a set of familiar phrases— "only emotion endures," "lower limit speech, upper limit music," "one *knows* in writing," "no ideas but in things"—that could then be adapted to the issue at hand. While this was by no means a systematic treatment of Hart Crane, it demonstrated how a poet thinks about and *through* other poets and, not insignificantly, his own quotidian experience.[v] One might describe his method, adapting Susan Howe's model, as "*My* Hart Crane."

Although I never took a class with him, Robert Hass was an important figure, someone who respected the poetry ferment represented by Olson and Creeley, but who came from a rather different poetics orientation (Stanford, Yvor Winters). He attended student readings, supported small magazines, and took time to hang out with students in the local watering holes. I used to babysit for his children, and when he and his wife returned from wherever they'd been, he'd sit down with me and go over my poems, providing the kind of formal analysis that I would never have gotten from anyone else. Since I was heavily invested in the Black Mountain habit of enjambing whenever I couldn't figure out where to go next, he patiently asked *why* a line break was necessary here or what an indentation meant there. He had a keen ear for small details of sound and rhetoric, and although I probably didn't follow much of his advice, his generosity and patience were a model for me, and I suspect for his other students.

A word about gender. SUNY Buffalo was hardly alone among American universities at that time in its scant representation of women faculty. Diane Christian and Ann Payne were, as I remember, the only women faculty members in the English department, and in the university at large the gender gap was pretty evident. Women poets were not taught—at least not in my courses—and the idea of a female epic or long poem that we associate with H.D., Muriel Rukeyser, or Gwendolyn Brooks—could not compete with Pound's *Cantos* or Williams's *Paterson*. Whitman was, of course a major figure, but not the queer Whitman we know much better today. And Emily Dickinson, so important to a later generation of students in the Buffalo Poetics Program, was never mentioned, even in my seminar on 19th century American literature. Within my student cohort there was a kind of male competitiveness that I found somewhat troubling. Some of this I suspect was a holdover from Olson's own rather patriarchal attitudes towards male creativity, but it was manifest in certain attitudes about heterosexual authority. In my book, *Guys Like Us* I try to revisit this homosocial poetics, recognizing the emancipatory nature of the new American poetry at the same time acknowledging its gendered restrictions and prohibitions.[vi]

"the city we create in our bartalk"[vii]

My cohort included students who were already accomplished poets: Duncan McNaughton, George Butterick, Ed Kissam, Shreela Ray, Albert Glover, Lewis MacAdams, Robert Hogg, Charles Martin, Daniel Zimmerman, and others, many of whom had published chapbooks or edited little magazines. I should also mention Bill Little (later Zonko), who was an older undergraduate whose knowledge of modernist poetry was a resource for me. It was a matter of pride among local poets that SUNY Buffalo had no formal creative writing program. There were writing workshops taught by Creeley, Robert Hass, Irving Feldman, John Logan, John Barth, Carl Dennis and others, but the emphasis remained on writing in more informal venues. Student readings were a regular feature of the non-curriculum, and with the advent of new photo offset and mimeo technologies, magazines were appearing on a fairly regular basis. There were numerous local outlets for publishing: *Intrepid* (Allen DeLoach), *Western Gate* (Daniel Zimmerman), *Fathar* and *Mother* (Duncan McNaughton), *Anonym* (Mark Robison), *Paunch* (Art Efron), *Mouth* (John Staley) plus the ongoing presence of Harvey Brown's Frontier Press and *Niagara Frontier Review* (Fred Wah) and the *Curriculum for the Soul* pamphlets, edited by Al Glover.[viii] Most actual discussion about the craft of writing happened in late-night conversations in bars and apartments. It would be hard to minimize the importance of local watering holes like Maxl's on West Ferry and Main,

Brinks on Elmwood, Bitterman's or Onetto's Fish Restaurant (Olson's favorite hangout) across from the Main campus and a number of places in Allentown, all of which offered a welcome (and warm) respite from Buffalo's brutal winters. And I shouldn't forget Ed Budowski's Student Bookshop across from campus which catered to small press publications and occasional readings.

These rather ephemeral factors constituted, in fine, a pre-institutional poetics program and posed an important alternative to the now-prevalent creative writing model. The benefit of the poetics-centered program that emerged much later, rather than a workshop-centered program, is that it avoids the fatal separation of writing from the study of literature and culture. With the rise of the MFA writing program, its institutionalization through the AWP, possibilities for collaboration across the disciplines diminishes. When the writing of poetry is separated from the poetics that grounds it, art is reified into its own monadic shell rather being than a participant in the production of meaning in the larger world. I once served as a reviewer of a distinguished university English department and was told proudly by the head of its creative writing program that in her workshops, at least, students don't have to do "all of that reading" and could concentrate on writing and publishing.

I've tried to describe my own personal recollections of Buffalo while I was a graduate student during a turbulent period. I realize that my experience will differ from others from that time and perhaps from other entries in this volume. But I wanted to give a sense of what the poetics program looked like before it appeared in capital letters as a distinct institutional element. The success of the Poetics Program is abundantly apparent in the roster of distinguished poets it has produced and faculty it has hired. As I look back on my experience at Buffalo I see many elements of a paradigm shift in literary study that led to that program as well as to what we would now recognize as cultural and critical studies. But I would still stress the importance of vernacular forms of education that occur at the margins of the campus and in solidarities formed through political activism. Buffalo—like the rest of the country—was undergoing huge demographic and political changes, but the "city we create in our bartalk," as Jack Spicer said, was being created in another realm.[ix]

---

i   Olson and Creeley were hired by Al Cook who continued to be a supporter of that legacy, even after Olson left. For an excellent short account of the Olson period, see Fred Wah's memoir in, *Dispatches* (June, 2017): (http://dispatchespoetrywars.com/)

ii   Robert Creeley, "The Pattern." *The Collected Poems of Robert Creeley 1945-1975* (University of California Press, 2006).

iii   Charles Olson, "The Songs of Maximus" 3. *The Maximus Poems*. Ed. George Butterick. Berkeley: University of California Press, 1983. 19.

iv   Charles Olson, "Bibliography on America for Ed Dorn." *Collected Prose*. Ed. Donald Allen and Benjamin Friedlander. Berkeley: University of California, 1997. 307.

v   Creeley's outlook can be summarized by a single word, *presence*. He advocated paying attention to where you are, what you're doing, how you're feeling. There was a politics to this that was evident in the midst of one of Buffalo's many student demonstrations. We were having dinner at his house in the rural town of Eden where he was living. The phone rang, and someone reported that a large number of his faculty colleagues were sitting in at the President's office, protesting his bringing police on campus to quell student demonstrations. Creeley wanted to go to campus (a long drive in the snow) to meet with students. I drove him to campus, and we went into the student center where a large rally was breaking up. He got on stage, and I remember that his first words were "We're all here. Don't forget, we're all here." He kept emphasizing that the fact that we are here, in this place, is a significant fact of this political moment. I think he was stressing the value of community and solidarity that tends to get lost in a chaotic moment when everyone is trying to figure out the next strategy.

[vi] Michael Davidson. *Guys Like Us: Citing Masculinity in Cold War Poetics*. Chicago: University of Chicago Press, 2004. I should add that a nascent feminist movement was developed among women graduate students who formed a reading group and then held open meetings with fellow students to discuss—and critique—sexist attitudes.

[vii] Jack Spicer, *Heads of the Town Up to the Aether*. *My Vocabulary Did this to Me: The Collected Poetry of Jack Spicer*. Ed. Peter Gizzi and Kevin Killian. Middletown: Wesleyan University Press. 306.

[viii] The active publishing scene in Buffalo expanded once the Poetics Program was inaugurated in 1991. James Maynard has published a bibliography of publications by graduate students in the Poetics program, *Among the Neighbors*. Buffalo: The Poetry Collection of the University Libraries University at Buffalo, 2016.

[ix] I am grateful to Peter Middleton, John Daley, Fred Wah, and Daniel Zimmerman for sharing their memories of Buffalo.

FRONTIER CITY

SOME POETIC DEBTS TO BUFFALO

Carl Dennis

When I came to Buffalo from graduate school at Berkeley in the fall of 1966 to teach at the State University of New York, I did not think of myself as a poet, just as someone who wrote poems now and then. I had been hired as an assistant professor of American literature, and though I had brought with me a couple of dozen poems written during the five years I spent at Berkeley, it was only after I had been in Buffalo for two years or so that I decided to try to make poetry my central concern. I would like to believe I would have come to this decision wherever I happened to be living, but it seems proper to acknowledge that the community I found in the English Department at Buffalo made it far easier than it might have been elsewhere.

There were, first of all, several full-time poets on the faculty, including John Logan, Irving Feldman, and Mac Hammond, who were followed soon afterwards by Robert Creeley. Their presence here was mainly due to the hiring policies of the chairman of the Department, Albert Cook, who had been appointed a few years earlier to oversee a major expansion of the Department as part of the process of transforming the private University of Buffalo into one of the central campuses in the newly established State University of New York. Al believed that a vital English Department should be a home for writers of poetry and fiction as well as for scholars and critics, that each group benefited from the presence of the other. It's true that he didn't think universities should offer advanced degrees in writing, reasoning that the only valid credential for a writer of fiction or poetry was a published book. But he did believe that students who were interested in writing should have the opportunity to be guided by people who defined themselves as writers primarily. Al himself wrote both poems and novels, as well as works of scholarship, and several other members of the faculty wrote and published poetry, including Aaron Rosen, William Sylvester, Lyle Glazier, and Max Wickert, and Howard Wolf. And a few years after I arrived Al was eager to welcome Robert Hass as a young Assistant Professor who was both a poet and a critic. It turned out, then, that I had come to one of the few English Departments in the country where shifting from writing criticism to writing poetry was considered perfectly proper, not frowned on as an unprofessional eccentricity.

With so many people on the faculty who wrote poetry, it was natural for small workshops to spring up, and I joined one or two early on, which, like many, kept shifting and dissolving as people hunted about for the colleagues whose criticism seemed most useful. The group I was part of that lasted the longest and meant the most to me met every other week in Mac Hammond's kitchen, and consisted, for the most part, of Mac and me, as the core faculty members, and two or three graduate students, including Charles Baxter, who was later to devote himself to the writing of fiction, and Alan Feldman, who already was hoping to make writing poetry his vocation. Though the workshop lasted only a couple of years (1971 and 1972), it ended up having an important impact on my writing, for Mac and Alan had distinctive styles that widened my range of possibilities. I think of Alan in particular in this regard, for he had studied with Kenneth Koch at Columbia and was already writing refreshingly open conversational poems in the mode of what had become known as the New York School. Alan and I never stopped exchanging poems after he left Buffalo for a teaching job in Framingham, Massachusetts over forty years ago, and we continue to do so now as old friends.

In setting up a workshop that was open to both faculty and graduate students,

Mac was exemplifying a freedom from conventional hierarchies that the English Department at the State University of New York was noted for, which showed itself most obviously in its efforts to include graduate students in making decisions about Departmental policy. I was sometimes critical of this effort, because I had trouble seeing our graduate students as disenfranchised electorate. To me they seemed more like apprentices in a guild system that was based on an inequality of skills and experience. But in this particular situation, that of a poetry workshop, where all of us were learning from each other, the result was liberating. Years later, when Mac was dying of cancer, I wrote a poem for him that tried to make clear how much the workshop he hosted meant to me.[i]

Numbers

Two hands may not always be better than one,
But four feet and more are likely to prove
More steady than two as we wade a stream
Holding above our heads the ark
Of our covenant with the true and beautiful,
A crowd of outlaw pagans hot on our heels,
The shades of our ancestors cheering us on.

Four friends with poems at Mac's this evening
Are closer than one to the truth if we lift our glasses
To the poet that Mac proposes
We toast before beginning, Li Po.

Three votes that the poem I've brought is finished
Versus one turn of the head too slight
For anyone not on the watch to notice
As Li Po demurs.

Is this America, land of one man, one vote,
I want to ask, or the China of one-man rule,
Of emperors who believe they're gods?

Li Po, now only a thin layer of dust
In Szechwan Province, though somehow
Still standing inches behind his lines.

Five of my lines, he suggests with a nod,
Out of the score I've written,
Are fine as they are if I provide them
The context that they deserve and speak them
Without misgivings and with greater gusto.

Five lead out from the kitchen
Past a dozen detours to a single bridge
That must be crossed in order to reach a homeland
Eager for my arrival.

This is the message I get from a prophet whose signs
Are a threadbare coat and an empty cupboard,
Proof he's never written for anyone but himself
And the dead teachers easy to count
On the stiff fingers of one hand.

Another sign of freedom from academic convention in the writers of the English Department was a deliberate effort to bring poetry into the community, which meant a concerted policy of organizing readings off campus. The most active leader of this effort was Max Wickert, who somehow managed to persuade the managers of many bars and cafes in Buffalo to host a regular reading once a week. From the late '60s through the '70s one could go to such readings almost every weekday evening, at spots where faculty and students in the Department could present their work to audiences that included not only fellow students and teachers but local writers as well, along with anyone who happened to be having a drink on the night of the reading and was willing to try something new. It's hard to say now how active the local poets were before the writers in the Department began reading off campus, but it's clear that when Just Buffalo was founded in 1975 to promote poetry in Buffalo and bring in writers outside the academy, it was serving an interest that had been developing for some time. The premise that the readers shared was not all that different from the premise that Wordsworth expressed in his preface to his *Lyrical Ballads*, that the language of poetry was not different in kind from the ordinary language of men and women, that poetry was not an esoteric discipline intended for a select few but open to anyone who was willing to pay attention.

This interest of poets in reaching into the larger community may be something of a surprise to those who think of the Buffalo English Department as the bastion of Language Poetry; for much Language Poetry is based on a poetics that begins with a distrust of ordinary discourse, that regards it as having become so corrupted by political and commercial rhetoric that the writer can't make use of it in poetry without first fracturing or distressing the lexical surface, with the resulting poems liable to provide few portals of entry for the common reader. But Language Poetry did not begin to become dominant in the Department until some years after the arrival of Charles Bernstein in 1989.[ii]

Till then it was the home of a poetry in a wide variety of styles and schools. It's true that its two more experimental poets, Charles Olson and Robert Creeley, in working out a poetics based on breath and line, as opposed to more traditional music, were later thought of as the forerunners of Language Poetry, but in fact their differences from each other suggest no one school could easily contain them. No one is likely to confuse Olson's expansive bardic poems embedded in place and time and Creeley's more abstracted poems of studied compression focused on the expressive subtleties of syntax.[iii] Meanwhile John Logan and Mac Hammond and Irving Feldman offered their distinctive versions of the confessional lyric. My point here is a simple one, that that the people who attended public readings in the '60s and '70s in Buffalo had to cultivate an open mind if they expected to enjoy themselves. There was no way for them to predict the kind of poetry that they would be hearing.

I don't have an explanation of why this active poetry scene found a home in a city like Buffalo, a working-class town that had seen better days, unless its lack of pretension made it seem like a place that would gladly welcome attempts to enliven it. At least Buffalo was not a secluded college town remote from the usual stresses of contemporary urban life. Its problems—poverty, homelessness, racial strife—were common to many cities in the northeast and mid-west that had grown, in the course of the nineteenth century, from small villages to be important centers of trade and manufacturing, only to lose their heavy industry in competition with global markets and to flounder somewhat in their efforts to regain their economic footing. At the same time, Buffalo was small enough for some of its citizens to believe in the possibility that the cooperation of concerned citizens might actually make a difference. This meant that poets who wanted to give their work a political dimension might have found it easier in Buffalo than in some larger cities to resist the feeling of powerlessness that makes political poetry hard to write. It was hard to settle for ironic elegies to Buffalo's lost grandeur as an important grain port when members of the City Council were willing to listen to residents who wanted to make the city more livable and more beautiful. It was hard to focus on bemoaning the lost beauty of the Buffalo river when several stalwarts were willing to give much of their leisure to restoring it.

The reluctance to be an ironic, detached observer of urban decay seemed to me to be expressed most obviously in the efforts to restore the system of parks and parkways that were planned and built by Frederic Law Olmsted and Calvert Vaux from 1868 to 1876.[iv] Though some of the parks when I arrived had been neglected and encroached upon, enough of the system remained intact to make it clear why Olmsted had remarked, with almost forgivable hyperbole, when the system was nearly completed, that Buffalo could claim to be "the best planned city, as to its streets, public places, and grounds, in the United States, if not the world." The difference between the project and the city that came to grow around it could make for some easy humor, but what could be more American than the gap between hope and fact, the imagined city and the actual one. Olmsted and Vaux were dreamers, but their dreams had been in good part achieved, though later compromised. In any case, I found it hard to live in Buffalo without thinking about civic issues, without asking what the role of citizen ought to entail. So, it seemed natural to make room in my poetry for political issues. In this regard, it seems proper to end these remarks with a poem that came out of my brief experience of working as a precinct Committeeman in Buffalo's Democratic Party, trying to drum up support for candidates I considered progressive. And it seems right to dedicate the poem to the memory of a late fellow-colleague in the English Department, Mark Shechner, whose political engagement sparked my own.[v]

The Canvasser Knocks

Sorry to pull you away from your dinner,
But to get George Wilmer's name on the ballot for mayor
I'm willing to be intrusive. Give me a minute
And I'll try to explain why you should sign my petition
Despite what you may have read in the papers.
Just because he wants a curfew on teens,
More police on the streets, and stiffer sentences
Doesn't mean he's only concerned with short-term answers.
He's got some long-range ideas about our neighborhoods—
Tenant buy-back programs and investment cooperatives—
Spelled out in the pamphlet I'd like to give you
If you think you'll find a moment before the election
To scan the particulars. As for backing the hockey rink
Over the new hall for the symphony, that's not the cold
Calculation for votes that it seems so much as a tactic
To pull more shoppers into the few stores downtown
Still trying to fight the malls.
What won his support for the downtown expressway
That sliced a corner off Delaware Park
Wasn't a check from the highway lobby.
A cut in commuting time means extra minutes
At home with the kids. How much the family
Is under the gun in these lean times
I don't have to tell you. It bothered me too
To see the number of Wilmers on his payroll
When he was a councilman, but at least they showed,
Unlike the relatives of the other candidates.
At least they punched in and pushed their papers.
Yes, he's got an arrogant streak. Better that
Than the sweet talk we get from our mayor now.
Do good manners mean so much?
Have it your way. I don't begrudge a man like Wilmer
My one free evening this week, talking to people
Like you, too stubborn to listen.
You tell me if you see a man on horseback
Riding up the street with a ten-point program
To rebuild the city with stone, not clapboard,
With a fountain on every corner and an academy.

Look at how many neighbors have signed my petition.
What document are you saving your signature for?
Where is it being written? Who's writing it?
How long will it take to reach your door?

All the details are fictitious, but I couldn't have written it without thinking of Buffalo as my fate and my project.

---

[i]   "Numbers" appeared in my book *Practical* Gods (New York: Penguin, 2001).

[ii] This essay on my debt to Buffalo doesn't seem the appropriate place to present my perspective on Language Poetry. Anyone interested in what ways I disagreed with some of its assumptions can read the introduction to my book of essays on poetic rhetoric, *Poetry as Persuasion* (Athens, GA: University of Georgia, 2001).

[iii] Charles Olson was a visiting professor from 1963 to 1965, and would likely have become a permanent member were it not for health problems that led to his death in 1970 at the age of 59.

[iv] For a thorough account of the work of Olmsted and Vaux in Buffalo, I recommend Francis R. Kowsky's fine book, *The Best Planned City in the World* (Boston: University of Massachusetts, 2013).

[v]   "The Canvasser Knocks" appeared in my book *Ranking the Wishes* (New York: Penguin, 1997). Mark Shechner's commitment to Buffalo later took the form of writing scores of book reviews for the Buffalo news in his long and serious effort to bring good books to the attention of readers on our Niagara frontier

BUFFALO'S OUTRIDERS POETRY PROJECT

Max Wickert

The following is an updated revision of Max Wickert's "Introduction" to his
An Outriders Anthology: Poetry in Buffalo 1969-1979 and After, *Outriders*
Poetry Project: Buffalo, NY 2013, pp. vi-xix; it is used with permission of the
author.

I came to Buffalo in the summer of 1966, a "callow youth" of twenty-eight, just hired by the UB English Department. Too late to meet Charles Olson, who had left the year before, I certainly felt the aftershocks of his presence. He had been a star appointment in Albert Cook's ambitious and audacious hiring plan and he had exploded onto the campus, changing heads and lives. I moved into the home vacated by Jack Clarke, a young Blake scholar; it was a Dutch-colonial bungalow crammed with all the books Jack would never read again: science fiction, investigations of flying saucers and the paranormal, crime thrillers, dissertations on codes, McLuhan, and a great deal of outdated New Criticism. Jack had arrived two years earlier from Western Reserve. He had immediately been swept into Olson's orbit and his Blake scholarship took a distinctly Black Mountainish turn. By the time I arrived, he was divorced, had taken over Olson's seminar on myth and was directing the Olson-founded Institute of Further Studies. Not much later my own marriage was on the rocks and my self-image as a scholar, in shambles. These two facts were not unrelated. I had come as a Yale-trained Victorianist, specializing in William Morris, and though I dutifully (and unsuccessfully) tried to cobble my Morris dissertation into a publishable book, and even taught a graduate seminar on the Pre-Raphaelites, my heart was no longer in it. I had by then met John Logan and under his spell began to re-imagine myself as a poet. My wife was meanwhile sitting in on John Barth's seminars with the notion of turning novelist. I was no longer your typical aspiring literary academic; she, no longer your typical faculty-spouse. (She eventually published a zippy whodunit). Within a year, we separated and were eventually divorced.

Divorce was, in fact, a Leitmotif all around, as was change in academic specialties. Roughly three-quarters of the colleagues who had arrived around my time were divorced five years later, and even more of them developed quite novel interests. In several cases, the change was from scholarship to poetry. Carl Dennis, for instance (though he, as a life-long bachelor, escaped divorce), was initially hired as a specialist on Sir Philip Sidney; nobody dreamt that a few decades later he would be known as a Pulitzer-Prize-winning poet. When Robert Hass applied for his Buffalo position, he did so as a novel-critic and did not (as he himself told me) think his handful of published poems worth mentioning on his application; a few years later, he won the Yale Younger Poets Award and eventually rose to become Poet Laureate of the United States and the winner of both a Pulitzer and a National Book Award. A young South African named J.M. Coetzee was hired at Buffalo on the basis of some brilliant critical essays on F.M. Ford, Lewis Carroll and Vladimir Nabokov. He was my office mate for a year, at which time I never knew that he was in fact writing a first novel. He left Buffalo and the States when his visa was revoked as a result of his arrest as a member of the Hayes Hall 45 (see below). In 2003, he received the Nobel Prize for Literature.

Early one chilly morning in March 1970, with the stink of tear gas wafting over the UB campus, a group of 45 faculty members—including Coetzee and three Outriders (myself, Martin Pops and Raymond Federman)—filed into the Hayes Hall University President's office. In the wake of student demonstrations, an injunction had been issued against unauthorized assembly. Police with helmets and guard dogs patrolled the campus to enforce it. Maintaining that, as faculty, we were simply doing our job in an academic space, we were, in fact, challenging the legitimacy of the injunction and protesting the presence of police on campus. We were at once confronted by a succession of law enforcers, sub-deans and acting vice presidents who told us to get out or be arrested. Arrested we were and hauled off in black Marias to a nearby precinct station where we were booked, finger-printed and locked up. When lunch time arrived, an officer went from cell to cell to take down our menu choices: beef, chicken or cheese sandwich to eat; cola, ginger ale or water to drink. The French-born Raymond Federman occupied the cell next to mine, along with the painter Jason Berger, who promptly asked for: "Boeuf à l'eaux!" The whole cell block echoed with guffaws at the pun.

We only spent a few more hours in the hoosegow before being sprung on bail, but we spent months slogging through court appearances and trials before being acquitted. Poetry and the other arts turned out to be a big help in raising the funds needed for our defense. The most elaborate defense fund event was organized by Esther Harriott. Almost a thousand well-wishers paid hefty ticket prices at Kleinhans Music Hall to hear Lukas Foss and two members of the Philharmonic play a Mozart trio (much too fast) and the writers John Barth, Robert Creeley, John Logan and Denise Levertov read from their work. I well remember Levertov, at the end of her gig—a tiny and elegant figure on the huge stage—raising her fist and crying out in her slightly lispy contralto: "Revolution!" (she pronounced it "revo-LOW-zhun.")

It is around midnight on a Saturday in 1971 Jack Clarke's apartment on Buffalo's West side—a drab, cavernous, nearly unfurnished den, not a book in sight, but crammed with people—Jack himself with his girlfriend. Debbie Daly (later Ott), the Director of Buffalo's Allentown Community Center, with her then-husband John, a countercultural lawyer. The graduate student poets Bill Cirocco, Mike Davidson, Ed Smallfield, Tony Petrosky, Shreela Ray. Robert Hass, not quite yet a Yale Younger Poet. Assorted other faculty (Angus Fletcher, Jerome Mazzaro, et al.) Plus the whole Institute of Further Studies and various local hippies, actors, painters, druggies and cultural sight-seers. Much drinking and/or inhaling, with Robert Creeley at the center of it all.

I've just piled in with John Logan and his minions, all of us also pretty far gone. I'm sort of in love with John, in an intensely Platonic way. (To put it bluntly, I'm besotted with him.) Also, I've recently been busted in a protest action with the rest of the Hayes Hall 45. My marriage is kaput. I'm having the first quarrel in my first affair. I'm sweating tenure. I've just published my first poems. And I'm very out of it, pickled and riding high on weed. As the evening progresses I seem to be having epiphanies: John Logan, flabby and plump and benign, has poured himself into the fraying sofa and is beginning to nod off. Right next to him, wide awake, one-eyed Creeley, very hard and skinny, straddles a chair in a peculiarly rigid position. The two of them are haloed in greenish light: a Halloween pumpkin perched next to a stalactite. Irreconcilable opposites. Twin archetypes of the new New American Poetry.

A little later I suddenly come to, hearing the door slam shut. Everybody has left and I find myself alone in the echoing room with Creeley—with Crow himself. The bare apartment seems vast, and we're sitting in the middle of it, facing each other. I stare at him. His eye fixes me back. Long, long silence. Then he mutters, querulously: "Hey man, what's your scene?"

I can think of nothing to say, my head crammed with hero worship and self-regard. I suppose I might have said: "Please, Bob, read me one of your poems. Read one of my poems. Ask me about my wife. Ask me how I got busted. Ask me about John Logan." But I just keep staring back into his eye and his eye keeps staring back. He's terrifically uncomfortable. So am I. We both still hear the sound of that slamming door. "Time to get out of here," I think and head for the door. But the handle isn't on it and the knob is on the floor.

Creeley takes a hard look at the knob and suddenly his one eye shimmers with panic. He starts dashing about; he actually scurries from wall to wall, utterly frantic. I think he thinks he's been locked up forever with a groupie and no exit. I think he thinks I think I want to kiss him, or maybe put my finger in his missing eye. Desperate situation. Another long pause, and suddenly there's grace. Tara! The door opens, framing Jack Clarke, cheerful and aloof, like Jesus at the Harrowing of Hell. I'm out of there before I know it.

That was my one time completely alone with Bob Creeley, and the only time that I ever saw him really lose his cool. It was, in a word he liked to use, a "particular" occasion. We came to know each other rather better by and by, but neither he nor I ever mentioned the episode to each other again.

The UB Department of English, before it moved to the Amherst campus, was housed in Annexes A and B of the old Main Street campus, temporary shacks erected in the days of the GI Bill. These two drab, single-story, earthbound barracks housed a faculty that (with some justification) considered itself occupying the intellectual stratosphere. The Annexes were too small for all but a few tiny classrooms. Larger events were often held in the second story conference rooms of the Norton Student Union. In 1972, one of the headiest academic seminars I ever attended was held there. The participants were Norman Holland, then department chair and author of the monumental *Psychoanalysis and Shakespeare*; René Girard, the renowned French philosopher of mimetic desire, who had just finished his masterpiece, *Violence and the Sacred*; C.L. Barber, whose *Shakespeare's Festive Comedy* was on all graduate school reading lists; and Murray Schwartz, co-inventor with Holland of the 'Delphi Seminar' method of reader-response teaching. The nominal subject of the session was Shakespeare's *King Lear*, but the ambitious discussion branched out to include *Oedipus Rex*, tragedy in general, the role of violence in civilization, and much else. By the end the heads of most of the audience—mostly graduate students and junior faculty—were spinning. Mine certainly was. Then a short, wiry man standing by the door spoke up. This was the poet Irving Feldman. In his characteristic Brooklyn-inflected hoarse whisper, he began by claiming that Oedipus was surely the only "person" without an Oedipus complex since he lived out what others wished, and somehow wound up concluding that, in a case like that of *Oedipus Rex*, knowing how things will end paradoxically enhances rather than defeats suspense. I have no recollection what he said in between, but his two-minute comment (which contained not a bit of academic jargon) seemed a logical sorites of brilliantly interconnected simple truths. At any rate, it left the entire room, including the celebrated panelists, slack-jawed and speechless. To my mind, Feldman's performance has ever since served as a pregnant example of how a poetic intelligence can break through academic shop talk.

Four years earlier, in 1968, John Logan had been invited by his friend Donald Justice to read at Syracuse University. Always a gregarious traveler, John traveled to Syracuse with four friends in tow, myself and four graduate students: the poets Dan Murray and Shreela Ray, and the poker-playing future Shakespearean, Joel Fineman. At the post-reading party, we met up with Doug Eichhorn, a young poet working on his Creative Writing M.A. under Justice. He and Dan and Shreela and I had recently published, or were about to publish, in John Logan's *Choice: A Magazine of Poetry and Photography*. We therefore invited Eichhorn to "ride out" to Buffalo for a joint reading of these new poems, and he suggested: "Why don't you all ride out to Syracuse, too." Thus Outriders was born (its original full title was "Outriders Inter-University Poetry Program") as a reading-exchange between young and not-yet-established poets residing at various colleges. That, at least, was the original idea.

The evening in Syracuse ended with Joel Fineman, whose poker game was on a professional level, cleaning out Donald Justice, who fancied himself an ace, in fine fettle; and with "Dangerous Dan" Murray scorching Justice's staircase carpeting while demonstrating his human-flamethrower trick of spouting burning lighter fluid. In the morning, the newly dubbed Outriders bid each other goodbye.

We thought up the Outriders moniker (academics that we were) as an allusion to the Monk in *The Canterbury Tales*, who, although vowed to stay cloistered by the Benedictine Rule, had license to travel as an "outridere" to far-flung monastic properties, and indeed to go on pilgrimages. Young twentieth-century American poets, who worked mostly in colleges in (we imagined) monk-like isolation, would surely benefit by visiting one another, especially if youth or obscurity prevented their being invited and paid to read under more prestigious auspices. We hoped to become an ever-growing pro bono network of creative writing students. Though unable to pay each other, we could at least help out with rides, meals, beds, publicity and minor expenses. Good will, in the absence of more tangible resources, would let us wing our way.

We got going a year later, when Eichhorn's Syracuse-based Salt Mound Press invited the Buffalo gang to read. The participants were, once again, John Logan, Shreela Ray, Dan Murray and myself, joined now by Robert Hass, a recent hire in the Buffalo English Department. The affair was a great success.

Somehow, however, a return engagement in Buffalo by Eichhorn's crew never materialized, and in early 1970, our agenda was modified. The Outriders Inter-University Program became the Outriders Poetry Project: Buffalo poets would still "ride out", but into the local community rather than to far-away colleges. There were to be weekly readings in local bars, ten each in the Spring and Fall every year. An invited poet of some distinction would start off, to be followed by an open reading. The events would be advertised not only on campus and in the city, but also to poet friends elsewhere, who (should they happen to visit town) were encouraged to drop in and read unannounced.

There was nothing very original about all this; it was standard in Greenwich Village and San Francisco. But this was Buffalo, and we had our doubts. In the event, it all worked out splendidly. The city and its colleges had by that time, and long after continued to have, an immense (and intense) poetic traffic from which Outriders certainly benefited. One night early on, for instance, when I was jotting down names for the open reading, a swarthy, dark-bearded, slightly balding beatnik-type came up and gently whispered: "May I read?" It was Allen Ginsberg.

The Outriders reading series in bars took place over a period of ten years (with some breaks) in frequently shifting venues. All of these places kept changing décor and management in response to changing clienteles, and none of them survive today. We were not charged rent for our reading space, since we attracted customers on otherwise dead Tuesday or Wednesday nights. Indeed, we often were the only clients, but a few dozen drinking poets were preferable to no paying customers at all.

The first series was held at Aliotta's Lounge, on Hertel Avenue, a dusty and grimy old gin mill in a Jewish-Italian neighborhood between the Main Street Campus and the city center. (Hertel was gradually changing in character. It had long featured the city's best kosher deli, Mastman's, which eventually closed as the neighborhood's Jewish population dwindled and made room for Lebanese and Arabs. Aliotta's later tried its luck as a comedy club, then as a karaoke bar, and finally folded.)

Outriders next moved farther downtown, to The One Eyed Cat on Bryant Street, a much hipper saloon with wicker-basket chairs hanging on chains from the ceiling (Creeley was highly amused) and Rock-star silk screened wall-paper.

Later that year, we had a brief summer season in the upstairs banqueting room of The Library: An Eating and Drinking Emporium (long since defunct) on Bailey Avenue near the old campus. The readings there memorably coincided with (and some were in support of) the Eugene McCarthy campaign.

By this time, Outriders was involved in various supplementary activities: the pilot program of Buffalo's Poetry-in-the-Schools program, initiated and eventually directed independently by Esther Harriott; a series of appearances on campus (co-sponsored with the Student Union Activities Committee) by C.W. Truesdale, Bill Zavatsky and others; two brief 'Third World Poetry Festivals' (the title is a misnomer, since, except for one African, the participants were all Latino); and the delegation of three Outriders to read at the Roycroft Foundation in East Aurora, NY.

Our fourth and last location was our happiest, the original Tralfamadore Café at the corner of Main and Amherst Streets. Ed Lawson, its owner-manager, was a man of considerable intelligence and resource. He scheduled literary readings alternating with jazz ensembles, such as the soon-to-be-famous Spyro Gyra. Outriders kicked off its season here with a hugely-successful benefit reading by Robert Creeley. We had also in the meantime secured some grant money, which allowed us to offer honoraria (if rather minimal ones) to writers from out-of-town, and we now had become fairly visible to the general community. Thus, the late '70s became climactic for us. However, if we thought of ourselves as successful, the success of the Tralfamadore as a jazz club was greater still and led to its relocation in a much larger and fancier building downtown. There poetry found no place. By 1979, the Outriders reading series were at an end.

The last sets of Outriders readings at the Tralfamadore overlapped with the 1978 and 1979 Buffalo Summer Poetry Festivals. During the late '60s and early '70s, the UB English Department had enjoyed the luxury of adding a prestigious visiting summer faculty to its already illustrious permanent one. The summer program was energetically administered first by Albert Cook, then by Thomas Connolly. Every year in the second of the three UB Summer Sessions, from four to seven visitors taught full six-week courses. These included poets of stellar reputation like Amiri Baraka, Basil Bunting, Gregory Corso, Ed Dorn, Robert Duncan, William Empson, Galway Kinnell, Kenneth Rexroth, Nathaniel Tarn and James Wright, to say nothing of novelists and critics like Kenneth Burke, Anthony Burgess, Hugh Kenner, Harvey Swados, and Tzvetan Todorov. In the increasingly tight budget squeeze of the '70s, fewer such visitors could be funded; by 1976 the summer visitor program was dead. Two years later, the department decided that a partial compensation for this setback might be a summer festival with visiting poets staying a few days each to supplement poetry courses taught by permanent faculty. An added feature would be to make these visitors accessible off-campus to the Buffalo community. In 1978, Artpark in nearby Lewiston was persuaded to co-sponsor this venture. Supporting grants were secured from the New York State Council on the Arts and Poets & Writers. On the basis of my long-time service (occasionally as chair) on the English Department's poetry committee and my experience with Outriders, I was asked to direct this UB/Artpark Summer Poetry Festival, with Outriders as a participating group. That summer, eleven visiting poets (including Marvin Bell, John Gill, Anselm Hollo, David Ignatow, Louis Simpson, and Gerald Stern) and several performance groups and collectives (including Canada's Four Horsemen), aided by a cadre of local writers (including Carl Dennis, Raymond Federman, Judith Kerman, Carlene Polite) staged a month of readings, workshops, poetry in performance, discussions and seminars in three locations: Artpark, the University, and the Tralfamadore Café. For Outriders, it was a gratifying culmination of a gratifying decade.

An encore came the following summer, though scaled down to two weeks and without Artpark participation, advertised under the ponderous title: "Trailblazers and Masters: Cross-Generational Exchanges in Contemporary Poetry." (I blush to admit that this was my idea). Four major poets were invited to bring along four younger poets of their choice. William Stafford brought Raymond Patterson; Gerald Stern brought Mark Rudman; David Ignatow brought Virginia Terris; and Anselm Hollo brought Allan Kornblum. In addition, John Frederick Nims, then Editor of Poetry, was invited as a kind of moderator-in-chief and Irving Feldman participated as a representative of the resident Creative Writing faculty. All gave readings and workshops, as well as visiting my summer seminar on "Poetry of the Present" and most stopped in at Outriders evenings as well.

This second Summer Festival featured a series of round table discussions at the UB Poetry Collection, each highlighting one of the young/ old pairs, J.F. Nims and myself moderating. The last round-table was given over to Anselm Hollo and Allen Kornblum. Hollo had appeared in the 1978 Festival. Before I then invited him, I was warned that he could be a problem, but he turned out to be unfailingly warm, erudite and courteous. I had met him often in earlier years, but now felt he was a friend and so was eager to have him back in 1979. This time was different. He had arrived, just hours before his scheduled seminar, from a nine-hour bus trip during which he had not slept but had ingested substances a-plenty. In short, he was flying. A group of us hurried him to lunch at a pretentious suburban restaurant, where he used the fake-Tiffany entrance lantern as a punching ball; he then imbibed freely and ate little. Arriving at the conference, he pulled a hip flask of vodka from his pocket and slammed it on the table, growling and muttering as I nervously introduced him. He then rose and launched into a tirade against the cultural and literary establishment, savagely turning on J.F. Nims as the representative *par excellence* of cultural officialdom. His language was coarse and impolite at best, and downright libelous at worst. Amid general consternation he kept up this rant, brooking no interruptions. Somehow or other J.F. Nims, with a courteous smile, managed to bring the affair to a more or less gracious conclusion. I was mortified, thinking "That's the end of our friendship!" and could scarcely look Anselm in the eye.

An hour later, he seemed more like his 1978 self, and we pretended that nothing untoward had happened. My own poetry reading concluded the day. Hollo and Nims were both in the audience, both amiable. I introduced myself as a schizophrenic poet and read two utterly different sets of my poems, one of rhymed sonnets (which Nims liked and eventually published), the other of semi-stoned free-verse experiments (which Hollo liked and later attempted, though without success, to get accepted by an editor he knew). I have rarely felt more ambivalent.

All the Festival conferences were taped and are available at the UB

Poetry Collection. I later listened to the recording of Anselm's explosion, expecting to hear nothing but vulgarities and insults. The insults are there all right, but I was surprised how much sense the whole thing makes. My memory of that episode now seems a fine parallel to my epiphany about the Logan-pumpkin and Creeley-stalactite at Jack Clarke's party. Such irreconcilable opposites are of the essence in contemporary poetry.

An Outriders Anthology, which I edited and published in 2013, bore the subtitle *Poetry in Buffalo 1969-1979 and After.* 1979 was the year in which the weekly Outriders readings ceased. Of course, most of our readers did not disappear, but remained energetic presences, not only at the university, but also in the community at Hallwalls, Just Buffalo or elsewhere. There were indeed a number of deaths—John Logan, Jack Clarke, William Stafford, Shreela Ray, Mac Hammond, Allen Ginsburg, David Ignatow, Albert Cook, J.F. Nims, Dan Murray, John Wieners, Leslie Fiedler, Robert Creeley, Carlene Polite, Ray Federman, Louis Simpson, Anselm Hollo—in fairly rapid succession. But many others continued writing. After a period of hibernation, I decided to revive Outriders, not as a reading series, but as a small press devoted to the Buffalo Outriders ambit. The brief final portion of the Anthology features the writers published by this press to date. Most of them were, as can readily be seen, already very much in evidence during the golden decade.

The Outriders core group consisted of writers on the UB faculty, especially Albert Cook, Robert Creeley, Carl Dennis, Raymond Federman, Irving Feldman, Robert Hass, John Logan, Mac Hammond, and William Sylvester. This group was seconded by a number of poet friends who, though not permanently teaching here, visited Buffalo very frequently, like Robert Bly, Allen Ginsberg, Anselm Hollo, David Ignatow, Milton Kessler and James Wright. By far the largest group was of those who got their start as poets while studying at UB and went on either to teach literature and/or creative writing elsewhere (Charles Baxter, Philip Dow, Alan Feldman, Charles Martin, Charles Molesworth, Jerry McGuire, Dan Murray, Tony Petrosky etc.) or to pursue other careers. Another important contingent is of Buffalo residents from various walks of life who also write poetry. Finally, there were the relatively few (about twenty of more than 130) who were one-time invited visiting readers.

The *Outriders Anthology* was definitely not a collection of regional verse, in the sense of poetry about a territory or written by natives. Very few poems in it explicitly refer to Buffalo, though there are some loving and perceptive evocations of the city's ambiance. Even fewer of the authors—only about half a dozen— were born in the area. Nor was it an anthology of a particular literary movement: the terms "San Francisco Movement" and "New York School" may make sense, but there is no such thing as a "Buffalo School." No particular poetic form, subject or technique dominated here. Poems range through traditional stanzas and meters to free and projective verse, *poesie concrète*, anti-poetry, poetic prose, children's verse; some are meditational, some satiric, romantic, anti-romantic, sci-fi, Nuyorican, descriptive, goofy, religious, prophetic, you name it. Though some of the authors clearly subscribe to particular orthodoxies, there is no orthodoxy that governs them all.

Least of all was this book a collection by "professional" writers. Yes, some of the authors are poets-in-residence and literature-and-writing professors in universities (this is virtually what being a professional poet means nowadays). I am one. But the range of callings among the rest was legion: actor, airman, arborist, archivist, bookseller, boxer, movie casting director, municipal councilman, dance critic, disk jockey, documentary film maker, elementary or high-school teacher, environmentalist, film critic, firefighter, guidance counselor, healthcare administrator, librarian, motel manager, journalist, landscape architect, literacy volunteer, merchant marine, museum curator, painter, performance artist, postal clerk, printer, prison staffer, psychotherapist, script writer, singer, social worker, software specialist, soldier, sports writer, theater director, trumpeter, yoga instructor etc. It was such amateurs (in the best sense) that found or made a community in reading and listening to each other.

In retrospect, I am struck by the relative absence of conflict and hostility in all this mutual reading and listening. Anselm Hollo's explosion at J.F. Nims was an exception. One might have expected more such upheavals in an array of writers-in-residence, formerly marginalized experimentalists, establishment poets, post-modern academicians and impatient-with-culture-as-usual townies thrown together at close quarters in the turbulent '60s and '70s. Certainly, there was some violence and abusive language around, but it generally came from right-wing onlookers or over-zealous policemen, almost never from the poets themselves.

Creeley, for one, had arrived with a reputation for a chip-on-the-shoulder temper and a knife in his pocket. Yet I never saw the slightest evidence for this, except perhaps much later on, in his white-faced fury when his biographer Ekbert Faas suggested that his change from counter-cultural firebrand to chair-holding professor had made him soft. Creeley was in a rage at being suspected of losing his rage. But on the whole, enmity was scarcely in evidence, despite oppositional stances on philosophy, life-style or poetics. And sometimes, to speak the truth, English department politics.

Still, the fact that people do not fight does not necessarily mean that they understand one another. In fact, I suspect that much of the Buffalo writers' crew during the '70s was composed of men and women who were often mutually baffled by, but preserved a principled if bemused curiosity about, each other. In this sense, too, my vague pumpkin-and-stalactite epiphany about Creeley and Logan seems about right. Irving Feldman's poem, "How Wonderful," splendidly articulates the frame of mind that can make such a suspension of opposition possible, pleasant and fruitful.

Looking back on the *Anthology* half a decade after its publication, and almost half a century after the golden decade of ca. 1965-1975, I now see it very much as a historical document, in the sense that most of its contributors (myself included—I am pushing eighty) belong to the past. Even the most experimental of its contributors—Wieners, Clarke, Harwood, Hollo, Federman, Creeley—are now largely viewed as long-ago trailblazers. Very few good poets write even remotely like them. Time moves very quickly in the twenty-first century. I think I began to sense a palpable break from that past in the change that gradually overtook the University of Buffalo's Poetics Program beginning in the1980s, as it moved from its founder Robert Creeley to its later luminaries Susan Howe, Charles Bernstein, Steve McCaffery and Myung Wa Kim. Outriders as a small press made a few attempts reflect this change by publishing monographs by Jeremiah Rush Bowen (*Consolations*, 2011), Jacob Schepers (*A Bundle of Careful Compromises*, 2014) and, perhaps most significantly, Edric Mesmer (*of monodies and homophony*, 2015). Still I, as its editor, must confess my incapacity to enter into the spirit of the most advanced poetry today. I therefore remain content to give visibility to some wonderful writers who do not pretend to move beyond the aesthetics of the late twentieth century: Linda Zisquit (*Return from Elsewhere*, 2014), Ansie Baird, Ann Goldsmith, David Landrey, and Sam Magavern (*Four Buffalo Poets*, 2016), and Carole Southwood (*Listen and See*, 2017 and *Abdoo*, 2018 forthcoming).

EXCERPT FROM THE INTRODUCTION TO
JUST IN TIME: POEMS 1984-1994

Robert Creeley

The following is an excerpt from an interview between Charles Bernstein and Robert Creeley, "Poetry in Search of Itself," recorded on Pearl Harbor Day, 1995, a transcription of which originally appeared as the introduction to his selected poems, Just in Time: Poems 1984-1994 *(New Directions 2001). It is used with permission of Charles Bernstein, who has kindly provided a brief introduction to the piece.*

Along with his poetic hero, William Carlos Williams, Robert Creeley is the great 20th century American poet of the everyday. For Creeley the ordinary is not something represented but rather something enacted word by word in each poem. His works combine searing emotional intensity and mind-boggling linguistic invention, proof that lyric intensity is dependent on formal ingenuity (and the other way around). Creeley was exemplary in his support of younger poets who rejected a poetics of complacency that reigns now, as it did in his time. He championed the radical modernists of the generation before him. And most important, he was necessary company to those of his own generation who risked the most in their successful transformation of postwar poetic thinking.

      Charles Bernstein

    C.B.: *It seems like suffused violence is something you deal with in a lot of your work, in many different ways, and in many different contexts. So, you know, we could start with Pearl Harbor Day, but it comes in the mention of words itself, and the violence of words and communication. Are there particular other poets, or ways in which violence is dealt with, that were useful to you in that way for your own work? Did you feel like you just had to start from whole cloth?*

    R.C.: Williams was classically useful to me in that way, and Lawrence to some real extent also. Just that both were remarkably and engagingly, if that's possible, angry men. In the sense that Lawrence was both sponsored and provoked by his imagination that the world was a meager and unresponding place. That people were too often persuaded by the most ugly, and curiously, not even despicable...I mean, simply, the most sullen and sodden kinds of motive. So that the tone in his writing is most often, not chiding, but a responding anger that people could so feel and so do things. Williams—I think the predominant emotion in Williams is one of a kind of repulsion and anger. And I thought, "Here are my two terrific heroes." Each had also, without question, an extraordinary intimacy, or a "contact" as Williams would say. But they were "classic," to my mind, they were classic Puritans, as I was—who moved in response, rather than in openness or direct accommodation.

    Weren't the models that were presented to you, that were available to you at first, in fact, the kinds of poetry that did not deal with...

Initially, I was probably most engaged or persuaded by prose writers. They were, almost without exception, dealing with violence in one form or another. Whether, say, it was Defoe, going back to that time, or particularly the kind of violence active in Dostoevsky, or Kafka, or Gide, for example.

But what's interesting is taking those fictions writers, who deal with struggle and conflict and so on, as the themes of their work. It seems like your work deals with this violence and antagonism within the form, within the structure of writing. And that's why I say it's suffused. I mean, how do you get to that transformation? Reading novelists who write about the subject matter of violence, and yet you've managed—it's not so much that you write about that as a subject, although sometimes you do…

I think it's the curious construction of the…almost of a "Trojan Horse," it's something…a cart, or a wagon, or something that…a conveyance that can carry this particular load in all its implications to whatever point I have in mind, and for whatever point I have in mind or can discover then more actively. I feel as though I don't have "a point" of any remarkable interest, to myself at least. But I do have an activity that's very interesting to me, and that activity, so to speak, is the peculiar recognition of things through the writing itself.

A lot of your work is involved with pulling things apart, and then putting them together, but that "pulling apart" is a very tactile, a very sensual thing. But it also is, you know, kind of a splitting open and rending, or "cleaving," in this marvelous double sense of cleaving, which I think is very much at the heart of it. That both separates, but also it brings back together… that you work out in the line structure of your work. It is absolutely modulated at every…

I was very attracted to Williams's way of positioning his line breaks. I mean he would "strike into the middle of some trenchant phrase"—whatever, or however, he says it—but the way he so characteristically breaks the line at a point least—not just least expected—but least permitted by the syntactical order. I don't know, I've never known, particularly, what he thought he was doing. I remember my own confusion when I heard a recording of him reading, say, in the early '40's. To recognize that he did not use these line breaks as any evident pause in his reading at all. Whether he thought of them intelligently or intellectually as being units, I don't know. Whether he was reading syllabically, I could not tell. I knew he put a lot of emphasis—stress—when he read "The tulips / bright tips / sidle and toss"—like that. But the line endings seemed, frankly, the least of his particular concerns. And so I had made a whole procedure out of my reading of him, which served me then very well, in fact, and still in obvious ways does. But it doesn't seem to have been his much at all.

There's a way in which people will doubly read your own line breaks. Reading it on the page it seems a very formal way of breaking apart the syntax, and at the same time when one hears you read something else happens. There's an emotional valence...there's a kind of existential quality, a temporal quality, moving from moment to moment, almost in anguish at times in the way that words break, especially recordings from the '50's and '60's. That doubleness is very much related. It's a relation of inside to outside. How do you react to that?

It makes good sense to me. I recall that there's a surviving record of Olson and myself reading. We had gone to a local place for such recordings outside of Ashville, N.C., when I was first there at Black Mountain as a visiting teacher. And I don't know whether it was my interest or his but, in any case, we determined to make a small record. I think it was mine, because I wanted to send it to Williams, so that Williams might hear Olson's...

Was this in one of those little recording booths?

Yeah. Exactly.

Like you'd have in a penny arcade?

Yeah, almost. It was a little more sophisticated. It was an actual studio, but it was that kind. So, a single small record. And we sent it to Williams, and it was useful. He could therefore hear what Olson's line was proposing to do, because here now was Olson literally reading it. And he was an extraordinary reader.

I love the term "record," as we now have here very sophisticated equipment. The idea of making a record is very much like making a mark. The line breaks are a very important part of the visual mark, and a very important part of the acoustic mark, of your work. Are you conscious of that in reading? I mean Williams, when one hears him read, we don't hear the breaks, as so often is remarked, there's not space in there. But you read the breaks.

I read the breaks. To me, like percussive or contrapuntal agencies, they give me a chance to get a syncopation into the classic emptiness: "it sits out there / edge of / hierarchic rooftop / it..." I mean it gives me, not drumming precisely, but it's a rhythm of that character. "It marks with acid fine edge / of apparent difference / It is there / here here that sky / so up and up / and where...," you know. It's also an agency for a lot of half-rhyming or accidental echoing, that I really enjoy. It's also sort of like water sloshing in a pan, not just like that—but that would be an apt analogy. Lapping at the edges.

Which is also a play between inside and outside, that works both to describe the form of the poem and the content. Also, I think it has to do again with where the violence is. The violence is within yourself. It's not just in somebody else, it's not always directed outside...

No. Would that it were, would that it would also settle down and forget it. I wrote a poem called "Anger" years ago, which is probably as accurate a sense of it as I ever managed. And then too, in the early stories, *The Gold Diggers*, it's always there that the anger is very explicit. It's clear in the one novel I wrote—*The Island*—it's a complicated, impacted, it isn't despair. I don't think I ever felt significant despair, but I certainly felt anger.

Can you read "What"?

Yeah.

Or, as they would say in England, "Can you read, what?"

I could read "What."

You have all those in your catalogue of poems, like "What," "It." I was going to ask you what "it" meant in the poem you read before. What is "it"?

[He reads the poem, "WHAT"]

Your work often plays off the lyric poem, the solitary self-expressing. It/his/your/my failings. But overpowering this expressive individual is a sense of company, and you use the word "company," you have a poem called, "Company," that maybe you'll read in a second, but "company" in the work of poetry. How is your work affected or influenced by this company?

Well, it's not a…it's not necessarily a team, although it probably would like to be…

It's true that your use of the word "company" is always and forever never like a corporation. It's never that sense of company.

If you read it, you recognize that it's not simply name-dropping—not at all—it's locating "the company." I remember one of our friends here had shown me a curious page or two from a journal of John Cheever's that was being published by the Paris Review. And Cheever is remembering my coming to Briarcliffe, to read. And it speaks about my hair, and my hands constantly running through it, etc. But, more to the point, he says, "he talks so much about the people that he knows…not only that he likes them obviously, he talks about Leslie Fiedler, he talks about X, Y, or Z as though he is proud of them." Not that he knows them simply, but that he's proud of them. And that sense of company, almost like "The Musicians of Bremen," I really love that sense. You know, that one could drink the ocean, another could live in the fiery furnaces, one could take seven league strides. I love that sense of a company. And I felt that way extraordinarily with friends at that time. I guess I had little "company," in one sense, in poetry at first, and then terrifically, I had a lot of company. Whatever its occasion or literary value, it was great.

It has another effect, as a reader, in that for me, the work provides company. One could be very moved by a lyric poem and the feelings the individual is expressing or the beauty of the expression. But this is different. There is something about reading your work which seems to provide company.

That's great! My work is done.

I don't think I'm alone in that. It's a formal experience of the work, and the way in which one enters into it, I think.

I was moved, as they say, in England recently at some wildly and pleasantly particular occasion, somewhere way out on the edge on the way to Cornwall. I'd take a train across the country, from Durham actually, all the way across to Reading, and then to Exeter, and then had gone from Exeter, driven by car another hour or so, down to Torrington, and was now to read. The point was, afterwards, someone said it was just as though one were sitting in one's living room or something. And I thought, that's precisely the place I'd love to have it all be. I love that sense of "Come closer and I'll tell you a story..."

And even as you say "living room," it takes on a literal sense. Could you read "The Company?"

Yeah. This was written, one might note, for what I presumed would be a company of the young...

I can't imagine the Signet Society...

I thought I knew a little of the Signet Society, having—as you had—gone to Harvard, but I didn't. Seymour Lawrence, I believe, was the only friend ever in it. But it was much more august, we realized, than the *Advocate* or any of the more public clubs, like the *Lampoon* or whatever. But in any case, I was invited to be the poet, I think they paid some money and I got a meal, and so on and so forth. So I went very innocently. I remember everything on my body was rented, except my underwear, literally.

This was 1985. I can't imagine going totally innocently in 1985...

My shoes were rented, my tie, my shirt, my pants. It was formal dress.

Oh, it was formal dress. I should emphasize to the radio listeners that you are in informal dress, but with a full head of hair here today...

Thank you. In any case, I had expected that this would be an occasion primarily for the undergraduates who were members of the society. Not so. There was a reception prior to it, in which we were told that they were raising something like...they were raising money for the society. I think the proposed goal was $2 million. I was thinking of some of our usefully humble enterprises here in Buffalo. Theirs was to take literary people to lunch! Not to publish anything, but to literally provide food and entertainment for the visitors and themselves. So anyhow, all the proceedings were in Latin.

In Latin?

In Latin.

How's your Latin?

Not too good. But anyhow, this poem was written, as I say, for the imagination—my imagination—of the young. Trying to tell them, in a funny sense, what it had been like to be a student at Harvard in the early '40s.

[He reads the poem, "THE COMPANY"]

EXCERPT FROM "ROBERT AND BOOKS [ON CREELEY'S LIBRARY]"

Penelope Creeley

This essay originally appeared as part of a Symposium on Robert Creeley's Library on February 7ᵗʰ, 2014, in association with an exhibit at Notre Dame's Special Collection; it is excerpted here with permission of the author.

One of the many things Robert and I had in common was a sense of domesticity. Robert and I hung pictures together in many, many places, as we moved and moved, made home where we found ourselves. Hanging pictures was one way we did it. Another, equally or more important way was making bookshelves. Robert, it turned out somewhat to my surprise, was a master bookshelf-builder. It came from years of practice, long before I ever showed up, that was driven by a need for order, and a need to keep his beloved books safe, sorted, out of harm's way. When I first arrived in Buffalo, books were in boxes still, in the unused, unfurnished living room. Robert had a worktable with his typewriter in the kitchen, and a few books in the bedroom. That was in July. By the end of August, as the new semester approached, a tiny, embryonic sense of permanence and potential routine began to enter our lives. It was marked by the building of the bookshelves, followed by the opening of the boxes, and the arranging of the books, the works of Robert's "beloved company." We had got to know the spaces of the living room by lying on the floor in there, listening to jazz in an attempt to educate me, and imagining the room. The old white VW bug we drove then, came home from a visit to the lumberyard with pine planks sticking out the windows. We lugged them upstairs, Robert set up some chairs as saw horses, and set intently to work. I sat about being, I hoped, helpful, but soon he asked me, reasonably politely, to go for a walk. I went down to the old Armory near the Niagara River, sat on its wide warm sandstone steps and watched the towering spirals of bugs whirl into the soft humid night air above the neighborhood's peaked rooftops. When I came home, the bookshelves were finished. Robert was sweeping up the little piles of sawdust, looking triumphant. He had thought he was out of practice, had been anxious to "prove himself." We loved the sense of permanence and place the shelves gave. There was room for the stereo, a tall deep shelf for the LPs, and all the rest for books. The rest of the room soon followed: we used a bed covered by an India print for a sofa, I covered cardboard boxes with corduroy, or spray-painted them, for side-tables, and we painted a variety of found chairs. The bookshelves were the most solid and satisfying thing in the apartment. Life formed around them. Not long after, Robert made me a daybed in the kitchen, so when he woke me up with a cup of coffee at an hour I still considered unthinkable, I would have a place to slowly surface. Soon another bookshelf materialized beside it, so I would have a place to keep the books I was reading safe, not lying around, vulnerable. Really, it meant that I would know where to look for them after Robert had picked them up and put them away. On the end of that bookshelf Robert hung a beautiful little Joe Brainard collage, shining blues and silvers, intricate and dear. I loved it. We were home.

Clearly the question now is, What were the books? Do I remember? I wish I did. If I were a real book person I would know. Some I do know. Olson. It can't have been the Collected, because George Butterick was working away at all that still. But Robert would read great chunks of Maximus to me, often with tears running down his face. Olson had died in '70. There was still great missing, confusion, hurt there. But there were the words, the magnificent poems. There were the stories attached, the memories, the love. The admiration, the awe. Robert was teaching me America through his beloved books. Williams. Williams was immediate to me. Straight to the heart, through Robert's voice. I could get it, I could see Williams's America out the windows, in the streets of Buffalo's West side, hear his rhythms and tensions in Robert's own voice. And there was the complicated relationship with Flossie and the boys. I looked for that behind the words, and was delighted by his novels with the portraits of immigrant families in New York City. In them Williams articulated some of the confusions I was also experiencing as a new immigrant.

Then there were the lyrical mysteries of Robert Duncan. There was Kerouac, exciting and naïve. His boyish eagerness brought Robert to stories of his own boyhood in Acton, not far from Lowell. And there was Ginsberg, great crusading Allen who wanted to change a country I had no idea of yet, but wanted to change too because it had such a huge effect on my little New Zealand. Then the books would lead to music. Robert would read me his own work, and play Charlie Parker, say, or Miles Davis, try to get me to hear the sounds and the pace of his head. Dig it. Dexter Gordon. Sonny Rollins. Sometimes the speed would bounce right off me. I could hear Bill Evans, Chet Baker. I wanted voice. I got the whole lazy river of Lush Life, Johnny Hartman and then Sarah Vaughn and Dinah Washington. And early reggae, from then terrific WBFO. And lots of country music. Hank Williams, and strange things, like "The Great Speckled Bird that is the Bible," and "Drop Kick Me Jesus." That last one was so funny we could hardly believe we could get so lucky, as we drove to New Mexico from Buffalo, listening to AM radio all the way. Soon Robert would record a lot of radio music, once cassette recorders were available. He delighted in their portability, their discrete size. The little plastic boxes of tapes would soon require their own shelves. Robert would build them their own mini-bookcases, to fit on the shelves among the books themselves. Neat, proper, a little fiddly, but they too were satisfying.

Those very early first days brought another education for me, regarding books. This time it was about the book as a physical object, and about Robert's friendships and loyalty. Before I left New Zealand, Robert had sent me a beautiful, newly-minted copy of *Presences*, his book with Marisol. Everything about it delighted him. He told me in detail all about its production, from its elegant design by Bill Katz to negotiations as to who the publishers would be. It had been a harrowing process, but the end-product was entirely satisfying. Bill's mock-up for the book's front page was one of the first things we ever framed. I still enjoy its tender presaging of the book-to-be.

In contrast, Robert's first, greatly anticipated *Selected Poems*, published by Scribner's, was a shattering disaster. The hurt, the let-down, the sense of betrayal that Robert felt when he saw the book was appalling. He hated the green and white cover with the gothic script. He hated the fact that Scribner's had not wanted Bob Grenier to write the introduction, had instead favored some other, better-known academic personage. He hated the typeface, the spacing, the paper, everything. He knew he had to leave Scribner's as soon as he saw the book, knew they did not understand him at all, knew that although he had felt so deeply honored to have been published by them at first, and would gladly have spent the rest of his writing life there, everything had changed as the firm became more corporate instead of remaining the family house it had been for many years. Soon after that *Selected Poems* came out, Robert's editor there was fired, almost co-incidentally with his having a heart attack. We went for lunch with him, in his New York apartment. The dismay and disillusionment was shared, although they both had fond memories of Charles Scribner, Jr. Soon after, the editor died. And I can't even remember his name. When Robert decided to accept an offer from New Directions to be his publisher, the relief was enormous. Although he did not feel their books were exactly beautiful, Robert loved the company of writers they published. He could himself now pay intense attention to spacing, placement, type and cover. He was allowed to speak, and was heard.

Of course, I now know about the passionate delight Robert had in the books he himself published in Mallorca with Ann McKinnon, at their Divers Press. The press was the practical expression of the life-force that poetry was for him. In his isolation, there it was a way to participate, to find a company beyond the island, but still to be part of the local community by having the books printed by the fine craftsman at Mossen Alcover in Palma de Mallorca. Robert loved the old man who owned the business, had great respect for its cottage industry, handmade integrity. Eventually ownership passed to the son. When we visited Mallorca in 2000, we found the shop again. It had closed down. But a faded sign still hung in the stone wall. The *Black Mountain Review* had been printed in that workshop. I have some recollection too of Robert's telling me the first book he ever published was a small volume about poultry, perhaps more specifically about pigeons, which had been his childhood love. (When Robert went to boarding school at 14, he took his pigeons with him). I can see where that book would have been in the shelves in his room here in Maine, can see it small, hardback I think, with a paper cover with a black and white photograph of a strutting pigeon on it. I believe the book was printed at Mossen Alcover, too, and had an article by a friend from New Hampshire, an older man also a pigeon-fancier, for whom Robert had great respect. Another company, another world, and still a book.

How I wish I could ask about all this, hear the stories one more time. I just went upstairs, into the back of Robert's closet. There, behind the clothes, behind the tattered tweed dressing gown (made by a tailor in Mallorca, kept through so many many many moves, loved for the quality of the cloth, the craftsmanship) are still boxes of books. Among them is a parcel of thick brown paper tied with string. In it are copies of Douglas Woolf's *The Hypocritic Days*, with cover by Kitasono Katue, printed at Mossen Alcover in January 1955. There are several layers of address labels on the parcel. The first label, printed in heavy black type, is to Black Mountain College. I think it must have been sent from Mossen Alcover in Palma de Mallorca to Black Mountain, then forwarded to Douglas Woolf, who was then in California. Douglas Woolf then sent it to Robert, who by that time was in Albuquerque, New Mexico. The parcel was still sealed, never opened, when I had to make an inventory of Robert's things after he died. It took me a while to bring myself to cut the string and look inside. I feel that its still being closed after all those years was a completely loving act of Robert's. To me it speaks of love for Douglas Woolf, for Mossen Alcover, for Kitasono Katue, and for the whole process. By the time Robert received the parcel that turn of the kaleidoscope had gone, shifted to other patterns. Keeping the parcel unopened was a way of remembering the time, keeping it whole.

Sometimes Robert wished he didn't have to ever open a book at all, even take off its shrink-wrap. He would say so with a laugh and a shrug, but there was truth to it too. He loved the perfect pristine fact of a book, its elegant containedness, its sense of pure potential. Was it like the way my brother and sister would hoard their chocolate Easter eggs, wallowing in the luxury of knowing they were there to be enjoyed eventually? I was always the one to eat my Easter eggs right up, and that attitude often troubled Robert. I had no hesitation in using things, including books. I would read them in ways that were comfortable to me, sometimes bending the spine too far, often laying them face down when I took a break. A bookmark was never at hand, anyway I would be back soon. Oh no! I pretty quickly learnt not to do that. At least not with Robert's books. And often, if I didn't get back to them quickly enough, they would have disappeared, been neatly reshelved, put away where they belonged.

Once we had this house here in Maine, many of the books lived here. Robert would refer to coming back, reacquainting ourselves with our stuff after an absence, as being like an archeological dig. For him the books had become a beloved record of his life. They contained the ideas, the thoughts, the speaking breath of his friends. He did not write in books, but he kept things in them. Letters, announcements, tickets, brochures, mementos of contact in the world with increasingly scattered, always dear friends. These were his bookmarks. These were the books wherein he had found his life. One of them was a copy of Pound's *Cantos*. He had taken it with him to the Second World War. To Burma. Another was a book handmade by Robert Duncan and Jess Collins. The tape of the box cover they had made for it was fragile, yellowing, but the handwritten poem inside was unfaded. I understand now why we sometimes had to rush home from the beach if a sudden thunderstorm was threatening and we weren't sure we had closed the windows before we left. A whole bookcase full of books was ruined one winter when the door adjacent blew open while we were away. They were soaked, warped. Robert was hurt, hurt. But he didn't fuss. Like when he cut himself, he hated it, would put a bandaid over it as fast as possible, then try to forget about it. This time we dried out the wet books, put them back in the shelves. A book specialist would deem them worthless, but Robert still loved them.

I would be completely untruthful to say that Robert was unconcerned by a book's "value" as object, however. He grew up with very little money, in a household where every penny counted. He worked hard to support his families, worried about being able to do so to the point of making himself ill with anxiety. He thought of himself as a teacher, which stemmed for him from writing, that core which sustained him through all else. Gradually he became aware that the accumulated artifacts of his life were part of a cultural history. His amazement was overwhelming when one morning he read that a ditto copy of Ginsberg's *Howl*, that Robert had typed out and made, then distributed at a reading of the poem in San Francisco, had sold for I think $20,000.00. He could hardly believe it, of course had not kept a copy for himself. The dittos were made "to get the word out," he said. Why would he have kept one? Equally he did not keep copies of magazines. Something's got to go, he said. He did not make collections or scour bookshops. Books sprang from his life, and came to it, were generated and generative.

Books with artists, the collaborations, were an exceptional source of excitement and energy for Robert. I think the sense of joined envisioning, call it, took him outside himself in a different way. The work of writing the poems, when he was responding to an existing picture, would call up a new concentration, a new way of seeing or thinking, but use his own particular tools too. Once, when he was working on something for Francesco Clemente, he saw the images only as big photographic slides. We were in Helsinki, Finland. Raymond Foye had sent the images in plastic sleeves. Robert kept them propped in the window of his study near the kitchen, using the grey light outside to light the slides. I would see him standing there right up at the window, peering at them intently as I passed by the open door or changed the laundry in the passageway. He was never more thrilled than when Francesco wrote him that he "gave his painting a voice." The link between them was intuitive, a breath.

Every book with an artist had its own power. *Famous Last Words* with John Chamberlain brought a big challenge and a sense of bringing his and Robert's long, lively friendship into their older, changed work lives. *Gnomic Verses* came one afternoon with Cletus Johnson. At first Robert had proposed loops of words for Cletus's beautiful little "theatre" marquees. Later, the Verses streamed out of Robert into his notebook as we drove back to Cletus's Ellington farmhouse, laughing and playing after lunch at the local Rod and Gun Club. The book *Drawn and Quartered* with Archie Rand also came in one inspired ninety-minute spree at the Castellani Museum, as Robert and Archie prepared for the "Collaborations" show. There was the mad dash to Germany to meet Georg Baselitz, the fun of the writing despite language barriers, or because of them. Robert wrote funny, playful poems which Rosmarie Waldrop somehow managed to translate to give Baselitz an inkling of what was going on in the originals. The work with Alex Katz came from summer days and summer dinners here in Maine. The field with its edges and paths is still the same, the clump of daylilies Alex and Ada gave us still bloom to mark August's ease and good talk.

Robert's particularity about books, all aspects of books, was as remarkable as Aldo Crommelynck's about prints, a passionate giving of form to a great love. He would often quote Charles Olson's "Limits are what any of us are inside of." Robert's editorial and critical rigor, ferocious as it was, left him free to imagine and then realize beautiful books inside and out, both in form and in content. The idea of book was a limit that both freed him and contained him. Finally, they became a part of him, inseparable. He would say "I can't remember whether I read it or wrote it." During the Iraq War, towards the end of his life, he would often include Matthew Arnold's "Dover Beach" among his own poems during a reading. Books and poetry, passing life on, teaching and learning, looking in, looking out. Staying open, trying it out.

When Steve Clay and I packed up the books from this house, to be sent to Notre Dame, I felt as though Robert's brain was leaving the house, his mind. I was bereft again, until I realized it was not gone. I have my own portal to Robert's mind through my own memories. So many of them are associated with books. And I have his own books. Robert always believed knowledge, wisdom, experience could not be owned, was not something to be kept to oneself like a miser, but to be used and shared, built on and passed on. His way of doing that was through books, both the reading of them and the writing of them. Robert had loved the generosity of his elders to him. If his books can go on being read, can give a picture of his diversity even in some small way, can go on teaching, then he is still alive, will always be alive, among those pages.

I HAVE FORGOTTEN ALL HUMAN RELATIONS, BUT NOT POETRY

Debora Ott

I first met Robert Creeley in the air when the disembodied voice of an actor read one of his poems as part of a PBS special. I was 14, and "Love Comes Quietly" stopped me in pace on my way to get water once home after a grueling basketball game. Made me want to hear, as never before, a poem hanging brightly and tuned to my ear. We'd studied poetry in New York City's public schools as part of some ones' idea of Language Arts curriculum, and the printed portraits of bearded dead white men circled the walls where they met the ceiling in my classroom, but this poem was different. Even at that tender age – maybe not so tender, I was precocious – the poem's emotional truth resonated, for it said something about what it means to be human, what it means to love. I followed the sound and found my mother sitting in bed, legs outstretched, with a newspaper masking her face. Casually she asked, "How was your game?" I remained mute, sitting inches away from the TV's black & white street scenes of New York. Cross-legged and wide-eyed, staring, waiting for the credits to roll. I needed to know who wrote that poem.

I got my hands on *For Love* at the Donnell Library at age 16 when I finally was allowed to ride the number 7 train alone into Manhattan. The ache of that wait and my unabated curiosity to know Robert Creeley led me to SUNY/Buffalo, or UB as it's called, years later as a transfer student. I'd studied Anthropology, Psychology and Sociology as a CUNY freshman and sophomore. Tired of considering the norm and eager to experience the exceptional, I imagined I'd discover it in contemporary American poetry, and I headed up to Buffalo. This was the late '60s. The campus was in turmoil, and Bob used the news of the day as a jumping off point to speak about what mattered – in poetry, on campus and in the world. He'd tilt his chair back, prop his feet on the desk, and read headlines and copy from the *Times* – sweeping back his hair with his hand when its silk threatened to cover his one good eye.

I only took one of Bob's classes. However, we became friends and collaborators and he remained my teacher. His important lessons included: a plan allows you to be present; always take your keys; and, *manipulate* means to shape with one's hands. One night after a reading, we were across the street from Just Buffalo's home on Elmwood Avenue, seated at the bar of Justine's. Bottles of spirits backed up against an enormous mirror across from the long wooden bar, and the light from crystal sconces dappled the room. Bob told me the power was *in* my hands, and I took his directive seriously as I shaped Just Buffalo. In the mid-70s, I began with a reading series, picking up where UB left off when it shifted attention and support from poetry to film and media. Writing workshops, a radio show on WBFO, publications, Poetry & Sign, and interdisciplinary programs in poetry and jazz followed. My vision was to build community through the literary arts, and I was driven to create occasions for public engagement and exchange with writers that honored them as contributing members of the community, all while ensuring that diverse voices would be heard.

Not having had access to poets whose work inspired me as a child, I was intent on placing writers in schools that looked like and spoke like the kids they were teaching. Buffalo native Lucille Clifton spoke of the distinction between Family English and Standard English at a talk she gave for Just Buffalo at the downtown Buffalo & Erie County Library. Family English, she explained – Ebonics, Chinglish, Spanglish – for example, informs our speech and keeps language alive. Standard English, by contrast, is the language of business and education. In either case, language is a portal. We learn to better understand each other through poems and stories, and in this way, literature is vital to the workings of a democratic society. Yet, literature is the least funded arts discipline in the US, and this makes resource sharing key. Just Buffalo presented Rita Dove/1995, Toni Morrison/1997, and Maya Angelou/1998 in collaborative partnership with UB's Distinguished Speaker Series, and Rita, in high demand as the new US Poet Laureate, only responded to UB's invitation once I reached out to her, since I'd invited her to read for Just Buffalo early in her career.

Unabashedly town not gown, Just Buffalo engaged UB faculty who reveled in community. John Clarke, Carl Dennis, Leslie Fiedler, Raymond Federman, Jorge Guitart, Mac Hammond, Anne Haskell, John Logan, Carlene Hatcher Polite, Martin Pops and William Sylvester read and taught for us. After her 4-month writer's residency at Just Buffalo, Alexis De Veaux went to UB to earn her PhD. Jimmie Gilliam, whose *Women of the Crooked Circle* writing workshop endures, also earned her PhD at UB, and Ansie Baird, long time Writers-in-Education teaching artist, earned her Master's. Poetics Program Fellows drafted grant proposals, gave readings, and led workshops. Some, like Ed Baxter III, Ann Goldsmith, and Liz Willis, won Just Buffalo writing awards. Sherry Robbins, Cass Clarke and Paul Hogan coordinated Just Buffalo's Writers-in-Education program, and Paul and Martin Spinelli hosted Spoken Arts Radio. Sue Mann Dolce and Michael Kelleher coordinated our readings and workshops series, and in1997, just prior to my moving to Atlanta, Mike, creator of Just Buffalo's beloved Babel series and now program director of the Windham-Campbell prizes at Yale, became Just Buffalo's first Artistic Director.

Fast forward, and the talent pipeline from UB continues with Laurie Dean Torrell, Just Buffalo's Executive Director, Barbara Cole, Artistic/ Associate Executive Director, and UB Distinguished Professor Bruce Jackson a photographer for Babel. *Onward!* as Bob would say. What a whirl. Bob remained my advisor and mentor, always generous with his time and open to assignments. In 1990, he traveled with Victor Hernandez Cruz to Buffalo, Detroit, Milwaukee and San Francisco as part of *Across State Lines*, a national reading tour I'd put together. By virtue of our connection, Bob's extended company of writers – Black Mountain, Beats, Brits, New York School –

were regularly featured on Just Buffalo's stage: Amiri Baraka, Ted Berrigan, Josephine Clare, Fielding Dawson, Diane DiPrima, Ed Dorn, Robert Duncan, Allen Ginsberg, Bobbie Louise Hawkins, Anselm Hollo, Ted Joans, Joanne Kyger, Bernadette Mayer, Michael McClure, Eileen Miles, Hilda Morely, Alice Notley, Joel Oppenheimer, Maureen Owen, Tom Pickard, Jeremy H. Prynne, Tom Raworth, Ed Sanders, Anne Waldman and John Wieners.

Bob was the featured reader at benefits when Just Buffalo needed to raise money. He participated in *Contemporary Poets Connection*, a project in which middle schoolers studied the work of poets, learned about the creative process by corresponding with them, and wrote their own poems. The anthology *Poets at Work: Contemporary Poets – Lives, Poems, Process* (Just Buffalo Press, 1995) was the project's culmination. Michael Morgulis, UB American Studies, designed the cover for that book, our broadsides and posters, and much more. In 1995, Bob received a Lila Wallace-Reader's Digest Fund Writers' Award. This Community Connection grant allowed him to work with Just Buffalo at City Honors High School, helping students develop an electronic poetry magazine that was available online. Poetics Program Fellow Ken Sherwood directed the project, and a 56kb modem – a big deal at the time – was installed in the school, a true gift, since students at City Honors did not have access to the Internet.

Bob was a provocateur and a raconteur. We spent his 50th birthday together, eventually getting thrown out of the Club Utica, at Five Points, after the strange man who'd coaxed us out of our cozy booth conversation and onto the dance floor spun by armed with his wife and smiled, "Now aren't you glad to be dancing with your wife?" To which Bob replied, "She's not my wife. She's my friend's wife," and we were summarily propelled out the Club door laughing and into the Buffalo night. It was 1976, it may have been two in the morning, and we had clearly violated a gentlemen's agreement at that country & western bar. Bob drove me home to Cottage Street in Allentown taking every conceivable one-way street the wrong way. DUI's were not a thing then, and when we were stopped by a cop on the southwest corner of the intersection of Maryland and Allen, Bob got out of the car, a VW Beetle, and regaled the officer with stories...it was his birthday, he'd been celebrating with his young friend, etc. The officer glanced through the windshield at me, I smiled and waved, and he gave Bob a pass. Another kind of gentlemen's agreement.

In those days, prior to the State Department tour of the South Pacific where Bob met Pen in New Zealand and she subsequently came to America, he often sat at my dining room table drinking, smoking and talking pretty much nonstop while we listened to music. He rolled out a dream of me and my then husband John and our five-year-old daughter Sabina moving to New Mexico. What our life could be there at his home in Placitas. It took some bravery on my part to interject, a relief for him I later realized, and question how he could detail this future when his instruction in art and in life was to be in the present moment. He explained that one wouldn't want to show up with nowhere to go and nothing to do. A plan allows for spontaneity. It's the structure that presence is built upon.

Days after getting settled in his Fargo Street apartment, Bob brought Pen over to Cottage. Ours was the first American family Pen met, and she told me years later how she'd thought us typical. Indeed! Sabina, decked out in an Indian print skirt I'd fashioned from a bedspread, glided from room to room singing stories. John Coltrane, Sonny Rollins, Dexter Gordon, Art Tatum, Charlie Parker, Thelonius Monk or any of the many Bob introduced us to – Lester Young, Art Blakely, Billy Strayhorn, Billy Eckstine, Chet Baker, Miles Davis – streamed from the stereo. Our dining room oak wainscoting reverberated with music and story. The following year, Bob, Pen, John and I went to see *Cousin Cousine* at the Allendale Theatre. Bob noticed how audience members laughed at different points in the film. My laughter brought on labor, and I held on so that Alice May could be born at home before dawn.

This is a story of the old days, *then*, when passion and purpose fueled *the scene*, as Bob called it, and time and attention was given over to what's new. What remains is poetry. The word. Its power to spin a teen's mind and make real what can only be imagined. To connect, inspire, and ignite in the working air. One Christmas, I gave Bob the gift of a rubber stamp with Chinese characters on it that translated read: *I have forgotten all human relations but not poetry.* As a gift back, he wrote me a poem. We were and are chosen family, dispersed like dandelion now, and Bob gone.

EDITING, NOT A DEMOCRACY: WORKING (OR MY SMALL PRESS MENTORSHIP) WITH ROBERT CREELEY ON THE BLACK MOUNTAIN II REVIEW

Stephanie Weisman

I met with Robert Creeley, for one hour every week for the three years that I was a graduate student in the Creative Writing Master's program at the State University of New York at Buffalo

Our time together, without a doubt, formed the basis, the backdrop for my own life journey; a trajectory to a life in the arts through his mentorship.

Through our weekly meetings, by sharing his stories, his knowledge, his experiences of the poets of that time, the small press publishing genre, he opened a world and the possibility for me and I'm sure so many others, to forge forward. His landscape seeped with individuals and communities making their way, working around the systems, not being diverted, or stymied by gatekeepers. Mavericks who became instigators, innovators and then yes, gatekeepers.

I graduated from SUNY Buffalo in 1978 with a degree in psychology. Poetry was my first go to, but my conservative side protested. It said, "no livelihood there." It was a great time to be a student at UB. Post-student riots, the Gen Ed requirements were minimal. I was able to race through my psychology degree in a year-and-a-half. But I decided against being a therapist. Realizing that if I was going to listen to people's problems, their life stories, I wanted it to be by choice. I also didn't want to research subjects what I imagined had very small focus. I veered towards journalism, again the practical choice.

I was both right and wrong about what I would end up doing in my life. As Founder and Artistic Director of The Marsh, a breeding ground for new performance in San Francisco and now in Berkeley, I have spent almost three decades, developing people's solo performances. For all these years, I still enthusiastically listen to their stories, all within the sociological, psychological, and cultural context of our times. And ultimately, I suppose I did indeed become a researcher of a small slice of theater called solo performance.

Another aspect of post-student riot SUNY Buffalo was "the colleges:" a system of collegiate units based on a theme; offering programs, classes and even a dorm living setting for the general student population. So, for example, Rachel Carson College focused on the environment. College B, which was right then in the process of changing its name to Black Mountain College II, was the arts college.

Black Mountain College II offered courses in the arts, drawing, theater, painting, it provided a student theater group that put on plays, its own version of community theater, an art gallery, and the option to live in a dorm section in the new Ellicott complex. It held the focus of the original Black Mountain College of living, learning and working on art within community. It was a natural fit for Robert Creeley, then holding the David Gray Professor of Poetry and the Humanities, who was happy to be an advisor to the new journal, the

Black Mountain II Review, published by the college.

A Job listing crossed my desk. Wanted: Editor for a new arts journal at Black Mountain College II. Graduate assistantship.

Every six months or so, I made a call to find out about applying to the Creative Writing program, but it hadn't gone anywhere. But to apply for this assistantship, I needed to be a graduate student. I typed up my poems, submitted my application to the English department's MA program in Creative Writing, was accepted and was awarded the graduate assistantship.

I had no idea that this would include an ongoing mentorship, an independent study, with Robert Creeley, the famed poet and editor of the original and *Black Mountain Review*.

Our discussions, my education, began in earnest. This was fall of 1980. Volume 1 of the *Black Mountain II Review* would be published in the spring. Bob's task was to support me in becoming an editor. From his perspective, this process would focus on the genre of the small press. Which he thought was paramount. I was 24. But back then, he seemed like a great uncle. What a revelation now, to realize he was only 54 years old, younger then I am now.

I was being mentored by an incredible editor. Each week, Creeley pulled out issues of small press publications. I remember one in particular, *Floating Bear*, originally edited by Diane di Prima and LeRoi Jones (Imamu Amira Baraka) and later just di Prima. It was mimeographed and sent out by mail. The editors vision, goal, was to get new poetry out as fast as possible. Hence, 37 issues were published between 1961-1969, (plus one additional guest edited issue in 1971), mimeographed and sent by US mail. It included prose and poems by Creeley, Paul Blackburn, Robin Blaser, Ed Dorn, Charles Olson and Philip Whalen.[i]

Floating Bear, stands out in my mind to this day because it was such a great example of making a high-quality publication so inexpensively. It was "printed" by mimeograph technology, so new poem/prose/art delivery was fast. Just a postage stamp away.

Creeley and I talked about the world, the culture of small press publishing. How important it was to go for it. Make the publications happen, no matter what it took. Both editorially, as well as the production and financial aspects. He told stories of his travails and solutions; like printing issues of the *Black Mountain Review* in Mallorca to save money.

I listened. I asked questions. We discussed. I had the great gift of soaking up all the history he had been part of and the skill set he had developed. A magnanimous imparting of knowledge to the next generation.

He was very clear about what he thought made a good editor. His basic tenet was that editing is not a democracy. That editing by committee blurs the vision. The editor, the leader, needs to holds the vision and direction of the publication.

And one more thing. As important as anything. I felt fully supported and protected by Creeley. He had my back. Also, he was so in it with me. He contributed poems. He got Joel Oppenheimer, a fellow black mountaineer, to contribute. He wrote the foreword to the first volume.

FOREWORD

A magazine such as this one has a specific possibility and rationale, call it, in that it can make a case particular only to the abilities and commitments of its contributors. There is no reason, here least of all, to practice satisfactions which are not very literally one's own. No one gets paid. No one's life is remarkably changed. Yet there is an immense difference in any world that takes on these self-evident determinations — which constitute an art and its practice, whatever else — and states a company of one's own recognitions and loyalties, no matter what may come of it.

Charles Olson told me years ago that Melville had over his writing table what I'd presume was a framed motto: *Be True To The Dreams of Thy Youth* . . . At thirty, I shyly embraced that hope and wondered if it might not be self-deceiving. But now I haven't the least doubt that it's all indeed that ever matters. Your dream of the world is the world you will get, however altered its reality in fact may seem to you.

Black Mountain — the college that gives this magazine its title and gave the former Black Mountain Review its name back then (1954-1957) — is long gone, having closed in 1956. But possible you'll remember Donovan's Song:

First there is a mountain.

Then there is no mountain.

Then there is . . .

Nothing more extraordinary in that fact than that the days are presently lengthening, and spring's come round again. I recall Willem de Kooning once saying, *The only trouble with Black Mountain is that if you go there, they want to give it to you* . . . Happily it's ended up in good hands.

ROBERT CREELEY[ii]

And we were wonderfully supported by the community that made up the Black Mountain College II. Visual artist and professor, James Pappas, Headmaster of the college, designed the first cover. Jeanne Noel Mahoney, Director, was fully supportive. Fantastic artist, Betsy Offerman, offered her graphic design and layout skills *pro bono*. The BMCII drawing teacher, Norine Spurling, was generous with her submissions. The Colleges and College Chairman, Murray Schwartz, the English Department, The Gray Chair (Creeley's chair), and the University, all supported the magazine. It was truly a community effort.

With my fledgling, but definitely not democratic editing approach, we put together a publication of poems, prose, photos and artwork from students, and the Buffalo community of writers and artists. We did national outreach soliciting and including submissions from across the country. I was introduced to amazing writers and artists.

When I realized that I really didn't know what it took to produce and publish the magazine, Creeley fully supported my idea to offer a "soup to nuts" undergraduate class in small press publishing through Black Mountain College II. The fundamental course notion was that each class would determine, produce and publish an in-class publication to learn the fundamentals of small press publishing, both about the genre, as well as the fundamentals of publication production.

Together the class decided on the publication and its content. I taught them what I was learning about the importance and role of small press publishing, issues of censorship, and editorial approach. Then to support the production end, guest speakers were invited to teach about finances, advertising, graphic arts, etc. Each semester, we would print the publication ourselves at an underground political press who offered us free use of their basement offset printer. (Remember this was before the days of desktop publishing so it was far more complicated. You actually had to be able to line up the text with a t-square!) Students would do the camera work, make the metal plates, and print it. One semester we did a university-wide calendar; another semester, a chapbook of the student's writing called *One Potato Chip*, which also included a poem by Robert Creeley.

On a trip to San Francisco, I saw Spalding Gray perform his solo performance, *Swimming to Cambodia*. I was blown away and decided this was what I wanted. Authentic storytelling from the personal perspective; embedded with the social, cultural and political impact of the times. I realized how close this was to the aesthetic vision that Creeley had offered me through his poetry and mentorship.

That performance spurred me on to attempt my own first solo. A performance of *Dancemasters*, a long poem that I submitted as part of my Master's thesis. The poem had been awarded a NYSCA grant and residency through Just Buffalo. Part of the residency supported a one-night performance of *Dancemasters* at a small Buffalo theater.

While still in Buffalo, I followed my interest in the small press genre, and wrote an article for *Small Press Publishing* magazine about Coach House Press, the Canadian literary publishing company who was at the forefront of digital/desktop publishing. My eyes were opened to this burgeoning world.

Within a week of moving to the Bay Area in 1984, I walked into the first Berkeley store renting hourly access to Macintosh computers. Eureka, I thought! Here it is. The missing link. Access to the technology that would open up a whole new level of small press publishing, Mimeography evolves! I talked my way into a job based on my small press publishing teaching experience and immediately started learning and teaching the basics of desktop publishing. (Imagine my shock and delight when Diane di Prima took one of my classes.)

From making posters to database development, this technology has allowed me to take the tenets I learned from Robert Creeley to another level. Another sphere. They form the basis of what I have gone on to do in my life. Not a replica, but an evolution of what I learned about small press publishing and editing from Creeley, translated into my creating, starting and artistic directing The Marsh, now presenting over 600 shows a year on its San Francisco and Berkeley stages.

It has come so far, Robert Creeley, since 1980, almost 40 years ago.

But your stories, your life's work, writing and making a place for poetry, and community have formed the bedrock, the undertow, the current that have moved ideas and creations forward, just as you moved the poetry, and the university world forward with your generosity, your brilliant work and your creative spirit.

---

[i]   di Prima, Diane. Jones, LeRoi. "The Floating Bear." *from a secret location.* http://fromasecretlocation.com/floating-bear/

[ii] Weisman, Stephanie, Editor. Black Mountain II Review. Spring 1981. Volume 1. Number 1. Page 5.

POETRY ON THE MOON: BUFFALO 1977

Peter Middleton

English at Buffalo was in eclipse, or so it seemed to a visitor from Britain. A mood of aftermath prevailed when I arrived in 1977: everyone who had been astir with the new poetry in the 1960s was now exhausted, the great moment when a poetry could land on the moon had passed. Even the heavy snow that buried automobiles and left deep trenches on the sidewalks was lesser than that of the previous year's great blizzard. Snow, revolution, open field poetry, and hope were all diminished now. Albert Cook, who had been at Buffalo since 1963, and hired both Charles Olson and Robert Creeley, was planning to leave for Brown the following summer because, according to the campus newspaper, he was dissatisfied by the "reduction in the amount of intellectual stimulation and vitality."[1] Theory was taking over. Much self-congratulation was aired in the same paper when Provost George Levine announced that they had hired four professors from Johns Hopkins - Carol Jacobs, Rodolphe Gasché, Louis Marin, and Henry Sussman - to start in fall 1978 with the aim of creating "a center of critical theory for literature." The Poetry Collection faced an uncertain future. Karl Gay, Librarian at the Poetry Collection was planning to leave for retirement in Majorca at the same time as the archive was to be moved to new quarters in Capen Hall. In an interview illustrated by a blurry photograph dominated by his thick rimmed spectacles above the caption "Karl Gay: protective, proud," he explained that it rested on him to decide which poets to collect, a task made increasingly difficult by the vast expansion of little magazines and small presses over the previous decade, although he was confident that "everything that is worthwhile is here." He had other reasons too. When I worked as an assistant there I learned that he feared that if New York State politicians discovered the true value of the poetry and rare books archive they were quite capable of selling it to help pay the enormous costs of the state highways program. The poet I most wanted to study with, Robert Creeley, was just re-establishing himself after emerging from a difficult period in his personal life, a time when he could write – "Moon, moon, / when you leave me alone / all the darkness is / an utter blackness" – and expect his readers to accept that he was talking about what the title of the poem calls "A Form of Women." In 1977, it looked as if he was not yet able, as he was so brilliantly later, to give the department his full attention.

SUNY Buffalo as a whole felt vast and as confident as a skyscraper corporation. It boasted an enrollment of 27,000 students, and was immensely pleased with the newly opened Ellicott Complex. "'Most academics haven't in their wildest dreams seen themselves working in such superb surroundings,'" is how Dr. Clifton K. Yearley, chairman of the Department of History, the Complex's first occupant, described Ellicott earlier this summer. Dr. John A. Neal, assistant vice-president for facilities planning, was equally smug: "Ellicott is going to be an exciting place to be. The kids will like it...It's not your typical educational plant." Others were less impressed. After John Gardner, under consideration for a prestigious chair in creative writing, was quoted in an interview in the campus paper to be repelled by the "ugly" new site, saying "they've built the new campus on the moon," the appointment fell through.

Whether he rejected the university offer, or they rejected him, was not clear. I was sympathetic with Gardner, after attempting to walk all the way across windswept Amherst, still awaiting state funding for expansion, promised by Nelson Rockefeller before his demise.

Even Buffalo English in eclipse was a very exciting place for a young would-be poet. Several inspiring resident lunar baedekers were teaching the history and writing of poetry. Diane Christian taught a course on William Blake, John Clarke taught a course that continued Olson's legacy, Albert Cook taught a more conventional comp lit course on the Poetic Image, and the poets Carl Dennis, Irving Feldman, and John Logan all taught creative writing courses in poetry, mainly to MA students. Creeley taught an unnamed course also primarily taken by the Master's students, ENG 634, for which the course catalog reprovingly said, "Course description not available at this time." I don't think it ever had a name. Various poets visited the campus, including Margaret Atwood, Maureen Owen, and James Koller, there were writers in residence including Tom Weatherly and Walter Abish, while downtown Allen de Loach was inviting Ted Berrigan, Joanne Kyger, Fielding Dawson and others to the Just Buffalo series. Even professors who did not teach poetry at all were interested in the psychology of writing. Norman Holland taught Supervised Teaching, or "Superteach" that year, and I spent much of the time arguing for a Marxist social interpretation against his theory that each of us construct our personality around a thematic processing of experience unique to ourselves. His evaluation of me reads: "If I read your characteristic strategy right, it is to create your life through outside sense-impressions, chiefly of language—a perfect identity theme for someone hoping to spend his life writing and talking about writing." He also gently noted that my own writing was associative rather than reliant on "topic sentences or paragraph organization."

Much of the time, however, poetry seemed a slightly embarrassing, old-fashioned activity, in face of the surge of interest in literary theory amongst the doctoral students. A few students, like Jerry McGuire were clear that they intended to be poets, but most were far more excited by the new developments in literary theory, the publication of a selection from Jacques Lacan's *Ecrits*, and Gayatri Spivak's translation of Jacques Derrida's *Of Grammatology*.[ii] Poetry was associated in most minds with the Beat era, and its lingering representatives such as Creeley. Now lyric had added rock music to itself, and intellectual linguistic feats were performed by the new French philosophers. No one seemed interested in the vision of poetry that I had been encountered back in England in exotic imports of Jerome Rothenberg's *America: A Prophecy*, Harvey Brown's Frontier Press and the west coast Black Sparrow imprint, or Richard Grossinger's amazing syntheses of science, magic and poetry in *Io* magazine. Tellingly, no one mentioned the new Language Writing emerging in the salt water cities.

I spent just the year 1977-1978 on a $3000 Teaching Fellowship in the doctoral program. Money was so short when I arrived that we had to go out and knock on doors to borrow cooking utensils for our tiny apartment. What made it worthwhile was the freedom to study what we wanted. Most doctoral students were also on these subsidized Teaching Fellowships, "in order," as the Department put it, "to free students for the kind of intensive yet independent work that this program entails," having also decided to abandon "the assumption that a full, methodical coverage of one particular discipline is the primary objective of graduate training." I am still grateful to Buffalo's idiosyncratic poetry teaching for starting me on the path to an understanding of poetry that made it possible to write my own poetry, and participate in the culture of little magazines and poetry readings. When I arrived, I was a cultural Marxist, with allegiances to Stuart Hall's CCCS in Birmingham, deeply influenced by the socialist thought of Raymond Williams, seeing in poetry structures of feeling rather than Machereyan ideology. Poetry, I believed, was not just finials on the superstructure; it could help instigate fundamental social change. Buffalo was not my first choice, but the graduate entry deadlines for universities in the far more attractive cities of New York and San Francisco had passed by the time I began to make plans to go to the States. And I was far too timid simply to just turn up and hustle my way into the poetry scenes of those far-away places. In Sheffield I had been writing a dissertation (on D. H. Lawrence) with which I was thoroughly disenchanted, and was also newly married.

What Buffalo poetry offered and what I had expected of poetry were far apart. Here surely was where I could find out if the poetics of Olson, Creeley, Dorn and Spicer were still viable, capable of transmission to a new generation, of their anti-conformist honesty, their ambitious vision of a transformed human knowledge, their sense of the mystery and potential for new understanding that could be found in their language arts. Poetry was inspiring but also mystifying to me, and nowhere more so than at the end of the line, the varying free verse line break whose rightness of location – why here and not there? – appeared to depend on a special knowledge that I lacked. I hoped to meet teachers or poets who could persuade me that I was right to believe that poetry was as valuable as political activism, as intellectually rigorous as mathematics, and as capable of social reach as cultural theory. Learning to become a poet would be a spiritual vocation, perhaps like training with a zen master, where you sat at their feet and listened, meditated on their works and put up with their idiosyncrasies and occasional cuffs round the ear. I wanted to meet prophets not ordinary scribblers, and must have been irritating to the established poets I did meet. The first was Carl Dennis, whom I met only once, at a welcome party for graduate students, where he asked me why I had come to Buffalo from Sheffield. Because Creeley is teaching here, I told him, not just a great poet, also an excellent critic of poetry. With some confusion I noticed that Dennis, of whom I had never heard, was smiling, politely signaling skeptical amusement at what was to him such an improbable claim. But it would turn out that it would be such pragmatic attitudes that would eventually make the year worthwhile.

In the end, I spent only a year in this strange city, where no one walked, where the snows created deep trenches and obliterated automobiles for weeks at a time, and where the factories were idle ruins. Lived experience appeared to be improvised around electric typewriters, vinyl scented automobiles, tidy jeans, pills and whisky. Graduate students were friendly, invited us to their apartments and even their family homes. Just as the rhythms of the day were hard to catch – just when did these people eat meals? – so were the patterns of their other lives before graduate school. Our apartment hot air vents circulated a friend's joint smoke into a disapproving upper unit, and the shaggy living room carpet was the nearest thing to grass that we saw for months. You could be made a job offer during a lift between campuses. I spent only a year because anomalously I had already written a thesis at the University of Sheffield, though at the time of applying to Buffalo it was not a doctoral thesis at all, but a Master's, and only upgraded while I was in America, so it awaited my attendance at a Ph.D. viva back in England. To add to the pressure to return, my then partner was unable to get a work permit and she had to register as a student in order to find any paid work. Though I was told that the department were considering making me Bob Creeley's RA, by the spring of 1978 it was regrettably clear that leaving was inevitable. So my experience of Buffalo, though powerfully formative, was more brief than that of most Ph.D. students, and as must be obvious, my memories will be somewhat unreliable.

*

John or "Jack" Clarke was my main source of information about Buffalo's recent history. He looked at once young and old, a boyish eager face on a large, clumsy body with a polio limp that gave him the walk of a much older man. I took a course with him that meandered around a series of poetry topics of which I remember only one, the importance of the rhetorical device of the "enthymeme," the undeclared premise. He generously invited me and my partner to visit him in Bowling Green, Ohio where he had a family house. We didn't really know what to do with ourselves when we there, and I doubt that he and his wife Cass knew either. He piled jazz records on the floor in a half-hearted attempt to sort them and instigate a conversation, but it was quickly apparent that I knew almost nothing about the music. We watched him play a set in a local group.

When it came to asking questions about other poets and the history of Olson at Buffalo he was elusive. He had created a whole imaginary Blakean cosmos around Olson's ideas, and his own theories about American history, and this cosmology inflected much of what he said. When I tried asking him about my favorite poets I made no headway. What did he think of Philip Whalen? No sexuality in his poetry, no awareness of desire. What about Creeley? Creeley had been awful to have as a colleague in the years after his break with his wife, always complaining, talking for hours about his failings, his anger, and sometimes breaking into tears. We all spent enormous amounts of time listening to him, said Jack, to my ear sounding not entirely sympathetic.

Jack was promoting Blake in both his teaching and in the sonnets he had begun writing.[iii] Ed Sanders explains in his introduction to a collection of these published by Jim Garmhausen, that Jack told him, "I'm simply applying what I've learned from Blake's method to all of mythology."[iv] The result was an almost private mythological language, which I spent a great deal of time trying to decode, not much helped by the two page reading list of esoterica provided by Sanders. A typical sonnet, "The Whorfian Hypothesis," begins: "Future & past are extraordinarily confused / in my mind as well, & if the shape of time / is a woman, then are women to be held in fear," and after some astrological speculations ends with a typical apocalyptic rhetoric: "for only the pustule-ridden can / redeem the Sun, when the heart of the mountain opens."[v] Entanglement of past and future was also evident in a pamphlet he gave me, *Lots of Doom*, a transcript of a lecture he'd given in 1971, in which he attempted to prophesy in metaphysical dimensions what happened in the '60s, and what the '70s were about to release – "It's now the man's responsibility to provide, in speech, the unknown."[vi] Clarke goes all around his non-topic, digresses, works his audience, tells anecdotes including a melancholic account of his "last night with Olson," and concludes what sounds to my unamerican ear as an Emersonian replay with Heideggerian abstractions: "You have to invent actually the ground of your being."[vii] Clarke's sonnets were not entirely convincing, tentative yet rigid affirmations of his cosmology. Eventually I wrote a poem for him, the last line of which was "take up your pen and write," a presumptuous instruction that arose from an intuition that he hid behind his physical awkwardness and was far too intimidated by the example of the dead poets he so much admired.

Why not take a course in how to write poetry? We had nothing like this in England. I applied on arrival to join John Logan's poetry class but was turned down, not surprisingly, since I had no idea how to write a poem and had none with me. Irving Feldman was less popular and I had no difficulty joining his class, "Creative Writing: Poetry," described in the catalog as "A workshop course in which primary emphasis will be placed on the discussion of the students' original works." Once or twice he taught the class still dressed in his tennis-playing clothes, and this outfit became associated with his approach to poetry, a sport that required effort and technique, but not soul-baring inspiration or world-changing ambitions. For the first time, I saw that it was possible to write a poem without waiting to be inspired by mysterious spiritual forces, if you crafted its form with some understanding and skill. I owe my understanding of how to run a poetry workshop to these classes, though at the time I suspect I arrogantly felt that we were all merely playing with poems.

Feldman was utterly opposed to prophets and mystics who commandeered poetry, and made no secret of his impatience with the acolytes, the "choir of eternal boys," who constantly praised Charles Olson. Now with the help of search engine access to the archives I can see the impressions he made at the time in his acerbic satire "My Olson Elegy" (1972), where he calls Olson the "bard of bigthink," a false prophet whose "steamy stupendous sputtering" was "all apocalypse and no end."[viii] A much later poem, "How Wonderful," published in *The Nation* in 1992, also recalls to me Feldman's resistance to any sort of poetic mysticism or poetics of communication or ideology critique. The first stanza imagines the narcissistic rewards of being fully understood, and the second the unexpected freedoms of being completely misunderstood; the symmetry between stanzas is broken in final lines that picture the poet's self "like a root growing wise in darkness," presumably away from the dazzle of mystical illumination or political enlightenment of poetic schools. As far as he seemed concerned, poets did not need to align themselves with any group at all.

My then partner and I often felt isolated in that long Buffalo winter, and were grateful for the brief friendship of the poet Tom Weatherly, a visiting writer for that year. He appeared to adopt us for a while, lonely as he was in the city, ignored by faculty and unsure of his role there. An impressively dedicated cyclist, he rode across the hard-packed snowy roads to our apartment for conversations with the English outsiders. At times, he wanted to relive his anguish at a failed marriage to a white woman, at others, his puzzlement at the culture at Buffalo, and sometimes just to talk about poetry. I read his *Mau Mau American Cantos* – a mix of showy verbal dexterity, impatience with political dogmatism, and satirical rewritings of the canon. After he left Buffalo he improvised his own version of black identity out of an amazing range of constituents, his early experiences in the marines and as a preacher, from poetry, from Republican politics, conversion to Judaism. With us this transformation was halfway along, as he looked downwards from his considerable height.

No one at Buffalo appeared to pay much attention to him. Al Cook offended me one day by saying that he had "invented" Tom Weatherly, an absurd claim that at first I didn't understand, until Al explained that he had written an imaginary comic portrait of a would-be radical black poet. Patronizing indifference to black politics and aesthetics appeared to be the norm. We went to hear Angela Davis, a legendary figure to the English left, speak on campus, assuming that many of our supposedly left-wing student compatriots would be there. Instead we were two of about six white listeners in an audience of several hundred young black Americans. When Davis arrived in the large hall she was attended by at least thirty young people dressed in paramilitary style, lined up against the side walls while she delivered a powerful speech. When I tried to discuss her lecture the next day with other graduate students they appeared uninterested, and the event shifted into the category of discrepant memories that have an edge of dream about them. For a while after Davis I noticed that a different English was spoken by the young black undergraduates talking in clusters around the cafe seating areas.

During the Christmas vacation, I worked in the Poetry Collection, as much an education as anything that happened in the classroom. The sheer variety and visible bulk, the wonders and absurdities, of the printed poetry, watched over by the rituals and restrictions of the librarians, made visits to the collection extraordinarily instructive. Standing beside two separately indexed sets of miscellaneous poetry chapbooks that I was supposed to integrate into one sequence, I learned a useful skill, to read poems on the run. Reading the poetry was discouraged, and I was always looking over my shoulder; Karl Gay might pop out of his office at any moment and complain that I was malingering. Vancouver poetry caught my attention, and I worked my way through *Georgia Straight* and many other pamphlets, noticing how a poetry scene could establish itself in a city other than the great metropolises. One day I was greeted with much excitement: "Untermeyer has croaked, Untermeyer has croaked," repeated one of the assistants to explain why the usual gloom had lifted, as she bustled about closing Louis Untermeyer's record now that his long career was over. Living poets required constant tiresome monitoring.

Personally, I owe much to Diane Christian, a young professor (and former nun I believe), who taught an inspiring course that meticulously took us through a reading of William Blake, poem by poem, book by book. This intensive immersion in Blake later enabled me to write a conference paper on a post-structuralist Blake for the Essex Conference on 1789, and there to catch the ear of a couple of academics from the University of Southampton, who recommended me for a lectureship. Her Blake was very different to Clarke's esoteric mythographer; her Blake "retains and reshapes the diction of the holy" and "works an inversion which does not destroy physical eroticism." This is a poetry in which "desire and sexual love also mirror what Blake called mental war, the energetic exercise of art."[ix]

Christian's short film (also credited to Bruce Jackson) of Creeley reading from *Mirrors*, made a few years after I left, is as much a tacit portrait of Christian's own vision of poetry, as a powerful image of Creeley himself (a still from the film showing Creeley smiling at his infant son on Penelope's lap appears as the cover for his *Collected Later Poems*). She manages to show how this poetry mirrors the love embodied in the infant's lunging presence, and even titles the film "Willy's Reading." The camera begins rolling before Creeley has readied himself with a drink of white wine, a few disconnected remarks – "This is written 11.13.78" - and stabilizing glances at Penelope and Willy. Then he manages to catch hold of a line of thought that coalesces out of a stutter: "You see, I like, I like, I like poe, poetry. Not that I even like poetry, I like it because I thought it's a way of working or having the use of words that's free and fun particularizing let's one say things both meaning them and not necessarily paying the dues it has in meaning them - I like that playfulness that's characteristic of John Ashbery - I didn't ever have an extraordinary theory of language - if the thing said was or wasn't true was paradoxically not finally the point it was whether it was experienced as true."[x] As he reads he criticizes his poems; one of them is dismissed with a laugh as "too rhetorically vague." He tickles the baby's toes. During my semester with him he was evidently impatient with poetry, once suggesting that if he had our opportunities as he put it, he would probably study genetics. His attention to the strange diremptions of assertortic force made possible in poetry had a lasting influence on me, eventually sending me to the American pragmatist tradition and its recent reinvention.

*

I have written elsewhere about my encounters with Creeley during that year in Buffalo, and will only summarize them here.[xi] He arrived in the classroom with no notes and with no guidance to his students as to how to prepare for the class. Then he talked for two hours, following lines of thought that we almost never interrupted, and that he only infrequently paused for questions or responses. He didn't try to get to know our names or draw out our different interests. Yet his teaching had an enormous impact on me because for the first time in my life I felt that I had been invited inside the poet's workshop, was listening to the primary reasonings out of which poems might come. Much of the time I and the rest of the class were bemused by the discourse that mixed complex abstractions with an unusually plain vocabulary, though one that was often subject to intricate syntactical manipulations. In an earlier essay, I tried to capture the mood of the classroom: "The highlight of each week was the graduate seminar on poetics with Creeley. I wish that I had kept much fuller notes of what he said than I did. What I kept are isolated sentences and phrases from each session, because it was hard to identify in this raga of musings the usual kind of statements that a student is expected to record. In an attempt to make sense of what he was saying I began to note down odd sentences or phrases as exactly as possible in order to retain their idiosyncratic precision, the reasons for which often eluded me. Gradually certain words began to crystallize out. He talked repeatedly about the 'information' one takes from reading a poem, adding that we badly need 'some imagining of the activity of poetry other than the usual standpoint of criticism as text, new, postmodern, or other'."[xii]

Creeley's office at Clemens was bare. Was he making a point about the loss of familiar rooms on the Main Street campus, or too preoccupied with changes in his own life to bother with decoration? We met there for independent study. I was 27 (he was nearly twice that), and full of questions. What was it like to have Olson as a friend? How does one write poetry now? He avoided answering. Instead he pictured Olson acolytes following in the wake of the poet's rocket finding themselves left up in the air. What do you think of Richard Grossinger? His alchemical memoirs had inspired me back in Sheffield. Creeley told me a lengthy, seemingly irrelevant story about Grossinger's vegetarian cooking, a soup that despite its variety of ingredients was uniformly brown. What I learned? That the indirections of anecdote could be more precise than focused analysis. That answers might not be what were needed.

Out of curiosity I went along to a short farewell celebration for Leslie Fiedler, a slightly chaotic affair at which people milled about, and various faculty spoke about him. Creeley spoke towards the end, and read a poem about which he was very self-deprecating, just a piece of "doggerel," he said, he had not been able to write a proper poem, but he wanted to pay tribute to his friend so he offered this. Listening to the poem, that I recall was structured around a car journey, I tried and failed to hear the signs of doggerel. What was it that made this verse fail to be a poem? If I could get this I might better understand how Creeley's poetry worked.

Creeley tried to interest me in my own national literature, the British poets and avant-garde writers that he had met, lending me (or giving - I was uneasily unsure) copies of Tom Raworth's *Serial Biography* and Ann Quin's *Berg*. His investment in Quin only became clear many years later when I discovered that they had had a relationship in the '60s, and he had been shocked by her alleged suicide in 1973. The only time he became angry with me, in a jazz bar to which he had taken us after a generous lunch in his small apartment where we sat on the floor, he suddenly lashed out saying harshly that I ought to pay more attention to British writers. Hurt for a few moments I consoled myself by blaming his outburst on the alcohol he had been drinking for several hours, rather than admitting my own neediness for approval, and my excessive adulation of Americanism in poetry.

His belief that the starting point should be one's own place found its strongest expression in an anecdote he told me several times about Basil Bunting's practicality. After staying at Kitaj's house in Spain where he read all forty seven books in the house, leaving *Middlemarch* to the last because he knew he'd dislike its fussy editorializing, he and Penelope had gone to England and hired a car to drive over to see Bunting at his home Corn Close in Northumberland. On the day the Creeleys were to leave, their car engine failed to spark into life, giving out only a damp, hoarse cough. Bunting had the answer immediately. He opened the bonnet (hood) and wafted across it a spray can of something he mysteriously called WD40, told Creeley to try again, and the engine started into life at once. I was unimpressed with this story, because everyone who owned an older car carried this oil mist spray – as a teenager I drove a black "sit up and beg" Ford Popular that needed constant encouragement.

Back in England in 1979 I saw that Creeley had published a poem about the visit to Bunting, that ends triumphantly when the "car starts / by god." Creeley moralizes in what is for him an unusually explicit manner on the importance of this crucial visit to Bunting for him: "What wonder / more than // to be where you are, / and to know it?"[xiii] Failing to be able to start the car felt to Creeley like a further reminder of his own incompetence, which he had been feeling strongly during their stay, his head full of self-reproaches – "Am I useful / today? Will I fuck up / the fireplace" - or it is understood, mess up his new marriage, or his own future work as a poet. Will he be able to keep the home fires and poetic inspiration burning?

"Corn Close" is a tiny mid-life *künstlerroman* that now resonates strongly for me with my own attempts at Buffalo to start up a literary engine of my own. The poem's exploration of the questions it poses also, I think, goes to the heart of much of what I saw more generally of poetry in Buffalo, of the widespread sense of needing to relocate its happenstance. "Corn Close" is Creeley's own version of what he kept saying to me in the bar and in our brief tutorials, and to all his students in the classroom, that we should try to be present to the places where we find ourselves, to the poetry and people around us.

The poem starts with a blast of italics, dashes, wordplay, and puns signaling considerable apprehensive and self-conscious uncertainty about the very act of initiating a poem that even after four stanzas could be heading in almost any direction, or even be about to end in a self-contained reflexive halt. This section could have been titled "One:"

> Words again, rehearsal—
> "Are we going to
> get up *into*
>
> heaven, after all?"
> What's
> the sound of *that*,
>
> who, where—

and how.
One wonder,

one wonders, sees
the world—
specifically, this one.

So far, it's a poem similar to a number of other earlier ruminations on the being of being, of how the I ("one") acts as subject as it wonders (or punningly, as it "oneders," as it were, brings a self into being through the wonderment of linguistic awareness), a twist on the Cartesian "cogito ergo sum." Creeley was always interested in his own and others' tendency to rehearse an event before it happens, to create temporal delays and sidesteps with verbal anticipations, to live in anticipation of a heavenly reward, whose falsity is evident in its sneaky reliance on impossible prepositions. How could we possibly imagine this future, this heaven, as a world, a place that could be gotten "into"? What possible actuality would valid the idea of an act of entering implied by the preposition?

Here the poem swerves abruptly. It turns out that there is a specific rainy-day world on hand, a locale very like that at the opening of Bunting's poem "Briggflatts," sheep on a steep hillside above the stream that will have its own local noun, and we are looking out a window with the poet still inert in bed while Bunting is already out and about. In comparison to Bunting's omni-competence, even when carrying the heavy garbage can up the hill, the poet feels his head is full of "vague palaver." Bunting is confident enough to criticize the Queen for the poor organization of her garden party (a regular event to which up to a thousand people are invited by the crown as a mark of recognition for exceptional achievement - my father was eventually invited to one for his work at GCHQ), and prefers music with a clear outline rather than the sort of "tonal blather" created by Charles Ives, a favorite of Creeley's.

For about the next dozen stanzas the poem returns to the angry self-criticism of the opening, interwoven with what may be asides from Bunting's conversation, on topics varying from the inevitability of bodily decline and mortality, to the relation between language and the world, to the sounds our bodies make by being alive. "Back on the track, / you asshole," says an unidentified vicious superego-like voice: "No excuses, / no / 'other things to do'—." A quotation from Sir Thomas Wyatt's poem, "They Flee from me," evoking the paranoia and despair of the Henrician court, is interpreted in a self-pitying way as a warning about the loss of friends and old relationships, and modulates suddenly into more constructive self-reproach about Creeley's expectations of the visit, that they would be able to help out Bunting. Now the gesture of bringing cheap whisky to someone who drinks single malt is exposed as a ruse of his own ego. Had Creeley been afraid that this aging poet was "broken" or his poetry "gone sour"? With hindsight, it is all too obvious to him that his fear for Bunting was really fear for his own situation. At this point the poem shifts straight from the lines "My fear / is my own" to Bunting's display of resilience when "He got / the car started." Resilience. Behind the spray can anecdote I heard and would firmly remember that poetry can be lost, that its persistence requires resilience and a whiff of penetrating oil.

*

Buffalo's brief poetry interregnum was not solely of its own making. Avant-garde poetry in America was in the middle of its own reorientations after the death of Olson and the withdrawal of Robert Duncan, the increased visibility of the first generation of New York poets and the growing reputation of the second generation, and a slow loss of public momentum by many of the second generation Olsonians. The arrival of structuralism in 1967, the introduction of textuality and signifiers by *Yale French Studies* in the early 1970s, and the sudden abundance of translations of post-structuralists (though often clunky or opaque with translator's literalese), gave social theory and philosophy new influence on literary practice, and in the process displaced older confidences in the political and cultural scope of poetry: not the "end of the age of poetry" but certainly an end of the centrality it briefly achieved in the sixties. Political separatism had walled off much black and feminist poetry. What place should poetry have in the academy? Creative writing deliberately neutralized larger aspirations for poetry in favor of craft, form, and semantics. Literary theory adhered dogmatically to a theory of language that displaced authorial agency. Linking poetry directly to sexual or spiritual revolution looked implausible.

My year of Buffalo poetry changed everything for me. The lunar dissociation of poetry teaching at Buffalo in 1977-1978 was just what a young idealist needed. Poetry was still possible, poems start with conscious acts of practiced hand, the mythic heroes had gone if indeed they ever existed, poetry could be a career as long as you had a job, poems could diffuse themselves in rhetorical vagueness or stumble clumsily, and still be worthwhile. Poetry at Buffalo felt to my youthfully distorted sense of human time to be middle-aged, and I sensed a generation of younger poets had gone missing, though I had then no idea where to find them. If I try now to codify the disparate impressions of Buffalo poetics they would be: that poetry arose from outside the ego; that a poem's language was not to be taken to be prosodic epistemology; that there was a valuable continuing quarrel about whether poetry should be apocalyptic or domestic; and above all that poetics needed to take account of the turbulent new philosophies of language. We left the States, spent a year in Swansea where I held my first university job, and just as importantly met Peter Hodgkiss, the editor of a crucial radical poetry magazine, *Poetry Information*, who published the paper on Edward Dorn I had written for Al Cook as well as filled me in on what the poets in my own country were achieving, and inevitably then moved to London where my partner went to work for the feminist magazine *Spare Rib*, and I finally began to write and participate in a thriving poetry scene. Literary theory captured my imagination, I learned how to write topic sentences, and I began to find that missing generation, some of whom were Language writers, reading them at first with puzzlement and then with enthusiasm. Buffalo receded into memory until I revisited in 1989, and discovered the Poetics

Program in full swing, all quite unlike anything that had been happening while I was there.

---

i   PrimThis and other quotations are taken from the Buffalo campus newspaper, *The Spectrum*, found in cuttings in a scrapbook of the year 1977-1978, so I cannot verify the exact dates and page numbers.

ii   I am indebted to Jerry for comments on an earlier draft of this essay, and for sharing his own memories of that time. He has written a witty elegy for Creeley that begins, "Hey, Bob, sorry / this is late and you / too and in // Texas for Christ / sake." Jerry McGuire, "Robert Creeley in Texas, March 31, 2005," Venus Transit (Buffalo, NY: Outriders Poetry Project, 2013,), 59.

iii   Vincent Ferrini describes Clarke as a "Mona Lisa man" in his sonnet "The Ghost of Rocky Neck," and also refers to the phenomenon of Olson acolytes: "few have the wheel whirring as / he does, even when loyalists go astray." Vincent Ferrini, Collected Poems (REF NEEDED).

iv   John Clarke, The End of This Side, Black Book 4 (1979), vi.

v   Ibid, 44.

vi   John Clarke, Lots of Doom: The Canton Reading December 12, 1971 (Castlegar, British Columbia: Cotinneh Books, 1973), 10.

vii   Ibid, 47.

viii   Irving Feldman, Collected Poems 1954-2004 (New York: Schocken Books, 2004). Accessed on Poetry Foundation website: https://www.poetryfoundation.org/poems/43377/my-olson-elegy. 8.2.2017

ix   Diane Christian, "Inversion and the Erotic: The Case of William Blake," in The Reversible World: Symbolic Inversion in Art and Society, ed. Barbara A. Babcock (Ithaca, NY: Cornell University Press, 1978), 125.

x   This is my own transcript of Creeley speaking on film. Bruce Jackson and Diane Christian, Willy's Reading, 1982. http://writing.upenn.edu/pennsound/x/Creeley.php

xi   I have written two essays about Creeley that draw partly from memories of Creeley in 1977, and notes taken in his seminar. Peter Middleton, "Robert Creeley's Reflexive Poems," The Gig 18 (2005): 43-59; Peter Middleton, "Scenes of Instruction: Robert Creeley's Reflexive Poetics," in Form, Power, and Person in Robert Creeley's Life and Work, eds. Steve McCaffery and Stephen Fredman (Iowa City: Iowa University Press, 2010).

xii   Quotations from Creeley are verbatim statements recorded in my notes from the classes, Fall 1977. The passage quoted comes from "Scenes of Instruction."

xiii   Robert Creeley, "Corn Close," Collected Poems 1975-2005 (Berkeley, CA: University of California Press, 2006), 157-162. First published in Later (New York, NY: New Directions, 1979).

ACROSS THE FRONTIER:
BUFFALO'S BORDER POETIC COMMUNITIES

Steve McCaffery

Let me attempt to outline my own history in Buffalo poetry and poetics and start with my arrival in North America from England in the Summer of 1968. Having gained a B.A. with joint Honors in English and Philosophy at Hull, I married, graduated and left the UK in the same week, destined to enter the MA program at Toronto's recently established York University. Poetry at Hull (and in the UK in general) was stultifying at the time of my departure. Philip Larkin was the university's Head Librarian and C. Day Lewis Poet-in-Residence during my last year's tenure there. I had started a poetry magazine called *Poet's Eye* which ran to three issues and successfully solicited contributions from both Larkin and Day Lewis; the final issue was devoted to Concrete Poetry, a genre which I had just discovered and which opened my mind to the possibilities of both a non-linear poetics and of being part of an international movement.

As I learnt subsequently, the Canadian poetry scene when I arrived in Toronto in the summer of 1968 was divisive to say the least. 1967 had been Canada's centenary year and the nationalist push for all things Canadian was obsessive. One Canadian poet, Dorothy Livesay, poked me in the stomach with her umbrella at a government sponsored event in Ottawa and denounced me as non-Canadian. A simplified poetic mapping of that time would reveal a sharp bi-coastal division between Vancouver and Toronto poets. Montreal was somewhat egregious in being stridently bi-lingual and would require a lengthy essay in itself. In Vancouver, the cultural conduit was north-south rather than west-east and the New American Poetries of the Bay area, and Black Mountain had been welcomed by a community of younger Canuck poets (Daphne Marlatt, Frank Davey, George Bowering among others). The 1963 Vancouver Poetry Festival brought up Denise Levertov, Philip Whalen, Charles Olson, Robert Duncan and Allen Ginsberg is now legendary. "Toronto the Good," by contrast, seemed staunchly nationalistic and mythopoetic. That its local influence was Norththrop Frye's reductive critical method as outlined in *Anatomy of Criticism* could and can be felt in the early work of Margaret Atwood, and Michael Ondaatje, and such older poets as Eli Mandel. In 1972 a poisonous text to internationalists like me found publication through Toronto's Anansi Press: Margaret Atwood's *Survival: A Thematic Guide to Canadian Literature*. In it Atwood argued for a "garrison" mentality and advanced the case for Canada's "victim status," owing to a lack of solid national identity comparable to those of the UK and the USA.

Among more singular poets of an older generation I should mention Toronto-based Raymond Souster, who edited *Contact* magazine (1952-54) and later *Combustion* (1957-60). Souster arranged a reading for Charles Olson in Toronto in 1960 and the two poets were in correspondence from 1952 to at least 1965. In Montreal, poet Louis Dudek had launched *Delta* magazine (1957-66) and entered a brief but intense correspondence with Ezra Pound. Prior to 1967 then, there was a certain border porosity between Canada and the States and a "North-American" modernism seemed to be emerging. For example, Irving Layton's volume *The Improved Binoculars* was launched simultaneously in 1956 by both the Toronto-based Ryerson Press and in the US by Jonathan Williams's Jargon Society. Two poets in particular were germane to my own developing practice: Bill Bisset in Vancouver and bpNichol in Toronto. Both of them were committed to the strident internationalism that I also embraced. Bissett's *blewointment* mimeo magazine was a melting pot for European concretists and North American visual poetics, as well as the New American Poetry and ethnically inflected chant poems. His guiding rules for acceptance were no rules at all. Many of the issues were neo-Dada chance assemblages of mimeographed poems, line drawings, diner menus, torn sheets of newsprint and magazines, and commodity labels such as soup cans or cigarette packets. Each copy was unique. In Toronto, Nichol co-founded with fellow-poet David Aylwood in 1964 a magazine called *Ganglia* which ceased publication in 1967. It reemerged under the new name of *grOnk*. The latter was self-published and mailed out free to a mailing list of I believe 300, which included the actress Audrey Hepburn (then living in Switzerland). Its first issue in 1967 included work by the French "spatialiste" poets Pierre and Ilse Garnier, as well as work by American poets D. A. Levy and D. R. Wagner. It lasted for 100 issues in various formats. The afternoon of my first meeting with Nichol was taken up discussing recent trends in Concrete poetry and in showing him some of my recent work. I had come across some of Nichol's own poems in magazines in England before I left and was keen to meet him in Toronto. The afternoon ended in him choosing three pieces of mine (including a prototype to Carnival), which he published later that day. In 1969, the Four Horsemen emerged, and its first public performance (January 1, 1970 is listed as the first ever manifestation of Canadian Performance Art; a date shared with Toronto's other collective General Idea. As well as concretism, Nichol found inspiration in the work of Gertrude Stein, Pound, Zukofsky, Williams, Olson, and Creeley. Nichol also acted as Canadian publisher and distributor of the work and magazines of a Cleveland-based poet D. A. Levy, whose Renegade and Seven Flowers presses served as the *zeitgeist* for an alternative counter culture that saw enlightenment through drugs and sex (not necessarily in that order). Through Nichol's connection, such Cleveland publications found a Canadian readership, just as Canadian poets were exposed on the shelves of Jim Lowell's Asphodel Bookshop. Levy died in mysterious circumstances. He was embroiled 1966-68 in a protracted obscenity trial which he eventually won. In late 1968, he was found dead of a self-inflicted gunshot wound to the head but rumors still circulate that he was shot by the Cleveland police.

The Four Horsemen's first visit to Buffalo followed in (I believe) 1975. Through the auspices of Max Wickert. We were invited to perform at the second annual arts festival at Art Park in Lewistown. We did our hour-long set in a tent of some kind and it was there I first met Anselm Hollo; Mike Basinski was also in attendance. The Buffalo poetry scene then seemed lively. Olson had been a visiting professor at UB 1963-65 and Creeley joined the UB English faculty in 1967. Another faculty member, Allen De Loach, edited a fabulous magazine *Intrepid*. For his part, Robert Bertholf, curator of the

UB Poetry Collection published the magazine *Credences* which ran, I believe, for eight issues in thick format. In October 1980, Robert Creeley organized a festival of Canadian Poetry at UB's North Campus. His connections to Toronto were largely through Victor Coleman, co-founder of Coach House Press and ex-patriot American Warren Tallman then teaching at the University of British Columbia. It was an almost all-male cast, as I recall, including Fred Wah (who had studied with Olson at UB in the 60s), Gerry Gilbert, Bill Bissett, bpNichol, Victor Coleman, and myself; the lone woman poet being Daphne Marlatt. Stan Bevington of Coach House Press designed the poster (one of which, I believe, survives in the Poetry Collection and one was on the wall of Creeley's office in 438 Clemens when I arrived in 2004). The design was taken from the Canadian $50 note depicting a group of RCMP offices on horseback with spears and in full regalia in tattoo formation. (I later told Creeley that Canadian's referred to the circular arrangement as a "Newfoundland Firing Squad" which tickled him pink.) In the evening Nichol and I performed as the Toronto Research Group in Darwin Martin House.

The Just Buffalo Literary Center reading series began in February 1976 with readings by British poet Tom Pickard and Michael McClure. Event were generally held in the Allentown Community Center at 111 Elmwood Ave. I drove down from Toronto with bp Nichol as part of a reading to launch the International edition of the magazine *Ink* (4/5, in April 1982). That issue included (as well as some of our own work) contributions by Alice Notley, Michael McClure, Victor Hernandez Cruz and Robert Creeley. Another important reading series in Buffalo was the Steel Bar Readings, curated by ex-Poetics Program student Jonathan Skinner. Organized on a monthly basis and held at the Tri-Main building a little south of the Central Park Grill on Main Street, I came down to read there with Fiona Templeton on 24 February 2001. Later that same year, in April, I believe, Skinner organized "Poetry Across the Frontier" (from which I take my title) that featured eight Canadian poets: (Steven King, Natalie Caple, Neil Hennessey, Mark Sullivan, Steve Venwright, Alana Wilcox (a novelist), Paul Dutton and Christian Bök). That year alone the series brought several people to Buffalo including Alice Notley, Judy Patton, Bruce Andrews, Tom Raworth and Humberto Ak'abal (for an Ethnopoetics seminar).

My next appearance at UB was in 1988 when the late Dennis Tedlock (newly appointed James McNulty Professor) invited me down for a three-day residency. Dennis had become familiar with my solo and group work in sound poetry through our joint friendships with Jerome Rothenberg. The emergence of Ethnopoetics in 1967-68 and the appearance of *Alcheringa* magazine and subsequent textual gatherings like *Shaking the Pumpkin* and *Technicians of the Sacred*, all chimed with the Horsemen's rejection of a reflective poetics for a stridently performative, physiological and participatory one. I duly took the residency but never met Tedlock; he was out of town on another engagement.

I moved to Buffalo in the Summer of 2004 on news of my appointment as David Gray Professor of Poetry and Letters and Director of the UB Poetics Program. The weekly readings that Charles Bernstein put on under the banner name of "Wednesdays at 4+" (the time of their happening) was changed to

Poetics Plus. A mandate of mine (and one too of my current colleagues) was to make the events accessible to a downtown audience always free of charge. The range of venues varied; two were held in the Big Orbit Gallery on Essex (Michael Davidson and a post-Katrina reading by New Orleans poets Bill Lavender and Camille Martin.) The problem with that space for Winter events was the lack of heating. Other readings took and take place at the Karpeles Manuscript Museum on Porter Ave., the Cinema at Hallwall's, Rust Belt Books, and WNYBAC.

I should emphasize, as a final word, the ongoing poetic transits across the borders. With Gregory Betts presence at Brock University in St. Catharines, Ontario (the closest Canadian campus to UB and only 25 minutes away) group exchange, cross-border readings began to take place. Mike Boughn, an American and former student of Bob Creeley's made Toronto his home many years ago. He edited, with Victor Coleman, the long-awaited, seminal *HD Book* of Robert Duncan. Published by University of California Press in 2012 it was launched in the Poetry Collection at UB in the same year. Another energetic presence in Toronto is Jay Millar whose BookThug press has published several titles by American and Buffalonians, including Steve Zultanski, a vital presence in the Poetics Program for many years. As Heidegger reminds us, "Poetically man dwells," and borders are meant for crossing. The Toronto-Buffalo corridor is one that proves it can be done. And recall too the Windsor-Detroit doublet that offers a thriving regional poetic community. I sometimes harbor the thought of a new school of Lake Poets that would include Ontarian, New York and Michigan communities. A topic at least for a lively symposium on Poetic Border Cultures.

FOUNDING THE POETICS PROGRAM

POETICS AT BUFFALO

Core Faculty

The Poetics Program is composed of five literary artists who make up its core faculty:

Charles Bernstein, David Gray Professor of Poetry and Letters, is the author of *Content's Dream: Essays 1975-1984* and *A Poetics*, as well as many works of poetry, most recently *Rough Trades* and *The Sophist*. He coedited *L=A=N=G=U=A=G=E* and edited *The Politics of Poetic Form: Poetry and Public Policy*.

Robert Creeley, Director of the Poetics Program, Distinguished Professor, holds the Samuel P. Capen Chair of Poetry and Humanities. His *Collected Poems, Collected Essays*, and *Collected Prose* are published by the University of California Press.

Raymond Federman, Distinguished Professor, has written many novels, including *Take It or Leave It, Double or Nothing*, and *To Whom It May Concern*. A native of France, Federman has written extensively on "surfiction" and on the work of Samuel Beckett.

Susan Howe, Professor, is the author of *My Emily Dickinson*, as well as a number of studies of early American literature. Her recent collections of poetry include *Europe of Trusts, A Bibliography of the King's Book or, Eikon Basilike*, and *Singularities*.

Dennis Tedlock, James H. McNulty Professor, is the translator of *Popol Vuh*, a Mayan book, and of *Finding the Center: Narrative Poetry of the Zuni Indians*. He coedited *Alcheringa/Ethnopoetics* and has written numerous studies of oral performances. His latest book is a long poem, *Days from a Dream Almanac*.

Program

The Poetics Program has an interdisciplinary approach to literary, cultural, and textual studies. Our programs include:

•Visiting Writer Residencies. Readings by and seminar visits with both American and foreign poets, fiction writers, critics, theorists, and philosophers. Recent visitors have included Michael Palmer, Robin Blaser, Jerome McGann, Rachel DuPlessis, Lyn Hejinian, Tom Raworth, Nathaniel Mackey, Clark Coolidge, Lorenzo Thomas, Leslie Scalapino, and Jackson Mac Low.

•"Common Place." A meeting ground for discussion and review of poetics and the poetics program with Poetics Program Director Robert Creeley, "Common Place," which meets monthly, provides an informal opportunity for exchanges on range, qualification, definition, and bibliographies.

•State of the Art. A series of lectures and talks by prominent UB faculty in all fields—the sciences, law, medicine, social sciences, arts, and humanities—on the poetics of each discipline as it relates to questions of human knowledge and action.

•Poetry/Rare Books Collection. The Collection has one of North America's most extensive holdings of twentieth century poetry books and manuscripts and continues to acquire archives from innovative contemporary poets. Professor Robert Bertholf, Curator of the Collection, is both a primary advisor to the Poetics Program and an active participant in its programs. Each year, a few graduate students have the opportunity to work in the Collection, placements that are integral to the goals of the Poetics Program.

•Graduate Seminars. The essence of the Poetics Program is the series of interrelated graduate seminars offered by the Core Faculty in such areas as ethnopoetics and native American verbal arts; the European tradition from Mallarmé to present; twentieth century English-language poetry and poetics, with emphasis on the radical modernist approaches and the relation of poetry to the other arts; the American traditions of the seventeenth, eighteenth, and nineteenth century; twentieth century innovative prose, fiction, and surfiction; philosophy, ideology, and literature; and "core poetics"—a history of poetics from the pre-Socratic to the present.

•The Art of Nonfiction Writing. Through a series of prose writing workshops and individual consultations, the Poetics Program provides support for investigating and developing new approaches to critical writing. By emphasizing the importance of the mode and style of all types of writing, the program encourages—and supports—students in writing essays and dissertations in creative, exploratory, dialogic, and self-constructed forms.

•The Poetics of Translation. The passage from one language toward another requires an experimental poetics. The Poetics Program offers courses, readings, and talks that explore the verbal arts in languages other than English and open the possibility of altering or extending the verbal arts of English itself.

•The Art of Teaching. Through its various offerings, the Poetics Program emphasizes teaching of the arts at the college level, with special emphasis on how to teach innovative works of literary arts to undergraduates.

•Graduate Assistantships are available for a few students to assist in Poetics Program activities, including events, research, and library work.

•Individual Consultation. Core faculty members are available for individual consultation on course selection, oral examinations, dissertation topics, and all aspects of writing and poetics.

•Fellowships. Poetics Program Fellows are funded for up to one academic year to participate in seminars and other program activities, present readings and lectures, and continue with ongoing research and writing. The Poetics Program also welcomes Fulbright and ACLS scholars to spend the term of their fellowships at UB.

Philosophies

While *poetics* suggests a long history of laws of composition, the Poetics Program stresses *poiesis*—the actual making or doing: poetry as process. Every doing carries the potential of something new, emergent, something not already predicated by poetics. Practice overtakes theory, practice changes theory. And not just writing practice, but performance practice, the practice of *sound*.

To write is to produce meaning and not reproduce a pre-existing meaning. To write is to progress and not remain subjected (by habits or reflexes) to the meaning that supposedly precedes language. To write is always first to rewrite, and to rewrite does not mean to revert to a previous form of writing, no more than an anteriority of speech, or of presence, or of meaning. The book creates meaning, and meaning creates life (and not vice versa). Fiction or poetry is never about something, it is something. Writing is not the living repetition of life. The author is that which gives the disquieting language of fiction or poetry its unities and disunities, its knot of coherence and chaos, its insertion into the real. All reading is done haphazardly. Now some people might say the situation (of poetry and fiction) is not very encouraging, but one must reply that it is not meant to encourage those who say that!

Poetics is "an unruly, multisubjective activity"; the reading of poetry, just as the writing of poetry, is beyond the control of any authority. Poetics opens the space of a page to interplay and contradiction, to many voices, a complexity of words. A poet brushes scraps of themes against the continuum of history. Language surrounds chaos. Poetry brings similitude and representation to configurations waiting from forever to be spoken. A poet is writing from inside the opening where the writing subject disappeared without writing. The search for traces is a polyphony of stories.

Ethnopoetics is not simply the poetics of exotic others but calls attention to the ethnicity—the particularity and nongeneralizability—of all poetic practices. Oral poetry is best thought of as something not older than or prior to or simpler than the written, but as something that goes on coexisting with, and interacting with, the written. Thus, our attention is to both alphabetic and nonalphabetic writing, to codes of the historical past and imaginary codes of a potential present.

Poetics stays grounded in the fact of making, the complex of that which has so made such "it," inside and out, the intimately present (oneself, like they say), else the vastness of all possible dimension. "To measure is all we know..." Such reference proposes world in all its times and places, in determined labors of common body, constructs of passage and echo. "Only the imagination is real..." (As in New England—*to work...*)

Admission

The Poetics Program is an integral part of the graduate program in English at the University at Buffalo, with special affiliation with the Program in Comparative Literature and the Poetry Collection.

Any graduate student in Arts and Letters at UB can participate in Poetics seminars and special programs. In addition, special one- and two-semester Poetics Fellowships are available for U.S. and foreign poets, critics, scholars, and students who wish to work with the Core Faculty and to do research in the Poetry/Rare Books Collection.

Applicants applying for admission to the Ph.D. program should contact the Director of Graduate Admissions, Department of English, 302 Clemens Hall, SUNY, Buffalo, NY 14260. Applicants applying for admission to the university's one-year M.A.H. Program should write to that program at 305 Clemens Hall.

Requests for information about Poetics Program Fellowships should be made to the Director, Poetics Program, Department of English, 438 Clemens Hall, (716) 636-3810.

EXCERPT FROM "A BLOW IS LIKE AN INSTRUMENT: THE POETIC IMAGINARY AND CURRICULAR PRACTICES"

Charles Bernstein

Used by permission of the author from Attack of the Difficult Poems *(University of Chicago Press, 2011).*

There are no core subjects, no core texts in the humanities, and this is the grand democratic vista of our mutual endeavor in arts and letters, the source of our greatest anxiety and our greatest possibilities. In literary studies, it is not enough to show what has been done but also what it is possible to do. Art works are not just monuments of the past but investments in the present, investments we squander with our penurious insistence on taking such works as cultural capital rather than capital expenditure. For the most part, our programs of Great Books amount to little more than lip service to an idea of Culture that is encapsulated into tokens and affixed to curricular charm bracelets to be taken out at parties for display – but never employed in the workings of our present culture. Ideas are dead except in use. And for use you don't need a preset list of ideas or Great Works: almost any will do if enactment not prescription is the aim.

I often teach works that raise, for many students, some of the most basic questions about poetry: What is poetry? How can this work be a poem? How and what does it mean? These are not questions that I especially want to talk about nor ones that the works at hand continue to raise for me. Whatever questions I may have of this sort, I have either resolved or put aside as I listen for quite different, much more particular, things. My own familiarity with the poetry I teach puts me at some distance from most students, who are coming to this work for the first time. And yet, when I overcome my resistance and engage in the discussion, which I often find becomes contentious and emotional, I am reminded that when a text is dressed in the costume of poetry, that, in and of itself, is a provocation to consider these basic questions of language, meaning, and art. Inevitably, raising such questions is one of the uses of the poetry to which I am committed; that is, poetry marked by its aversion to conformity, to received ideas, to the expected or mandated or regulated form. These aversions and resistances have their history, they are never entirely novel nor free of traditions, including the traditions of the new; that history is nothing less than literary history. But the point of literary history is not just that a selected sequence of works was created nor that they are enduring or great (or deplorable and hideous) nor that they form a part of a cultural fabric of that time or a tradition that extends to the present. All that is well and good, but aesthetically secondary. The point, that is, is not (not just) the transcendental or cultural or historical or ideological or psychoanalytic deduction of a work of art but how that works plays itself out: its performance not (just) its interpretation. But as history is written by the victors, so art (as a matter of professional imperatives) is taught by the explainers.

It needn't be so, for we are professors not deducers: our work is as much to promote as to dispel, to generate as much as document. I am not – I know it sounds like I am – professing the virtue of art over the deadness of criticism but rather the aversion of virtue that is a first principle of the arts and an inherent, if generally discredited, possibility for the humanities.

I suspect part of the problem may be in the way a certain idea of philosophy as critique, rather than art as practice, has been the model for the best defense of the university. I don't say critique as opposed to aesthetics but critique without aesthetics – that is, the sort of institutionalized critique that dominates the American university – is empty, a shell game of Great Books and Big Methods full of solutions and cultural capital, signifying nothing. That is, Professionalized Critique dogs every school of criticism when as a matter of routine (and perhaps against its most radical impulses), it turns art into artifact, asking not what it does but what it means; much as its own methods are, and quicker than a wink, turned from tools to artifacts. Like I told the man at the agency, if you want the guy to talk maybe you need to remove your hand from his throat, even if it looks to you like that's the only thing keeping him upright.

Poetry, and the arts, are living entities in our culture. It is not enough to know the work of a particular moment in history, removed from the context of our contemporary culture; such knowledge risks being transmitted stillborn. Just as we now insist that literary works need to be read in their socio-historical context, so we must also insist that they be read into the present aesthetic context. So while I lament the lack of cultural and historical information on the part of students, I also lament the often proud illiteracy of contemporary culture on the part of the faculty.

I do not suggest that the (contemporary) practice of poetry should eclipse literary history (as, for a time, the contemporary practice of analytic philosophy eclipsed the history of philosophy). I do believe, however, that literary history or theory uninformed by the newly emerging forms of poetic practice is as problematic as literary criticism or literary history uninformed by contemporary theoretical or methodological practices. I realize that my insistence on the aesthetic function of poetry and the significance for literary studies of contemporary literature has an odd echo with some of the tenets of the New Critics. But I point this out mainly to debunk the dogma that works that "create linguistic difficulty and density and therefore make meaning problematic" have remained, or were ever, the center of attention of literary studies from the New Critics until the present, as Catherine Gallagher suggests. As far as English literary studies of this century is concerned, *The Waste Land* and *Ulysses* have had to bear most of the weight of this claim. But these cease to be difficult texts insofar as they are fetishized as Arnoldian tokens of "bestness," a process that replaces their linguistic, aesthetic, and socio-historical complexity with the very unambiguous status of cultural treasure; in any case, they have not been contemporary texts for well over half a century. Despite the homage, "difficult" or "ambiguous" literature has not, as a rule, meant teaching disorienting or unfamiliar works of literature to college students, and especially not works that challenged the professor's critical or ideological paradigms or were written in unfamiliar or disruptive dictions, dialects, or lexicons. Rather it has meant turning a narrow range of designated difficulties into puzzles resolvable by checking off the boxes on the "Understanding Poetry" worksheet, while rejecting ways of reading poetry that do not produce "understanding" but rather response, questions, disorientation, interaction, more poems. In fact, if you look at the anthologies of English and American literature that have been used in humanities classes over the past fifty years, you will see that if "difficulty" is a criterion at all, it is as likely to be one for the exclusion of a work as for its inclusion; a tendency that has only accelerated in recent years as "accessibility" and moral uplift have taken on both a political and pedagogic imperative. In the end, despite their defense of difficulty, the New Critics were primarily responsible for defanging radical modernism and enthroning its milquetoast other, High Antimodernism (a reference to their own work certainly, but also bringing to mind the work they abjured). Moreover, as Gallagher accurately points out, and it is also a point made with synoptic brilliance by Jed Rasula in *The American Poetry Wax Museum*, the New Critics and their heirs actively discounted much of the demotic, folk, vulgar, idiosyncratic, ethnic, erotic, black, "women's," and genre poetry for which its reading methods were inadequate. This is not, I would insist, because this work was not ambiguous or difficult enough but because it posed the wrong kind of difficulties and ambiguities.

The academic profession is not a unified body but a composite of many dissimilar individuals and groups pursuing projects ranging from the valiantly idiosyncratic to the proscriptively conventional. Most of the popular generalizations about what professors do or don't do are unsupported by facts; for example, it turns out that, as a whole, professors work very long hours, generally beyond anything required of them. Moreover, there is a disturbing trend to equate classroom hours with work hours, leading to a fundamental misrepresentation of the nature of academic labor. It's as if you measured the work of a lawyer only by the hours spent in her client's presence, or the work of a cook by how long it takes to eat his soufflé, or the work of a legislator by the number of pages of legislation he or she has written. Yet comparable misrepresentations of the academic profession are having dire consequences, most specifically in abetting the increase in non-tenured part-time employment that is eroding not only the working conditions of the university but the quality of education that universities can provide.

Misinformation feeds on misinformation, so it is particularly unfortunate that political expediency has encouraged many of those who speak in the name of the university to abandon any vision of the radically democratic role the university can, but too often does not, play in this culture. That is to say, tenure and academic freedom are not primarily valuable because they provide job security to individual faculty members but because they serve the public good. There is no conflict between the public interest and full-time tenured employment: short-term cost savings cannot justify the long-term economic folly of compromising one of the most substantial intellectual and cultural resources this society has created. The question is not whether our society can afford to maintain the intellectual and cultural space of the university at present levels but whether it afford not to.

The greatest benefit of the university is not that it trains students for anything in particular, nor that it imbues in them a particular set of ideas, but that it is a place for open-ended research that can just as well lead nowhere as somewhere, that is wasteful and inefficient by short-term socioeconomic standards but is practically a steal as a long-term research and development investment in democracy, freedom, and creativity – without which we won't have much of an economic future or the one we have won't be worth flesh it's imprinted on. At its most effective, the university is not oriented toward market-place discipline and employment training, but rather toward maximizing the capacity for reflection and creativity. When it is most fully achieving its potential, university classes are not goal-oriented or pre-professional but self-defining and exploratory. Attempts to regulate the university according to market values only pervert what is best and least accountable about these cultural spaces. We cannot make education more efficient without making it more deficient.

My plea then is for enriched content, especially aesthetic and conceptual content, over a streamlined vocational goal orientation. There is an educational payoff but it has to do with degrees of intellectual resonance and creativity not measurable (always) in immediate job readiness (for which, as Silicon Valley has shown, college may be unnecessary). Almost everyone agrees there is a practical value in students being able to write in conventional business English but minimum standards are notoriously hard to achieve, as even those who emphasize basics skills realize. To create good writers you need to create good readers. There is no short cut. A correction-oriented expository writing drill might produce barely competent writers (it often doesn't) but such competence may come at the cost of alienating students from their own language practices (talking and writing and reading). Taking an image from Rousseau's *Emile*, if we swaddle the young scholar in the strictures of grammatical correctness, we may induce immobility while fostering uprightness. And mobility is a practical skill for a "people in transition," to use a phrase from Langston Hughes that speaks to our American social space at the beginning of the twenty-first century. In correcting a perceived deficit, we must keep in mind that teachers, just as doctors, need to be sure to do no harm.

Arthur Levine, then president of Teachers College, suggested, at the meeting where I first presented this essay, that we imagine our relation to our constituents on the model of a bank's relation to its depositors. With a bank, you deposit something you have already acquired. With education, you are seeking to acquire something you don't already have. For at its best,

education delivers nothing—it enables, animates. That is, the information imparted is embedded in an interaction. Information stripped of this interaction is largely inert: it is as if you are given the database but not software to use it, or, perhaps more accurately, you are given the data and the software but not tools to question the collection method, reframe the categories, or collect new data. Let the buyer beware: the new "consumer-oriented" education may be cheap, but it also may not be worth very much.

The university I envision is more imaginary than actual, for everywhere the tried and sometimes true pushes out the untried but possible.

Within the academic profession, fights are often intramural as new disciplinary and methodological projects threaten older ones, the new and old both claiming to be the victims of unprecedented dogmatism, bad faith, and lack of intellectual or cultural values. In literary studies, these conflicts tend to be among three different conceptions of the field. One group defines literary studies in terms of its traditional subject matter, that is, the literary works that have traditionally served as the principal object of study in the field. This group maintains relative consensus among its constituents. A second group accepts the idea of the field as defined by its subject matter, but proposes a new range of subject matters – from works underrepresented in traditional literary study to works that challenge the very idea of the literary. There is consensus among the constituents of this second group on broadening the subject matter of the field but necessarily no consensus on exactly what the new subjects should be. A third group consists of those who define the field primarily in terms of a particular method of analyses, critique, or interpretation. There is little consensus among the constituents of this third group since the approaches adopted are often seen to be mutually exclusive. No doubt many in the profession are sympathetic, to varying degrees, with all three of these conceptions of the field. The danger for the academic profession is not that one side or another will "win" – that the new barbarians will become the olds boys or the traditionalists will block innovation. Rather, the problem is the idea that consensus should prevail. The manufacturing of consent always involves the devaluing or exclusion of that which doesn't fit the frame. What I value is not temperance but tolerance, for an insistence on temperance can mark an intolerance not only of the intemperate but also of unconventional – or unassimilated – forms of expression. We don't need to agree – or even converse – so long as we tolerate the possibility of radically different approaches, even to our most cherished ideas of decorum, methodology, rationality, subject matter. The university that I value leaves all of these matters open, undecided – and not just open for debate, but open for multiple practices. The point is not to replace one approach with another but to reorient ourselves toward a kind of inquiry in which there are no final solutions, no universally mandated protocols – an orientation that is fundamental to the essays collected in this book. The point is not to administer culture but to participate in it.

In discussions about the state of the university, complaints about "tenured radicals" abound. I am more worried about tenured smugness and tenured burnout. While I respect the authority of scholarship I reject the authoritativeness of any prescribed set of books, methods, experts, standards. The problem is not that there has been too much reform but that there has hardly been any at all: the content has shifted, but this reflects demographic changes more than ideological ones; the structure of authority remains the same. Given the passionate engagement with their research of most of the graduate students I know, the often deanimating mandates of perceived professional success are the surest symptom of the problem. From the time they enter graduate school, the passions, commitments, and creativity of the young scholar are routinely reoriented toward a cynical professional wiliness that emphasizes who it is opportune to quote or what best fits market prospects rather than what the young scholar is most capable of doing or what best suits her or his passions or aesthetic proclivities. The profession, both panicked by the market and temperamentally conservative (even in its apparently non-conservative guises) seems bent on shaping young scholars in its own image rather than encouraging the production of new and unexpected images. In these circumstance, professors – sometimes unintentionally, sometimes with the best intentions – often seem less inclined to offer themselves as aids to the young scholar's research than to act as living roadblocks.

While specialization is appropriate for a scholar's own work – and there is nothing more sublime about the university than those obsessive scholars who seems to know everything about a specific subject, writer, or period – specialization is too often projected out on students at large, as the same few books get taught over and again, while the vast wealth of new books and old books remain "outside my field" (why not take a walk on the adjacent fields from time to time?). The problem may well be that many professors do not feel they have the authority to teach or supervise work in which they do not have expertise. I suppose imagining I have no expertise at all may be my greatest advantage: I can consider teaching or discussing almost anything if a student makes a compelling proposal for its necessity. My subject is contemporary poetry, but I find it stretches from there to almost anywhere – by which I mean to say that whatever time students have in the university, in college or graduate school, should be a time of indiscriminate, prodigal, voracious, reading and searching: one text must lead directly to the next. Against the mandated hypotactic, rationalized logic of conventional syllabi, I suggest we go avagabonding: let our curriculums spin out into paratactic sagas. I propose we focus less on adducing the meaning of a homogenous sequence of works and more on addressing the relation of heterogeneous series of works (Li Po next to Oulipo, "Jabberwocky" with Newton's Optics). Nor is this another appeal to interdisciplinarity, which assumes the constituent disciplines that are already established and carefully preserves their distinctness through the process. Indeed, I've come to realize that poetry is one of the most intradisciplinary topics in the humanities, but this is because – since well before Lucretius – poetry already potentially encompasses all the disciplines of the humanities.

I realize my approach will not be to everyone's taste, nor do I wish to impose my sensibilities on the academic profession at large. What I ask for is greater tolerance for such approaches in a university that allows for the multiple and even incommensurable not just in its theories but in its practices.

It's not that I overstate my case, I am making a case for overstatement.

This wild adventure in learning is surely what inspired many of us to make the arts or humanities our calling, yet we lose the passion as we go from this adventure in texts to administering culture by teaspoon. And this is very like what we do when we imagine our graduate programs primarily in terms of vocational training in narrowly predefined fields, rather than opportunities for open-ended research, centers for the study of the arts, lavish emporiums of further thinking. Does anyone doubt that we deaden the potential of future research and future teaching with our cramped, vocational/preprofessional disciplinary fantasies? And what a travesty, in particular, this training for jobs that do not even exist: though we must all do all we can to reverse the pernicious trend toward poorly paid adjunct work in place of full-time, tenured employment. Yet I must disagree with those who, with great probity, advise that we reduce graduate programs to make them conform more precisely to the job market so as to avoid overproduction of Ph.D.s. Rather we should welcome into our graduate programs those whose goal is not to have the same job as their teachers, but who, for a number of reasons, want to take one, two, or five years, modestly funded in exchange for some teaching, to pursue their studies, in ways they must be primarily responsible to define.

And what of academic standards? Aren't these the dikes that protect us from the flood of unregulated thought? Or are they like the narrow Chinese shoe that deforms our thinking to fit its image of rigor? When I examine the formats and implied standards for peer-reviewed journals and academic conferences, they suggest to me a preference for a lifeless prose, bloated with the compulsory repetitive explanation of what every other "important" piece on this subject has said. Of course, many professors will insist that they do not subscribe to this, but the point is not what any one of us does but the institutional culture we accept. It seems to me that the academic culture of the humanities places more emphasis on learning its ropes, on professional conformity, than it does on any actual research, writing, thinking, or teaching of the people who make up the profession. Indeed, it doesn't really matter what constitutes this conformity: the distinction being made is an important sense antipathetic to substance. This is the chief function of anonymous peer review: not ensuring quality or objectivity but compliance.

Anonymous peer reviewing enforces prevalent disciplinary standards, especially standards about the tone or manner of an argument, even while permitting the publication of a wide range of ideas – as long as the ideas are expressed in the dominant style. While it might seem that anonymous review would encourage greater textual freedom, in practice the submission of an anonymous article to multiple anonymous readers ends up favoring work that comes closest to conforming to accepted norms of argument and writing style – indeed such a procedure is one of the best ways of determine what these norms are. Of course, it's not big surprise that institutions perpetuate their institutional styles. But perhaps what may make what I am saying sound – to some in the profession – exaggerated is that I find it deplorable that academic profession is, well, too academic. Maybe this is because I am more accustomed to a form of cultural exchange and production among poets and through independently produced "small press" books and magazines that seems more vital, and more committed to the values often ascribed to the academic profession, – that is, more committed to fomenting imagination than controlling imagination – than is the academic profession itself. The academic profession has a lot to learn from such communities of independent artists and scholars. I also feel that the academic profession has an obligation to provide a sanctuary for the arts, especially in a period of devastating defunding of government support for the arts.

What I object to is disciplinarity for the sake of disciplinarity and not in the service of inquiry. Too often, the procedures developed by the academic profession to ensure fairness and rigor end up creating a game that rewards routinized learning over risk. Blind peer reviewing, like its cousins standardized testing and evaluation, is certainly an advantage when it comes to discouraging preferential treatment for individuals, but the price it often pays for this is bolstering preferential treatment for the most acceptable types of discourse and fostering the bureaucratization of knowledge production. Anonymous peer review, like standardized testing and uniform assessment, encourages blandness and conformity in the style of presentation and response, leading those whose futures are dependent on such reviews and evaluations to shy away from taking risks with their writing styles or modes of argument or ideas. The policy is to reward the best test-takers but not necessarily the most engaging or culturally significant achievements. The result is that academic prose, like the career patterns it reflects, tends to avoid animation in favor of caution and to defer exuberance in favor of interminable self-justification and self-glossing that are unrelated to the needs of documentation or communication, research or teaching. I am not saying there is no place for anonymous peer reviewing, nor that it should be abolished, but that there is far too much deference given to a system that in trying to eliminate one kind of bias actually institutes another kind. In contrast, not enough recognition is given to those activities of the members of the academic profession that question the rules of the game, that champion rather than adjudicate, that see universities as places for wild questions and not just the prescribed answers.

Emphasis on conventional testing is antipathetic to an aesthetically charged encounter with art. Testing students on their ability to memorize names or dates or on their skill at identifying passages taken out of context encourages them to focus on mastering information rather than on reading literary works: the two goals are in opposition.

The best way I can describe how I teach is by calling it a reading workshop, for I am less concerned with analysis or explanation of individual poems than with finding ways to intensify the experience of poetry, of the poetic, through a consideration of how the different styles and structures and forms of contemporary poetry can affect the way we see and understand the world. No previous experience with poetry is necessary. More important is a willingness to consider the implausible, to try out alternative ways of thinking, to listen to the way language sounds before trying to figure out what it means, to lose yourself in a flurry of syllables and regain your bearings in dimensions otherwise imagined as out of reach, to hear how poems work to delight, inform, redress, lament, extol, oppose, renew, rhapsodize, imagine, foment . . .
. . . .

At the SUNY-Buffalo, I am the director of the Poetics Program, co-founded in 1991 by Robert Creeley (our first director), Susan Howe, Raymond Federman, Dennis Tedlock, and myself, with the support of Robert Bertholf, Curator of the Poetry Collection.

I came to Buffalo as Butler Chair visiting professor in the fall of 1989; Susan Howe had been Butler chair the year before. I had scant teaching experience. I first taught in the winter quarter of 1987 at the University of California – San Diego's writing program. In the summer of 1988, I taught my first literature class at Queens College. I also had taught a class in Princeton's Creative Writing Program for two semesters (spring 1989 and spring 1990). I was appointed David Gray Professor of Poetry and Letters in the fall of 1990 (Creeley had been the first Gray Chair, but had been promoted to the Capen Chair a couple of years earlier). We hired Susan Howe and she came back to Buffalo in the fall of 1991. In Buffalo that first year, Bob and I cooked up the idea for the Poetics Program, though Bob had wanted to secede from the English Department and move to the Center for the Arts then under construction. I argued that we should use the administrative support of the English degree and have our students receive the generic English PhD. In 2003, I was appointed Donald T. Regan Professor of English at the University of Pennsylvania.

The Poetics Program at Buffalo has its roots in the formation of the English Department at Buffalo in the early 1960s by Albert Cook. Cook had the idea that you could hire literary artists to teach not creative writing but literature classes, and in particular literature classes in a Ph.D. program. It was with this in mind that he hired Creeley, Charles Olson, and others; it marked a decisively other path from far more prevalent graduate (usually M.A. and M.F.A.) "creative writing" programs that emerged at the same time.

By formalizing this concept in the early 90s, shortly after Howe and I came to UB, we were suggesting an alternative model for poets teaching in graduate, but also undergraduate, programs. The Poetics faculty teaches in the English Department's doctoral program, supervising orals and directing scholarly/critical dissertations, even if our license to this is more poetic than formal. A frequent question I get from students applying to the program is whether they can write a creative dissertation. I always do a double take: "I hope it will be creative, but it can't be a collection of poems or a novel." For the fact is that Poetics students have the same requirements as all other graduate students and are admitted by the same departmental committee. And while we encourage active questioning of the conventions of critical and scholarly writing, we remain committed to the practice of poetics as something distinct from, even though intersecting with, the practice of poetry. The implications of this perspective are perhaps more pragmatic, not to say programmatic, than theoretical: while the "creative writing" approach at universities often debunks the significance of critical reflection, sometimes pitting creativity against conceptual thinking, the Poetics Program insists that scholarship, historical research, and critical writing are at the core of graduate education.

This is not to say that a Ph.D. program is appropriate for most poets. I tend to discourage people who ask my advice from pursuing this degree at any institution, partly to ensure that they have considered the limitations of the academic environment in terms of artistic freedom, compensation, and future employment. But if this is the choice they make, it is likely because they want to be teachers, editors, and writers and their writing is as likely to be criticism or poetics as poetry.

The Poetics Program is fully integrated into the English Department, presenting seminars and sponsoring events within that context, even while marking such offerings as our own. We also provide modest funding to students to publish magazines and books (print and electronic) as well as to organize their own poetry readings, talks series, and conferences: over the past decade, this has resulted in dozens of magazines, scores of books, and numerous visitors, not to mention our web site, the Electronic Poetry Center, created by Loss Pequeño Glazier (epc.buffalo.edu).

While many doctoral programs in English expect students to choose between being poets and scholars, we suggest that the one activity may enhance the other, for those so inclined. The poets, as I've suggested, do their poetry and their editing on their own: it informs their graduate work but is never the explicit content of it. And, equally significant, the Poetics graduate students form a vital community among themselves, where their shared interest in criticism and scholarship, poetry writing, and teaching make for an active bond. As it turns out, this mix seems to produce PhDs who are eager and well qualified to teach literature as well as writing.

....

My commitment is to public education: the education of the public at large and an education about the public, how it is constituted. Yet we are writing off our large public institutions of learning with the cynical assumption that graduates of such colleges have no practical need for the sort of open-ended education in the arts and sciences that most of us in the humanities support. "I never learned anything in college so why should they." Indeed, from a corporate point of view, having too many people in the workforce who think too much may be detrimental if they are to end up in dead-end jobs that require little thought. Such ideas are fundamentally anti-democratic of course; they are breeding ground for a passive and malinformed citizenry that is unable to make sense of the complex issues that confront the nation. What price do we have to pay for an informed citizenry, one that can understand the complex multiplicity of American culture, can read into events not simply register them as a series of fated accomplishments? What sort of investment are we willing to make in the intellectual and cultural development of our citizens so that we can remain, as a country, innovative, vibrant, socially responsible? How can we prepare ourselves for the unexpected, the difficult, the troubling events that are sure to lie ahead for all of us? Will we spend billions for defense while begrudging any money spent on what we are defending? The great experiment in mass education is not even a hundred years old: it has had virtually no downside. That we teeter on abandoning this commitment now is a testament to a smallness, to a lack of generosity, and to a contempt for noncommercial values that can only make us poorer – not only cultural, but economically.

SOME QUESTIONS AND ANSWERS FOR RAYMOND FEDERMAN

Charles Bernstein & Raymond Federman

The following questions and answers were adapted by Charles Bernstein from an interview he performed with Raymond Federman, first published in Journal of Experimental Fiction 23 / *Writers Club Press, 2002, as 'The Laugh that Laughs at the Laugh: Writing from and about the Pen Man, Raymond Federman', ed. Eckhard Gerdes.*

Some questions for Raymond Federman

Raymond, what is the use of fiction? What is the use of stories? And what is the use of telling them, the same ones or different ones, over and again?

How about historical memory? Collective memory? Does fiction serve to spark or to spank memory? To make sure people don't forget or to be sure they remember the right things, and also remember the right things about the right things? You are a survivor of the Holocaust, your family was killed during the systematic extermination of the European Jews during World War II. We have many memorials of this systematic extermination. What do you think that such memorials should represent? Your work, which I would say is one of the most significant of the memorials to the systematic extermination process, in many ways veers into abstraction and digression — it refuses to represent those events. Why do you evade history? Is it that facts, or not any facts but those facts, refuse representation? But then do they refuse memory too? In any case, you make light of facts rooted (or is it rotting?) in that dark history. But whose history? Your history? Our history? You refuse to be solemn in the face of those horrendous events that have, in all actuality, in living color and dead black and white, occurred historically, but also hysterically. What gives you the right ¬— moreover, what gives you the nerve — to be funny about this? Why aren't you, not only a real survivor but a famous one, terribly solemn and profoundly serious, like the memorials that we have all grown accustomed to, that make us weep and in our weeping comfort us? Your work seems to mock not only the possibility of accurate representation, but also the idea that mourning should be dignified. Do you think mourning is a joke? Why do you make readers so uncomfortable with your laughter, your self-consciousness? Why do you still kick up a fuss instead of writing with poignant, eloquent, tearful resignation?

What is 'The Voice in the Closet'? Whose voice? What is the voice saying?

When you speak of *Federman*, is that you? If so, why do you refer to yourself in the third person? Or are you not you to yourself? Did you lose that you in the closet? Or later? Who or what are you calling attention to when you name yourself, as you do so often, so insistently? Why do you call so much attention to this anxious act of self-naming? Is it because the name names an absence? Or is because in the absence of this naming you cease to exist to yourself, for yourself? Or for "us"?

Do you think your work is better understood in Germany or in Europe than it is in the United States? In Germany, do you represent a response to a

German catastrophe and is that why you take a place of honor as a witness of, and commentator on, that catastrophe? In the U.S., are you seen as just another unintelligible experimental novelist refusing to give the dignity of sense to the catastrophes of your lifetime? Is your work *American* in its refusal to represent, in its insistence that response and representation are mutually exclusive? Were your works made possible because they are grounded in a cultural space that is non-European or anyway (for you) post-European? In what ways would you say your works portray a coming of age in America that is also the coming of age of America?

Ray, are you a poet or are you a fiction writer, and does it make any difference?

Your work is often immersed in some of the seamier sides of male culture, and it has sometimes been read as sexist. Yet, why is there is so little reference to the outdoors, to men doing virile things in open spaces? Why is there so little male bonding? And what about the sexual desperation of the men in your books? How do you imagine male sexuality?

Who is this guy who drops down by parachute into an Army barracks in the South in the 1950s? Why tell your story from the point of view of the man who fell to earth, or let's say to America? Why do you blur memoir with fiction? Why don't you take out the rough edges of that first encounter with America? Why does what is most 'experimental' about your books – the typography, the digressions, the multiple point of view, the insistent intrusion of aesthetics and philosophy – seem at first playful and then deadly, uncannily serious?

How about improvisation, Raymond? Your work plays a lot with a feeling of spontaneity, of just going on, with the pleasure of telling the story as it is happening. But if that's true, why does your work seem so composed that it decomposes in its own afterburn?

Some Answers for Raymond Federman

For Raymond Federman fiction is useless.

Fiction is a delusion we use to screen ourselves from reality and reality is largely, though not entirely, delusional. This is why Federman is a story teller and not a novelist. And assuredly not a writer of fiction.

And if he tells the same stories over and again it is because the story is never the same in any telling because, if it were, *that* would be fiction. And Federman writes nonfiction. Historical nonfiction.

Or else what he writes is a bed of lies. (A hole inside a gap.)

And anyway it is never the same story and Federman tells it over and again because what he has to tell, like history, cannot be told once and for all.

Like the same dream you keep having only it's not the same and this time you can't wake up.

Federman wakes us up.

Federman is a spelunker of either historical memory or collective forgetting, depending on the reader. He is not interested in the well-lit paths through the cave nor even the once-marked off-roads. What's a cave to him or he to a cave that we should weep so? Memory has become a way of forgetting, the recovered forgetting of the professional memoirist. Federman prefers the musings of Stan and Oliver, or Vladimir and Estragon. He speaks of his life like a defrocked poet at a coroner's inquest.

O, inconstant heart!

Digression is as much a foil as progression. Federman's digressions are as direct as "an arrow from the Almighty's bow." They pierce but don't wound. The wound is the condition, the voice in the closet that comes out, like Tinker Bell, only if you say you believe it. And you believe it only at your peril. (Pauline will fend for herself.)

The elementary error of the literature of self-help and affirmation, the preferred fiction of the mediocracy, is that trauma is overcome, that you get better, that there is healing. That there can be understanding. Federman neither dwells on the abyss, nor theatricalizes it, nor explains it, nor looks away.

The Dark is the ground of his being and his becoming.

Go nameless so that the name you are called by becomes you.

Federman is an improper noun full of signs and stories signifying (precisely) nothing. *Federman* names that which is *(k)not here.*

He is our American Jabès, only the rabbis have been subsumed into the bouillabaisse and the ladder loaned to the roofer.

And from that roof we shout to the crowd assembling below: Break it up! Go back to where you came from, if you can find it! *There is nothing to see here.*

The truth you seek is not on this earth nor in Heaven either.

Then Federman begins again.

One more time.

The words, at least the words, are indelible, even if we are not.

Or so the story goes ....

"THERE ARE NOT LEAVES ENOUGH TO CROWN TO COVER TO CROWN TO COVER"

Susan Howe

The following first appeared as the introduction to The Europe of Trusts *(1990); it is reprinted here with permission of the author and of New Directions.*

For me there was no silence before armies.

I was born in Boston Massachusetts on June 10th, 1937, to an Irish mother and an American father. My mother had come to Boston on a short trip two years earlier. My father had never been to Europe. She is a wit and he was a scholar. They met at a dinner party when her earring dropped into his soup.

By 1939 the Nazi dictatorship was well-established in Germany. All the dissenting political parties had been liquidated and Concentration camps had already been set up to hold political prisoners. The Berlin-Rome axis was a year old. So was the Spanish Civil War. On April 25th Franco's Lufftwaffe pilots bombed the village of Guernica. That November Hitler and the leaders of his armed forces made secret plans to invade Austria, Czechoslovakia, Poland, and Russia.

In the summer of 1938 my mother and I were staying with my grandmother, uncle, aunt, great-aunts, cousins, and friends in Ireland, and I had just learned to walk, when Czechoslovakia was dismembered by Hitler, Ribbentrop, Mussolini, Chamberlin, and Daladier, during the Conference and Agreement at Munich. That October we sailed home on a ship crowded with refugees fleeing various countries in Europe.

When I was two the German army invaded Poland and World War II began in the West.

The fledgling Republic of Ireland distrusted English with good reason, and remained neutral during the struggle. But there was the Battle of the Atlantic to be won, so we couldn't cross the sea again until after 1945. That half of the family was temporarily cut off.

In Buffalo New York, where we lived at first, we seemed to be safe. We were there when my sister was born and the Japanese bombed Pearl Harbor.

Now there were armies in the west called East.

American fathers marched off into the hot Chronicle of global struggle but mothers were left. Our law-professor father, a man of pure principles, quickly included violence in his principles, put on a soldier suit and disappeared with the others into the thick of the threat to the east called West.

Buffalo

> 12. 7. 41
> (Late afternoon light.)
> (Going to meet him in snow.)

HE

> (Comes through the hall door.)

The research of scholars, lawyers, investigators, judges Demands!

SHE

> (With her arms around his neck whispers.)

Herod had all the little children murdered!

It is dark
The floor is ice

they stand on the edge of a hole singing—

In Rama
Rachel weeping for his children

refuses
to be comforted

because they *are* not.

Malice dominates the history of Power and Progress. History is the record of winners. Documents were written by the Masters. But fright is formed by what we see not by what they say.

From 1939 until 1946 in news photographs, day after day I saw signs of culture exploding into murder. Shots of children being herded into trucks by hideous helmeted conquerors—shots of children who were orphaned and lost—shots of the emaciated bodies of Jews dumped into mass graves on top of more emaciated bodies—nameless numberless men women and children, uprooted in a world almost demented. God had abandoned them to history's sovereign Necessity.

If to see is to *have* at a distance, I had so many dead Innocents distance was abolished. Substance broke loose from the domain of time and obedient intention. I became part of the ruin. In the blank skies over Europe I was Strife represented.

Things overlap in space and are hidden. Those black and white picture shots—moving or fixed—were a subversive generation. "The hawk, with his long claws / Pulled down the stones. / The dove, with her rough bill / Brought me them home."

Buffalo roam in herds
up the broad streets connected by boulevards

and fences

their eyes are ancient and a thousand years
too old

hear murder throng their muting

Old as time in the center of a room
doubt is spun

and measured

Throned wrath
I know your worth

a chain of parks encircles the city

Pain is nailed to the landscape in time. Bombs are seeds of Science and the sun.

2,000 years ago the dictator Creon said to Antigone who was the daughter of Oedipus and Jocasta: "Go to the dead and love them."

Life opens into conceptless perspectives. Language surrounds Chaos.

During World War II my father's letters were a sign he was safe. A miniature photographic negative of his handwritten message was reproduced by the army and a microfilm copy forwarded to us. In the top left-hand corner someone always stamped PASSED BY EXAMINER.

This is my historical consciousness. I have no choice in it. In my poetry, time and again, questions of assigning *the cause* of history dictate the sound of what is thought.

Summary of fleeting summary
Pseudonym cast across empty

Peak proud heart

Majestic caparisoned cloud cumuli
East sweeps hewn flank

Scion on a ledge of Constitution
Wedged sequences of system

Causeway of fainted famed city
Human ferocity

Dim mirror Naught formula

archaic hallucinatory laughter

Kneel to intellect in our work
Chaos cast cold intellect back

Poetry brings similitude and representation to configurations waiting from forever to be spoken. North Americans have tended to confuse human fate with their own salvation. In this I am North American. "We are coming Father Abraham, three hundred thousand more," sang the Union troops at Gettysburg.

I write to break out into perfect primeval Consent. I wish I could tenderly lift from the dark side of history, voices that are anonymous, slighted—inarticulate.

ZWISCHEN DEN LINDEN: THE ELECTRONIC POETRY CENTER & THE TECHNOLOGIES OF IMAGINATION

Loss Pequeño Glazier

The city's name, "Buffalo," most likely does not come from the animal, which may have only ever appeared in the Buffalo zoo, but perhaps more probably from the French, "Beau Fleuve" named for what was then called Buffalo Creek. (The first mention of "Buffalo Creek" was made by British military engineer Captain John Montresor in his journal of 1764.) "Beau Fleuve" is "beautiful river," in Buffalo, itself caught between lakes, in Seneca, the Language of the indigenous peoples at the time "Dosoweh," or "between the linden," the lakes themselves often shimmering like thinly frozen seas. Indeed, it is as if Buffalo bears "frost flowers," "a never-ending sea of ice flowers quietly floating over a thinly frozen sea."[i]

"Buffalo" thus is a multiple, a misnomer, a cross-reading of itself, constantly misrepresented, where the play of words determines the air, exists in a space in-between; we inhale the air, then are not only in the air, but the air is inside us.

In the same way Poetics at Buffalo is not now what it was – or ever will be again. And yet, employing a circular sort of logic, those who were there, have had the first Poetics at Buffalo in mind and in that sense what once and no longer is remains a fact that presently *is*, now widely dispersed geographically. And where it once was, still is, and bears its own particular relation to what it once was.

But in my reading, Buffalo was Buffalo because of Robert Creeley. Of course, before Creeley there was Al Cook and before Al Cook, who envisioned an avant-garde English faculty, was Thomas B. Lockwood, whose personal collection formed the basis for the UB Libraries' celebrated Poetry Collection. Buffalo was buzzing with the innovative. In a nearby building, Gerald O'Grady founded a media study program that is now legendary. Artists – including avant-garde filmmakers Hollis Frampton, Tony Conrad, and Paul Sharits, documentary maker James Blue, video artists Woody Vasulka and Steina, and Viennese action artist Peter Weibel – investigated, taught, and made media art in all forms, and founded the first Digital Arts Laboratory. It all laid a foundation, a hum of innovation in the air, my contact "there" was a path that began with Creeley and from thence to the field that would yield a richness of presence, so expansive that one cannot even imagine it. When I arrived in Buffalo in 1988, the Olson Lectures series was just wrapping up. I was fortunate to subsequently work individually with Creeley (as others, also through a once-in-a-lifetime independent study), and then extensively and across decades experience the meticulous, benevolent presence of Charles Bernstein, nearly my contemporary, and company. "Company" in Creeley's sense is a group of peers who precipitate their own flourishing through their interaction, or a group of compañeros in spirit, and the Poetics Program of the time offered just that: the pacing and space between the words of Creeley, the leadership and range of cutting edge literary engagement of Bernstein, and the radiant musings of Susan Howe, who in her particular process of close reading traces emergent coastlines of thinking in itself. I brought to the group my own process of poiesis, both on and off the screen, my mestizo inventiveness, a touch of timid gregariousness, earnest goodwill, and my organizing skills to related events. Amazingly, I somehow had also become part of "the company."

How Creeley? In the first place Buffalo was what Creeley would have called a "haunt." A place that is not only where one is, but a place that somehow makes us *what* we are. It is the "here" in a world of "there"; a momentary pause, in good company, on the long trek through the snow to the ice shore. It is where the company gathers. His way of being fomented such a sprit, in an "enchantment of ... crooked litanies," as the *Los Angeles Times* refers to his articulations, was his tremendous gift to all:[ii]

> You have to reach
> Out more it's
> Farther away from
> You it's here
> (Creeley, "Here")[iii]

Though really I was one of the company from the beginning, at the same time I always felt marginal. Nonetheless, I was at the center of the Electronic Poetry Center (EPC), I was an exuberant adviser to Bernstein's Poetics List, I relished human-built-code, I was the writer of "Mayapán: A Poetics of the Web," numerous online works under the rubric "W3 Reports/Tributes/Posts" (including "The Charles Olson Festival," "Transgeographies: Vancouver Report" on Robin Blaser, "Robert Creeley: A 70th Birthday Celebration" (an extraordinary event), "Assembling Alternatives," "Oh No Orono," and "For Larry Eigner," reports from festivals standing at the formation of new conscious imaginings of word, performance, transmission, mission, transience, and the book/digital word/works (all available in the EPC's "Library"), leading to the E-Poetry Festivals (Bernstein appeared at the first E-Poetry and at its Ten Year Anniversary as well as at the 20th Anniversary celebration of the EPC); this activity, along with my work building the EPC, culminated in my *Digital Poetics: the Making of the Web* (Alabama UP 2002), the first full-length book on digital poetry. In one sense the EPC's founding (1994) and the first E-Poetry (2001) had little formal relation with the Poetics Program, though there were multiple areas of cross-over, convergence, and co-sponsorship. Thus the EPC. Though Poetics at Buffalo was energized by the digital medium (especially in the transformational role of Bernstein's Poetics list and of the EPC itself), members of the Poetics at Buffalo community were simply less than connected with the nuts and bolts of the operation than I would have hoped. Code was "Greek" to many. I was astonished. How could:

> \<i>*italic*\</i>
> **bold**\
> \underline\

be difficult to understand? The brackets open like a curtain for the phrase to enter, enact the typographic theatrical performance for the audience, then close the curtain for the exit.

To extend this very elementary example of code, <a> tags with an attribute, the "href" or "hypertext referent" raises the enactment to a slightly more nuanced level:

<a href="destination">link</a>.

Here is where language play can begin to enter in. It's not far-fetched to think of adding a bit of irony to this, however one wishes, as in the difference between: "There's a speck on your nose" and "There's a speck on your big nose." Thus, irony, metaphor, and invention can enter into something as simple as the link above, even with these placeholders:

<a href="destination">no exit</a>.)

To me, code was not an enigma but a theater of inscription. And typography is not just telling what is, but resonates with Dickinson's: "Tell all the truth but tell it slant." Code is inextricable from human communication. As participants in the Poetics Program, weren't we all addressing multiple codes on many levels?

In a curious way, folks having little interest in coding held much in common with small press publishing, where folks love to have chapbooks done but hardly ever ask how they can help. For me, making poetry happen goes hand in hand with being a poet. It's not just about making one's own poetry but to ALSO provide a platform for the transmission of poetry, a kind of community commitment. It was rare that there was any help – even to this day – when it is so clear that some hands-on digital work will be part of our combined efforts over the years to come.

This account nonetheless does not intend to underestimate the contribution of many poetics community members producing a plethora of Poetics-spawned small press publishing, readings, a gallery, conversations, and interactions with the exemplary list of visiting poets to Buffalo under Bernstein's tenure as David Gray Chair. (See the "Historical set of Wednesday at 4 posters and calendars, 1990-2005" available at the EPC). Thus, the mix, in those days, was richer and more varied than the digital slice might imply. The digital, however, extends availability and reach that words can be broadcast (as my own fruitless recent search for a print copy of Jonathan Skinner's *Ecopoetics* 1 demonstrates): this brings many rewards, for example when a student told me he became interested in new poetries reading them at an isolated outpost on the polar circle in the Canadian artic. The EPC was there for him!)

Nonetheless, I still felt marginal. I mean, maybe it's my own ethnic humility, but a lot of folks were so self-important! Curiously, I have not heard of most of them since those days, though assuredly Bernstein has, always seemingly a nexus between generations, national literatures, and media movements, especially the treasure of archival poetry sound resources he has curated. Nonetheless being marginal is not really a bad thing (like Groucho Marx said about any club that would have him as a member) and, aside from the slightly denigrating feel, it provided a crucially important perspective, a terrain of distance or as Blaser might have it, a practice of outside – a real haunt. (I'd love my tombstone to be at the edge of a graveyard with the inscription, "Thus he lies where he lived. May the margins embrace him.")

The general feel of isolation made sense as I had come to Buffalo with the background of a literary bibliographer. (Not one worker, not even in the Poetry Collection, was a librarian.) My focus was on small presses, the Mimeo Revolution, the ability of people to engage machines like printing presses and Xerox machines to shape the changing face of poetry (see Glazier, *Small Press: An Annotated Guide*. Greenwood, 1992). Next, I took one forging poetry objects through JavaScript, FTP, and Telnet, to create new spaces in the painfully fertile, fleshy folds of crisscrossing continuums, continuities, and disconnects. It was just the way the line would drop, or the file transmission would freeze, or the IRC would start scrolling unintelligible strings of control characters, frustrating to say the least. But overcoming those obstacles, overcoming the up-front code tantrums of text only machine tantrums – pure ecstasy!

As to being on the margins, the librarians in the libraries did not take to me (unsure of how to evaluate new writing), the English establishment distrusted me (years after Al Cook, not eager to embrace new media forms), and the Computing Center barely tolerated a project like the EPC (not wanting to veer from conventional paths.) Indeed, the Computing Center was hesitant to– the first ones at Buffalo – but agreed to do so if Martin Spinelli, host of the LINEbreak series with Bernstein – would supply a copy of the server-side software of RealAudio. Spinelli managed to do so, one day bursting into my office with the software in a box. I negotiated with the Computing Center. I was also helpful on the helm of the launching of LINEbreak, Bernstein's Poetics List, and, I with Kenneth Sherwood, launched *RIF/T*, perhaps the first online literary small press magazine.

As to digital poetry Creeley was immediately, irrevocably supportive of the new medium and one of my earliest enthusiastic supporters. My work was seemingly a delight to him. He loved all the possibilities and was totally cognizant that I had unearthed a new forge for pounding out words in an unbound sense, boundless, buoyant. Creeley was a man who used words sparingly, each one mattered; each was capable of endless slippage, shape-shifting to new hues, colors, and echoes. About the digital, he was enthusiastic, proactive, positive, even working on a digital project with Buffalo high school students.[iv]

One can see how the technical provides a wellspring of energy and metaphoric ply that bends language into a an object of reflective metaphoric angles in this passage from my 2003 book, *Anatman, Pumpkin Seed, Algorithm*:

We're the unacknowledged shaman in
the CPU cycle, the traces of pattern when

the screens refresh. We pick up the
pieces, bind your binary, put the boost in
your bouillabaisse. We're the salt in the
shaker & the spice in the puritan; we're
the lumens that crawl between the
windows the hesitations allow.[v]

Here the poetic soil is fertile offering, as Duncan might have called it, an "opening of the field." The field is the screen that hovers luminous in front of your face as you write. There is a powerful Sun mainframe in the background, its disks as powerful as a thousand Arabian stallions. The images flit in and out with the refresh rate of the screen. It may be those blank moments, moments of sheer blankness, bending Genet's thoughts about the space around words, cited later, that the real thinking emerges. Needless to say, I am honored that a self-avowed techie writer writing from the queen of techie sites would take time to muse over my words from the Niagara frontier.

So I think there's room to say here, that the poetics of the EPC fed into the poetics discovery and into the poetics of my poetry snowballing into the Buffalo Poetic of the time; all of the material picked up as the snowball rolled became a mass of energy, at once beaming, gleaming new, in another sense a continuation of New Poetries from decades ago, with the glittering sparks of Language Practice and the youthful, fervent engagements of the collection of brilliant students that all seemed to be hammering away, some in actual converted steel-town Buffalo factories, in some cases literally working in steel with blow torches and welding machines.

This was maybe how Creeley and Bernstein teamed up so excellently for the Poetics Program. New language (making) in formation. Bernstein was strikingly receptive to the digital medium. It began with me explaining every nuance I could to him; we passed hours in his office on campus in a delirium of discovery. He appreciated my reports from inside the belly of the whale: that massive bone structure, it was HTML!

You see, I had entered the Internet business before there was even a Web. I will never forget the space alien animal embrace of the dial up connection, the glorious starkness of Telnet, the tickertape parade of files flying through FTP, the bare, menu-driven honesty of gopher. No graphics, no gimmicks, no pop-ups, no visual sales pitches. Having the property of being itself, not as contemporary Websites, being, as Sartre wrote of Genet, "Both itself and the reflection of itself."[vi] Gopher was straight up. But various investigations allowed me to understand that it was not to rest here: the Web would be unleashed one day. So I began building pages, hundreds of them, in gopher. In 1994 the World Wide opened its doors. I unleashed my serpents and for seconds, for mere seconds but for real, the EPC was not just the largest poetry site in the world but the largest site of any type in the world! Of course, all those companies with hundreds of coders overtook me in short order. But a definitive victory, no matter how small, forever remains a victory.

As Creeley later wrote, musing over a Delmore Schwartz title:

I dreamt – in dreams. *In dreams,*
the poet wrote, *begin responsibilities.*
I thought that was like going to
some wondrous place and all was
waiting there just for you to come
and do what had to be done.[vii]

This began a commitment to the EPC that has now surpassed twenty years of work. From the start, it was a breakthrough! There was a featured article in *The Chronicle of Higher Education;* it became the talk of poetry organizations across the Northeastern U.S. The EPC was the largest and most extensive project of its sort. As such, I was invited to speak to the New York Council for the Arts and at New York's Poet House. I also met with Kenneth Goldsmith in New York who was eager to get information to begin building his impressive UbuWeb site. Goldsmith is an EPC affiliated site to this day. Goldsmith also contributed author pages to the EPC, helping the EPC grow in content, size, and relevance.

The EPC was intended, not as a passing flash in the pan, but like a 1956 Chevy on a Havana side street, built to last, solid and substantial, then rebuilt, rewired, reinvented, held together by willpower, imagination code work-arounds, and zip files, tarred, untarred, and re-permissioned. Using knowledge and insights from my librarianship studies, my programming experience and comfort in the wilderness of computer source code, and my Ironworker's knowledge of structural steel. The concept was simple. The directories branched off a main entry page in an orderly and logical manner. There was the root EPC directory. Under that were directories for such logical branches as authors (where author pages are located), the library (full text materials), poetics (the poetics page when Creeley and Bernstein were at UB), and magazines, publishers, and sites, etc. The URLs were geared to human reading, allowing the user to know what to expect from the URL itself (e.g., http://epc.buffalo. edu/authors/glazier/essays), without being on the one hand abstruse or on the other so literal that they were an endless string composed of the title of the article with dashes instead of spaces. One of my objectives, after my studies as a literary bibliographer and special collections librarian, considering that most library special collections are only open from 9 to 5 on weekdays, when most unfunded, independent, and/or employed poet/researchers cannot access them, was to establish a 24-hours-a-day Special Collections that was open and accessible to any person for any reason at any time.

Further, the EPC was not just a poetry site, but a curated location in cyberspace where poetic materials in all genres could be gathered according to the same type of guidelines that inform a library Special Collection. It is true that, for teaching, one value of EPC Author pages was to offer select works to introduce specific authors to students. At the same time, however, as many materials are ephemeral or go out of print quickly, the EPC was able to make texts available that might have been totally tucked away in special collections vaults. (This is also an exemplary contribution, allowing preservation of the material context of these works.) Here the emphasis on access through the digital medium also made possible the user's reading, notetaking, copying, and immersion into fleeting texts that might prove critical to multiple investigations, interests, poetic obsessions, poetic democracy, wanderings, digressions, and discoveries.

The EPC is a project that has taken two decades to build its foundation, and it is a massive poetic-enabling resource created, maintained, and directed, not in the spirit of financial gain, but in rock solid benevolence and as a commit to the presence of the living word amid explosions of data in the digital world. This was, is, and will always be an extension into the material world of Poetics at Buffalo, regardless of its physical location as well.

Surprisingly, as the site grew during its early years, it became clear that, like any conceptual breakthrough, the EPC was greater than the sum of its parts. English students, faculty, and many of those even in the libraries, did not really understand the momentum that was snowballing in these 30,000 pages. It was a poetic of parts put together for a machine of literary vision in a Net context. Moving this forward, through long stretches, fell directly on my shoulders, a trek across what often seemed like an endless desert with the occasional oasis of a student interested in a specific project (the occasional Ph.D. students would contribute author pages as natural by-products of their studies of specific authors, such work offering them a natural reason to begin to correspond with those authors, as well), and the constant support of Bernstein's David Gray Chair. The Center was built entirely from volunteer labor, often it was me making a page for a visiting poet to the Poetics reading series and working with insightful contributors, beginning with Spinelli and Sherwood, with Kenneth Goldsmith, later with Senior Editor Jack Krick, singularly responsible dozens of author pages, and the constant, meticulous, dedicated contributions of Charles Bernstein. Thus, brick by brick, over decades, the EPC site continued to grow, often from my initiative, always with Bernstein's support, and with input from a multitude of contributors, those mentioned above and many others. I think it's fair to say that, on the technical side, I was consistently on guard, typing raw HTML mark-up by hand, crystal clean code being as important to me as any poetic expression, late into the night on many occasions. It is certain that all in all, thousands of pages were written by my hands, an absolute Buddhist buzz of text-only in-the-moment egoless-auto-open-bracket-code-close-bracket-apotheosis, with good words from many gracious supporters along the trail. Though I, personally, may have used a good deal of time that might have been employed in my own ego-oriented practice, altruism was the key and at the same time, the excitement of writing code and watching it work, a poetic practice itself, induces its own sort of poetic ecstasy, one that only the Mac-Low-dizzy, non-intentional whirring whirling dervish might know.

Additionally, I began to write digital poetry, poetic texts that engaged code and its constructs in their constitution. These will be detailed in depth in my almost-competed book, "Array Poetics." In brief, such digital concepts can be seen operating with precision in a poem as spare as "White Faced Bromeliads on 20 Hectares," a sequence of eight poems in which each line in each poem has two alternate possibilities. As it turns out, each 8-line poem has

512 possible iterations, giving the sequence perhaps 4,000 possible readings. Such a concept grew out of my work with author manuscripts where a line is crossed out and another put in its place. In some cases, the author would then strike the inserted line putting back in its original version. This made me think of what it might produce to have a poem where each line consisted on two variants; you could have the original line and the alternate line in the same text, displayed at unpredictably as the computer periodically refreshed the screen. EPC-building made me aware of such possibilities. As the texts themselves, like those of P. Inman or Bernstein's "Veil" or Gertrude Stein's *Tender Buttons* might equally suggest. There are a lot of ways to articulate a poetic approach as if, stumbling through interwoven codes, utterance is made real. Truly, code is writing "as real as thinking" as code is writing-thought-through to be fed to a "thinking machine" to result in expressive articulation.

Regarding some of the Poetics Programs founding structures, such as the idea of Poetics

"Core faculty," a concept that Creeley and Bernstein put forward, was one that drew objections from affiliated faculty. "Core faculty" simply meant writers that write both creative and theoretical texts. As I understand it, "Poetics" itself was a goal of Creeley's before 1991 when he, Charles Olson, and John Barth were in the UB English Department at the same time. As to the "Core Faculty" issue, some colleagues were unhappy about the concept, suggesting their work was equal to poetry and to poetic theory/critical work. I never argued that point nor their other argument, that they did not believe in the idea of "core" faculty, that everyone was "core." Of course, this is true but that does not mean that there can't be areas of specialty within various faculty endeavors in a department. Thus, being "core faculty" in poetics a mark of privilege a higher tier of university appointment. In the case of "Core faculty" in the Poetics Program as it was, simply indicated a creative writer who also wrote critically. In any case, a title could never equal the spirit of having built the EPC; it was a simple gift to a community, a spirit of collaboration, as well as a learning experience, no recognition required:

> Dreaming back thru life, Your time—and mine accelerating toward Apocalypse, the final moment—the flower burning in the Day—and what comes after ....[viii]

Thus, even as Core faculty, I was on the margin again, the only one of the group to not be in the English Department. (I had been considered for it but there was some unwarranted controversy about this, based on unfounded narratives. It worked out much better anyway for the EPC to find its location in the media-rich Department of Media Study, bursting with the technologies of imagination, and for me, especially, to work with Tony Conrad, an original Fluxus artist, founding member of the inception of Buffalo's avant-garde art scene, and enduring benevolent spirit after the departure of Howe and Bernstein.)

Though three Core Faculty members remain alive from the original Poetics at Buffalo, only two remain active EPC contributors. None are at

Buffalo any more. As to the dispersed members of the original Poetics Program team, the centrifugal pull has cast their words around the globe, Bernstein and Howe most notably. It will always have been a good thing to have been part of Poetics at Buffalo as it was, and no one wishes the present Poetics Program any ill will ever, in whatever configuration it may continue to be instantiated. As to its legacy, there will always have been the radiance of the presence of language as in itself and of itself, both inside and outside itself, in the drawer and on the table, buried in the warp and weave of the code whose company we continue to keep.

My philosophy is that writing, in whatever medium, is an engagement with an attempt to see half-objects in the crescent-light of a waxing moon. Rather than label myself "poet," "digital poet," or "poet programmer," I prefer to let my artistic vision float, like a ribbon of moonlight on the sea. There is a density to the movements of that light that passes all understanding, and keeps the edge of articulation in rhythm with the dark expanses between the stars; poetic thought is a ligature wound through all practice, print, digital, visual, concrete, sculptural, moving image, multi-dimensional, and in forms as yet unimagined. The lyrical is itself a liquid, pliable, renewable resource. My materials remain the rhythm of the heart and the engagement of the lungs: breath made flesh; flesh-contoured bellows. La Fragua of Guanajuato, its fruit sellers, roast chicken, ninety-year-old peanut vendors, bicycle vendors laden with desert wildflower honey and plums. "La luna vino a la fragua / The moon came to the forge" wrote García Lorca.[ix] The forge of Los, Blake's job, not his "Job" but his job, day-labor, beating the letters from the red-hot metal, pounding the mark-up into fanciful, dancing shapes to hardened into iron. Later to die broke. Like the iron inside the skyscraper upon which Los strides, Blake's Lotaburger Los Lunas, Blake's Basque farms, at no loss for words against the gloss of cumulus-embellished skies.

Huye luna, luna, luna.	Flee moon, moon, moon.
Si vinieran los gitanos,	If the Others come
harían con tu corazón	they would make with your heart
collares y anillos blancos.	necklaces and rings moon-white.[x]

And this is what happens after so many years. A poetic that is more structural steel than poetic fabrication, invention as a force independent of gravity, the timelessness of the present moment, all living sentience, though long dead, now free from time, independent, and conversing with me through the page. Yes, I said the page. In the present middle way, particular expressive possibilities can only be transmitted through the page. The page and the digital as manifestations of multiple ways of seeing, independent of any totalizing medium, indeed, impossible to even record except for fleeting moments determined only by the tolerance of the medium which whispers the first letter of the first word of the manifestoes made mostly of dark matter, code, quantum-condensation, coalescence. We are merely grateful we are allowed one of their prolific polysemous-colossal-conglomerate sensations, its types of lizards a-to-z, the bilingual, multicultural, eclipse-imagined totality, the way that red soil has all the past and all the future sandwiched in a single gleam of light across its face reflected by the setting sun.

Burying myself in snowfalls of magnolia petals, I watch them float on the glossy surface of the North Oconee River. The EPC lives on. We salute all in the Company and wish you a beau fleuve of poetic blessings, that these chronicles will help in any endeavor you undertake, that you always go in glee.

I am what I learned from Poetics at Buffalo. It is the white light that ripples across the moon-touched sea-lake, dosoweh. Having been a plus to Poetics at Buffalo, in its finest moment, has landed me on this mountain, with the oaks, towering ponderosa pines, and explosions of fragrant flowers, magnolias trees blushing across rugged slopes like your own moments of déjà vu. (See how the accents on the "e" and the "a" almost make a little house for your past present premonition? In HTML, "déjà vu," nearly as expressive! At least I, personally, see a landscape of barbs and agave with the short past participle "vu" ("seen") – it is what I saw – a volcanic peak on the distant horizon.) In a short time, a once-in-99-year event will occur. With the ceremonial élan of a regal sash across the North American continent: the moon will block the sun's blaze like Creeley's closed eye, birds will stutter somnambulantly, Lorca's crickets, low-toned, deep forest owls, and Southern katydids will begin to wail, and the world will be seen as it is, a speck under avalanche of stars, unfettered by the mere fact of day. To this moment it has led.

i   Diaz, Jesus. "Did You Know that These Strange Fields of Ice Flowers Exist At Sea?" *Gizmodo*. http://gizmodo.com/5968768/did-you-know-that-these-fields-of-ice-flowers-exist-at-sea/

ii   Dukes, Carol Muske. "Straight from the Hearth." *Los Angeles Times*. http://articles.latimes.com/1991-06-23/books/bk-1840_1_robert-creeley

iii   "Gnomic Verses" from *The Collected Poems of Robert Creeley, 1975-2005* (2006).

iv   Most of Creeley's personal activity in the new online space was largely with e-mail, though he keenly appreciated the precision, power, and rapid transmission that it, and its associated media, made possible. As to my work, I'm certain that his sixth sense fueled a keen excitement about language living in a new form. See "UB's Creeley helps City Honors develop own Web site on Internet." UB Reporter, March 13, 1997, http://www.buffalo.edu/ubreporter/archive/vol28/vol28n24/partner1.html, accessed 6 August, 2017.

v   Glazier, "One Server, One Tablet, and a Diskless Sun," *Anatman*, 69

vi   *The Thief's Journal*, 7

vii   Robert Creeley, "After School," On Earth (UC Press, 2005)

viii   Allen Ginsberg, "Kaddish." City Lights.

ix   Federico García Lorca, "Romance de la Luna," Glazier, trans.

x   Federico García Lorca, "Romance de la Luna," Glazier, trans.

BUFFALO SYMPHYSIS: A GROWING TOGETHER OF SITE AND SMALL PRESS POETRY

Geoffrey Gatza

The physical setting for a small press is crucial to its creative development, perception and reception. There is a dynamic interaction in which poetic practice and the city of Buffalo enjoy a unique collaboration which is not readily transferable to another location: the city is the poetry and the poetry is the city. Unlike a dialectical relationship, in which contact between the work and its site brings about a product of this interaction. In the city of Buffalo there is a growing together of ideas, energy and connectivity between reader, writers and scholars to produce a symphysis, of sorts. Here we are spoiled for choice through its people, local resources, library and archive materials and technological hubs of information. In Buffalo, this symphysis fuses together place and thought to produce meaning and an identity that seeps beneath the surface of things, bringing about a notion of poetry.

There are many forms of poetry the flourish here; there is no one school of thought. There is not one kind of Buffalo poetry; traditional poets and poetry meet the non-traditional quite often. Although we are joined together by space there is no one sphere of influence. Here we have an overlap of locations where experimental poets perform in reading spaces where a few days earlier a spoken-word reading had just taken place.

This fusing is especially true for my small press BlazeVOX.[i] We are an independent press located in Buffalo, New York, which is often referred to as Poetry City. We specialize in innovative fictions and wide-ranging fields of innovative forms of poetry and prose. Our goal is to publish works that are challenging, creative, attractive, and yet affordable to individual readers.

BlazeVOX began life in 1998 as an undergraduate project, while I was studying at Daemen College. I found something in poetry that motivated me to become more active in its creation and production so I helped recreate the student newspaper, which had been out of circulation for many years. In our first issue, I interviewed Robert Creeley through email. In our dialog, I asked him about his poem "Citizen."[ii]

It is a fine poem that makes mention of LSD, Peter Orlovsky and the need to clean up the world by writing a "giddy little ode." It also alludes to the classical character of Oedipus having carnal knowledge of his mother. As accurate as that detail is towards the play, the publication of a stanza that included the word "motherfucker" was deemed to be inappropriate by the Student Activity offices. I was directed to remove it from the article. Being mildly annoyed, in place of the poem I placed a large white blank space in the place where the excerpt of the poem should have been printed and I included a small explanatory footnote for the blank space. It was, of course, a very small issue of little consequence, but it gave me a taste of the interesting nature of publishing. It also was how I met Robert Creeley and was introduced to the UB Poetics Program and the vibrant poetic community in Buffalo.

The first issue of BlazeVOX, an online journal of voice, appeared in the fall of 2000. I had developed a love for coding and designing webpages, which matched my increasing fascination with poetry. I found an importance in contemporary, non-traditional poetry and its ability to speak directly to readers. There is an elusive quality that cements connections and meanings that is at once obvious yet resoundingly fresh and new.

I have always been enamored with the essays and early poetic work of Ezra Pound, less so of his deplorable views he developed later in his life. Online publishing captured the zeal of his dictum make it new. Placing a literary journal online held a vibrant prospect to change the development of the book and the printed page from its centuries old traditions. This is why, beginning with our first issue, we made Ezra Pound the honorary editor-in-chief.

Our goal of the journal was to escape answers but rather to examine questions. With a minimalistic style, each issue of BlazeVOX focuses on the idea of expression, and more specifically on writings where anyone can express anything at any given moment. The works collected feature coincidental, accidental and unexpected connections, which make it possible for a subtle diversity and firebreaks to ignite and combust. We consciously make an effort and take chances on works aimed at expanding and questioning the medium of poetry.

In our early years, the Internet was a very new development for publishing literary journals. Today it is clear how important an online presence is but at the time we were greeted with skepticisms. It is difficult even for me to recall a time, not long ago, when print was the only way to receive literature. If someone wanted to find poetry in Buffalo they would have to go to libraries or bookstores like Talking Leaves or Rust Belt books or attend reading hosted by Just Buffalo Literary Center to find like-minded people. You would have the visit coffee houses like Spot, Coffee Bean Café or Stimulance to find other poets. The University Heights area was a hot bed for artists, writers, undergraduate students, graduate students and professors to associate and discuss ideas.

At the time, the hypertext novel was going to overtake the linear, paper-based version. Flash-based video poems and programs animated the landscape of writing. It was in this environment that Charles Bernstein and Loss Pequeño Glazier hosted the E-Poetry 2001. The digital literature festival, presented by Just Buffalo Literary Center and UB's Electronic Poetry Center emphasized the art, performance, scholarly and artistic conversations that surround innovative practices that were taking place throughout the world. In attendance were Christian Bök, Jennifer Ley, Kenneth Goldsmith, Katherine Parrish, Brian Kim Stefans, Marie Damon, Juan José Diaz Infante, and Barrett Watten.

The conference was instrumental in the development of our online presence. There was an electric atmosphere throughout that week. People were meeting face to face rather than over a modem. Most of the people had known each other from the Buffalo Poetics LISTSERV, which was founded by Charles Bernstein in late 1993.[iii]

It is important to mention how much of an influence Charles Bernstein has been on our press and how we approach publishing. As the David Gray Professor of Poetry and Letters at the University at Buffalo, his friendly open style and enthusiastic personality encouraged very many people in varied ways. The Wednesday@4 series brought in poets and scholars to Buffalo that expanded the frontiers of our city but also the networking abilities of those in Buffalo. Many of the ideas that I firmly believe about poetry and publishing come directly from his talks, books and interactions with his students.

We moved into book production in 2006. There was a real market for us to expand our horizons. Once we found a viable technology to bring out printed books, we hopped right on board. From our first run of ten books we have tried to push at the frontiers of what is possible with our innovative poetry, fiction and select non-fiction and literary criticism. Our fundamental mission has been to disseminate poetry, through print and digital media, both within academic spheres and to society at large. We seek to publish the innovative works of the greatest minds writing poetry today, from the most respected senior poets to extraordinarily promising young writers. We select for publication only the highest quality of writing on all levels regardless of commercial viability. Our outlets of publication strive to enrich cultural and intellectual life and foster regional pride and accomplishments.

To date we have published over 500 books. Our family of fine writers includes Bill Berkson, Anne Waldman, Clayton Eshleman, Anne Tardos, Tom Clark, John Tranter, and national book award winner Daniel Borzutzky. We publish 25 to 40 books a year. There is no real logic behind this number except for amount of interesting projects that become available.

In this city small presses are relevant cultural institutions. Our local audiences have developed and grown over many decades. Michael Basinski, the recently retired curator of The Poetry Collection at the University at Buffalo, often says, *all poetry is small press poetry*, and that certainly seems true. There have been hundreds of small presses and journal that have come into existence in Buffalo. Many have come about through projects begun by students of the UB Poetics Program and many others are startups from local poets who employ letterpress chapbooks and art books, zines and digital magazines. Many were on display in the Buffalo Small Press Book Fair. Kevin Thurston and Chris Fritton founded the yearly two-day event that brought together booksellers, bookmakers, small presses, authors and poets. It was a wonderful event that enjoyed a successful ten-year run, ultimately ending as a project in 2016.

Our small press has had a wonderful run for the past seventeen years and we hope to continue to be relevant for any years to come. One of BlazeVOX's axioms is that we are *publishers of weird little books*, so I am a firm believer that the strong force that binds all of our books together could be found in the odder experimental side of the literary landscape. There is so much that is exciting about poetry, from its discourses to its execution to its futile utilities. It is the human cost of poetry – the energy in its expression on the page and or the vocalizations that occur in the spoken breathe that provoke me into paying close attention to what is occurring. This is all very broad discursiveness about very specific artistries, but there is always something fascinating and unique in a new project, be it a full-scale book or a chapbook.

There is a real disadvantage in being a poet. Poetry does not sell well and has little cultural capital. So the notion of tangible remuneration as a reward for ones writing is never the motivating force for being published. Having one's book of poems published is its own end and for the poet, a job well done. Since we cannot succeed simply by writing better to produce more commercial materials we succeed by spending our energy embracing what needs to be written.

It's difficult to say exactly what's currently happening in the literary landscape our region today, but it's definitely something exhilarating. There is a new resurgence in economic development, which has been labeled *New* Buffalo. In the past few years the old and dirty has been cleaned up and power-washed. There are new buildings where old ones once stood. There are new veneers and fresh coats of paint. There are new businesses that are breathing new life into the old and derelict. But with all of the change that is taking place, things are still very much the same. There is still plenty flourishing in hybrid forms and experimentation that matches, inch for inch, the same kind of innovative spirit one thinks of when they think of Buffalo.

---

[i]   Gatza, Geoffrey, ed. n.d. *BlazeVOX [books]*. http://www.blazevox.org.

[ii]   Creeley, Robert. 1981. *The Collected Poems of Robert Creeley, 1945-1975, Volume 1*.Berkeley, CA: University of California Press.

[iii]   A LISTSERV is a legacy technology that was a forerunner to social media sites. At any time there were over a thousand poets and scholars corresponding through email. At its best times the Poetry List was a space to share, discuss and interact, collaborate and promote projects and readings. The list continued until late January 2014 when it finally closed.

GENDER TROUBLE

Juliana Spahr

1.

We meant our fellow graduate students and ourselves, when Chris Nealon and I discussed doing this. We were talking about those moments in graduate school when everyone was teaching things like the postcard never arrives to its sender or the deep meaning behind a term like "always already" or whatever to their introductory composition classes. We were talking about a moment that seemed slightly absurd to us. But there were other things to talk about also. Like how the '90s moved from Act Up and queer nation in the beginning of the decade to protests demanding global justice at the end. Chris suggested that we both write something on *Gender Trouble*, that Judith Butler book. I'm not sure I wrote something on *Gender Trouble*. I am not sure Chris did either. This piece, the piece that I wrote, is less about gender and more about graduate school and literary lineage. But no matter. I wrote the original version of this in 2006. And then gender keeps changing, in good ways. So I rewrote this. I think of these things that I have learned, unevenly and still learning, as the things that come after *Gender Trouble*. Rereading *Gender Trouble* last year I kept thinking of *Gender Trouble* as a foundational part of a movement that ends up making *Gender Trouble* feel somewhat old fashioned in how it understands gender. That book did some work, in other words. And then some other books did more work. And that work continues.

2.

I went to graduate school from 1989-1995 in Buffalo. So a lot of my vision of the 90s is limited and defined by this experience. It was cold in Buffalo about 8 months of the year and so I and some of my femme colleagues often wore under the short slightly flouncy skirts that were popular at that time either thick, dark tights or tight-fitting long underwear and then usually some sort of boot, not the kind with heels that are popular today but the more practical kind commonly used in our culture for tromping around in snow, a Doc Marten sort of boot or a combat boot. I usually combined this with some girly top, like maybe a cut off slip or some sort of camisole that I bought at Victoria's Secret in the mall, and then as many thrift store sweaters as were necessary to stay warm—often a pull over and then a men's cardigan on top of this.

What I am saying is that the performance of gender that Butler so astutely describes in *Gender Trouble* didn't feel like it got at how I performed gender as much as the cold performed gender for me.

3.

As graduate students we wore these sweaters out to various bars late at night, after we had done some reading and some writing alone in our large yet cold rented apartments, and warm in these sweaters we talked about things like radical modernism. And legacies. And masculine poets. We talked not reflectively about masculine poets as masculine poets, but just compulsively about masculine poets as if we were not even noticing that we just talked about masculine poets. We couldn't help ourselves. The heroic masculine literary tradition for some reason that remains unclear to me felt as if it was a warm breeze in the middle of a cold Buffalo winter. A warmth that maybe came from the ghosts of the living and the dead, the warm breath left behind by Charles Olson and Al Cook, and Michael Davidson and Jack Clarke and Gregory Corso and John Weiners and Robert Haas and Charlie Altieri and Steven Rodefer. Warmth came out of our mouths as we talked about this tradition. And this tradition merged in our minds with the heroic myths the city told about itself, such as that it wasn't for the weak because it dealt with the cold and snow more than most other places in the nation.

Those of us who studied the poetry of fragmentation, quotation, disruption, disjunction, agrammatical syntax, and so on were a group, a herd, and we were well known among our peers in the program for being annoying in how we built networks of burrows and lived collectively within them, lived in the breath of the warm masculine heroic tradition. But while we looked a herd to others, among ourselves we felt divided, split, uneven, uneasy. The masculine heroic literary tradition for sure shaped us and as it did this there was no denying that it shaped us into divisions that often felt uncomfortable to all of us. It was as if every so often a large hand would descend, pick us up by the neck, hold us upside down so as to hypnotize us, and then use a forefinger and middle finger to press down the vent area just in front of our anus so as to make our sex organs protrude. If what protruded had a more circular shape and a rounded tip, the hand declared us a jack-kit bunny. If what protruded had a groove on each side and a pointed shape, the hand declared us a jill-kit bunny. It was easy though to tell who was a buck rabbit and who a doe rabbit. No hand had to press the vent area just in front of their anus. Buck rabbits—there were five of them—had endowed chairs with budget lines for travel and to bring people to the university to read and dole out to graduate student projects as they saw fit. The one who did not have such a line was a doe rabbit. This was all the more noticeable because the one doe rabbit was actually better known and more established than some of the buck rabbits. And this was called a "shame" and "an accident of hiring" and was blamed on the English Department's hiring practices, not the Poetics Program or the heroic masculine literary tradition that haunted it.

This was how the tradition divided us into buck rabbits, doe rabbits, jack-kit bunnies, and jill-kit bunnies. We couldn't see our way out of these categorical impositions. We couldn't hold on to the heroic masculine literary tradition if we didn't give in to these divisions and for some reason we refused to give up the heroic masculine literary tradition, maybe because it was the only thing we really had.

The divisions were larger than all of us. They were structural. Every year a fresh new group of students would arrive to attend the English Department. Every year the admissions committee would have admitted a femme or maybe two who said in their application that they were interested in studying twentieth century poetry. Every year, by the second semester, this femme or two would have changed the focus of their study.

But in contrast, the study of poetry of the masculine heroic literary tradition that used fragmentation, quotation, disruption, disjunction, agrammatical syntax, and so on seemed to be a magnet for those masculine. They would enter the program planning to do the muck racking, hard hitting masculinist American literature dissertation that Buffalo was so famous for. Leslie Fiedler—a cult academic because of both his arrest for possession of pot in the 70s and his "Come Back to the Raft Ag'in, Huck Honey" article that looked at the raft of Huck and Jim as a homosocial space, an article that I have to admit has not aged very well—drew them to the program. But once they got there they would quickly decide to write a dissertation on the early works of some masculine poet; the field is wide open, they would exclaim; there has been no full-length study on the early works of this masculine poet.

4.

While probably all of us would say we were feminists of the most basic equal pay for equal work sort of feminism, the hand felt otherwise. For instance, there were two sorts of jobs available for bunnies. One of them involved nothing more than doing errands, like picking up poets at the airport that the buck rabbits had invited to read. The other position involved teaching two courses a year, which while it wasn't a lot of work it wasn't something like picking up poets, poets that we thought were famous or sometimes good writers and thus would be more than willing to pick them up at the airport. The teaching felt more like work. And even though we all just looked like bunnies in our thrift store sweaters, some of us looking more masculine and some more feminine, it was very clear to all of us that buck rabbits did not care much about whether we looked more masculine or feminine. They instead felt the most comfortable with those bunnies who showed a round tip when the vent area just in front of their anus was pressed down, no matter how they presented. And so those bunnies became their assistants and because they could, they paid those who did the errand job $2000 more a year than the bunnies who showed a pointed shape when the vent area just in front of their anus was pressed down and who did the teaching jobs. When those who showed a pointed shape complained because they couldn't even apply to be rejected, the buck rabbits said that because the pointed shapes were so devoted to teaching and the rounded tips did such a bad job of it, that it made more sense for the rounded tips to do the easier and fancier job and be paid more for it. Or when a buck rabbit decided it would be a nice favor for someone to live in his huge rented burrow rent free because he was only in it for a few days a week, and he was right it was a nice favor, he let a rounded tip live there. This was again probably because it would be inappropriate for a buck rabbit to be living in a house with a pointed shape and maybe no pointed shape wanted to live in the huge burrow, but it was another example of the complicated financing system that the heroic masculine literary tradition left behind. When a buck rabbit had so called favors like typesetting jobs that he billed out at a fairly decent freelance rate and then subcontracted to bunnies at minimum wage, he almost always subcontracted this work out to the pointed shapes and they almost always took it, because they needed the money.

We talked about the hand that picked us all up and put us all on our backs all the time. We talked about the small differential in our pay. In these moments we used essentialism as an epithet. We were stuck together in a burrow with narrow mud walls that had been dug out before we got there and we knew it. It was hard for us to figure out where to dig to expand the burrow or how to make new openings into it because we had not created it. Those of us who thought of ourselves as doe rabbits were experienced with closing down openings to the burrow in order to protect the young, not with building new openings. We couldn't see our way into the things that get talked about in *Gender Trouble*, a book which we could have read as a how to guide on something as simple as a way to insist that what poked out when the hand pressed down on the vent area just in front of our anus did not tell determining stories about who we were.

5.

In 1992 the anti-abortion group Operation Rescue came to Buffalo with their "Spring of Life" action and, again, many bunnies spent their mornings doing clinic defense (which I have to confess started at some ungodly hour in the morning and so I wasn't as diligent as some of my fellow bunnies). Mainly those who had a pointed shape poke out when the vent area just in front of their anus was pressed showed up at these events. But some with a rounded tip did too. Still this was an event where once again a story was told about the pointed shape from which there was no escaping. And at the same time there was at SUNY Buffalo a graduate student unionization drive and many of the bunnies who did clinic defense began to work on the unionization drive. Because the Poetics Program buck rabbits preferred to fund the bunnies with a rounded tip, many bunnies with a pointed shape found refuge and funded positions in the union, the organizing ranks of which were almost exclusively pointed shapes. Most of the bunnies with a rounded tip didn't find the union as interesting as the early works of some masculine poet. I am remembering that it was hard to get a number of them to join the union.

Eventually this union drive culminated in the graduate students being affiliated with CWA and out of this came a contract with health benefits. I learned a lot from this work that I couldn't have learned in graduate school. A huge amount of economic changes happened in the name of free trade in the nineties. The fact that CWA was mucking around organizing a labor force that made $8,000 a year is a sign of how complicated the time was for unions. For several years many of my weekends were spent walking picket lines for other CWA affiliates like health care workers and bus drivers. I learned from the discussion on these picket lines some details about the larger world of international economics that were not at all evident in my seminars which tended to concentrate on the revolutionary politics of fractured language practices. I began to notice the IMF and the World Bank and structural realignment and outsourcing and those other things that would be grouped under the term "globalization" and would contribute to the 1999 Seattle World Trade Organization protests. Basically, the world beyond the burrows of the masculine heroic literary tradition entered into my vision.

In 1995 I left Buffalo and moved to New York City. The poetry world there was not divided into buck rabbits and doe rabbits and jack-kit bunnies and jill-kit bunnies. It had some other formation with badgers and swans and coyotes and wrens and whales and grasshoppers. I remember the year of 1995-1996 as one of the most productive I've ever had poetically. I wrote no literary criticism, walked no picket lines, and worked as a bartender and then as a secretary. It was not that during these years no one was there doing something that was the equivalent of pressing on the vent in front of my anus. I think of these years as the years in which I became a duck, as in a sitting duck. When the bar hired me, the manager took an oiled tube, touching it to a pair of sensitive spots that if I had a corkscrew penis would immediately trigger an explosive erection and ejaculation. Because nothing happened when the oiled tube touched me, I was hired. I felt caught behind the bar, was constantly screwing my vagina clockwise to keep things out of it. In 1997 I moved to Hawai'i for a job at the University of Hawai'i at Manoa and there became an octopus.

TOWARD A TELLING:
NOTES IN MEMORY OF DENNIS TEDLOCK

Rosa Alcalá

"...I don't know how to begin this story," Dennis Tedlock writes at the outset of on essay on Quiché Maya storytelling, explaining that since the stories of the Quiché Maya "occur naturally in conversation," they can't simply be produced on demand.[i] And I, too, now being asked to write this, feel unable to tell a story that might succinctly describe Dennis, what it was like to be taught and mentored by him. Perhaps the reason I am unsure of where to begin is that I suspect Dennis would not have wanted to be the object of discussion. For Dennis, the real story was not about him; it was in the act of listening, in letting the story be heard. This is evident in his description of how he found himself "looking at the Quiché text of the *Popol Vuh*, a text written some centuries ago, over the shoulders of a Quiché who was not only very much alive, but who was laughing at something he had read there." It was this interaction, of witnessing the *Popol Vuh* as something living and in dialogue with a community, that guided Tedlock's own immersive and collaborative approach to translation. Given this, it seems fitting that my first encounter with Dennis was not face to face, but translation to translation, as I rendered into English Cecilia Vicuña's *Cloud-net* and found several references to his *Popol Vuh*. This dialogue, initiated in 1998, would continue for years to come, as I picked up several more threads of his work—and also of Barbara Tedlock's— while translating Vicuña's poems and transcribing her performances.

And so, when I think of Dennis, it's not in the form of a story, but in the ways he made other stories possible, including the work of his students. As a teacher, he encouraged heterodox approaches to academic research and writing, and mostly tried to get out of the way of his students' own interests and approaches, listening to us as much as he had taught us to listen ourselves. There is an image that has returned to me again and again since Dennis's passing—it is of his finger pressing the play button on a cassette player during the first seminar I took with him in 1999. We were being asked to listen to Andrew Peynetsa telling the Zuni story of "The Boy and the Deer" and then transcribe it.[ii]   He gave us no instruction beyond that, but still I felt I had to impress him by somehow replicating his methods. He was, after all, the person who had opened up the possibility of giving oral performances life beyond anthropology journals, offering on the page the full dimension and vibrancy of the telling itself, so that it could no longer be ignored or categorized as "folklore" or "artifact" and had to be discussed as part of the full range of contemporary poetics. But the aim, it soon became clear, wasn't to impart a particular method of transcription or have us assume the Ethnopoetics mantle, it was instead to teach us to listen—and to take seriously the responsibility of that listening, in striving to understand both what was being heard and not heard—in the real sense of pauses in speech, but also in regard to cultural context and its relation to place and time and audience. He was also teaching us to think of all the bodies, including our own, involved in the telling, and how "listening," as Eleni Stecopolous recalls, "is performative too."[iii]   At the time, I was thinking a lot about Federico García Lorca's "Play and Theory of Duende," its positing of duende as earthly, as entering through the feet, rather than hovering overhead like the angel or muse, as something visceral rather than intellectual. The playing of the tape recorder felt very earthly to me, our ears serving an equivalent function to the feet, in that they rooted us, our bodies, in what was happening, as it happened.

I never recovered from that first listening, from the recognition that poetry didn't just exist on the page, and spent much of my time in his seminars rethinking what it meant to translate Cecilia Vicuña's work. The result was *Spit Temple: The Selected Performances of Cecilia Vicuña*, which owes much to Dennis, not just in the ways he represented typographically and in translation an oral performance, but also for funding my early research through his McNulty Chair in English.

In an essay included in *Spit Temple*, Dennis Tedlock tells us that when Vicuña, known for her whisper-like delivery, asks her audience, "Can you hear me?," she's not asking whether the microphone should be adjusted, but instead suggesting to the audience that they adjust their hearing.[iv] This also describes what it felt like to be in the presence of Dennis, who at times seemed as if he were listening to his own thoughts, tuning into what he was thinking, either by speaking quietly, almost as if to himself, or remaining silent. I had learned over time in his presence to adjust my hearing, waiting to catch that moment when his eyes would widen slightly and, as Yunte Huang writes, the silence would give way "to the poetic or a moment of illumination."[v] These were important moments. Barbara Tedlock once kindly "translated"—sensing that a year into working on my dissertation with Dennis I hadn't learned to tune into his subtle manner of praise—that he felt very confident in my abilities. I learned eventually to read his low-key gestures of generosity, and also his silences. When I grew increasingly nervous that Dennis had yet to respond to a request and the deadline was looming, I had to remind myself that he always came through, and often, when I least expected it (but most needed it), he'd deliver a long and thoughtful response that provided career advice, encouragement, and sometimes the date on the Mayan calendar and what it signified.

In one of his last acts of generosity, Dennis organized in 2015 a Translation Symposium in Buffalo's Rare Poetry Library to showcase the work of his former students and mentees, and flew us all out to talk about our current research. It was clear to me that we, the presenters, owed much of what we were doing—our careers in fact—to Dennis, and I tried to repay this debt by publically acknowledging the impact of his influence. And while Dennis seemed pleased, he didn't comment on my praise and prolong this focus on him. Later, at the dinner reception that Dennis and Barbara Tedlock organized for a large group, Myung Mi Kim tried to drive the point home again, telling him to look around and take in how important he was for those in attendance, and he just sort of nodded and did this *hmmm* thing and changed the subject. I do remember, however, spending a good deal of time that evening discussing with him the prevalence of the diminutive suffix in Spanish.

It strikes me now more than ever how significant it is that Dennis was not only a co-founder of the Poetics Program, but that his seminars were taught in an English department and not in, say, Anthropology or Linguistics, Cultural Studies or Comparative Literature. They served as a reminder of the range of aesthetic possibilities of what we might call "American" "experimental" poetry, and put into question what it meant to "make it new." Ethnopoetics, as Dennis taught it, is not the study of a "minority" literature, or of something that has long disappeared, or is "living in the past," or was "produced in isolation from other languages and cultures." "Ethnopoetics," he explains in his seminar description, "does not merely contrast the poetics of 'ethnics' with just plain poetics, but implies that any poetics is always an ethnopoetics."[vi] As such, Dennis's seminars were attended by a devoted group of students, Stecopolous and Huang among them, who went on to produce some of the most innovative work –both poetry and scholarship–to come out of the Poetics Program.

What kind of translator and poet would I be now, I often wonder, had I not heeded Cecilia Vicuña's advice, when I was applying for PhD programs, to go work with "The Tedlocks." What I do know is that what I learned from Dennis Tedlock was not just wrought in the classroom, but in witness to a shared commitment between he and Barbara, in life and in work, that extended beyond the scholarly or even literary into a place of greater consequence, a place—how can I say it otherwise—of love. Two people side by side in their fieldwork, each writing separate accounts of what they observed and took part in, each citing the other's work, each listening to the other. Maybe that's the real story, for which there is no beginning or end.

---

[i] The essay, "Beyond Logocentrism: Trace & Voice Among the Quiché Maya," appears in Dennis Tedlock's *The Spoken Word and the Work of Interpretation* (1983).

[ii] This is the first story in *Finding the Center: The Art of the Zuni Storyteller*, which includes Tedlock's transcriptions and translations of live performances in Zuni by Andrew Peynetsa and Walter Sanchez (U of NE Press, 1999).

[iii] See Bernstein, Charles. "Dennis Tedlock (June 19, 1939 – June 3, 2016)," *Jacket2*. https://jacket2.org/commentary/dennis-tedlock-1939-2016

[iv] See Tedlock's "Handspun Syllables/ Handwoven Words." *Spit Temple: The Selected Performances of Cecilia Vicuña*, ed. Rosa Alcalá. NY: Ugly Duckling, 2013.

[v] See https://jacket2.org/commentary/dennis-tedlock-1939-2016

[vi] See Tedlock, Dennis. "Ethnopoetics," *Electronic Poetry Center*. http://epc.buffalo.edu/authors/tedlock/syllabi/ethnopoetics.html

POETICS FOR THE MILLENNIUM

EXCERPT FROM "EAR TURNED TOWARD THE EMERGENT"

Myung Mi Kim

The following is an excerpt from an interview with Myung Mi Kim, conducted in 2007 by Charles Bernstein and various graduate students as part of the "Close Listening" series at the University of Pennsylvania, the transcription of which is hosted at Jacket2; the excerpt is used with permission of Myung Mi Kim and Charles Bernstein, who has kindly provided a brief introduction to the piece.

Myung Mi Kim came to Buffalo and the Poetics Program just as Robert Creeley, Susan Howe, and I were leaving. I still regret that I didn't have the chance to work with her. But the three of us recognized that Myung's radical work in teaching creative writing and her focus on the poetics of cultural dislocation were vital for the future of the program.

Myung's books — *Under Flag, The Bounty, Dura, Commons,* and *Penury* — are of the highest order of American poetry. Together these works provide not reports of what the poet has discovered, summarized or expressed, but an active thinking field for the reader to enter and explore. Using half-remembered revenants of Korean, her mother's mother tongue, along with historical documents, and lyric fragment, Myung's poems work to displace displacement. Myung's work is formally radical not so much in its abstraction but in the new forms it creates for socially conscious engagement.

Charles Bernstein

Pauline Baniqued: *Hi. I really enjoyed reading Commons. I started to think about the process involved in writing this, so my questions are mostly related. Maybe I could just put them out there for you?*

Your poetry is charged with meaning and double meaning, and open to multiple interpretations. How is this seemingly less smooth-flowing and more intellectual approach received by those in poetry, for example, in academia or by those who actually practice poetry? Do you find yourself having to decide whether certain material qualifies for poetry? Are you self-conscious about it when you write, and if so, do you sift out things to include in your poetry? How do you differentiate or judge?

Kim: What I'm hearing in that question, or at least the direction I want to take that question, is the interrogation of archive. There may be two things to consider here. One: what is material for the poem? This question is immediately conjoined with: what are the possibilities of the poem? The work or thinking through the interrogation of the archive immediately signals both the problem of what belongs in a poem, what is extra to the poem, and therefore, because of that excess, perhaps needs to be considered as belonging to the poem. For me, the question of what belongs and what doesn't belong in some really foundational sense is a question of what has been excluded in terms of the sociohistorical index, and therefore the question of what belongs or doesn't is one that needs to keep being opened up. There's got to be some kind of pressure on the question of what closes down the archive, who has authority to create archive. I'm hoping that I'm at least hearing one aspect of your question. Do you want to keep going?

Baniqued: *Yes. You use a lot of primary text, direct images, and lines in the poem as if taking the most objective photograph or stand towards the experience or the thought. Do you think that this is a "better" form of poetry, or a good direction towards the development of poetry? That poets remain more faithful to the experience that's being documented, and thus write more "effective" poems? What do you say to people who may think this is BS or think of it as stripping the essence of "again" writing poetry?*

Kim: Let me make sure I heard the first part of the question. When you are talking about the objective photograph — do you want to say a little more about that?

Baniqued: *That was the sense that I got when I was reading these poems, probably because there weren't as many adjectives as is common in more traditional kinds of poetry. There were just snapshots of what was there. The words were very precise.*

Kim: Actually, that is a useful question to follow up the first question about material, because for me it is a question about materiality. And what you're saying is the lack of modifiers, right? There are no adjectives, very few. That's fascinating to me because it's not a description for the thing. It is the thing. What is it to have perception that is unfettered from description?

Bernstein: *There's an aspect to what Pauline is asking though that's slightly different, which is what do people think when you write stuff that's difficult to understand? People like me with a limited horizon, vocabulary, you know, who say, "What is she talking about? I don't understand. I understand the words, but I don't understand what the words are doing. Do I have to read other poems? I mean, I open this book for the first time and it makes no sense to me." Are you trying to write for the broad masses of the people?*

Kim: I think the question here is: can the masses actually have a lot more to say about what's scrutable and readable and intelligible than what someone else external to the broad masses has determined. In other words, who has the privilege to say "this is transparent," "this is being rendered transparently," "I understand this"? What's at stake, it seems to me, in poetry or any sort of writing practice, is to keep asking under what terms and conditions do we understand legibility? Who has the authority to invest and divest in formulating what's scrutable, what's readable? These are questions about exclusion, inclusion, and social affiliation. What are the orders of exclusion and inclusion that get rehearsed when we consider: do I understand this? what does it mean? Is it possible to keep extending the meaning of meaning, the terms by which we understand anything at all, and especially language, because that's what we use all the time, every day, every second? How is it possible to keep extending the terms of meaning-making and of sense-making?

Julie Charbonnier: *You mentioned yesterday how each reading is different and how you would have other people come up and read your work. If you could just elaborate on that. And how would someone who doesn't speak another language experience repercussions while reading?*

Kim: Let me start with the second part of your question first, because I think it dovetails usefully with what I've just been saying about the demands on sense and sense-making that are politically and socially and culturally driven. When you ask about a person who doesn't speak another language, and what kind of condition would be produced for that reader, my question in return is always whether one can produce an approximation of the condition of language again unhooked from the givens of communication and communicability and transparency. Would it be possible to suggest/evoke/amplify/proliferate different ways of being inside and listening to and activating the space that we call language, which doesn't belong to any one language group, doesn't belong to any one particular set of ideas about the benchmarks of language such as rhythm, syntax, intonation, inflection? Even if there were no identifiable second language, an experience of language is produced, and I think everyone has access to that.

Charbonnier: *So, you think that when phrases can't be translated, these other limits of syntax, that there are actually more resources, is what you're saying?*

Kim: I think the whole notion of untranslatability, unsayability, the unsayable remains a profound interest linguistically, culturally, and politically. That kind of immanence and the emergence implied in that state of the unsaid mobilizes a certain social force.

...

Heather Gorn: *In listening to you last night and then a reading you did at Buffalo, I guess before* Commons *was printed officially, I was noticing a lot of differences in what you were reading and what I was reading along with in the text version. I was wondering if you would speak a little about versions of text, and when you do or don't think something is finished. Also, you mentioned last night about conceiving of your works as one long continuum, and sort of how that might play into how you think about a finished product.*

Kim: When I finish the text, in fact, that is the finished text. However, I feel that when I'm giving readings from the finished text, it's as if the text literally re-presents itself to you. Even if you are the maker of that particular text, there's a way in which you're greeting it and reading it. So, the occasion of the reading creates a space in which that re-listening and re-making initiates itself, and sometimes that happens, say, before the event, that I'll sit down and wonder, in a sense, out loud to myself, what will I be reading. In that process, something gets kicked up, something is re-initiated. Sometimes it happens in the reading itself, at the instance of the performance. I don't think of them necessarily as revisions. I do think of them as reformulations, re-takes, re-assembling, which is a lot how I work in the first place, a kind of process of accretion and assemblage and reconfiguration. So, in a way, every time you come back to the text, the process can re-kindle itself. That's been of some interest to me simply because it opens up the question of what is real time, what is compositional time, and what is the time of making a text. I think they are all different filtrations of what it means to produce a written text, which is not to refuse or in any way empty out the meaning of the book or the text that might come to some kind of rest. These elements are being held in a conversation with each other so that no one part, processually speaking, forecloses on any other part.

Gorn: *And your reformulations, do they change according to the atmosphere or your state of mind? Because you say sometimes you craft them before, sometimes right then —*

Kim: Right.

Gorn: *Given a kind of dynamic in the air, or, I guess, a little bit of both?*

Kim: I think a lot of it is like elaboration and re-elaboration, and sometimes it's quite physical. There are certain things on certain days you can render, there are certain days that certain parts of text seem difficult to produce on a physiological level.

Gorn: *I asked just earlier about Latin in general, and was noticing that various titles of your sections or works will be Latin-oriented, and then also in the Buffalo reading, I think you mentioned one of the working titles for* Commons *was* Works and Days, *which was obviously a less-than-slight nod to Hesiod. So, I'm just wondering if Latin is anything more than a kind of linguistic ghost, as you said, or a kind of treasure trove? Is it strictly that? Or what is your relationship with it?*

Kim: It's really amazing your timing in asking this question because the other day I thought maybe I should just learn Latin. Latin seems to be a particular kind of magnet for English. I am interested in that phenomenon. It's the ungraspable in English that sometimes seems to be embodied in Latin. I need to keep thinking about why that is, and why my ear hears that and not, say, French roots, you know? My "listening" for/toward Latin is overlaid with having an acquaintance with something you don't quite recognize. It's a strangeness that becomes an acquaintance, which in turn is familiar and unfamiliar.

Gorn: *It seemed a little elegiac also in your general use of it. Even with things, or later things, like Vesalius. Anyway, thanks.*

Kim: Thank you.

Damien Bright: *So we've been talking about accretion, assemblage, and reconfiguration, and all of this speaks to a certain -ism: postmodernism, poststructuralism, if you will. I mean you use various sources. We were talking about the archive and these kinds of to-ing and fro-ing between various levels of temporality. And you just said a strangeness that becomes an acquaintance, and so this almost spectral nature of language, and all of this has me thinking in a Derridean fashion, and you quote Helene Cixous's* Stigmata *in the postscript, or that's how I conceive of it, to* Commons: *poets as "agents for the most arduous, most dangerous cause there is: to love the other, even before being loved." And so, I guess I was wondering about the purpose behind your writing in terms of this friendship: is it a gesture of friendship? A critical gesture, a historically critical gesture with a view to a friendship that would annul certain ills of the past, I guess? Yes.*

Kim: Yes. I'll see if I can unpack some of that. There's a lot there, wonderfully a lot there. I think, at least I would like to hope, that writing does not identify its object. In other words, yes, I think there's an imbrication of historical critique. At least asking how is it possible, especially in formally radical practices, to imagine form already itself as critique. And so, yes, that calls up again by implication and imbrication and complicity, historical radical practices, as a means of addressing ... I don't think you said social ills, but something with the word ill ... I mean, what is that circuitry between form as critique as a kind of interrogative space, which is an action, not a decision. I don't think aesthetics and ethical engagements rise from a decision. One is making an intervention. One is addressing an ill. One is recuperating. These are all possible modes and drives, but the practice is infinitely open. It's not a determinable space. You don't arrive at it. It's the ongoing, unnameable returning to an earlier moment — the unsayable, the unspeakable, the ear turned toward the emergent, which is not about a decision to recuperate the erased, for example, however you might want to formulate that sort of impulse. Alternative ways of knowing might be a useful phrase here. How is it possible to take the resources of poetry, especially a formally radical, unpositioned, and unacculturated mode of inquiry that we attempt to name almost always awkwardly. Whatever identification we come up with — whether it's assemblage, accretion — my instinct would be to ask: And then what? What else? How else? The work of writing and reading and thinking is the tending of the otherwise, revitalizing the interconnection between form and form-as-critique or potential for critique. Does this help? At least respond to parts of your question?

Bright: *Yes, it does. And perhaps then on a more prosaic level this drive that you mentioned to relate, this almost constant conversation between form* *and form-as-critique, is that, and perhaps I'm being too forward here, a drive specific to you as a poet? Or do you think that is a drive that reaches beyond you as a poet, that is socially engaged, as in, how should I put my question more clearly —*

Kim: No, I think you said it.

Bright: *Is your vocation mandated by that drive or does it go further?*

Kim: Initially, I would want to question a word like mandated, because, yes, there is a mandate. Yes, there absolutely is, I think, something at stake. No question about it. However, I think what I'm trying to perhaps pose here is this: can that space be left undetermined? Would it be possible to disengage the impulse to have art perform an equal translation or transparent rendering into the social?

Sarah Yeung: *Earlier, you spoke about how some of your work was technically unreadable, like the birdsong: you can't read that out loud. What are your thoughts on how your work translates from being read on paper to being read out loud? What do you feel is lost and what do you feel is gained? You use spaces in different ways, the hybrid characters of Korean and Roman characters, and different entities that can be read, but, I suppose, have a very different effect out loud than on paper.*

Kim: It's the question of what can be seen, heard, read, spoken, received, transmitted in relation to (in proximity to) the idea of tracking language in which mutable, roaming, fugitive connections and disconnections and ruptures also generate meaning. Dis-ease is useful to me, or the dis-abling of habituated practices of language. The idea of something not working, something not being sayable or reproduceable, (re)printable, carries its own charge.

Yeung: *My other question is about themes in your work. In Commons, you have a lot of references to specific wartime incidents. There are many different places and times, and I was wondering why different incidents aren't more clearly demarcated in the work, and also if there are any in particular that are of significance to you.*

Kim: I think, especially in the earlier books like *Under Flag*, there's very clearly a kind of matrix that holds things together, the Korean War, for example, or the militarism in Korea subsequent to the Korean War. There's a much more clearly demarcated — and I'm using that word on purpose — clearly demarcated notion of nation: Korea, as a place, as a geographical reality, a material reality. And if you walk through the other books, it's almost as if that particular condition begins to call forward and speak with all the other conditions of war. It's a terrific question. I mean, what does it mean to both identify and unidentify or not locate? I'm trying to get at that conjunction between every specificity as its own, inviolable, intractably itself, and also the kind of global social-economic-political forces that produce conditions of war that are huge, not necessarily taggable to an instance. Or convert that or invert that, and say how can you understand that by — it's not an absence, right, it's not taking away the location. I'm trying to understand both. When you do the locating one by one, what's produced? What are the politics of that? What's the potential work that that can do, differently from understanding the condition of war transhistorically, transculturally?

Yeung: *All the wartime references did seem to be located in Asia, though, right?*

Kim: For the most part, yes. But *Commons* enfolds the presence of various wars, from many parts of the globe. This might be taking your question in too different of a direction, but the question here may also be: what does it mean to document anything? How does document, to document, take place?

Bernstein: *Let me extend the question that Sarah is asking. I'll ask a question I know the answer to in part because I read other interviews with you, but talk a little about your relationship to Korea in terms of your parents, grandparents, diaspora. Have you gone back to Korea? What's your own personal history in respect to Korea and to Korean?*

Kim: In many ways, I think I'm a fairly typical, if not overtly conventional, immigrant subject.

Bernstein: *Funny, you don't look typical.*

Kim: Yeah, that's what they all say. [Laughter.] I think maybe one of the things that's behind Sarah's question —

Bernstein: *I love that I asked you an absolutely factual question and you're hesitating more than you would with an abstract Derrida question.*

Kim [talking at the same time]: The facts are so uninteresting, Charles. Post-immigrant subject. A certain mode of the post-sixties immigration of the professional class from Korea. My father was an MD. What are the facts here? I hardly know. I do know that I have a strange — talking about ghostly and spectral — I mean, that's mostly what my relationship to Korea looks like. It is, in some sense, the most real and most constructed place I can possibly imagine. So the facts pale in relationship to that dynamic or that phenomenon. The facts are very straightforward: immigration to the US with my nuclear family —

Bernstein: *What year was that and how old were you?*

Kim: 1967 and I was nine. In terms of certain kinds of language propositions, I was once told by someone who works as a speech therapist that age twelve is apparently the cutoff for whether you have an enduring accent or not. So, if you look at my siblings — I'm the youngest — this bears out. The oldest sibling, maybe, has more trace of an accent. Anyway, why am I telling you this? Because you asked me for a fact. So, these are facts.

Bernstein: *That's very interesting to me. The accent, of course.*

Kim: But that sense of proximity and removal … family stories … already a generation or two removed … The [family stories] are particular to me; they are particular to my mother's experience. Yet, they are already arriving in a condition of history. They are already subjects of a history, of a [new] place and a [new] time. [So the result is that you get] the kind of collision and elision and wonderful richness, and yet absence of [the] real places, real times, which have been, in some sense [for the later generation], made by words. So, it's both delicious to report the words that one is told, but you also realize it has a real relationship to bear, bearing with what is no longer.

Johnathan Liebembuk: *I think a lot of the questions that have been posed deal with binary relationships of different things: translatability, untranslatability, one language versus another, or in relation to another, space and time even. I guess my question — I want to work from the ground up maybe — deals with one language in another, Korean, English, and even further down to the ground, the characters in each of these languages and how you use them in* Commons *in particular. I wanted to know what you perceive, anticipate, or hope the effect of Korean characters and Roman ones will be on readers with little or no knowledge of the Korean language, specifically the written aspect of Korean for someone not even being exposed to the poem, to the sounds the Korean characters are making. Do you expect the readers to be playful with these characters? Uneasy, and have some aversion to them? Maybe attempt to draw common features between the character and phoneme systems? And overall, what are the effects of these unfamiliar written characters on readers with no exposure to their phonetic mappings?*

Kim: I love it when questions answer themselves. Your question, by including this very intriguing trio of words — aversion, play, and commonality — begins to answer the question the way that I would respond to it. In another conversation I was having today someone said, "When I encounter a text I can't read, I just basically run away." I believe this sense of the turning away (or aversion) is part of reading. But the turning away signals a sense of convolution or evolution or revolution. Something is happening. Something is taking place. Something is under transformation. This is where the notions of play and potential commonality come in. I can't think of any other conjunction as generative as aversion and play.

Liebembuk: *I think that makes sense and leads into me trying to tie that together. Julie also mentioned the untranslatable, and you mentioned these aversions that people may have to the untranslatable as resources for meaning.*

Kim: Yes.

Liebembuk: *My question centers around the very last sentence you wrote in your afterword, which I think you mentioned was a pain for you to actually write, but is very useful in a lot of ways to mobilize the notion of our responsibility to one another in social space. That alone sums up what I got from* Commons *very well, but my question is, specifically, do the poetic images found between languages in whatever space, be it sounded or visual, serve as a pilot light for any human prosody to arise? And I emphasize any there. In other words, in reading* Commons, *studying languages, and hearing stories from varied cultural backgrounds, I personally feel that a prosody emerges in the interplay of two or more languages. Is this what you were dealing with in most of your work? That is, the emergence of poetic forms and praxis from between languages, and, if so, I think this ties in with what a Sioux writer, Vine Deloria, once really hit hard in one of his books,* God Is Red. *It seems to challenge... time in poetry as hegemony and brings space, poetic space, language space into focus. A Romanticist lyric-space can't not be treated in your interplay of Korean and English, where a Myung Mi Kim poem might be set next to a Shelley poem, not because of how they relate in time, but how they relate in poetic space, and how the aversions that maybe a native Korean reader might have to a Shelley poem are different but similar than what I might have to a Myung Mi Kim poem.*

Kim: Let me first respond by saying, yes, absolutely, most of my work is devoted to the emergent prosodies, poetic forms, and praxis prompted by the interplay of plural languages. The conversation that we've been having today, I hope, is precisely in the service of tracking and rendering the complexities of lived time and historical time, potentializing new modes of relation.

"ONCE WE LEAVE A PLACE IS IT THERE": RADICAL PEDAGOGY

Andrew Rippeon

Myung Mi Kim poses the question, early in *Under Flag*, early in her writing: "Once we leave a place is it there."[i] In my reading of Myung's work, and having worked with her in her seminar room, this question is for me an early register of what we might call her radical pedagogical practice. "Once we leave a place is it there"—this marks a pedagogy not simply in the thought-exercise it presents, or in its interrogative character, but in its recognition of the constitutive inter-relationship of space and time and plural subject.

> Pedagogy: the art or science of teaching. [Latin *paedagōgus*: teacher, schoolmaster, slave who took children to and from school...Ancient Greek παιδαγωγός: slave who took children to and from school...παιδ-, παῖς boy, child...ἀγωγός: leading][ii]

So what's come to mean "the art or science of teaching" was once an identity conferred—also questioned—by movement through a particular space. That is, on the way from the home to the school, and *only* on the way from where we rest to where we learn and back, the *paidagogos*, slave, becomes the leader: the *paidagogos* is enslaved by leadership, leads through enslavement. It's important that this jumble of identities occurs in the movement—an ushering of the other—from comfort to concept, and nei¬ther comfort nor concept, at least in their familiar forms ("home"; "school"), appear on the road itself. "Once we leave a place is it there"—we could modify this, imagine it in the mouth of the plural *paidagogos*, and ask: "Once we set out on the way who are we"...

To say Myung's practice is radically pedagogical, then, is to say that it wants to make the primary scene of pedagogy—that dislocation of the plural subject by positioning it in a spatial-temporal interval, rather than at a particular location and time—the very place to which we're being taken, the very matter of the way we've set out upon: "A time of writing as a time of reception. Relativizing."[iii] The epistolary *Spelt*, with Susan Gevirtz, is one example, in more ways than one, of this bringing of the interval to itself. Writing as on the way to *each other*. Writing as the ground upon which each sets out *with the other*. Writing as on the way *to itself*—*Spelt* is bound in transparent endpapers, each side filled with barely legible handwritten notes to the exchange they bind. "This exchange began out of the hope for contact in which the speed of scrawl could be registered..."[iv]

In such a gesture as *Spelt* is in its entirety, the writing becomes the *paidagogos*: plural, restive, led and leading, facilitator of later transformations for other subjects. This is to say that the gesture of *Spelt* is to keep clear the way *between* two subjects and the way *before* the single subject, while yet also calling the subject to an interval somewhere between her own self and work. "Once we leave a place is it there"—who leads and who follows at this point is as potently confused as ever.

In *The Coming Community*, Agamben writes of "the supreme power" of that which "is capable of both power and impotence."[v] This capability to not-be is in fact *the* supreme power: the potentiality that such power reserves for itself—to be able to not-be—is a greater potential than that of the potential to be. Though this might read as a compelling formulation for the lyric poem, or art in general, Agamben, via Aristotle's comparison to the act of writing, moves directly to thought:

> ...thought, in its essence, is pure potentiality; in other words, it is also the potentiality to not think, and, as such, as possible or material intellect, Aristotle compares it to a writing tablet on which nothing is written...[vi]

Perhaps the pedagogical scene I'm trying to evoke shares this rich potentiality: thought reserves itself somewhere on the way between Agamben's "to think" and "to not think." Becoming a plural potential only in so far as, like the *paidagogos*, it can remain unarrived at either end, thought refrains from, resists, the ossified concept as much as cognitive dissolution. Like thought that arrives at concept or falls into void, the pluralizing and qualitative alchemy that pedagogy *was* (was *then*) evaporates into rigid positions if we attempt to say who or what we were during our time between.

But what does this look like? We do go to school (some of us). Myung is a poet and teacher, and "This is the study book."[vii] All of these are some form of arrival, no matter their resistance to or reservation from precisely such. But as we think of the original scene of pedagogy, or Agamben's blank writing tablet—themselves incompletely figuring the potential they as objects can't represent—these arrivals call, through their humility, to the powerful potential of which they now are only a trace. In a practice such as this, writing and thought become indistinguishable from one another: each the back of the other. Agamben again:

> Thanks to this potentiality to not-think, thought can turn back to itself (to its pure potentiality) and be, at its apex, the thought of thought. What it thinks here, however, is not an object, a being-in-an-act, but that layer of wax, that *rasum tabulae* that is nothing but its own passivity, its own pure potentiality (to not-think): In the potentiality that thinks itself, action and passion coincide and the writing tablet writes by itself or, rather, writes its own passivity.[viii]

Each—writing and thought—moving through the other, each leading and led, *paidagogos*-like, by the other. This is what it means to figure Myung's practice as and at a radical pedagogical scene. And the back of this arrival, in turn, is the seminar room itself, a ready wax impressed upon by action and passion. Thus a thinking-writing in the room, the characters of which are wrought through the process of their own heat. And wiped clean by the very same gesture of impress.

The *why* of this un-inscribing inscription—heat of action-passion at once inscribing and obliterating the inscribed to make room for later inscription—is probably clear; or, how I understand this *why* is clear from the way I've moved through this piece. The radical potential in the now-lost original scene of pedagogy was itself only a potential under—only a potential *through*—complete domination. And as the *paidagogos* walked beside the child on the way from home to school, whatever change was wrought among subjects on the way was wrought in and only in the *paidagogos* alone. But it is perhaps the child's voice asking, in *Under Flag*, "Once we leave a place is it there." No longer for the *paidagogos* alone, the plurality of the pedagogical scene is here opened to more than one subject, while power relations among these subjects are disrupted. And the power of this potential, this opening of the scene, is that it might pass unrecognized, that it remain illegible, that it might not-happen.

Pedagogy has today shifted from relationship on the way, to a science of the practice in schools. But as Myung's writing brings its own scene to itself-in-process (and in this is radically pedagogical), her teaching practice is likewise a setting in itself of the practice of the seminar room—a redistribution of responsibility and relationship, and an unsettling of power and production. The practice of her seminar room itself takes into account, counts upon, our individuation from one another prior to both entries to the seminar: as immediate daily event and as periodic, ongoing process. This texture of individuals is complicated and complemented by a deliberate manifold of material, counting again upon difference and the impossibility of mastery, and the inevitable overlaps and lacunae in a plural experience of a poetic field. This calling to and creation of difference becomes, in conversation, a practice of pedagogically shifting positions—leading, following, creating and un-creating, forgetting, recalling. That we arrive as already differentiated subjects, and that the place of the seminar is a place where those differences might contribute to a collective motion toward (yet never an arrival at) a future destination, a collective building (yet never completion) of an edifice in active thought is the most literalized case I can imagine of *entering into* a conversation. "To mobilize the notion of our responsibility to one another in social space."[ix]

In such a radical practice of it as Myung's, pedagogy—which was originally, primarily a relationship in and through space, and is here a scene of self-inscribing and -effacing action-passion—becomes a movement of one space, a space of pure potential, into other spaces via the distribution and pluralization of responsibility. And as with the child's address to the *paidagogos*, plural potentialities on the way trace residues into "home" and "school": "What is the work of household—the moral and just education of a child."[x]

Myung's is a practice of the poem and the classroom that resists arrival and completion in order to reserve for itself transformative potentialities and in order for it to resist oppressive systems of authority and culture: "within a few years it learns to read—if it is a boy—and in this place a catalogue of books may be inserted."[xi] Rather than such a catalogue as constitutive of the subject, rather than subject *as* catalogue as even an enlightened academy sometimes forgets to avoid, instead a writing-thinking as poem as classroom where the heat of creation returns the material to its uncreated potentiality:

> The perfect act of writing comes not from a power to write, but from an impotence that turns back on itself and in this way comes to itself as a pure act...[xii]

> Contemplate the generative power of the designation "illegible" coming to speech[xiii]

Pedagogy, in text and practice, where in no case is it clear where we *are* going, only that we are going. That *we* are going. Pedagogy, where it remains clear that we are a *we*, but who is leading and who is following is thoroughly undone:

> Addressed to no one. Globe and a model
> of the planets. Book of perpetual. Book
> of boulders. Ascending numbers. After
> each enunciation. In the first, what kind
> of education. In the second, crested jay
> to the front, *wasah*, *wabasah*, to the left.
> Sound as it comes. Alkali. Snag snag sang.
> *Usher liberty.*[xiv]

---

[i] Myung Mi Kim. Under Flag (Berkeley, CA: Kelsey St. Press, 1991), 14.

[ii] "Pedagogy" and Pedagogue." The Oxford English Dictionary. oed.com, 21 August 2017.

[iii] Susan Gevirtz and Myung Mi Kim. Spelt (San Francisco, CA: a+bend press, 1999), n.p..

[iv] Ibid, n.p.

[v] Giorgio Agamben. The Coming Community (Minneapolis, MN: The University of Minnesota Pres, 1993), 36.

[vi] Ibid, 36 – 37.

[vii] Myung Mi Kim. The Bounty (Tuscon, AZ: Chax Press, 1996), 13.

[viii] Giorgio Agamben. The Coming Community (Minneapolis, MN: The University of Minnesota Pres, 1993), 37.

[ix] Myung Mi Kim. Commons (Berkeley, CA: The University of California Press, 2002), 111.

[x] Ibid, 108.

[xi] Myung Mi Kim. River Antes (Buffalo, NY: Atticus/Finch Chapbooks, 2006), n.p.

xii   Giorgio Agamben. The Coming Community (Minneapolis, MN: The University of Minnesota Pres, 1993), 37.

xiii   Myung Mi Kim. Commons (Berkeley, CA: The University of California Press, 2002), 110.

xiv   Ibid, 110.

ROUTES IN "THIS ECSTATIC NATION": THE ABCS OF GROWING AS A POET-TRANSLATOR-CRITIC IN BUFFALO

Eun-Gwi Chung

> One is the Population / Numerous enough
> This Ecstatic Nation / Seek – it is Yourself
> Emily Dickinson

1. from A to Z

Arrival is Apart is Access is Abyss is Anti-war Poetry Reading is Alternative is Buffalo is Blank is Broken English is Bleeding is Blob-like is Between is Community is Construction is Clearing is Concrete is Clemens Hall is Context is Content is Capital is Condition is Choosing is Crisis is Diction is Dictation is Dream is Deform is Deconstruction is Design is Death is Difference is English is english is Expectation is Evacuation is Editing is Flower is Form is fuck is Fragment is Flight is Gender is Grids is High is Hello is Hell low is Horizon is Identification is Interlude is Jet lag is Korean is Language is Lake Erie is Memory is Margin is Niagara is Niagara is Niawanda is Opaque is Path is Pronunciation is Passing is Past is Politics is Population is Public is Practical is Press is Pushing is Plurality is Question is Queer is Rust Belt is Repetition is Relation I Response is Responsibility is Stutter is Sound is Sense is Slant is Structure is Signpost is Small Press is Talking Leaves is Leaving is Transnational is Translation is Tying is Universal is Not universal is Urgency is Vernacular is Verizon is Ways of Seeing is Wednesday @ 4 is Writing is Writing @ 4 Plus is Whatever is Xrossing is Yellow is Zero

2. B u f f a l o / June 28 00

Arrival. Late afternoon. Sunlight. A tarred road, torn, turned, and shattered. Arrival is not arrival till you get the right name of the place. In quest of irresistible dictation and destination, if there be. Arrival understands itself on that dazzling day with language, dictation with talking, with a word of commanding. When I am asked about my destination at the airport immigration desk, I say, "Buffalo," and the guy at the desk angrily retorts, "What?" and I say without noticing his tiresome anger, "Oh, Buffalo. You know, Buffalo, the city of Niagara." And after a good while, I realize that I mispronounced the word as buh-fah-loh as is frequently called in Korea, not **buhf-*uh*-loh**, the right pronunciation in the United States.

Apart from my language, day 1, a clean, shiny, dazzling, shiny day, a typical Summer Buffalo. Day 2, I spend the whole day at the Niagara Falls. I am ill in bed for the whole night. Sublime, I come to know what it means, really. The one who is loved "to be astonished" in this new city, I am shocked and recovered, quickly and quietly. And yet, I don't know that my Buffalo summers would be filled with many new and old visitors playing in water wearing disposable blue raincoats on the "maid of the mist" under the falls. Day 3 is allotted for the Allegany State Park. I don't have to think about the nation, people, and family I left temporarily, just a road and another road and another road, all in straight lines, and trees are enough and enough for me. Yes, I am happy. Day 4, I go out by myself with a dog-eared map that my friend gave to me. I am enough and wet with the pleasure that I finally succeed in getting into my lovable city to read and write poetry. I don't know yet. I arrive at the City Buffalo but I am not reached yet, but anyway, arrival is arrival, enough is enough.

Access denied. For the years I stayed in Buffalo, my friends in Korea would think that Buffalo is part of New York City, not New York States. From time to time I would get a call from this and that friend saying "I just arrived in New York for business, would you come and meet me, if not busy?" I have to say, "Why not? I will come and meet you if you give me 9 hours. Would you wait for me there?" Our conversation always ends with some sigh and giggling. Next time, I would tell like a tour guide that Buffalo is a city in western New York State and the county seat of Erie County, on the eastern shore of Lake Erie at the head of the Niagara River. And later, I would tell my friends that I live in "An All America City" borrowing the phrase in the big road sign somewhere in the Highway 90.

In Buffalo, every reading and writing activity is a social, political event that marks the days indelible, endurable, and prolonged. It is also very concrete and private. So many poetry readings and gatherings at Wednesday @ 4 Plus, Rust Belt Books, Just Buffalo Literary Center, and Gender Week poetry reading, and Anti-war poetry reading after 911, etc. The many unexpected meetings with unexpected facts, faces, and voices tell us that Buffalo is the city of poetry. I spend the hours at Rust Belt Books, 202 Allen Street, Buffalo, browsing the stack and sniffing the scent of old books. Special events include Rust Belt Books poetry reading with Anna Reckin, Sandra Guerreiro, on Oct. 25, 2001, and the reading with Kimiko Hahn on Sep. 19, 2002 is also unforgettable. In Gender week poetry reading, jokes that gender does not referring to male, gender is just permitted to female are floating here and there. Once, I read my poem on "comfort women."

> *"Poem 1"*
> *Silence Broken shatters a half-century of silence for*
> *Korean women forced into sexual servitude by the*
> *Japanese Imperial Army during World War II. .Jungun*
> *Wianbu in Korea, literally military comfort women.*
> *"comfort women" is a euphemism for women forced to*
> *serve as sex slaves for Japanese Imperial soldiers during*
> *World War II. Many advocates want to replace the*
> *term, "comfort women" with military sex slaves (MSS).*
> *I choose to keep the term, because "comfort" is closer*
> *to the horrendous dehumanization with such a chilling*
> *casualness. (by Dai Sil Kim-Gibson in -Silence Broken-)*
>
> *Mr. Chairman, how much compensation do you think*
> *ought to be paid to a woman who was raped 7,500*

> *times. (by Karen Parker in UNITED NATIONS*
> *COMMISSION ON HUMAN RIGHTS)*

after kidnapped from their home, shipped like military supplies to far-off places,

after suffering the insufferable, they went home

only to be silenced.

HENCE, HEREBY

Her sealed voice was heard on that day it was broken out

through the secrets of a half-century,

Not for whom not for what

Not for who said what what is said by whom

To untie the tied to tie the untied to seal the unsealed to unseal the sealed

Han(한/恨)

is the word, the tangled knot in your heart

is not sorrow, not anger, harrowing is the word

undeniable is the word, is riveting is the word

is intolerable is the word, the world, is powerful is gut-wrenching

is the word the world is moving is stunning is stirring is affecting is horrible

is touching is cutting is compelling is chilling it   is   it

is but it isn't   but it isn't   it isn't

I am sorry. Does it hurt you? I don't want to move you I don't want to touch you

I want to untie the tied I want to break the unbroken, the silence of my blood, of my body, the silence of my lips the memory of my thighs

shattering my flesh and blood knotting your body and flesh, I don't want to tie I don't want to break

> *Sometimes I wish I had died in Rabaul. If I had died, I would not have brought my children into this world and given them such hardship. My last hope is to buy a house for*

> *my uneducated son, the poor thing. That's all.*

> *When my cuts and bruises had healed slightly, they put me back*

> *into the same room. And another soldier raped me in the room.*

the word of memory, the world of absence, flowing in the endless forgetting,

marked in that room with the brutal soldiers, inscribed in us, you and I, in my moms and your grandmas,

engraved in this living room.

the word

possible only by being silenced

being a hurt, a taboo, being a lethal dart into your own being

It is

it isn't   (e. gwi)

Pain generally lacks a voice, disgrace and horror, too. It is a dangerous route, obviously, for a poet, to voice a taboo, to touch the realm you never know. Without any expectations you just wait for the moment when some other voice knocks and awakens you in the form of poetry. It is a route that can't never be fully realized, can't never be safely fulfilled. It becomes present just in writing as blank, as reverie. I am a little bit scared facing the impossibility of voicing a person whose presence is marked only in its blank erasure and mourning, in the form of afterlife. Yes, voicing others' experience quite unknown to me is like standing in front of abysmal silence and touching, fumbling an unseen screen. The answer to the hesitating touch arrives at rather unexpected moments. I try to weave the moments of endless forgetting and mourning between two different temporal spaces then and here, two different languages here and there. How can I find the form of discovery from the wide, still latent, territory of the buried lives? Is the language of witness and testimony, risky and foolhardy, enough for putting her painful body and humiliation with no compromise in the new frontline of history? There is no definite way to write and talk, no linear line of memory in that buried body of witness. Waiting, listening, and gazing are all you need.

Day after day, each of us responds to the signs of Buffalo Poetics culture experimenting unexpected routes, forms, and records. The population of reading and listening to poetry is one and one is enough and enough for "this ecstatic nation" that occupies our curiosity, uncertain vastness. Shots of memories are piled as poems and spread beyond the isolated walls in 102, Robert Drive, North Tonawanda. Holding the hours, days, months, and years in Buffalo in language needs an interpretable reminder and we are happy by being each other's witness and critical listener. My double consciousness then and now is still lingering in a margin of the city, in the trail roads of the Niagara River and Falls. Arrival is arrival. Arrival is not arrival. It's nowhere and everywhere. The very fact that there is no origin in the middle perplexes me but it is also an omen and oath to be a poet-translator.

3. Interlude

> The term 'origin' does not mean the process by which the existent came into being, but rather what emerges from the process of becoming and disappearing.
> Origin is an eddy in the stream of becoming.
> --Walter Benjamin

To be a translator is far different from being a poet or critic. Why do I translate, for what? To translate is to repeat something in difference. It is to return to a certain spot of language, the term origin becomes problematic in translation. As is origin "Returning," a poem by Korean modern poet Kim Jiha, is the first translation of my Buffalo day. "Magnolia blossoms, / its white light flies into the sky lonely, / Torn by the wind, / petals one by one / go back to the soil // Going back, the young days," Here the poet calls forth the young souls who died for democracy during the April 19 Revolution in Korea. Fullness of petals, of youth is scattered, corporeal things in this world are transposed into the language of engagement.

When I am invited to translate some modern Korean poems into English and introduce them in the Modern Poetry Class, I realize translation is a creative activity of hospitality, an event of imagining community that nobody knows its final results. The question of community and creativity is engaged with interrelated issues of the public and the private, the origin and the original, viable and unnegotiable. Translating poems is not easy; there is an inevitable conflict between the source and the target language.

Translators very often feel torn caught in conflicts between the source and the target. The language of translation is the language of process and inquiry, not the language of close and termination. It's to build once the hermit's cave where a translator constructs a space in the void, the *third* space, responsive and responsible, and a new form of 'after-life' is the body-territory where concern and aspiration are changed into reciprocal relationships. As a poet, I am happily apprehensive. As a translator, I am unhappily happy. I become a betrayer who steals its own language from the original land and gives it to her quite unknown lover. Yes, aspiration always beats concern. May your tongue be twisted and your home lost forever, but most of your tongue would be alive again.

4. Tonawanda / Aug. 7 05

A good word comes with a headache. On August, 2005, I get an email saying that I am chosen as the recipient of 2005 Korean Literature Translation by the Daesan Foundation in Seoul. I am very lucky to have Myung Mi Kim as a co-translator for the project. I remember the wide room where I and Myung shared our mutual understanding and interest on poetics and translation. The room is rather dark. Something drapes the walls. It's a short day of Buffalo winter Buffalo and then it's a long day of short summer Buffalo. Myung has a right eye to understand the Korean poems by Lee Seong-bok and a right ear to listen to the voices of the "Mouthless Things." We talk and talk on how can we make the double voices and sometimes contradictory stories heard and presented in translation? How to do with the passages that refuse translation? In every poem, there is refusal to be defined and translated. How to address the foregrounded incompletion and leakage in another language?

Up to a point, translation is a process that realizes the dream of the audience. Translating modern Korean poems into English, we try to dismantle and invert the hierarchy of the original, and in the process, we find that the place of translation always offers the space of interpretation, embracing and being tormented by the virtues of the excess of meanings. It is in this critical dialogue with Myung, coupled with a continual attention to lived experience of different languages that I confirm my role as a translator-poet-critic. Myung, articulating her questions about the original poem in Korean, helps me to construct a possible wall of resistance against both the fixed meaning of a sentence and boundless extension of meanings. Once dwelling in possibility and danger of choosing and not choosing, we happily travel untraveled routes that few try to do.

Translation is not a passive way of reading a given text. It is always connected to a very lively, critical way of thinking. My translation always begins with a question; as a mode of thinking, as a constructive site for returning, where can poetry in translation be found? What is it to be a poet-translator-critic in and out of academia? Calling out the questions of my Buffalo days again here and now, I can't help confessing to a sense of déjà vu in two aspects. To write something on Buffalo Poetics is to rethink about the role of poetry in the republic of anti-poetry, here and there, then and now. Poetry has always been in the excluded outskirts of main-culture in the most marginalized form. A poet-translator-critic is a person who displays a vast tolerance and merrily repeats the questions again and again and untiredly constitutes a relationship between different languages and nations.

Moreover, writing from the divided-country under the serious threat to everyday safety and national security, I feel weird as if I repeat the same questions entailed in translation for the politics, too, for example, what can Trump do, what can Kim Jong Eun do? This sense of déjà vu is, after all, changed into another question of poetry; crisis and poetry, poetry and politics, language and impassability. I can't understand what you mean, Trump, I can't follow you, Kim Jong Eun, and in quite the same way, I hear people's complaint about poetry; I can't get it. I can't do that. What is this one? What is this place? Or can I see and revive the flower of yesterday again in a different land for a different people?

In a poem "What is This Place" by Lee Seong-Bok, the question of location, "what is this place" is transposed into the recognition of violent returning. "The crimson sun, stubbed by mountain peaks, / Bleeds, soaking the sky with blood, / Its belly slashed with the saw blade of a rocky ridge, / No thought of sewing it up. / —What is this place? / — May I come by and bleed like this every day?[i]" With no expectation on recovering, we repeat the same pattern, the same route, we are incurable crossers. Contrary to what a first glance might have said, this poem is not about depicting the melancholy beauty of nature. It is about loss and mourning, the act of remembering, of repeating, of repenting, and of course, the act of resisting against erasure and extinction. The poet seeks to put poetry in a very complex provocation in rather a casual form of conversation.

Or, the act of translation is to gaze the flower in yesterday's sky, or blossoming as some other's body. "Love is not / inside a person loving. / Rather, a person loves / inside of love. // A flower stalks jammed / into the narrow neck of a vase / withers with the musty smell of a floor / and the flower is in yesterday's sky." It is to find the by-gone trace of yesterday's love, yesterday's glory, yesterday's sky, yesterday's language. I quite well know, as a translator, the endeavor is easy to stop somewhere in the middle, as if jammed in the narrow neck of a vase. There is, however, a huge consolation in translation. Even if my language remains incomplete, it's not the fault of poetry, its direction of desire is embraced within the consistent quest for alternative language.

5. 432, Clemens Hall, 2004

When I firstly groped the possibility of translating Korean poems into English in Buffalo, I just focused on conceptualizing the task of translation as being an access or a channel between two different languages. I didn't ask, for example, where and in what form does a literary translator reside. I thought of literary translation as an interpretation and exposition and I didn't have a fear about being against the grain of the original text. Yearning to cross two different languages was much fiercer than the fear on literary translation as transgression. But now, even after I saw the publication of my third poetry book of translation *Ah Mouthless Things!* (Green Integer, 2017) following *Fifteen Seconds Without Sorrow* (2016) and *The Colors of Dawn: Twentieth-*

Century Korean Poetry (2016), I find myself going back to the trace of the fallen petals of magnolia, or the numberless white petals that I see in the room 432, Clemens Hall.

Sitting under the painting of Susan Bee's "The Lighthouse" looking out of the window, I wonder whether the law of gravity is a right or not. Bob Creeley is sitting next to me. Out of the window, the wind blows from the little lake and I see dust and white shredded papers flowing high in the wind. It seems like that I can draw the wind map, a beautiful animated visualization of the air and the lake. Yes, translation, as the activity of hospitality, as the event of unexpected surprise, is to go against the law of gravity in languages, for me, I am firmly rooted in Korea, but again, both Korean and English is quite foreign to me. I can't find any suitable and stable space for poetry translation; I am alienated from both languages and 'after-life' born in translation resides in the undefinable zone like the white dust and shredded papers blowing in the air. Translation, like origin, is an eddy in the stream of becoming. It has a form, exerting some power for further questions with no end. Translation, repetition, origin, original, enough is not enough, enough is enough.

6. Seoul, Aug 24 2017

Despite my original plan to draw kind of analytic impulse on my writing, on my route to be a translator-poet-critic, I am keenly aware of the impossibility of drawing an entire map. At points where remembrance exerts a particular pressure here and now as a professor-scholar, my response easily stops in front of anxiety. Drawing the route here and then, I find landscape recurring and returning. Meanwhile, my mapping of Buffalo days extends beyond Buffalo to include Seoul, the past and the cities I never saw. All spots of time in the process reflect my reading of difference in the text, in everyday life, here in Seoul and there in Buffalo. The longing in the face of the lost becomes the force to maintain the missing.

Still I do not know how to build a proper relationship between Korean and American, between the living and the lost, how to get a grid of translation, a continuously imperiled and perpetually ongoing form. Ten more years have passed since I came back to my own country. But even here, arrival is not arrival yet. One obvious fact is that in the never-properly-reached arrival, I am happily dependent on my incomplete gesture, tongue, and deposits of time and memory that wait to become vocables. Fragments radically interrogate the by-gone moments and ask where the location of warps and wefts of geography is.

Still I fumble the unborn words of poetry in Korean and in English and still search for the physicality of this and that body, of this and that language in my everyday life. To mark the ABCs of my Buffalo days, I start with spots of time and prolong the span of time and place. Now I find both beginning and end are never simply given. Like translation. Like poetry. Please let me not be too hasty. Here at the end is the beginning. I keep looking and talking. Just Buffalo, "This ecstatic nation" is numerous here and there, then and now, like arrival, like urgency, like poetry, like translation.

i   Lee Seong-Bok, *Ah, Mouthless Things* (Los Angeles: Green Integer, 2017) 11.

THE POETICS PROGRAM AND THE POETRY
COLLECTION, 2001 TO PRESENT
(A PERSONAL HISTORY)

James Maynard

Since its first semester in the fall of 1991, the Poetics Program has enjoyed a mutually beneficial relationship with the Poetry Collection of the University Libraries, and together they have made the University at Buffalo (UB) an internationally renowned place for the study of modern and contemporary poetry and poetics. For my contribution to this volume I was asked by the editor to talk about the relationship between the Poetics Program and the Poetry Collection during my time at the university. As someone infinitely fortunate to have been involved as I have with both facets of poetry in Buffalo, it seems to me that the best way to do so is by starting with my own personal experience.

I arrived in Buffalo to begin a PhD in the English Department's Poetics Program in the summer of 2001 after completing an MA in Creative Writing at Temple University in Philadelphia. For many years the two schools have been something like sister programs, and having enjoyed Temple's focus on innovative writing and the social contexts in which it is produced, and especially my work with Rachel Blau DuPlessis and Jena Osman (herself a graduate of the Poetics Program), UB seemed the natural place to continue my studies. I immediately found myself within an intensely active poetry community created by students in the Poetics Program. From my visits to Rust Belt Books I was aware of earlier student presses and publications like *Leave Books, Meow Press*, and *apex of the M*, and by then Jena Osman and Juliana Spahr's *Chain*, although no longer published in Buffalo, had developed into a nationally renowned journal for innovative writing, but what so thoroughly impressed me was all that was happening in the present.

From the beginning it seemed like everyone I met was editing a magazine, printing chapbooks, and/or organizing readings. In my first two years alone there were new issues being produced for the magazines *Ecopoetics* (Jonathan Skinner), *Kenning* (Patrick Durgin), *Kiosk* (an older departmental publication revitalized by Gordon Hadfield, Sasha Steensen, and Kyle Schlesinger), *Rust Talks* (both a performance series and a publication edited by Kristen Gallagher and Tim Shaner), and *Verdure* (Chris Alexander and Linda Russo). Chapbooks were being stapled and stitched together, often with letterpressed covers and digitally printed texts—for a while each generation of printers would teach any new students who were interested how to use the Vandercook machine in the Art department, and now much of the letterpress printing takes place at the Western New York Book Arts Center—by presses such as *Cuneiform* (still in operation and run by Kyle Schlesinger), *Handwritten Press* (Kristen Gallagher), and *Little Scratch Pad* (Doug Manson). Among other publications, Michael Kelleher was continuing his collaborative Elevator box project featuring a different editor, artist, and writers each year. Terry Cuddy and Mirela Ivanciu, from UB's department of Media Studies and Fine Arts/Photography, respectively, had recorded performances from a number of Poetics students and others that they released on a VHS tape titled *Transient Views of Western*

New York (2001). In addition to the influx of visiting poets coming to read in Buffalo almost every week for the Poetics Program's departmental Wednesdays at 4 Plus schedule, there were at the same time student-run reading series like Another Reading Series (Barbara Cole, Gordon Hadfield, and Sasha Steensen), Exchange Rate (featuring poets traveling from Buffalo to Toronto to read and vice versa), and ñ (enye) (Rosa Alcalá) that would meet in students' apartments and feature readings by students in the program as well as others. Also taking place were student-organized events like the Prose Acts conference organized by Christopher Alexander and Brandon Stosuy during my first semester. As has always been the case with the Poetics Program, it was a community based in large part on the collaborative activity of making, and I loved it from the start. (Since then, I've had the immense pleasure of witnessing firsthand many more student magazines, presses, publications, reading series, and conferences during my sixteen years in Buffalo.)

My first real introduction to the Poetry Collection occurred in the winter of 2002. For my second semester I was organizing an independent reading group on the poet Robert Duncan with other students in the Poetics Program. We needed to find a faculty supervisor who would meet with us a few times and sign off on our work. I asked Robert Creeley and Charles Bernstein and both suggested I talk to Robert Bertholf, who at the time was Curator of the Poetry Collection and the executor of Duncan's literary estate. In hindsight, my approaching Bob to be our supervisor, and his agreement to meet with our group and introduce us to Duncan's papers, was a life-changing moment, although like most such moments it would take me years to realize it. That semester, Bob (or "Dr. Bertholf," as everyone called him; I think I can count on one hand the number of times I called him Bob before he passed away in February 2016) was extremely generous in sharing with us over several meetings his own particular appreciation of Duncan's poetry—an intimate understanding developed over decades of study, numerous editorial and critical publications, and a long friendship with the poet and his partner, the artist Jess—as seen through Duncan's manuscripts, notebooks, and correspondence. It was an inspiring tour of the collection, and my first time ever looking seriously at archival materials.

After our last meeting together, Bob told us all to keep in touch, and that there were an infinite number of dissertation projects to be found in the Poetry Collection as well as part-time jobs for graduate students. So that summer I took him at his word and asked about any opportunities for work. Unfortunately nothing was available. The next semester I asked again, and the answer was the same: nothing. I don't think I even asked the following spring, and so was surprised to get an email from him in May 2003 that simply read: "Jim, You asked about summer employment. Mike [Basinski, then his Assistant Curator] and I have a deal for you. Call up." The rest, as they say, is history, and I went on to enjoy a happy apprenticeship working with two of the Poetry Collection's former curators. After starting off assisting editorially on a number of Duncan projects with Bertholf, who was also a member of my dissertation committee, I became his graduate assistant in 2004. After he retired in 2007, I began working in a larger capacity with the entire collection with former curator Michael Basinski, and proceeded to serve as assistant to the curator (first as an instructor and then adjunct), visiting assistant curator, assistant curator, and associate curator before being named the collection's seventh curator in September 2016. If Bertholf introduced me to the fields of archival study in general and to Robert Duncan in particular, it was Basinski who gave me my full education in how to care for and continue building a collection like the Poetry Collection. Bertholf and Basinski: two debts I can never fully repay.

As my own story demonstrates, the Poetics Program and the Poetry Collection have enjoyed a healthy partnership over the years, and one that has provided both sides with tangible benefits. From the program's beginnings in the early 1990s, Robert Bertholf was a "primary advisor" to and frequent co-conspirator with the original core faculty of Charles Bernstein, Robert Creeley, Raymond Federman, Susan Howe, and Dennis Tedlock. Since then the curators have often worked closely with the faculty in the program as well as the English department in general; lectured to graduate and undergraduate seminars on different special topics and aspects of the collection; served on degree committees; mentored students working on class assignments as well as theses and dissertations; organized related exhibitions; and participated in Poetics programming. The Poetry Collection and the Poetics Program have regularly collaborated on events, with the collection often serving as the physical location for the program's readings, lectures, conferences, and other activities. Indeed, it has been wonderful to welcome many of the Wednesdays at 4 Plus and Poetics Plus visiting writers and scholars to the collection and to have them sign their books during their visit. We have also been extremely fortunate over the years to hire a number of Poetics students to work in the collection as student assistants and graduate assistants and to help with grants and other special projects, always benefiting from their individual expertise in modern and contemporary Anglophone poetry. Finally, in addition to serving as a repository for all of the program's student and faculty publications over the years (although undoubtedly, given the fugitive nature of some of these materials, there are items we are missing), the Poetry Collection also holds archival collections for such student presses and publications as *Chain, Kiosk, Handwritten Press, Meow Press*, and *Uprising Press*, as well as the radio show LINEbreak.

Given these overlapping relationships that have existed over the last 26 years, it was personally a great pleasure to organize the retrospective exhibition Poetry in the Making: The UB Poetics Program 1991-2016 from March 21 through August 29, 2016 in the Poetry Collection's reading room. Presented in conjunction with the Poetics Program's twenty-fifth anniversary conference Poetics: (The Next) 25 Years and serving as the site of its reception on April 9, the exhibition celebrated the history of the program through a selection of its faculty and student publications (including books, chapbooks, magazines, broadsides, and more); historical documents; reading and event posters; announcements for student-organized conferences and radio shows, magazines, and talk series; calendars for the Wednesday at 4 Plus (Fall 1990 – Fall 2004) and Poetics Plus (Spring 2005 – Spring 2016) reading series; photographs; and ephemera. As a supplement to the exhibition, which was only barely able to scratch the surface of the Poetics Program's history, the Poetry Collection published *Poetry in the Making*, the most complete bibliography of publications by graduate students in the Poetics Program that I could produce using the resources of the Poetry Collection. (This appeared as the inaugural issue of *Among the Neighbors*, a pamphlet series for the study of little magazines edited by the Poetry Collection's cataloger Edric Mesmer.) In my introduction to the bibliography, I suggest that, though the Poetics Program's history has been largely organized around provisional and situated responses to the open-ended question *what is poetics?*, the more particular question of *what has been the poetics of the UB Poetics Program?* can be best addressed empirically by looking at what its graduate students make while they are in Buffalo. "In my experience," I wrote, "biased as it surely is, I've always believed that the best indicator of the program's evolving poetics, not to mention its longstanding vitality, can be found in the activities of its students and especially their publications."

On a grander scale, this approach to studying the evolution of poetry through its many iterations in different material forms was at the heart of Charles Abbott's decision in the mid-1930s to begin assembling the Poetry Collection in the manner that he did. In his essay "Origins to 1978, The University at Buffalo's Poetry Collection," Curator Emeritus Michael Basinski outlines Abbott's early development of the Poetry Collection and its subsequent history through 1978. Today, as the library of record for twentieth- and twenty-first-century Anglophone poetry, we continue to expand (albeit more inclusively) Charles Abbott's attempt to capture all that is happening across the spectrum of poetry in English, a mission that from the beginning has been predicated on notions of totality and flux. Synchronically, our goal—impossible as it always is—is to document the sum total of Anglophone poetry at any given historical moment. Diachronically, we aim to provide researchers with all the primary and secondary sources necessary, among other uses, to be able to map out the evolution of writing over time by individual poets as well as in poetry itself as a living and social art form. In order to accomplish these goals, we collect almost all forms of print publication from the centers and the margins of poetic culture without prejudice and as exhaustively as funds allow. Today the library is comprehensive in its collection of first and other bibliographically significant editions (140,000+), little literary magazines and journals (9,000+ titles), broadsides (7,000+), anthologies, criticism, and reference materials. Additionally, the Poetry Collection holds more than 150 archives and manuscript collections from a wide range of poets, presses, magazines and organizations including James Joyce, William Carlos Williams, Helen Adam, Robert Duncan, Robert Graves, Dylan Thomas, Jargon, and Wyndham Lewis. The collection is also a regional repository for many of the publishers and arts organizations of Western New York. There are also substantial collections of artwork, audio recordings, posters, ephemera, photographs, visual poetry, mail art, and zines, making it one of the largest poetry libraries of its kind in the world. As an active research center for the study of modern and contemporary poetry, the Poetry Collection supports with its materials a wide range of scholarly publications; opens its doors to visiting researchers from around the world; assists with the educational activities of undergraduate and graduate students at UB and elsewhere; hosts lectures, conferences, readings and other events; and loans items to exhibitions.

On both a practical as well as a theoretical level, the Poetry Collection and the Poetics Program have been highly compatible with one another. In terms of practice, given its expansive collecting parameters, the Poetry Collection has amongst its holdings virtually all of the publications by and about those twentieth- and twenty-first-century Anglophone writers (and in some cases their select manuscripts too) associated with the innovative writing practices and communities that have long been of interest to the Poetics Program (e.g., high Modernism, Objectivism, Black Mountain and New American Poetry, New York School, Language Poetry, New Narrative, HOW(ever), electronic poetry, post-Language, Flarf, contemporary visual poetry, ecopoetics, Conceptualism, etc.). More generally, however, the two share in common a fundamentally progressive view of poetry as being in a constant state of transformation. "The defining vision of the program," as I wrote in the introduction to the Poetics Program student bibliography, in a statement that I believe applies equally to the Poetry Collection, "is based on an anti-foundational understanding of poetry— i.e., the processural activity of poiesis—as a liminal field always evolving out of its multiform past in response to the overlapping aesthetic, social, and political needs of the present. Its approach to poetry is a radical praxis in both senses of the word: rooted in particular theories and traditions and yet constantly branching out into progressively new and unforeseen directions." Certainly this view is at the heart of the program's "philosophies" as articulated by its five founders. In the Poetry Collection as originally conceived by Abbott, the physical evidence of such changes is largely the rationale for looking at the evolution of writing from drafts to little magazine appearances to chapbooks to first editions on through subsequent iterations. For me, as a former student and proponent of the Poetics Program's ethos (characterized generally by an openness to formal innovation, a respect for all forms of linguistic alterity, ethnopoetics' insistence on the significance of sound and oral performance, and an emphasis on writing as social practice) and as a curator who works specifically with writing's material history of multiplicity (variants and versions) and the various contexts (visual, historical, social, biographical, literary) in which it is always situated, poetry is most present in the process of its being made.

I would like to end here by describing a recent collaboration that I think demonstrates the transformative possibilities of both the Poetics Program and the Poetry Collection working together in concert. In the fall of 2015 a group of graduate students (Brandon Boudreault, Allison Cardon, George Life, Claire Nashar, Sean Pears, Jake Reber, Dan Swenson, and Corey Zielinski) asked me if I would supervise a reading group for those interested in discussing the significance of the Poetry Collection and its mutually constitutive relationship with the Poetics Program, its historical development and archival practices, and the importance of such a poetry archive in the twenty-first century. Their idea was that, after some collective discussion about the history of the Poetry Collection and its philosophies, each member of the group would then undertake a self-guided research project involving items from the archive or else otherwise in some particular relationship to it. My only requirements were that they design a project that would allow them to explore what most excited them about the Poetry Collection and/or its holdings, and that they ultimately presented their findings and ideas in whatever form of writing seemed best suited. So together we developed a reading list, and in the first week of December we met to discuss the history and curatorial practices of the Poetry Collection. Afterward each of the eight participants began designing a small research/writing project to be completed within the next three months, and we continued to meet accordingly on an individual basis.

The culmination of their work was the publication of *Launched in Context: Seven Essays on the Archive* (April 2016), which the graduate students edited and published and publicly introduced themselves as part of the Poetics Program's semester-long 25th anniversary celebration. (As a complement to the virtual exhibition performed in each of the essays, the students then had an opportunity the following September to design and present an actual physical exhibition of their projects.) Like all archival research, which regardless of where it begins can swerve unpredictably, each small project started as an experiment: tentative forays into manuscripts, speculative inductions, errancies in search of meaning. For some, this process involved examining unpublished manuscripts (or in one case the lack thereof) to learn something about the writing process and poetics of poets like William Carlos Williams, Marianne Moore, Robert Duncan, and Bob Kaufman. Others were more interested in staging readings of the archive itself and one's embodied experience of it. Issues of permission, order, race, coincidence, (mis)recognition, waste, quotation, gender, memory, anxiety, information, and authority were all variously addressed, and some of the writings intentionally contained traces of their initial uncertainty in order to bear witness to the conditions that make meaning possible in the first place. All are a pleasure to read, and testify to that larger adventure of thinking to which both the Poetry Collection and the Poetics Program are both committed: namely, the personal transformation of the past into new meanings.

ONCE AND FUTURE BUFFALO POETICS: (THE NEXT) 25 YEARS CONFERENCE

Evelyn Reilly

A Buffalo of the mind

In the late '90s and early '00s, the idea of "Buffalo" became part of my life as a poet on a course of self-education into the world of experimental poetics. I was working in a job with no connection to poetry or academia, but lived just off the Bowery in New York City. This made it possible to go to readings at St. Marks Poetry Project on Wednesday evenings, to the Segue Series at The Bowery Poetry Club on Saturdays, even catch the last productions of Richard Foreman's Ontological Hysteric Theater. In retrospect, all this was astonishing piece of good fortune. Part of the lucky brew were the many poets who had passed through the SUNY Buffalo Poetics Program, who, even with their inevitable critiques, carried its broadly intellectual and self-consciously avant garde aura. I was also aware of Buffalo's visual art and music scene and began to create a mental construct that was as much Cindy Sherman as Robert Creeley and Charles Bernstein. Sometimes I'd say to people that I would have lost less time in the dislocating wastelands of the mainstream poetry world if I'd gone to Buffalo. After all it was where the author of *My Emily Dickinson* taught.[i]

Fast forward to spring 2016 and a conference organized in celebration of the Poetics Program's 25th year anniversary. I was drawn to the idea of finally experiencing Buffalo "in the flesh," especially as the poetry of Judith Goldman and Myung Mi Kim, who were among the organizers, was important to me. I was also interested in the question posed—"What is the poetics of the next 25 years?"[ii]

In the intervening years between my Buffalo-as-Camelot construct and this conference much had happened in the poetry world as I experienced it. Experimental poetry by people of color overflowed the podium of the Poetry Project. The poetic hi-jinks of Flarf, then Conceptualism, and for a short period Flarfy-Conceptualism, morphed into Post-Conceptualism. To the continued vitality of what Joan Retallack named "the experimental feminine" in 1999,[iii] was added the expanding explorations of queer poetry and poetics. And so-called "ecopoetics," whose eponymous journal was launched in Buffalo by Jonathan Skinner,[iv] began to exit its genre-ghetto.

House of Hope?

One immediate regret I had about the conference was that I couldn't arrive early enough to attend the first night's discussion of Creeley and French poetry, which included Norma Cole and Jean Daive, among others. So I was pleased to encounter Cole's hanging sculpture House of *Hope—in Memoriam, Montien Boonma 1953-2000* in the exhibit space of the Poetry Collection. Composed of hundreds of quotations from artists, writers, and philosophers printed on streamers, which were suspended from an overhead armature, the piece was, as explained by Cole, "a book you could walk inside of, a book you could feel, touch."[v] Watching clusters of people playfully moving in and out of it, I felt it encapsulated many of my hopes for events such this conference—the interaction of actual poetic bodies with the words of others and the recombinations of those bodies, transposed from their usual habitats, into new social formations. Cole had stated that all the pieces of the original installation of which *House of Hope* had been a part engaged "with the nature of memory, the future-past," which also seemed relevant to the aspirations of such gatherings.

References to alternative tenses have taken on a distinct "Anthropocene ring" to me in recent years, as have many other expressions and phrases. Many of these filtered through the talks and conversations that weekend, as the very term Anthropocene has begun to haunt our communal imagination, conjuring as it does a vision of a rock formation in which our own fossil remains lie intermingled with evidence of extreme temperatures and mass extinctions. This is a "future-past" that can make Walter Benjamin's angel of history, with its backward look on the trail of human wreckage as it is propelled forward by a storm of progress, seem unintentionally prescient in an environmental sense.

There were many notions of present-future and future-past poetics at the conference. There were also, and I find this to be characteristic of our biocultural moment, the usual side references to impending catastrophe. I see this as a kind of nervous acknowledgement of the frailty of our current circumstances, in this case including our poetic circumstances, heightened by the almost quaint hopefulness represented by the carefully tended archives of the Poetry Collection.

A good example of this phenomenon took place during a panel titled "Landscapes, Mappings, Networks: Digital/Material Crossings."[vi] The papers given at this panel—one of two "ecopoetic" panels of the conference—made reference to many current coordinates of disaster: post-industrial waste sites, illness caused by urban power grids, global economics, and the dispiriting energy footprint of our digital lives. One of the panelists, Mark Wallace, ended his presentation by saying "The universe doesn't care, do we?" which elicited the usual uncomfortable laughter.

A similar tone and vocabulary were laced through the titles of numerous seminars and papers—bodies at risk, crisis, post-crisis, urgent, dire times, mourning, resistance, sick space, traumatic violence, in the breach, disembodiment—a collection of words notably drawn from all the panels and seminars, not just the ecopoetic panels or the seminar titled "New Poetic Ecologies." The latter, convened by Stephen Collis, turned out to be a very congenial conversation among self-identified Anthropocene cultural investigators, many of whom, I was pleased to discover, were young and impressively smart.

My own panel, titled "Constructive Alterities in Feminist Ecological Poetics," proposed a re-drawing of the lineage of an evolving ecological poetics, asserting that "a radically inclusive and cross-gender dynamic, has long informed the ecological imagination and the invention of ecological forms and themes in poetry." This panel included Brenda Hillman's charting of the fruitful and diverse terrain of women's work in ecopoetry in the experimental mode, Angela Hume's discussion of Audre Lorde's "survival poetics" as a strategy against erasure of the environmental and social context of her lyric practice, and my own discussion of the "feminine ecopoetics" of the art of Camille Henrot. It concluded with an important talk by Joan Retallack on the patriarchal relationship to and metaphors of the natural world (with special emphasis on the misogyny of Emmanuel Levinas's notions of freedom and futurity). As alternative, she proposed the "experimental feminine" as a practice, aesthetics and poethics available to poets of all gender identifications.[vii]

"Who is Speaking?" redux

I've long carried with me questions about the power dynamics among poets in public settings raised by Lyn Hejinian's essay "Who is Speaking?" published in *The Language of Inquiry* in 2000. This essay begins by explaining that its title was a question "first posed in the early 1980s as a topic for discussion by a group of Bay Area women poets and intellectuals," which then led to a panel discussion in San Francisco at Intersection for the Arts in 1983.[viii]

A few quotes:

The question "Who is speaking?" was intended as a challenge to a perceived style of asserting power and to the structures of power that were being created by it. It was directed not at any specific group of persons but at the problem of power itself...

[The question "Who is speaking?"] constituted a challenge to certain styles of discourse, lest they begin to circumscribe possibilities in the public life of the poetry community. Erudite, authoritative, contentious—that was one of the public voices of poetry.... That this generally came more easily to men than to women was not unpredictable, though not all of the women in the scene felt ungrounded and not all the men in the scene were speaking. The men and women who weren't speaking did not feel powerless, however. To invent other public formations—even to enact an ungrounding—seemed desirable, even necessary, and it certainly seemed possible.

for, as she continues:

At stake in the public life of a writer are the invention of a writing community; the invention of the writer (as writer and as person) in that community; and the invention of the meanings and meaningfulness of his or her writing.

I quote these passages because the question of who is and isn't speaking remains critically important and also because of a disorienting episode at the end of my own panel, which seemed minor, perhaps even accidental, at the time, but which resulted in shutting down discussion of the only explicitly feminist panel in a conference with a stated emphasis on dialog. After only a single question, a prominent poet raised his hands, a gesture mistaken by the moderator as a question, but which the poet explained was not, saying that he just meant to clap. At this point the moderator, probably due to stresses of "keeping to schedule," but also perhaps, consciously or not, due to the power dynamics of the moment acceded to this signal of "time to move on" and closed the Q and A period. We on the panel were a bit stunned by the impression of not being worth much response, an impression only enhanced by an animated discussion following the next panel, which included a talk on the subject of the archiving of poets' papers. The result was the distinct feeling that the desire to be read long into the future, as manifested by the safekeeping of the individual poet's archives, was of much greater interest than our engagement with gender, poetics and environmental destruction, intended or not.

The phrase "intended or not" is of course extremely fraught. Lately I've been pondering the workings of "intent" in the context of the dynamics of systemic exclusions and vulnerabilities, and the resulting legacy of damage and distrust. Inside "intended or not," "consciously or unconsciously," lurk so many elements of privilege, complicity, blindness, normalization, indifference, rationalization, guilt, confusion, awkwardness, fear, self-satisfaction, delusion. One could go on.

To continue to reference Hejinian:

Silencing in a community, of course, does not always come from the community's terms. Silencings occur that are manifestations of a drama whose history is longer than that of any community.

This incident ended up in a confusing zone for me where it joined other occasions in which I've found myself playing a part in this communal drama, filled as it is with ambiguous gestures, inattentions, and unintentional intentions. I'm certain for other conference participants there were parallel incidents and ironies, as these are indeed systemic and continue to feed various styles of what I called in my own talk "we(a)ryness," as in "feminist eco-we(a) ryness," but which could be used to describe other states of the worn-down social self.

Of course, the question "Who is speaking?" brings with it the question "Who is not speaking and why?" I, myself, can often shrink from the dynamics of the public Q and A as an audience member and wonder about my sometimes need for privacy of thought or time to digest, my unwillingness to expose half-formed thoughts. To what degree can this be construed as a lack of generosity and engagement, a failure of responsibility to the writing of others and to the sustenance of an engaged community? Perhaps most importantly, what do speaking and not speaking mean in terms of what ends up included or not among the poetry and poetics of the next 25 years?

Ojalá

When I was invited to write these reflections on the conference, I agreed even though more than a year had passed since it had taken place and, after a quick search, I discovered I had lost whatever notes I'd taken. I agreed partly because of a suggestion in the invitation that ecopoetics might have been an immerging *telos* of the conference, which I liked to think might be the case, but also because I am grateful for having been a beneficiary of the Buffalo poetry and poetics world.

The result is this admittedly very subjective collection of partial memories highly colored by my own biases of interest. In no way can I adequately do justice to the history of influences, life-long interactions and other aspects of communal memory, which were eloquently evoked by Charles Bernstein, Elizabeth Willis, and others. This "institutional memory" was also at the center of the event called "Remembering Creeley," which took place on the same evening as a keynote lecture on breath, black music traditions and experimental poetics by Nathaniel Mackey.[ix]

I did manage to keep the list of panels and seminars from the conference and can see the many threads of discussion I inevitably missed. The subjects reflect the breadth of interest of the organizers, ranging from poetic explorations of hierarchy and social difference to digital and hybrid poetries to cross-cultural, polyvocal and postnational poetics. In looking through these materials, I also see that the original conference description included its own version of what I'm coming to think of as the "Anthropocene squirm:"

The conference is not at all meant to focus on the SUNY, Buffalo Poetics Program, but rather on poetry and poetics tout court as you envision/ propose/speculate upon them for (ojalá) the quarter-century to come.

"Ojalá." The Spanish "hopefully," with its etymological echo of the Islamic "God-willing." A wish that the next quarter-century of poetry and poetics will be both productive and possible.

Ojalá.

---

[i] Susan Howe, *My Emily Dickinson*, New Directions, 1985.

[ii] The "Poetics: (The Next) 25 Years" conference was organized by Judith Goldman, Myung Mi Kim, Cristanne Miller, and Allison Cardon, and took place April 9-10, 2016.

[iii] Joan Retallack, "The Experimental Feminine," published in The Poethical Wager, University of California Press, 2003.

[iv] *Ecopoetics* was edited by Jonathan Skinner from 2001 to 2005.

[v] Quotes are from an interview with Norma Cole by Robin Twemblay-McGaw, published by X Poetics (xpoetics.blogspot.com), March 2009. *House of Hope—in Memoriam, Montien Boonma 1953-2000* was originally part of a larger installation by Cole titled *Collective Memory* at the California Historical Society in San Francisco. A fine arts book based on *Collective Memory* has been co-published by Granary Books and the Poetry Center, San Francisco State University, 2006.

[vi] In addition to Mark Wallace, panel participants included Stephen Voyce & Adalaide Morris, Jennifer Scappettone, and Heriberto Yepez.

[vii] A revised version of this talk will be published in *Poetics and Precarity*, edited by Myung Mi Kim and Cristanne Miller, forthcoming from SUNY Press, 2018.

[viii] Lyn Hejinian, *The Language of Inquiry*, University of California Press, 2000.

[ix] Nathanial Mackey's talk, "Breath and Precarity," constituted the first annual Robert Creeley Lecture on Poetry and Poetics. It will also be published in *Poetics and Precarity*, ibid.

APPENDIX A:

TIMELINE OF THE UNIVERSITY AT BUFFALO POETRY AND POETICS

The following timeline includes the founding of institutions relevant to the history of poetry and poetics at the university, the hiring of major faculty members who taught contemporary poetry, and a sample of important publications prior to 1990. Publications by graduate students in the Poetics Program from 1990 to 2016 can be found in Appendix D. This timeline is constructed from information collated from the various essays contained within this collection, as well as "Poetry & Poetics at Buffalo: a timeline 1960-1990," edited by Cynthia Kimball and Taylor Brady, published in Chloroform: An Aesthetics of Critical Writing *(1997). Revised versions of portions of that timeline are used here with permission of the editors.*

1929 – Thomas and Marion Lockwood pledge $500,000 to build a library

1935 – Lockwood Memorial Library opens

1937 – Charles Abbott begins letter-writing campaign asking poets for their work sheets

1949 – Oscar Silverman convinces Abbott to purchase James Joyce Collection

1956 – Oscar Silverman named Chair of the English department

1960 – Ralph Maud begins publishing *Audit*, a journal of criticism and literature

1961 – Charles Abbott dies

1962 – private University of Buffalo joins State University of New York

1963 – Albert Cook named Chair of the English department

1963 – Professor Arthur Efron begins publishing *Paunch*, a journal devoted to Romantic criticism and poetry

1963 – Charles Olson hired as Visiting Professor

1963 – Audit/Poetry founded by Michael Anania and Charles Doria

1964 – Raymond Federman hired by English department

1964 – Irving Feldman hired by English department

1964 – First Buffalo Summer Program in Modern Literature (Teachers include Ed Dorn, Robert Kelly, LeRoi Jones, Leslie Fiedler, Robert Creeley)

1964 – Harvey Brown publishes first issue of *Niagara Frontier Review*

1964 – Revision of the English departments "Statement on Poets and their Function in the Department of English" states that professional poets "may be regarded as academic professionals" but that the department does not plan "to follow the Iowa and Johns Hopkins plans of formal graduate degrees in Creative Writing"

1965 – Charles Olson teaches only two weeks of the fall semester, then returns to Gloucester

1965 – Albert Glover, Jack Clarke, George Butterick, and Fred Wah launch *The Magazine of Further Studies*

1965 – William Sylvester hired by English department

1966 – John Logan hired by English department

1966 – Carl Dennis hired by English department

1966 – Robert Creeley begins teaching part-time at Buffalo

1967 – Karl Gay hired as curator of Poetry Collection

1967 – Robert Hass hired by English department

1967 – Professor Leslie Fiedler arrested for possession of marijuana

1968 – Robert Creeley hired by English department as a full-time professor

1968 – Faculty and students cancel classes or hold them off campus to protest Vietnam War

1969 – Mac Hammond's *Cold Turkey* published with an accompanying record of multi-track poetry

1970 – Charles Olson dies

1970 – Clarke and Glover begin assigning portions for *Curriculum of the Soul* project

1970 – 45 faculty members arrested for trespassing and ignoring a court injunction against demonstrations

1970 – Max Wickert founds the Outriders Poetry Program

1971 – Douglas Calhoun publishes first issue of *Athanor*, a poetry journal

1971 – Judith Kerman publishes first issue of *Earth's Daughters*, a feminist poetry journal

1973 – *White Pine Press*, an independent publisher of world literature, founded in Buffalo

1975 – Ishmael Reed hired by English department as Visiting Professor

1975 – Debora Ott founds the Just Buffalo Literary Center

1976 – Albert Cook leaves Buffalo for Brown University

1977 – Oscar Silverman dies

1978 – Joy Walsh and Michael Basinski publish first issue of *Moody Street Irregulars*

1979 – Robert Bertholf hired as curator of Poetry Collection

1980 – Buffalo's art-focused residential college, "College B," renamed "Black Mountain College II"

1981 – First issue of resuscitated *Black Mountain Review* published

1981 – First issue of *Credences: A Journal of Twentieth Century Poetry and Poetics* published out of the Poetry Collection

1982 – John Logan leaves Buffalo for San Francisco

1988 – Susan Howe hired by English department as Butler Fellow

1988 – Joseph Conte hired by English department, with a specialty in modern and contemporary poetry

1989 – Susan Howe hired as Visiting Professor

1990 – Charles Bernstein hired by the English department as Gray Chair of Poetry and Letters

1990 – Susan Howe hired as full-time professor

1991 – Charles Bernstein, Robert Creeley, Raymond Federman, Susan Howe, and Dennis Tedlock found the Poetics Program

1994 – Los Pequeno Glazier launches the Electronic Poetry Center

1997 – Steve McCaffery receives his PhD in the Poetics Program

1997 – Nick Lawrence and Alisa Messer publish *Choloform: An Aesthetics of Critical Writing*

2001 – Ming-Qian Ma hired by the English department, with a specialty in contemporary innovative poetry and poetics in relation to philosophy, science, and arts

2001 – Carl Dennis retires

2003 – Charles Bernstein leaves Buffalo for the University of Pennsylvania

2003 – Robert Creeley leaves Buffalo for Brown University

2003 – Myung Mi Kim hired as a member of the Poetics Core Faculty

2004 – Steve McCaffery hired as the Gray Chair, and a Poetics Core Faculty member

2004 – Michael Basinski becomes curator of the Poetry Collection

2006 – Susan Howe retires

2006 – Cristanne Miller hired by English department, with a specialty in Emily Dickinson and Marianne Moore

2007 – *I have imagined a center, wilder than this region*, a book on Susan Howe's pedagogy, published by Cuneiform

2008 – *Building is a Process: Light is an Element*, a book on Myung Mi Kim's pedagogy, published by P-Queue

2012 – Judith Goldman hired as a member of the Poetics Core Faculty

2016 – Poetics: (The Next) 25 Years Conference held at University at Buffalo

2016 – Dennis Tedlock dies

2016 – Robert Bertholf dies

2016 – James Maynard becomes curator of the Poetry Collection

2016 – Myung Mi Kim appointed as the McNulty Chair

APPENDIX B:

A CHECKLIST OF THE PUBLICATIONS OF FRONTIER PRESS, 1965-1972

Michael Boughn

The following checklist accompanies Boughn's essay, "Olson's Buffalo."

1. Dorn, Edward. *Rites of Passage.*

    a. First edition, 1965.

    THE RITES OF PASSAGE I a brief history I EDWARD DORN

    Perfect binding; pp. [i-vi] 1-155 [156]. 15 x 21.5 cm.

    On copyright page: "Cover by Raymond Obermayr".

    b. Second edition [retitled], 1971.

    By the Sound I [line drawing of a house by the sea] I Edward Dorn I Frontier

    Press I Mount Vernon, I Washington I 1971

    [1-13]4; pp. [i-vii] 1-199 [200]. 13.8 x 21 cm. Paper wrappers.

    On copyright page: "Drawings by Flavia Zortea I Design by Ron Caplan".

    Note: Ron Caplan writes: "The cover—an odd green, like a slash of light downward—that's not mine. . . . They tore off the 'old' ones and pasted the new ones on. Of course, the rest of the book was as I designed it."

2. Adams, Brooks. *The New Empire.*

    Second edition, 1967 [1902].

    [device] I *BROOKS ADAMS* I *THE NEW EMPIRE* I *Frontier Press* I *Cleveland, Ohio* [dot] *1967* I [to the left of the previous two lines] [publisher's logo]

    [1-6]16 [7]8 [8-9]16; pp. [i-vi] vii-ix [x-xii] xiii-xxxvii [xxxviii-xl] 1-197 [198] 199-228 [229-232]. 13.7 x 20.8 cm.

    On p. [iv]: a poem by Charles Olson. On copyright page [vi]: *"The book was composed and printed by the Crimson Printing Company, Cambridge, and bound by Stanhope Bindery, Boston."*

3. Sanders, Edward. *Peace eye.*

    Second (enlarged) edition, 1967.

    PEACE EYE I Ed Sanders I [device] I [publisher's logo] I FRONTIER PRESS I Cleveland, Ohio

Loose sheets triple-stapled through the spine and glued into paper wrappers; pp. [1-84]. 20.8 x 26.6 cm.

On p. [5]: introductory poem by Charles Olson. A 6.3 cm. wide strip of very red (C11) paper is folded around the cover, and on it [in black]: "2nd ENLARGED EDITION".

4. Woodward, W.E. *Years of Madness: A Reappraisal of the Civil War.*

First edition, second impression [photo offset], 1967 [1951].

[device] | years of madness | [device] | w.e. woodward | [publisher's logo] | frontier press, inc. | cleveland, ohio | 1967

Perfect binding; pp. i-vi [1-2] 3-311 [312-314]. 14.5 x 23 cm.

On copyright page: "Copyright Helen Woodward 1951 | Copyright Frontier Press 1967"

5. *The Decline & the Fall of the "Spectacular" Commodity-Economy.*

First edition, 1967.

THE DECLINE & THE FALL | of the | "SPECTACULAR" | COMMODITY-ECONOMY | [publisher's logo] | FRONTIER PAMPHLET NUMBER ONE | FRONTIER PRESS

[1]10; pp. [i-vi] [1] 2-10 [11-14]. A single triple-stapled gathering. 15 x 22.7 cm.

On verso of title page: "This essay, 'The Decline and the Fall of the 'Spectacular' Commodity-Economy', originally appeared in the *Situationist International*, December, 1965." At foot of back cover flap: "design: ron caplan".

6. Hulbert, Archer Butler. *Paths of the Mound-Building Indians and Great Game Animals.*

First edition, second impression (photo offset), 1967 [1902].

HISTORIC HIGHWAYS OF AMERICA | VOLUME 1 | [rule] | Paths of the Mound=Building Indians | and Great Game Animals | ARCHER BUTLER HULBERT | *With Maps and Illustrations* | [publisher's logo] | FRONTIER PRESS, Inc. | CLEVELAND, OHIO | 1967

[1-9]8; pp. [i-ii] [1-11] 12-13 [14-17] 18-34 [35-37] 38-42 [43] 44-46 [47-48] 49-50 [51-53] 54 [55-56] 57-67 [68] 69-76 [77-78] 79-93 [94] 95-98 [99-101] 102 [103] 104-109 [110] 111-127 [128] 129-140. 13.2 x 18.8 cm.

7. Long, Haniel. *If He Can Make Her So*

First edition, 1968

[first four lines in yellow green C120] IF | HE CAN | MAKE HER | SO | [black] Haniel Long | Selection and introduction by | Ron Caplan with a painting | from the work of John Kane | [green] [device] | [publisher's logo] | FRONTIER PRESS | PITTSBURGH, PA | U S A

[1-5]¬8 [6]6 [7]8; pp [i-viii] ix [x-xx] 1-3 [4] 5-16 [17-18] 19-23 [24] 25-27 [28]

29 [30] 31 [32] 33-35 [36] 37-42 [43-44] 45-49 [50] 51 [52-54] 55-79 [80] 81-83 [84] 85 [86-88]. 16 x 25 cm.

Contents: Introduction, "Haniel Long", by Ronald Caplan, Pittsburgh Memoranda (section title for the following 5 pieces) "Prologue," "Homestead 1892," "Mrs. Soffel 1902," "Henry George 1913," "Two Memoranda 1914," Notes for a New Mythology (section title for the following piece) "How Pittsburgh Returned to the Jungle," A Pittsburgher En Route (section title for the following piece) "New Mexico," Piñon Country (section title for the following piece) "The Bandits," The Grist Mill (section title for the following piece) "If He Can Make Her So," Malinche (Doña Marina) (section title for the following piece) "She who speaks to you . . . .," Atlantides (section title for the following piece) "The Simplest Way," Bibliography (section title for the following piece) "Selected Books of Haniel Long".

8. Dorn, Edward. *Twenty-Four Love Songs.*

First edition, 1969.

Twenty-four | Love songs by | Edward Dorn | frontier press | 1969 [slightly red C12] [device]

[1]16; pp. [1-32]. A single double-stapled gathering. Trim size 13.7 x 19.4 cm. Cream laid paper with vertical chain lines watermarked "LINWEAVE TAROTEXT". Cover size ± 15.2 x 22.6 cm., light olive (C106) stock with deckled fore edge.

On page 31: [slightly red] "Designed & printed in San Francisco by Graham Mackintosh".

Contains 24 numbered poems. The number at the head of each poem is printed in slightly red.

9. Long, Haniel. *Interlinear to Cabeza de Vaca.*

Second edition, 1969 [1936].

INTERLINEAR TO | [deep red (C14)] Cabeza | deVaca | [black] *His Relation of the Journey* | *Florida to the Pacific* | *1528-1536* | [deep red] [cross] | HANIEL LONG | FRONTIER PRESS

[1-2]8 [3]4 [4]8; pp. [i-vii] ix-xii [xiv-xvi] 1-34 [35-40]. 10.6 x 17.6 cm.

Colophon p. [37]: "INTERLINEAR TO | CABEZA DE VACA | was originally published in 1936 by Writers' Editions, 'a cooperative group of writers | living in the Southwest, who believe that | regional publication will foster growth | of american literature,' and is here pub- | lished by Frontier Press in an edition of 4000 | copies in monotype Bembo and handset | Perpetua on Mohawk Vellum. | Design: Ron Caplan. 1969."

10. [White, Bouck]. *The Book of Daniel Drew.*

Second [?]edition, second impression [photo offset], 1969 [1910, 1911, 1930, 1937, 1965].

THE BOOK OF | [photo of Daniel Drew] | DANIEL DREW | NEW YORK CITY | FRONTIER PRESS

[1-5]16 [6-7]14 [8-14]16; pp. [i-vi] vii-xii [1-2] 3-423 [424-428]. 13.7 x19.7 cm.

Contents include "Introduction" by Edward Dorn.

At the foot of the inside flap of the dust jacket: "COVER DESIGN : RON CAPLAN".

11. McClure, Michael. *The Surge.*

First edition, 1969.

Cover title: on a folio of deep orange [C51] wove paper folded quarto, ± 16.2 x 23.8 cm., with deckled fore-edge, [medium olive C107, upside down from right to left] "THE | SURGE". Inside front cover [medium olive] "MICHAEL | McCLURE | frontier | press | 1969

[1]6; pp. [1-12]. A single double-stapled gathering. 15.5 x 23.3 cm.

On p. [11]: "*The Surge* was first published in *Foot*, (1962)". On p. [12]: "DESIGNED & PRINTED BY GRAHAM MACKINTOSH".

12. Berkman, Alexander. *Prison Memoirs of an Ananrchist.*

Second edition, 1970 [1912].

PRISON MEMOIRS | of an | ANARCHIST | ALEXANDER BERKMAN | [publisher's logo] | FRONTIER PRESS | PITTSBURGH

[1-16]16 [17]8 [18]16; pp. [i-xx] [1-2] 3-98 [99-100] 101-488 [489-490] 491-498 [499-500] 501-533 [534] 535-538 [539-540]. 13.6 x 20.8 cm.

At foot of dust jacket front flap: "COVER DESIGN : RON CAPLAN".

Contents include "Introduction: Alexander Berkman" by Kenneth Rexroth.

13. Büchner, Georg. *Lenz.* **Translated by Michael Hamburger.**

Second English edition, 1969 [1947].

LENZ | Georg Büchner | TRANSLATION BY MICHAEL HAMBURGER | FRONTIER PRESS | 1969

[1-2]16; pp. [1-6] 7-52 i-v [vi-vii]. 10.5 x 17.7 cm. Paper wrappers.

On p. [6]: "DESIGN BY RON CAPLAN"; pp. i-iv, "Introduction," by Michael Hamburger; p. v, "Principle dates in the life of Georg Büchner".

The first of a series that includes items number 16 and 19, all with identical binding.

14. Dorn, Edward. *Songs Set Two—A Short Count.*

First edition, 1970.

[slightly red (C12)] SONGS | [medium brown (C58)] SET TWO | [black] A Short Count | [medium brown] This volume | is to honor | the Scald | [slightly red] EDWARD | DORN | [medium brown] frontier press 1970

Perfect binding; pp. [1-32]. 11.3 x 15 cm.

On p. [32]: "designed & printed by Graham Mackintosh"

Contains 19 numbered poems. 13 is blank.

15. Williams, William Carlos. *Spring and All.*

Second edition, 1970 [1923].

Spring | & All | William | Carlos Williams | FRONTIER PRESS | 1970

[1-7]8; pp. [i-viii] 1-98 [99-104]. 10.6 x 17.7 cm. Paper wrappers.

On p. [vi]: "SPRING AND ALL WAS FIRST PUBLISHED IN 1923 | BY THE CONTACT PUBLISHING COMPANY"

16. Brakhage, Stan. *A Moving Picture Giving and Taking Book.*

First edition, 1971.

A | MOVING | PICTURE | GIVING | AND | TAKING | BOOK | STAN BRAKHAGE | FRONTIER PRESS | West Newbury Mass 1971

[1-3]8 [4]6 [5]8; pp. [i-viii] 1-65 [66-68]. 10.7 x 15.2 cm. Bound in leather covers with gilt stamped title.

On p. [67]: "DESIGN BY PHILIP TRUSSELL | 1971".

17. Dorn, Edward. *The Cycle.*

First edition, 1971.

The Cycle | by | Edward Dorn | Frontier Press | West Newbury Mass | 1971

[1]16; pp. [1-32]. A single double-stapled gathering. 24.2 x 32 cm. Paper wrappers.

18. Dorn, Edward. *Some Business Recently Transacted in the White World.*

First edition, 1971.

SOME BUSINESS | RECENTLY | TRANSACTED IN | THE WHITE WORLD | FRONTIER PRESS 1971

[1-6]4; pp. [i-x] 1-83 [84-86]. 10.5 x 17.5 cm. Paper wrappers.

Contents: "A Narrative with Scattered Nouns," "A Epic," "Of Eastern Newfoundland, Its Inns & Outs," "C. B. & Q.," "The Terrific Refinery in Biafra," "Driving Across the Prairie," "The Garden of Birth," "The Sheriff of McTooth County, Kansas ," "Greene Arrives on the Set," "Some Business Recently Transacted in the White World."

19. Glover, Albert. *Trio in G.*

First edition, 1971.

A TRIO IN G | A| Glover | Frontier Press | West Newbury | Massachusetts | 1971

[1-4]8 [5]6 [6]8; pp. [1-92]. 15 x 20.8 cm. Paper wrappers.

On p. [6]: "Drawings and design by Philip Trussell".

20. H.D. *Hermetic Definitions.*

First edition, 1971.

[within an ornamental oval frame of roses in deep red (C13) and gray green (C122)] Hermetic Definitions | HD | [below] 1971

[1]4 [2-5]8; pp. [1-72]. 22.6 x 15 cm. Covers of heavy white stock glued at spine.

Contents: "Red Rose & A Beggar," "Grove of Academe," "Star of Day."

No imprint, no colophon, no copyright. This edition was printed from an autograph transcription of a manuscrirpt version at the Beinecke Library. The title, "Hermetic Definitions," is printed as it appears on the manuscript. Inserted in the copy at Yale is a note by Norman Holmes Pearson: "Illegally published by Harvey Brown Frontier Press West Newbury, Mass. 1971, in what Brown asserts was an edition of 1600 copies 'none for sale'. If so, most were hidden for later profit. Note that the title is *Hermetic Definitions* rather than *Definition* and that the text differs from the New Directions edition. Text from an earlier version surreptitiously obtained by Brown." Brown continued to distribute to book free until he died in 1990. Hundreds of copies mildewed in his mother's basement.

21. Kelly, Robert. *Cities.*

First edition, 1971.

[two large dots over the "i"s] CITIES | ROBERT KELLY | FRONTIER PRESS | 1971

[1-5]4; pp. [i-vii] 1-65 [66-72]. 10.7 x 17.6 cm. Paper wrappers.

On copyright page: "AN EARLIER VERSION OF THIS ACCOUNT APPEARED IN THE IOWA REVIEW." "DESIGN BY RON CAPLAN".

22. Kelly, Robert. *In Time.*

First edition, 1971.

Robert Kelly | IN TIME | FRONTIER PRESS | WEST NEWBURY, MASS *1971*

[1-6]8; pp. [i-viii] 1-11 [11a] 12 [12a] 13-33 [33a] 34-46 [46a-46c] 47 [47a] 48 [48a] 49 [49a] 50 [50a] 51 [51a] 52 [52a] 53 [53a] 54 [54a] 55 [55a] 56 [56a] 57 [57a] 58 [58a] 59 [59a] 60 [60a] 61[62-66]. 17 x 21.5 cm. Paper wrappers.

On p. [vi]: "DESIGN BY RON CAPLAN".

23. Anderson, Sherwood. *Mid-American Chants.*

Second edition, 1972 [1918].

Sherwood Anderson | Mid-American | Chants | FRONTIER PRESS | 1972

[1-9]4; pp. [i-viii] 1-62 [63-64]. 21.5 x 26 cm. Paper wrappers.

On p. [iv]: "Book Design by Ron Caplan"

24. Dorn, Edward. *Gunslinger: Book III.*

First edition, 1972.

Gunslinger | by | Edward Dorn | Frontier Press | West Newbury Mass | 1972

[1]20; pp. [1-40]. A single double-stapled gathering. 19.8 x 30.4 cm. Paper wrappers.

On p. [5]: "BOOK III | THE WINTERBOOK | prologue to the great | Book IIII Kornerstone".

APPENDIX C:

CHECKLIST OF THE PUBLICATIONS OF THE INSTITUTE OF FURTHER STUDIES, 1969-1997

Michael Boughn

The following checklist accompanies Boughn's essay, "Olson's Buffalo."

1.   Olson, Charles. ["That there was a woman"]. 1968.

   1 p., 15.5 x 20.2 cm.

   Dated, "March, 1968".

   Folded once in an envelope, 16 x 10.5 cm., with the printed return address, "THE INSTITUTE OF FURTHER STUDIES | [device] [to the right of device] Box 25 [dot] Kensington Station "Buffalo, New York [dot] 14215".

   Reprinted as *Maximus* III.189 (Butterick 583).

2. Olson, Charles. ["Added to making a Republic in gloom on Watchhouse Point"]. 1968.

   1 p., 15.5 x 20.2 cm.

   Dated, "March, 1968".

   Folded once in an envelope, 16 x 10.5 cm., with the printed return address, "THE INSTITUTE OF FURTHER STUDIES | [device] [to the right of device] Box 25 [dot] Kensington Station "Buffalo, New York [dot] 14215".

   Reprinted as *Maximus* III.190 (Butterick 584).

3. Olson, Charles. ["Wholly absorbed"]. 1968

   1 p., 15.5 x 20.2 cm.

   Dated, "'LX VIII".

   Folded once in an envelope, 16 x 10.5 cm., with the printed return address, "THE INSTITUTE OF FURTHER STUDIES | [device] [to the right of device] Box 25 [dot] Kensington Station "Buffalo, New York [dot] 14215".

   Reprinted as *Maximus* III.191 (Butterick 585).

4. Olson, Charles. ["I like something in the American which does honor a Hotspur of itself"]

   Postcard, 17.7 x 12.7 cm. Recto, a photograph of Jacqueline Kennedy Onassis and Alice Roosevelt Longworth. Verso, eight hand written lines in blue signed, "Charles Olson": "I like something in the American which does honor a Hotspur of itself, | and even defines it as in fact close to the | condition of valor. What does, though, always ultimately | show up though, in their skin, or the health of it, some sickness | through their eyes seen almost to have the right | color or '[?]' frrom the edge of known and admitted | danger—is some poverty (actually they have saved | themselves from the glories of god ism | Charles Olson"

At top left of verso, "SOME OF THE SUBTLEST OF ALL POSSIBLE TRAIL-BACK, Mrs. Aristotle | Onassis, left, attending the christening of Rory Catherine Elizabeth | Kennedy, 11th child of the late Sen. Robert Kennedy, at St. Luke's | Church, McLean, Va., Sunday, Jan. 12, 1969, chats with Mrs. Alice | Roosevelt Longworth."

5. Olson, Charles. "Clear Shining Water." 1968.

Postcard. 41.7 x 19 cm. The card is double folded to 14.2 x 19 cm. On the front of the folded card is a drawing of "The Judgement of Paris" from a Greek vase, reproduced from Jane Ellen Harrison's *Prolegomena to the Study of Greek Religion*, p. 295. On the back is the printed return address, "THE INSTITUTE OF FURTHER STUDIES | [device] [to the right of device] Box 25 [dot] Kensington Station "Buffalo, New York [dot] 14215." Printed across the inside of the unfolded in three panels, "CLEAR, SHINING WATER", De Vries says, Altgermanische". At foot of third panel, "CHARLES OLSON, | Institute of Further Studies, July 1st, | 1968".

Reprinted in *Additional Prose*. Ed. George Butterick (Bolinas, Four Seasons Foundation, 1974). 71.

6. Blake, William. *Milton*, pl. 25 [1968].

1 p., 18.5 x 26.2 cm.

Double folded in an envelope, 19 x 10 cm., with the printed return address, "THE INSTITUTE OF FURTHER STUDIES | [device] [to the right of device] Box 25 [dot] Kensington Station "Buffalo, New York [dot] 14215".

7. Pound Ezra. "The Child's Guide to Knowledge" [1970?].

2 pp., 18.5 x 26.2 cm.

12 line epigraph by William Blake. Double folded in an envelope, 19 x 10 cm., with the return address, "The Institute of Further Studies | BOX 482 | CANTON, NEW YORK 13617".

8. The Magazine of Further Studies. Buffalo, NY. 1965-1969.

All issues 22 x 28 cm. loose sheets wrapped in corrugated paper covers and triple stapled through the spine. The cover of each issue has a different art work.

a. No. 1: "Lament for the Makaris," by William Dunbar; "Berkeley," by Robert Hogg; "Seven," by John Clarke; "from Don Cherry," by Harvey Brown; "Four poems," by Albert Glover; "Mythology / Poetry, Bibliography 1" and "III Pleistocene Mythology, A Bibliographic Beginning," by John Clarke; "Five poems," by George Butterick; "Two poems," by Stephen Rodefer; "Jazz Clarke Poem," by Charles Doria; "You've lost that lovin' feeling," by David Cull; "from Mountain," by Fred Wah; "Three poems," by John Weiners; "Placemats," by John Clarke.

b. No. 2: "crow feather," by Ruth Fox; "Pleistocene Mythology," by John Clarke; "The Blue Garden," by Charles Doria; ""I'd call you sweet but," by Colette Butterick; "For Andrew Crozier—wherever he goes, the same way, always," by John Temple; "Notes on the Possibility of a Phenomenological Poetics—The Body's World," by Charles Sherry; "Two Poems," by Charles Sherry; "ISHMAEL:8:X:sixtyfive," by Daniel John Zimmerman; "Plus X," by Patricia Jamieson; "Notes from Class," by George Butterick; "Nothing Done," by Jim Braemer; "Three poems," by John Weiners; "2 songs for children," by John Temple; "The Canoe, Too," by Fred Wah; "Notes (for I. Massey 9/28/65 on C. Olson," by Albert Glover; "Poem for Planters," by Albert Glover; "It's no fun anymore," by Jack Clarke; "As to the Exomorphic," by J. Clarke; "The Lamo," by Charles Olson; "traitor poem," by Dave Cull; "Beasts of Burden," by Mac Hammond.

c. No. 3: "Al, I Imagine: simply to be an animal," by Charles Olson; "Furs," by Fred Wah; "Five poems," by John Weiners; "As I walked home last night," by John Temple; "Letter A," by Lewis MacAdams; "The Mountain, the creek, all ends in the lake," by Fred Wah; "from Black Creek," by Ruth Fox; "Sections from Subway," by George Butterick; "Two poems," by Duncan McNaughton; "Poem," by Robert Hogg; "The Lesbian is dead," by Duncan McNaughton; "Enough animus so it all has will," by John Clarke; "I see a whale in the South-sea, drinking my soul away," [review of *Sailing after Knowledge*, by George Dekker, and *The Savage Mind*, by Claude Levi-Strauss] by Albert Glover; [review of *Human Universe* and *Other Essays*, by Charles Olson] by John Clarke.

d. No. 4: "Hell and Heaven: Psychemimeisis to beyond the rainbow bridge," by David Tirrell; "The qanat spurts the geyser," by Ed Sanders; "By fixes only move," by John Clarke; "3 songs," by Robert Hogg; "for my friend," by Charles Olson; "Fingers of the Sun," by Ed Sanders; "Poem for Turning," by Fred Wah; "that otherwise than how the story goes," by Ron Caplan; "Proem," by George Butterick; "Drugs and the Unconscious" by John Weiners; "the mute," by Ed Billowitz; "by honor," by Ed Sanders; "Blake letter November 4 1967," by John Clarke; "Dear Royal Members my west view in this," by David Tirrell; "Letter, October 18, 1967," by Fred Wah; "Moon morning 6 Nov '67" by John Clarke; "A letter and a drawing for John Clarke 11/7/67," by Albert Glover.

e. No. 5: "Second tale: return," by Robin Blaser; "it is a dark cold hard tin forest," by Ron Caplan; "Letter, May 15, 1968," by Fred Wah; "La Barranca del Cobre," by Drummond Hadley; "Insulted," by John Weiners; "Where the daughter goes the mother must follow," by John Clarke; "The quality of goods, the explicitness," by George Butterick; "[review of *Megalithic Sites in Britain*, by A. Thom], by Peter Riley; "from *Art and Artist*" by Otto Rank; "Prophetic hieroglyphs: world forecasts," by Albert Glover; "Magic rite," by Ed Sanders; "A plan for a curriculum of the soul," by Charles Olson.

f. No. 6: ["letter to John Clarke"], by Charles Olson; "I am very glad and all alone in the world," by Mary Leary; "He said, that when he would step out into the street," by George Butterick; "I point to my own absolute (?) experience of," by Fred Wah; "it was all tainted with myself, I knew it all to start with," by John Clarke; "Three poems," by John Temple; "Thinking along the lines that," by John Clarke; "A lifetime," by Robert Hogg; "I shall never forget the maniacal horror of it all in the end," by Robert Creeley; "Lockd in a fiery Tree," by Duncan McNaughton; "the black dog is third dog," by Albert Glover; "'. . .we found marginal," by Buri; "But what's wrong with mortality?" by Albert Glover; "SO," by Fred Wah; "Thirty-six years after my birth was the time," by John Clarke; "At this point I would distinguish the following kinds of form," by Robert Duncan; "Dear Diana—Buga Nov. 4, 1968," by Ed Billowitz; "so I put my hand out further, a little further," by Buri; "Dear Jack & Mary," by David [Tirrell]; "Ah no, I cannot tell you what it is," by John Temple; ""Out of the well-heads of the new world," by Fred Wah; " . . . so much as there is a steady flow of breath," by Fred Wah; "So like   play," by Charles Olson.

9. *A Curriculum of the Soul* (in order of publication):

0 Pleistocene Man   Charles Olson

21 Vision.................................Drummond Hadley

22 Messages.............................James Koller

3 Woman.................................John Wieners

18 Ismaeli Muslimism................Michael Bylebyl

19 Alchemy .... David Tirrell

16 Dance .... Lewis MacAdams, Jr.

13 The Arabs .... Edward Kissam

27 Sensation .... Anselm Hollo

1 The Mushroom .... Albert Glover

14 American Indians .... Edgar Billowitz

11 Novalis' Subjects .... Robert Dalke

2 Dream .... Duncan McNaughton

7 Blake .... John Clarke

12 The Norse .... George F. Butterick

17 Egyptian Hieroglyphs .... Edward Sanders

6 Earth .... Fred Wah

24 Organism .... Michael McClure

20 Perspective .... Daniel Zimmerman

8 Dante .... Robert Duncan

25 Matter .... John Thorpe

15 Jazz Playing .... Harvey Brown

28 Attention .... Robert Grenier

23 Analytical Psychology .... Gerrit Lansing

26 Phenomenological .... Joanne Kyger

9 Homer's Art .... Alice Notley

10 Bach's Belief .... Robin Blaser

4 Mind .... Michael Boughn

5 Language .... Lisa Jarnot

APPENDIX D:

POETRY IN THE MAKING: A BIBLIOGRAPHY OF PUBLICATIONS BY GRADUATE STUDENTS IN THE POETICS PROGRAM, UNIVERSITY AT BUFFALO, 1991-2016

James Maynard

This Bibliography was originally published as a small booklet for the Poetics (The Next) 25 Years Conference *in April 2016. It will be reprinted by SUNY Press in June 2018 as part of a volume titled* Poetics and Precarity, *co-edited Myung Mi Kim and Cristanne Miller. It is reprinted here with permission by the author and by SUNY Press.*

From its beginning in the fall of 1991 up through today, the University at Buffalo English Department's Poetics Program has been largely organized around a single question: *what is poetics?* While far from the first to orient itself around such a pursuit, what has distinguished the program over the years is its assumption, shaped entirely in the image of its founders and continuing core faculty, that all answers to this question must invariably be experimentally derived, historically and culturally situated, and always plural. The defining vision of the program is based on an anti-foundational understanding of poetry—i.e. the processual activity of *poiesis*—as a liminal field always evolving out of its multiform past in response to the overlapping aesthetic, social, and political needs of the present. Its approach to poetry is a radical praxis in both senses of the word: rooted in particular theories and traditions and yet constantly branching out into progressively new and unforeseen directions. Pedagogically, the program has been heavily informed by former UB English Department Chair Albert Cook's practice in the 1960s of hiring poets and writers to teach literature classes based upon their experience as practitioners of language as well as by those poets (both on faculty and visiting) who had previously been associated with that other great educational experiment Black Mountain College. It is no coincidence that the Poetics Program developed in a rust belt city that historically has been welcoming to experimentation across the arts. Encouraging an interdisciplinary study of poetries often within and between different cultures and time periods, the program's ethos from inception has included an openness to formal innovation, a general respect for all forms of linguistic alterity, ethnopoetics' insistence on the significance of sound and oral performance, and an emphasis on writing as social practice.

But, to be more specific, *what has been / is the poetics of the UB Poetics Program?* Certainly one answer lies in the program's dedicated and engaged faculty who have each left an indelible mark on the students like me who have been fortunate enough to study with them, so much so that it is impossible to think of the program without thinking of its core faculty Charles Bernstein, Robert Creeley, Raymond Federman, Judith Goldman, Susan Howe, Myung Mi Kim, Steve McCaffery, and Dennis Tedlock; its extensive group of affiliate faculty in English and other departments; and the curators of the Poetry Collection who have been longtime collaborators and participants, not to mention the hundreds of writers—some of the most interesting and significant poets and prose writers and critics and theorists from the latter half of the twentieth and beginning of the twenty-first centuries—who have visited over the years to give readings and guest lectures. But in my experience, biased as it surely is, I've always believed that the best indicator of the program's evolving poetics, not to mention its longstanding vitality, can be found in the activities of its students and especially their publications. And this is as true today in 2016 as it was in 1991. When I first arrived in Buffalo as a new poetics student in the summer of 2001, it seemed to me like everyone I met here was publishing a magazine, sewing chapbooks, organizing readings and conferences, and/or printing letterpress covers and posters. It was a community based in large part on the collaborative activity of making, and I loved it from the start.

An empirical approach to answering the ongoing question of *what has been / is the poetics of the UB Poetics Program?*—which over the years has sometimes led to various tensions among the community—can be found in the rich history of publications produced here by its graduate students. Each of these titles—each made thing—offers its own articulation of a particular poetics, and their sum total demonstrates a wide variety of active traditions (e.g., Objectivism, Black Mountain poetry, New York School, Language poetry, New Narrative, HOW(ever)); a number of emerging aesthetic movements of the 1990s, 2000s, and 2010s (e.g., electronic poetry, post-Language, Flarf, contemporary visual poetry, ecopoetics, Conceptual poetry); and the broad reach of the program as inscribed within a large constellation of overlapping print networks centered in Buffalo and radiating outwards. As much as these publications offer in terms of their content and form, they are equally valuable in demonstrating how graduate students in the Poetics Program have been able to participate in the construction of their own literary communities through the activity of publishing themselves, their peers, their teachers, and their colleagues and mentors from around the world. Further extending the ground of poetics made manifest in these publications are the reading, talk, and performance series and the symposia organized over the years by Poetics graduate students. Viewed together these related projects allow one to begin mapping out the particular contributions of the program to the national and international discourses on poetry over the past twenty-five years.

The beginning of this bibliography's historical coverage coincides with the founding of the Poetics Program in the fall of 1991, and the first student publications begin to appear as early as that same semester. Looking through the pages of these chapbooks and magazines, one is continually reminded by their acknowledgements of all the forms of institutional support that made them possible. Certainly there would not have been so many titles without the generosity of those chairs and departments most often thanked, including the David Gray Chair of Poetry and Letters (Charles Bernstein, Steve McCaffery), James H. McNulty Chair (Dennis Tedlock), Samuel P. Capen Chair of Poetry and the Humanities (Robert Creeley, Susan Howe), Graduate Student Association (GSA), the Poetry/Rare Books Collection (now the Poetry Collection of the University Libraries), the English Graduate Student Association (EGSA), Department of English, the Samuel Clemens Chair (Leslie Fiedler), the Melodia Jones Chair (Raymond Federman), the Poetics Program, and others.

Whatever this bibliography may make visible about the history of the UB Poetics Program, it does so at the expense of ignoring the other magazines and presses in Buffalo with which these students and publications were often in dialogue. To present a more comprehensive picture then of a larger Buffalo poetics one would need to add at least the following: other Buffalo magazines (e.g., *Earth's Daughters, No Trees, Yellow Field*); other Buffalo publishers and presses (e.g., BlazeVOX, Blue Garrote, House Press, Just Buffalo Literary Center, shuffaloff, Starcherone, sunnyoutside, Weird Sisters, White Pine Press, Writer's Den); UB undergrad magazines and presses (e.g., *name, we the notorious pronouns*, PressBoardPress); UB faculty publication series (e.g. Buffalo Broadsides, Buffalo Vortex, Outriders) and magazines (*Intent, Becoming Poetics*); and publications from other schools, colleges, and organizations.

NOTES ON THE BIBLIOGRAPHY

My principle in selecting materials for these lists has been to identify those publications produced by students in the Poetics Program (often difficult to determine, as membership has always been largely the result of self-identification) and to list only those items that were published in Buffalo during their time here as students. Presses and magazines that started elsewhere and/or subsequently moved out of Buffalo to other locations are marked (*). Notable examples of magazines and presses edited by Poetics students and published outside of Buffalo (and therefore not included here) include Roberto Tejada's magazine *Mandorla* and Peter Gizzi's co-edited magazine *O·blék: A Journal of Language Arts* and its corresponding O·blék Editions.

Items marked (+) indicate that the archive for that particular magazine or press is held by the Poetry Collection as one of its manuscript collections.

CALL FOR CORRECTIONS AND ADDITIONS

Due to its nature this bibliography is undoubtedly guilty of inaccuracies, omissions, and partial information, especially in sections V. Reading, Talk, and Performance Series and VI. Student-Organized Symposia. For these I apologize in advance, and ask that anyone with any corrections and/or additions to suggest please send them to me at jlm46@ buffalo.edu. Also, since this collection was composed almost solely on the basis of the cataloged holdings of the Poetry Collection, anyone with additional materials not listed here is encouraged to donate them to the collection. We are continually looking for chapbooks, magazines, photographs, faculty syllabi, audio/video recordings, reading posters, and other ephemera that document the ongoing history of the Poetics Program.

ACKNOWLEDGMENTS

Thanks to Edric Mesmer for his enthusiasm in publishing this bibliography as the inaugural chapbook in his *Among the Neighbors* series, Michael Basinski for many years of sharing with me his endless knowledge of the history of poetry in Buffalo, Alison Fraser and Declan Gould for their help in gathering together these publications, everyone who helped provide information and/or donated materials for this publication (far too many to name individually), and the Poetry Collection for its dedication to collecting as completely as possible the publications of students and faculty in the Poetics Program. Two sources that were useful for their bibliographic information regarding publications from the first few years of the program are *Publications from Buffalo, NY* (Buffalo: Poetry/Rare Books Collection, n.d. [1994?]) and Kristin Prevallet, "A Selected Bibliography of Buffalo Publications in Poetry and Poetics 1960-1996," *Chloroform: An Aesthetics of Critical Writing* (1997): 272-287.

Finally, I'd like to dedicate this publication—printed in conjunction with a retrospective exhibition titled *Poetry in the Making: The UB Poetics Program 1991-2016* in the Poetry Collection coinciding with the conference *Poetics: (The Next) 25 Years* as part of the 25th anniversary of the program—*to all the faculty, staff, and students of the UB Poetics Program past, present, and future*. For almost fifteen years now, first as a graduate student and then as curator, I've had the pleasure of seeing these publications assembled, printed, launched, exchanged, discussed, and enjoyed, and I hope (expect!) that the making will continue for many decades more.

I. PRINT SERIALS

apex of the M
Editors: Lew Daly, Alan Gilbert, Kristin Prevallet, and Ram Rehm
Contributing advisors: Susan Howe, David Levi Strauss, John Taggart, Keith Waldrop, and Rosmarie Waldrop
    1 (Spring 1994)

2 (Fall 1994)
3 (Spring 1995)
4 (Winter 1996)
5 (Spring 1997)
6 (Fall 1997)

Broke
Editor: Andrea Strudensky
Layout and illustrations: Joel C Brenden
[Earlier issues?]
Vol. 2, no. 1 (Winter 2009)

Celery Flute: The Kenneth Patchen Newsletter
Editor: Douglas Manson
Editorial Board: Michael Basinski, William Howe III, Lisa Phillips, and Larry Smith
Vol. 1, no. 1 (June 2006)
Vol. 1, no. 2 (November 2006)
Vol. 1, no. 3 (July 2007)
Vol. 2, no. 1 (May 2009)

Chain (*) (+)
Editors: Jena Osman and Juliana Spahr
1: Gender and Editing (Summer 1994)
2: Documentary (Spring 1995)
3: Hybrid Genres/Mixed Media, Vol. 1 (Spring 1996)
3: Hybrid Genres/Mixed Media, Vol. 2 (Fall 1996)

Chloroform: An Aesthetics of Critical Writing
Editors: Nick Lawrence and Alisa Messer
Associate editors: Amy Nestor, Cynthia Kimball, Taylor Brady, Kristin Prevallet, Martin
Spinelli, Ken Sherwood, Michael Stancliff, Eleni Stecopoulos, and Yunte Huang
1997

Curricle Patterns: A Magazine of Poetry Manuscripts
Editor: Alicia Cohen
1 (November 1999)
2 (July 2000)

Damn the Caesars (*)
Editor: Richard Owens (Punch Press)
Vol. 1, no. 3 (Autumn 2005)
Vol. 1, no. 4 (Spring 2006)
Vol. 2 (2007)
Vol. 3 (2007)
Vol. 4 (2008)
Vol. 5 (2009)
Vol. N (2010)
Misc. ephemera

Displace: A Journal of Poetry & Translation
Editor: Yunte Huang
1 (1997)

Ecopoetics (*)
Editor: Jonathan Skinner (Periplum Editions)
1 (Winter 2001)
2 (Fall 2002)
3 (Winter 2003)

Essex
Editors: Scott Pound and William R. Howe (Essex Studios, Toronto, and Tailspin Press, Buffalo)

> Vol. 1, no. 1 (Spring 1997)
> Vol. 1, no. 2 (Summer/Fall 1997)
> Vol. 1, no. 3/4 (Fall 1997-Winter 1998)

Experimental Review: A Channel 500 Newsletter
Editor: Benjamin Friedlander (Channel 500)
> Vol. 1, no. 1 (March 2000)

I Am a Child: Poetry after Robert Duncan and Bruce Andrews
Editors: William R. Howe and Benjamin Friedlander (Tailspin Press)
> Vol. 1 (April 23, 1994)

Kadar Koli (*)
Editor: David Hadbawnik (Habenicht Press)
> 4 (Spring 2009)
> 5 (2010)
> 6 (2011)
> 7: On Violence (Summer 2012)
> 8: Dystranslation (Summer 2013)
> 9: The Archive (Summer 2014)

Kenning: A Newsletter of Contemporary Poetry Poetics and Nonfiction Writing (*)
Editor: Patrick F, Durgin
> 9 (Vol. 3, no. 3, Autumn 2000/Winter 20001)
> 10 (Vol. 4, no. 1, Spring 2001)
> 11 (Vol. 4, no. 2, July 2001): *Often: A Play* by Barbara Guest & Kevin Killian
> 12 (Vol. 4, no. 3, Autumn 2002/Winter 2003): The Audio Edition (cd)
> 13 (Vol. 5, no. 1, 2002)

Kiosk: A Journal of Poetry, Poetics, & Experimental Prose (+)
Editors: First published in March 1986 as *The Moral Kiosk* and continuing as *Kiosk: A Magazine of New Writing* through 9 volumes into 1996 as a UB English Department journal, *Kiosk's* editors over the years included a number of students from the Poetics Program. In 2002 Gordon Hadfield, Sasha Steensen, and Kyle Schlesinger restarted the magazine—and associated it more explicitly with the Poetics Program—as *Kiosk: A Journal of Poetry, Poetics, & Experimental Prose.*
> 1 (2002)
> 2 (2003)
> 3 (2004)
> 4 (2005)

P-Queue
Editors: Sarah Campbell, Andrew Rippeon, Holly Melgard, Joey Yearous-Algozin, and Amanda Montei
> 1: Statements of Poetics & Parole (2004)
> 2: Anomalies (2005)
> 3: Hybrids (2006)
> 4: Disobedient/s (2007)
> 5: Care (2008)
> 6: Space (2009)
> 7: Polemic (2010)
> 8: Document (2011)
> 9: Volume (2012)
> 10: Obsolescence (2013)
> 11: Natality (2014)

12: Fatality (2015)

13: Mourning (2016)

Pilot: A Journal of Contemporary Poetry
Editor: Matt Chambers and Andrea Strudensky

1 (2006)

2 (2007): a box set of chapbooks by 16 UK poets: Sean Bonney, Emily Critchley, matt ffytche, Kai Fierle-Hedrick, Giles Goodland, Jeff Hilson, Piers Hugill, Frances Kruk, Marianne Morris, Neil Pattison, Reitha Pattison, Simon Perril, Sophie Robinson, Natalie Scargill, Harriet Tarlo, and Scott Thurston

Poetic Briefs (*)
Editors: Jefferson Hansen, Elizabeth Burns, Juliana Spahr, Brigham Taylor, Bill C. Tuttle, and Mark Wallace

1 (December 1991)

2 (February 1992)

3 (March 1992)

4 (April 1992)

5 (May/June 1992)

6 (July 1992)

7 (August/September 1992)

8 (October 1992)

9 (December 1992)

10 (February 1993)

11 (April 1993)

12: Interview Issue: Dennis Tedlock, Masani Alexis de Veaux, Robert Creeley, Eric Mottram, Ge(of) Huth, Charles Bernstein, and Rosmarie Waldrop (nd)

President's Choice
Editor: Steven Zultanski

1 (2007)

Rust Talks
Editors: Kristen Gallagher and Tim Shaner

1: Logan Esdale and Graham Foust (June 15, 2000)

2: Eleni Stecopoulos and Jonathan Skinner (September 14, 2000)

3: Roberto Tejada and Richard Deming (October 26, 2000)

4: Kathryn Wichelns and Meghan Sweeney (November 16, 2000)

5: Michael Kelleher and Christopher W. Alexander (February 8, 2001)

6: Laura Penny and Peter Ramos (March 15, 2000)

7: Linda Russo and Greg Kinzer (April 12, 2001)

8: Barbara Cole and Thom Donovan (September 27, 2001)

9: Eun-Gwi Chung, Sandra Guerreiro, Anna Reckin (October 25, 2001)

10: Gregg Biglieri and Nick Lawrence (November 15, 2001)

11: Brandon Stosuy and Patrick F. Durgin (February 14, 2002)

12: Nathan Austin and Elizabeth Finnegan (April 11, 2002)

13: Kristen Gallagher and Tim Shaner (October 3, 2002)

14: ?

15: Martin Corless-Smith and Gordon Hadfield (n.d.)

16: Alicia Cohen and Sasha Steensen (April 17, 2003)

17: James Maynard and Jonathan Stalling (May 7, 2003)

18: ?

19: Thom Donovan and Michael Cross (March 11, 2004)

The Rusty Word
Editor: Joel Kuszai

1 (September 20, 1995)

Satellite Telephone (*)
Editor: Robert Dewhurst
    3 (Winter 2010)

Situation (*)
Editor: Mark Wallace
    1 (December 1992)
    2 (nd)
    3 (nd)
    4 (nd)
    5 (nd)
    6 (nd)
    7 (nd)

Small Press Collective
Editor: Taylor Brady
    1 (April 24, 1997)
    2 (November 10, 1997)

Uprising: An Occasional Journal (+)
Editor: Mark Hammer
    1 (nd)
    2 (nd)

Verdure
Editors: Linda Russo and Christopher W. Alexander
    1 (October-November 1999)
    2 (March-April 2000)
    3-4 (September 2000-Feburary 2001)
    5-6 (February 2002)

Wild Orchids
Editors: Sean Reynolds and Robert Dewhurst
    1: Melville (2009)
    2: Hannah Weiner (2010)
    3: William Blake (2011)

Working Papers
Editor: ?
    [1] (March 2010)
    [2] (May 2010)

II. ONLINE SERIALS:

a l y r i c m a i l e r

http://epc.buffalo.edu/ezines/alyric/
Editor: Michael Kelleher
    1: Dan Machlin (1998)
    2: Garrett Kalleberg (1998)
    3: Eléni Sikélianòs (1998)
    4: Laird Hunt (1998)
    5: Heather Fuller (1998)
    6: Stephen Mounkhall (1998)
    7: Carrie Ann Tocci (1998)
    8: Sheila E. Murphy (1998)

9: Notes from the Place(less Place) (1998)
10 & 11: Anselm Berrigan & Lisa Jarnot (1998)
12: Michael Basinski (1998)

Cartograffiti
URL no longer available
Editor: Taylor Brady and Small Press Collective

Deluxe Rubber Chicken
http://epc.buffalo.edu/ezines/deluxe/
Editor: Mark Peters
    1 (May 1998)
    2 (Feb. 1999)
    3 (May 1999)
    4 (Nov. 1999)
    5 (March 2000)
    6 (May 2000)
    7 (May 2001)

Lagniappe: Poetry and Poetics in Review
http://www.umit.maine.edu/~ben.friedlander/lagniappe.html
Editors: Graham Foust and Ben Friedlander
    Vol. 1, no. 1 (Fall 1998)
    Vol. 1, no. 2 (Winter/Spring 1999)
    Vol. 1, no. 3 (Summer 1999)
    Vol. 2, no. 1 (Fall 1999)
    Vol. 2, no. 2 (Spring/Summer/Millennium/Election 2000)

lume: a journal of electronic writing and art
http://epc.buffalo.edu/ezines/lume/
Editor: Michael Kelleher
    1 (May 2000)
    2 (February 2001)

RIF/T: An Electronic Space for Poetry, Prose, and Poetics
http://epc.buffalo.edu/rift/
Editors: Kenneth Sherwood and Loss Pequeño Glazier
    1.1 (Fall 1993)
    2.1 (Winter 1994)
    3.1 (Summer 1994)
    4.1 (Spring 1995)
    5.1 (Summer 1995)
    6.1: Local Effects for Robert Creeley @ 70 (Fall 1997)

III. BOOKS, CHAPBOOKS, BROADSIDES, AND OTHER PUBLICATIONS LISTED BY PUBLISHER

Allerwirklichste Miniatures Press
Editor: ?
    The World: A Pamphlet Made Especially for the Geoff Ward/Linda Russo Reading @ the Cornershop, Buffalo NY, Friday, 25 September 1998, 1998

Alyric Press
Editor: Michael Kelleher?
    Michael Kelleher, Jonathan Skinner, and Eleni Stecopoulos, *Three*, 1999

Atticus/Finch (*)
Editor: Michael Cross

Cynthia Sailers, *Rose Lungs*, 2003
Elizabeth Willis, *Meteoric Flowers*, 2004
Eli Drabman, *The Ground Running*, 2004
Tanya Brolaski, *The Daily Usonian*, 2004
Thom Donovan and Kyle Schlesinger, *Mantle*, 2005
Gregg Biglieri, *I Heart My Zeppelin*, 2005
Myung Mi Kim, *River Antes*, 2006
Lisa Jarnot, *Iliad* XXII, 2006
John Taggart, *Unveiling / Marianne Moore*, 2007
Patrick F. Durgin, *Imitation Poems*, 2007
Taylor Brady and Rob Halpern, *Snow Sensitive Skin*, 2007
C. J. Martin, *Lo, Bittern*, 2008

Bon Aire Projects
Editors: Amanda Montei and Jon Rutzmoser
Amanda Montei and Jon Rutzmoser, *Dinner Poems*, 2013
Joey Yearous-Algozin, *Holly Melgard's Friends & Family* (introduction by Teresa Carmody, footnotes to introduction by Vanessa Place), 2014
Teresa Carmody and Vanessa Place, *Maison Femme: A Fiction*, 2015

Channel 500
Editor: Benjamin Friedlander
Mark Wallace, *6/20: Poem for O.J.*, 1994?
Richard Roundy, *Inquiring Minds/Inside the White Bronco*, 1994?
Jena Osman, *Victor vs. Nebraska*, 1994?
Cynthia Kimball, *Proof*, 1994?
William R. Howe, *Scream Scream Scream All You Want*, 1994?
Benjamin Friedlander?, *Danger!! Warning!! Bar Your Office Doors and Classrooms!! Anti-Revolutionary Poetics! Anti-Poetic Revolutionaries!*, 1994?
Lucia W. Noi [Luca Crispi?], *Cult u 're tv*, 1994?
Alice Crimmins, *So a Husband Kills a Wife and We All Enter into the Conversation*, 1994?
Abby C. [Coykendall?], *If X Has That Spot*, 1994?
Victoria Lucas, *Social Fantasies*, 1995?
Ted Pearson, *The Fall Classic*, 1995?
Nick Lawrence, *Pensacola Shotgun*, 1995?
Benjamin Friedlander, *Jeff's Hulking Tan Toyota*, 1995?
Robert Creeley, *Help*, 1995?
Carla Billitteri, *Berlusconiana*, Nov. '94, 1995?
Charles Bernstein, *Mao Tse Tung Wore Khakis*, 1995?
Georges Bataille, *The Void* (translated by Victoria Tillotson), 1995?
Kristin Prevallet, *The Princess Is Dead*, 1997?
Benjamin Friedlander, *Crash*, 1997?
William Sylvester?, *Think Big Die*, 1998?
William Sylvester, *(Hesiod's She Who Poem, Eoia, Is in the Loeb Library.)*, 1998?
Mark Peters, *Bill, Bill, Bill*, 1998?
Michael Kelleher, *Immortality, a Jingle*, 1998?
William R. Howe?, *A Ship of the Crime Poplist*, 1998?
Cher Horowitz, *The Survivor Is the Worst Nazi*, 1998?
Photios Giovanis, *Haute Couture Killing*, 1998?
Benjamin Friedlander, *Memories of President Clinton*, 1998?
Benjamin Friedlander, *Ichabod!*, 1998?
Brent Cunningham, *Timely Is a Princess*, 1998?

Cuneiform Press (*)
Editor: Kyle Schlesinger
Luisa Giugliano, *Chapter in a Day Finch Journal*, 2000
Luisa Giugliano, *Chapter in a Day Finch Journal*, 2000 (broadside)

Nick Piombino, *The Boundary of Theory*, 2001
:*prose::acts:*, 2001 (limited and regular edition broadsides)
Michael Magee, *Leave the Light On*, 2002 (with Handwritten Press)
Patrick F. Durgin, *Color Music*, 2002
Patrick F. Durgin, *Color Music*, 2002 (broadside)
Gregg Biglieri, *Los Books*, 2002
Stacy Szymaszek, *Mummified Arm Indonesian*, 2003
David Pavelich, *Outlining*, 2003
Thom Donovan, *Love of Mother a Reason*, 2003
Gregg Biglieri, *Reading Keats to Sleep*, 2003
Derek Beaulieu, *With Wax*, 2003
Derek Beaulieu, *With Wax*, 2003 (deluxe edition)
Christopher W. Alexander, *Two Poems*, 2003?
Ron Silliman, *Woundwood*, 2004
Alan Loney, *Meditatio: The Printer Printed: Manifesto*, 2004
Andrew Levy, *Scratch Space*, 2004
Craig Dworkin, *Dure*, 2004
Robert Creeley, *Oh, Do You Remember*, 2004
Gill Ott and Christopher Webster (images), *The Amputated Toe*, 2005
Craig Dworkin, *Andy Warhol's Lost Portraits*, 2005?
Johanna Drucker, *From Now*, 2005
Gregg Biglieri, *Sleepy with Democracy*, 2006
Ulf Stolterfoht, *Lingos VI* (translated by Rosmarie Waldrop), 2007
I Have Imagined a Center // Wilder Than This Region: A Tribute to Susan Howe,
2007
Max Jacob and Larry Fagin, *Two Poems*, 2008

Curricle Patterns
Editor: Alicia Cohen?
Linda Russo, *Secret Silent Plan*, 2000

Dove | Tail
Editor: Victoria Brockmeier
Laura Mullen, *Turn: Essay*, 2006
Matthew Cooperman, *Still: (to be) Perpetual: Poems*, 2007?

Éditions Hérisson
Editor: ?
Bob Perelman, *Chaim Soutine*, 1994
Pam Rehm, Nick Lawrence, and Carla Billitteri, *Three Poets*, 1994

Elevator
Editor: Michael Kelleher
Sugar in the Raw, 2000 (anthology)
Ed. Brian Collier, *The Elevator Box*, 2000 (boxed set)
Eds. Michael Kelleher and Isabelle Pelissier, *The Postcard Project*, 2001 (boxed set)
Eds. Michael Kelleher and Isabelle Pelissier, *The Postcard Project*, 2001 (book
edition made and designed in collaboration with Handwritten Press)
Ed. Jonathan Skinner, *La Mitad: 11 from Buffalo*, 2001 (anthology)
Ed. Amy Stalling, *The Grid Project*, 2003 (different word grids and book edition)

Essex Publications
Editors: Scott Pound and William R. Howe
Scott Pound, *How Do You Like Your Blue-Eyed Text Now, Jacques Derrida?*,
1998? (no publisher information listed)

Habenicht Press (*)
Editor: David Hadbawnik

Micah Robbins, *Crass Songs of Sand & Brine*, 2010
David Hadbawnik, *Sir Gawain and the Green Knight*, 2011
The Rejection Group, *5 Works*, 2011
Sarah Jeanne Peters, *Triptych*, 2011
JodiAnn Stevenson, *Houses Don't Float*, 2011
Richard Owens, *Ballads*, 2012
John Hyland, *The Novice*, 2015
John Hyland, *The Novice*, 2015 (poem card)
David Hadbawnik, *Sports*, 2015
David Hadbawnik, *Sports*, 2015 (poem card)

Handwritten Press (*) (+)
Editor: Kristen Gallagher
Alicia Cohen, *bEAR*, 2000
Michael Magee, *Morning Constitutional*, 2001 (with Spencer Books)
Ikhyun Kim, *Il Jom Oh*, 2001
Aaron Levy, *Tombe: In Conversation with Kristen Gallagher*, 2001
Ed. Kristen Gallagher, *The Form of Our Uncertainty: A Tribute to Gil Ott,* 2001
(with Chax Press)
Michael Magee, *Leave the Light On*, 2002 (with Cuneiform Press)
Dan Featherston, *The Clock Maker's Memoir: 1-12*, 2002
Barbara Cole, *From "Situation Comedies,"* 2002
Nathan Austin, *(glost)*, 2002
Terrence Chiusano, *On Generation and Corruption: Parts I and II*, 2003
Gordon Hadfield and Sasha Steensen, *Correspondence: For La Paz*, 2004

Hostile Books
Editors: Joe Hall, Mike Flatt, Veronica Wong, and Ryan Sheldon
Joe Hall, *No*, 2015
Mike Flatt, *Asbestos*, Vol. 1, 2015
Ryan Sheldon, *Lemon*, 2015
Veronica Wong, *emmenagogue*, 2015

Leave Books
Editors: Kristin Prevallet, Juliana Spahr, Mark Wallace, Bill Tuttle, Elizabeth Burns,
Jefferson Hansen, and Brigham Taylor (began as a collective)
Keith Waldrop, *The Balustrade*, 1991
Bill Tuttle, *Private Residence*, 1991
Elizabeth Robinson, *Nearings: Two Poems*, 1991
Ann Pedone, *The Bird Happened*, 1991
Robert Kelly, *Manifesto: For the Next New York School*, 1991
Jefferson Hansen, *Gods to the Elbows*, 1991
Peter Ganick, *As Convenience*, 1991
Elizabeth Burns, *Letters to Elizabeth Bishop*, 1991
Susan Smith Nash, *Grammar of the Margin Road*, 1992 (published by Leave
Books? no publisher information listed)
Nina Zivancevic, *I Was This War Reporter in Egypt*, 1992
Mark Wallace, *You Bring Your Whole Life to the Material*, 1992
Joseph Torra, *Domino Sessions*, 1992
Juliana Spahr, *Nuclear*, 1992
Cathleen Shattuck, *The Three Queens*, 1992
Rena Rosenwasser, *Unplace . Place*, 1992
Pam Rehm, *Pollux*, 1992
Bin Ramke, *Catalogue Raisonné*, 1992
Nick Piombino, *Two Essays*, 1992
John Perlman, *Imperatives of Address*, 1992
Jena Osman, *Balance*, 1992
Gale Nelson, *Little Brass Pump*, 1992

Joyce Mansour, *Cris / Screams* (translated by Serge Gavronsky), 1992

Le Ann Jacobs, *Varieties of Inflorescence*, 1992

Susan Gevirtz, *Domino: Point of Entry*, 1992

Drew Gardner, *The Cover*, 1992

Tina Darragh, *Adv. Fans—The 1968 Series*, 1992

John Byrum, *Interalia: Among Other Things*, 1992

Dodie Bellamy, *Answer: From "The Letters of Mina Harker,"* 1992

Tom Beckett, *Economies of Pure Expenditure: A Notebook*, 1992

J. Battaglia, *Skin Problems*, 1992

Michael Basinski, *Mooon Bok: Petition, Invocation, & Homage*, 1992

Mark Wallace, *Complications from Standing in a Circle: The Dictionary Poems*, 1993

Susan M. Schultz, *Another Childhood*, 1993

Stephen Ratcliffe, *Private*, 1993

Lee Ann Brown, *Crush*, 1993

Julia Blumenreich, *Artificial Memory: 4 Ingathering Texts*, 1993

Bruce Andrews, *Divestiture—E*, 1993

Cole Swensen, *Walk*, 1994

Joe Ross, *Push*, 1994

Eléna Rivera, *Wale; Or, The Corse*, 1994

Joan Retallack, *Icarus Ffffalling*, 1994

Kristin Prevallet, *From "Perturbation, My Sister": (A Study of Max Ernst's "Hundred Headless Woman")*, 1994

Randall Potts, *Recant: (A Revision)*, 1994

Eds. Juliana Spahr, Mark Wallace, Kristin Prevallet, and Pam Rehm, *A Poetics of Criticism*, 1994

Sianne Ngai, *My Novel*, 1994

Kevin Magee, *Tedium Drum, Part II*, 1994

Kimberly Lyons, *Rhyme the Lake*, 1994

Lori Lubeski, *Stamina*, 1994

Cynthia Kimball, *Omen for a Birthday: Unravelled Poems*, 1994

Lisa Houston, *Liquid Amber*, 1994

Barbara Henning, *The Passion of Signs*, 1994

Sally Doyle, *Under the Neath*, 1994

Laynie Browne, *One Constellation*, 1994

Guy R. Beining, *Too Far to Hear*, 1994

Will Alexander, *Arcane Lavender Morals*, 1994

Kim Rosenfield, *Two Poems*, 1995

Mark McMorris, *Figures for a Hypothesis: (Suite)*, 1995

Ira Lightman, *Psychoanalysis of Oedipus*, 1995

Kevin Killian, *Santa*, 1995

C. S. Giscombe, *Two Sections from Giscome Road*, 1995

Marten Clibbens, *Sonet*, 1995

Little Scratch Pad Press / Little Scratch Pad Publications / Little Scratch Pad Editions / Little Scratch Pad Factory

Editor: Douglas Manson

Douglas Manson, *Edge of Perception: A Poem*, 2000

Douglas Manson, *Or VVV: Sinespoem 1-7*, 2003

Douglas Manson, *The Flatland Adventures of Blip and Ouch: A One-Act Closet Drama*, 2004

Douglas Manson, *A Book of Birthdays*, 2005

Aaron Lowinger, *Autobiography I: Perfect Game*, 2005 (with House Press)

Douglas Manson, *Sections in Four Seasons: From "To Becoming Normal: A Poem of Limit,"* 2006 (Bird in the Tree Edition)

Tom Yorty, *Words in Season: Poems*, 2007 (Little Scratch Pad Editions 6)

Nick Traenkner, *Accidental Thrust*, 2007 (Buff & Rust 2)

Kristianne Meal, *TwentyTwo: First Pallet*, 2007 (Buff & Rust 2)

Kristianne Meal, *TwentyTwo: First Pallet*, 2007 (Little Scratch Pad Editions 1)

Douglas Manson, *At Any Point: From "To Becoming Normal: A Poem of Limits,"* 2007 (Buff & Rust 4)

L. A. Howe, *NTR PIC E ST R*, 2007 (Little Scratch Pad Editions Chapbook 5)

Michael Basinski, *Of Venus 93*, 2007 (Little Scratch Pad Editions Chapbook 3)

Overherd at the River's Hip: 15 Buffalo Poets: Poems in Conversation, 2008 (Little Scratch Pad Editions number 2.3)

Jaye Bartell, *Ever After Never Under: 20 Choruses*, 2008 (Little Scratch Pad Editions second series 2)

Jonathan Skinner, *With Naked Foot*, 2009 (Little Scratch Pad Editions second series 4)

Geof Huth and Tom Beckett, Interpenetrations: Buffalo, 2009

Low Frequency

Editor: Michael Flatt

Please Welcome: Intros 14-15, 2015

a rawlings and Chris Turnbull, *The Great Canadian*, 2015

Nathaniel Mackey, *From "Blue Fasa,"* 2016

M Press

Editors: Alan Gilbert, Kristin Prevallet, Ram Rehm, and Lew Daly

Lew Daly, *Swallowing the Scroll: Late in a Prophetic Tradition with the Poetry of Susan Howe and John Taggart*, 1994 (*apex of the M* supplement #1)

Meow Press (+)

Editor: Joel Kuszai

Bill Tuttle, *Epistolary: First Series*, 1993

Elizabeth Robinson, *Iemanje*, 1993 (2nd printing March 1996)

Joel Kuszai?, *Brooklyn Yards*, 1993 (published by Meow Press? no author or publisher information listed)

Benjamin Friedlander, *Anterior Future*, 1993

Michael Basinski, *Cnyttan*, 1993 (2 states)

Misko Suvakovic, *Pas Tout: Fragments on Art, Culture, Politics, Poetics and Art Theory, 1994-1974*, 1994

Leslie Scalapino, *The Line*, 1994

Pierre Joris, *Winnetou Old*, 1994

Robert Fitterman, *Metropolis* (1-3), 1994

George Albon, *King*, 1994

Juliana Spahr, *Testimony*, 1995

James Sherry, *Four For*, 1995

Mark Johnson, *Three Bad Wishes*, 1995

Loss Pequeño Glazier, *The Parts*, 1995

Peter Gizzi, *New Picnic Time*, 1995

Benjamin Friedlander, *A Knot Is Not a Tangle*, 1995

Dubravka Djuric, *Cosmopolitan Alphabet*, 1995

Charles Bernstein, *The Subject*, 1995

Rachel Tzvia Back, *Litany*, 1995

Bruce Andrews, Charles Bernstein, and James Sherry, *Technology/Art: 20 Brief Proposals for Seminars on Art & Technology*, 1995 (no publisher information listed)

Gary Sullivan, *Dead Man*, 1996

Ron Silliman, *Xing*, 1996

Kenneth Sherwood, *That Risk*, 1996

Lisa Samuels, *Letters*, 1996

Lisa Robertson, *The Descent: A Light Comedy in Three Parts*, 1996

Meredith Quartermain, *Terms of Sale*, 1996

Kristin Prevallet, *28 for the Road*, 1996 (Meow Press Ephemera Series #6)

Jena Osman, *Jury*, 1996

Hank Lazer, *Early Days of the Lang Dynasty*, 1996

Wendy Kramer, *Patinas*, 1996
Cynthia Kimball, *Riven*, 1996 (Meow Press Ephemera Series #4)
Jorge Guitart, *Film Blanc*, 1996
Deanna Ferguson, *Rough Bush*, 1996
Robert Duncan, *Copy Book Entries* (transcribed by Robert J. Bertholf), 1996
Robert Creeley, *The Dogs of Auckland*, 1996
Natalee Caple, *The Price of Acorn*, 1996
Jonathan Brannen, *The Glass Man Left Waltzing*, 1996
Taylor Brady, *Is Placed Leaves*, 1996
Dodie Bellamy and Bob Harrison, *Broken English*, 1996
Natalie Basinski, *How the Cat Got Her Fur*, 1996 (Meow Press Ephemera Series #12)
Michael Basinski, *Barstokai*, 1996 (Meow Press Ephemera Series #5)
Michael Basinski, *Heebie-Jeebies*, 1996
Cynthia Kimball, *Annotations for Eliza*, 1997
Kevin Killian, *Argento Series*, 1997
William R. Howe, *A #'s: Onus*, 1997
Dodie Bellamy, *Hallucinations*, 1997
Charles Alexander, *Four Ninety Eight to Seven*, 1997
Susan M. Schultz, *Addenda*, 1998
Denise Newman, *Of Later Things Yet to Happen*, 1998
Noemie Maxwell, *Thrum*, 1998
Andrew Levy, *Elephant Surveillance to Thought*, 1998
Joel Kuszai, *Castle of Fun*, 1998 (Meow Press Ephemera Series #22)
Daniel Kanyandekwe, *One Plus One Is Three at Least: Selected Writings of Daniel Kanyandekwe* (edited by Julie Husband and Jim O'Loughlin), 1998
Benjamin Friedlander, *Selected Poems*, 1998
Stephen Cope, *Two Versions*, 1998 (Meow Press Ephemera Series #23)
Don Cheney, *The Qualms of Catallus & K-mart*, 1998
Graham Foust, *3 from Scissors*, 1998

Nickel City
Editor: Christopher W. Alexander
Christopher W. Alexander, *Admonitions*, 2000

Nominative Press Collective (*)
Editor: Christopher W. Alexander
Judy Roitman, *Diamond Notebooks 2*, 1998
Keston Sutherland, *Scratchcard Sally-Ann*, 1999
Matthias Regan, *The Most of It*, 1999
Christopher W. Alexander, *History Lesson*, 1999

Otamolloy
Editor: Michael Kelleher?
Michael Kelleher, *The Necessary Elephant*, 1998

Phylum Press (*)
Editors: Richard Deming and Nancy Kuhl
Richard Deming and Nancy Kuhl, *Winter 2000*, 2000
Roberto Tejada, *Amulet Anatomy*, 2001
Graham Foust, *6*, 2001
Joel Bettridge, *Shores*, 2001

Poetic Briefs
Editors: Editors: Jefferson Hansen, Elizabeth Burns, Juliana Spahr, Brigham Taylor, Bill C. Tuttle, and Mark Wallace?
Sterling D. Plumpp, *Blues for My Friend's Longings*, 1993 (Poetic Briefs Broadside #1)

Poetics Program
>Ed. Jena Osman, *Lab Book*, 1992
>Charles Bernstein, *What's Art Got to Do with It: The Status of the Subject of the Humanities in the Age of Cultural Studies*, 1992
>Brandon Boudreault, Allison Cardon, George Life, Claire Nashar, Sean Pears, Jacob Reber, and Corey Zielinski, *Launched in Context: Seven Essays on the Archive*, 2016 (published by Spring 2016 graduate student reading group on archives supervised by James Maynard)

Porci Con Le Ali (*)
Editor: Benjamin Friedlander
>Benjamin Friedlander, *Mininotes*, 1996
>Heiner Müller, *ABC*, 1996 (translated by Benjamin Friedlander)
>Benjamin Friedlander, *Period Piece*, 1998
>Benjamin Friedlander, *Partial Objects*, 1999

P-Queue / Queue Books
Editor: Andrew Rippeon
>Richard Taransky and Michelle Taransky, *The Plans Caution*, 2007
>Eds. Michael Cross and Andrew Rippeon, *Building Is a Process, Light Is an Element: Essays and Excursions for Myung Mi Kim*, 2008
>Erica Lewis (poems) and Mark Stephen Finein (artwork), *The Precipice of Jupiter*, 2009
>José Felipe Alvergue, *Us Look Up / There Red Dwells*, 2008
>Geof Huth, *Eyechart Poems*, 2009
>Jimbo Blachly and Lytle Shaw, *Pre-Chewed Tapas*, 2010
>Simone de Beauvoir and Vanessa Place, *The Father & Childhood*, 2011

Punch Press (*)
Editor: Richard Owens
>Richard Owens, *From "Bel & the Dragon,"* 2007
>Brian Mornar, *Repatterning*, 2007
>Bill Griffiths, *And the Life (The Motion) Is Always There*, 2007
>Dale Smith, *Susquehanna: Speculative Historical Commentary and Lyric*, 2008
>*Rave On: Punch Press, Damn the Caesars*, 2008
>Richard Owens, *Two Ballads*, 2008
>Ben Lyle Bedard, *Implicit Lyrics*, 2008
>Sotère Torregian, *Envoy*, 2009
>Richard Owens, *Punch Press*, 2009?
>Thomas Meyer, *Kintsugi*, 2009
>Natalie Knight, *Archipelagos*, 2009
>Carrie Etter, *Divinations*, 2010
>Richard Owens, *Cecilia Anne at One*, 2010

Quinella Press
Editor: Nicholas Laudadio
>Michael Kelleher, *Three Poems*, 1998
>Graham Foust, *Three Poems*, 1998
>Taylor Brady, *Three Poems*, 1998
>Joel Bettridge, *Three Poems*, 1998

RIF/T
Editors: Kenneth Sherwood and Loss Pequeño Glazier?
>Loss Pequeño Glazier, *Electronic Projection Poetries / Kenneth Sherwood, Hard [HRt] Return*, 1995

Rubba Ducky (*)
Editors: Christopher W. Alexander and Matthias Regan

William Fuller, *Avoid Activity*, 2003

Henry Card, *People's History Pop-Up: For the People by the People*, 2003? (published by Rubba Ducky? no publisher information listed)

Henry Card, *Freedom Fighter Portraits*, 2003? (published by Rubba Ducky? no publisher information listed)

Tailspin Press

Editor: William R. Howe

Mark Wallace, *The Sponge Has Holes: A Bibliophilic Event*, 1994 (Tailspin Press Chapbook 002)

William R. Howe, *Tripflea: (Book)*, 1994

Eds. Raymond Federman and William R. Howe, *Sam Changed Tense*, 1995 (with Weird Sisters Press)

Michael Basinski, *SleVep: A Performance*, 1995 (Tailspin Press Chapbook 003)

Michael Basinski and William R. Howe, *Place Your Text Here*, 1995

Nils Ya, *Chastisement Rewarded: A Poetics of the Fragment*, 1996

William R. Howe, *Pollywannahydral: A Shape*, 1996 (Tailspin Press Chapbook 006)

Kenneth Sherwood, *Text Squared: A Word-Sculpture*, 1997? (Tailspin Press Chapbook 004)

Peter Jaeger, *Stretch Conflates: An Exquisite Corpse*, 1997 (Tailspin Press Chapbook 007)

William R. Howe, *A*, 1997

Trifecta Press

Editor: Nicholas Laudadio

Graham Foust, *Endless Surgery*, 1997

Troll Thread (*)

Editors: Joey Yearous-Algozin, Holly Melgard, Chris Sylvester, Divya Victor

Joseph Yearous-Algozin, *The Lazarus Project: Alien vs. Predator*, 2010

Chris Sylvester, *The Republic*, 2010

Chris Sylvester, *Grid*, 2010?

Chris Sylvester, *Biography: There Past*, 2010?

Joseph Yearous-Algozin, *Buried*, 2011

Divya Victor, *Partial Dictionary of the Unnamable*, 2011

Divya Victor, *Partial Directory of the Unnamable*, 2011

Chris Sylvester, *Total Walkthrough*, 2011

Holly Melgard, *Colors for Baby*, 2011 (Poems for Baby Trilogy 1)

Holly Melgard, *Foods for Baby*, 2011(Poems for Baby Trilogy 2)

Holly Melgard, *Shapes for Baby*, 2011 (Poems for Baby Trilogy 3)

Shiv Kotecha, *Paint the Rock*, 2011

Joey Yearous-Algozin, *The Lazarus Project: Night and Fog*, 2012

Joey Yearous-Algozin, *The Lazarus Project: Faces of Death*, 2012

Joey Yearous-Algozin, *The Lazarus Project: Heaven*, 2012

Joey Yearous-Algozin, *911 9/11 Calls in 911 Pt. Font: Part 1*, 2012

Joey Yearous-Algozin, *9/11 911 Calls in 911 Pt. Font: Part 2*, 2012

Joey Yearous-Algozin, *The Lazarus Project: Nine Eleven*, 2012

Divya Victor, *Partial Derivative of the Unnamable*, 2012

Chris Sylvester, *Junk Rooms*, 2012

Chris Sylvester, *Still Life with Every Panda Express Food Item Three Times: For Chris Alexander's "Panda,"* 2012

Maker, *Poems for Money*, 2012

Holly Melgard, *The Making of the Americans*, 2012

Trisha Low, *Purge Vol. 1: The Last Will & Testament of Trisha Low*, 2012

Isaac Linder, *The Moviegoer*, 2012

Shiv Kotecha, *Outfits*, 2012

Josef Kaplan, *1-100*, 2012 (16 vols.)

Sarah Dowling, *Birds & Bees*, 2012

Jeremiah Rush Bowen, *Nazi (Argument on the Internet (5/31/11 - 8/31/11) vol. 1
)*, 2012

Jeremiah Rush Bowen, *Faggot (Argument on the Internet (5/31/11 - 8/31/11) vol.
2)*, 2012

Uprising Press (+)
Editor: Mark Hammer?

Barbara Tedlock, *From "The Beautiful and the Dangerous"* / Michael Basinski,
Egyptian Gods 6, 1991 (Uprising 1)

Elizabeth Willis, *From "Songs for (A)"* / Stephen Ratcliffe, *Nostalgia*, 1991
(Uprising 2)

Susan Howe, *From "Melville's Marginalia,"* 1991 (published by Uprising
Press? no publisher information listed)

Rachel Blau DuPlessis, *From "Draft 2: She,"* / Michael Boughn, *Stone Work
V* 1991 (Uprising 3)

Michael Basinski, *Her Roses*, 1992 (Uprising 9)

Edward Dorn, *The Denver Landing: 11 Aug 1993*, 1993

Vigilance Society (*)
Editor: Anonymous

Eli Drabman, *From "Daylight on the Wires,"* 2006?

Eli Drabman, *Daylight on the Wires*, 2007?

Wild Horses of Fire Press
Editor: Thom Donovan

Thom Donovan (with images by Abby Walton), *Tears Are These Veils*, 2004

IV. BOOKS, CHAPBOOKS, BROADSIDES, AND OTHER PUBLICATIONS PRINTED WITHOUT A PUBLISHER (ORGANIZED CHRONOLOGICALLY):

Ed. Mark Hammer, *The Image of Language, The Language of Image: UB Poetic
Voices: 1992*, 1992 (publisher unknown)

Jonathan Fernandez, *Ah! Thel Is Like a Watry Bow*, 1993? (published by the
author)

William R. Howe, *Projective Verse: A Preformance Script with/out Type Writer
in 5 Parts*, 1994 (published by the author)

Alan Gilbert and Kristin Prevallet, *A Selective Bibliography of French Poetry in
Translation Published in American Small Press Poetry Journals from 1980-1992*, 1995
(publisher unknown)

Joel Kuszai, *Filmic 10: Salt Series*, 1995 (published by the author)

Cynthia Kimball, *Song for a Handfasting: (For Two Voices)*, 1995 (publisher
unknown)

Benjamin Friedlander, *The Missing Occasion of Saying Yes*, 1996 (published by
the author)

Kristin Prevallet, *The Rhyme of the Ancient Mariner: An Interpretation of the
Poem by S. T. Coleridge*, 1997 (VHS recording)

William R. Howe, *Notions of Nationalistic Feverish Paradigmatic Coronal*, 1998
(published by the author)

Christopher W. Alexander, *Eschatology: A Reader*, 1999 (published by the
author)

Terrence Chiusano, Ikhyun Kim, and Brandon Stosuy, *Last Friday, May 12,
2000*, 2000 (publisher unknown)

Sandra Guerreiro, *Finger Print: Impressão Digital*, 2001 (published by the
author)

Terry Cuddy and Mirela Ivanciu, *Transient Views of Western New York*, 2001
(VHS recording)

A Degraded Textual Affair, 2002 (edited by William R. Howe?)

Linda Russo, *Solvency*, 2005 (publisher unknown?)

Susan Howe, *Loving Friends and Kindred*, 2006 (printed by Sarah Campbell?)

Steve McCaffery, *Appelle's Cut*, 2007 (printed by Matt Chambers, Michael Cross, and Richard Owens?)

Michael Cross, *Foresting*, 2007 (printed by Andrew Rippeon?)

George Oppen, *The Poem*, 2008 (printed by Andrew Rippeon?)

Susan Howe, *I heard myself as if you*, 2008 (printed by Richard Owens and Andrew Rippeon)

Michael Sikkema, David Hadbawnik, and Nava Fader, *Sideways*, 2009? (printed by David Hadbawnik)

Scrap Paper: A Small Press Portfolio, 2009

Richard Owens, *Archer Disowns*, 2010 (printed by Andrew Rippeon?)

Andrew Rippeon, *The hill I am of* / Julia Bloch, *The Selfist*, 2010? (printed by Andrew Rippeon)

Andrew Rippeon, *5 from "Flights,"* 2010? (printed by Andrew Rippeon?)

Divya Victor, *From "Sutures 3.11.10,"* 2010? (printed by Andrew Rippeon?)

V. READING, TALK, AND PERFORMANCE SERIES

[These student-organized series have been in addition to the Poetics Program's departmental series Wednesdays at 4 Plus (Fall 1990-Fall 2004) and Poetics Plus (Spring 2005-present)]

Another Reading Series
Organizers: Barbara Cole, Gordon Hadfield, and Sasha Steensen
Early 2000s

BYOB
Organizer: ?
2011

(co)ludere
Organizer: Divya Victor
2008

Cornershop
Organizer: Anya Lewin
1998

Deluxe Rubber Reading Series
Organizer: Mark Peters
1999

Dove | Tail
Organizer: Victoria Brockmeier
2014

Emergency Poetry Reading
Organizer: ?
Dates?

Exchange Rate
Organizer: ?
2004?

Last Friday
Organizers: Linda Russo and Christopher W. Alexander
1999

ñ (enye), Poesía y Crítica en la SUNY-Búfalo: A Non-Unilingual Reading Series of Poetry, Criticism and Translation
Organizers: Rosa Alcala and Kristin Dykstra
2000-2002

Opening Night
Organizers: ?
Fall 2008-present

Poetics Plus Plus
Ogranizers: Graduate Poetics Group
2015

Poets Theater
Organizer: David Hadbawnik
2009-2012

Portable Lecture Series / Portable Talk
Organizer: ?
Dates?

Red Flannel (+)
Organizer: Mark Hammer
1988-1995

Refer
Organizer: Divya Victor
2009, 2011

Rust Talks
Organizers: Kristen Gallagher and Tim Shaner
2000-2004

Saloon Conversation Series
Organizer: ?
2006

Scratch and Dent
Organizers: Cornershop and Small Press Collective
Dates?

Small Press in the Archive
Organizers: Margaret Konkol (founder), Nicholas Morris, and Ronan Crowley
2007-2014

Steel Bar
Organizer: Jonathan Skinner
2001

VI. STUDENT-ORGANIZED SYMPOSIA:

Writing from the New Coast: First Festival of New Poetry at SUNY Buffalo
Organizers: Juliana Spahr and Peter Gizzi
March 31-April 3, 1993

Place(less Place): A Gathering of Poets
Organizers: Small Press Collective

June 19-20, 1998

Eye, Ear & Mind: A Conference on the Poetry of Ronald Johnson
Organizer: Joel Bettridge
March 15-18, 2000

Prose Acts
Organizers: Christopher W. Alexander and Brandon Stosuy?
October 18-21, 2001

A Degraded Textual Affair
Organizer: William R. Howe?
June 6, 2002

Re-reading Louis Zukofsky's *Bottom: On Shakespeare*: A Symposium for Students, Poets
& Scholars
Organizers: Kyle Schlesinger and Thom Donovan?
October 31-November 1, 2003

(Re:)Working the Ground: A Conference on the Late Writings of Robert Duncan
Organizers: James Maynard, Robert J. Bertholf, and Michael Basinski
April 20-22, 2006

Contemporary British Poets
Organizer: Matthew Chambers
April 12, 2007

George Oppen: A Centenary Conversation
Organizers: Andrew Rippeon and ?
April 23-25, 2008

A Symposium on *Dura*
Organizer: Andrew Rippeon
November 21, 2008

Poet-publishers: A Small Press Symposium
Organizers: Richard Owens and Andrew Rippeon?
April 19-20, 2009

Modes of Love and Reason: A Bernadette Mayer Symposium
Organizer: Robert Dewhurst?
April 1, 2011

Clairvoyant Codes: A Symposium on the Work of Hannah Weiner
Organizers: Robert Dewhurst and Sean Reynolds?
October 19, 2012

VII. RADIO SHOWS

T-n-T Broadcasts
Edited by Martin Spinelli
1995

LINEbreak (+)
Hosted by Charles Bernstein; co-produced by Charles Bernstein and Martin Spinelli
Recorded 1996-1996 in Buffalo and elsewhere

Inks Audible (WHLD 1270 AM, Buffalo)
Hosted and produced by Doug Manson
Broadcast ca. 2005

Spoken Arts (WBFO 88.7 FM, Buffalo)
Hosted by Sarah Campbell
Broadcast ca. 2006

CONTRIBUTORS

Rosa Alcalá is the author of three books of poetry, most recently *MyOTHER TONGUE* (Futurepoem, 2017). Her poems, along with critical perspectives on her work, are included in Stephen Burt's The Poem is You: 60 Contemporary American Poems and How to Read Them (Harvard UP, 2016) and other anthologies. The recipient of an NEA Translation Fellowship and runner-up for a PEN Translation Award, she is the editor and co-translator of *Cecilia Vicuña: New & Selected Poems* (Kelsey Street Press, forthcoming). She has taught for CantoMundo, and was the 2016 Allen Ginsberg Fellow at Naropa's Jack Kerouac School of Disembodied Poetics. She teaches in UTEP's Bilingual MFA Program.

Michael Anania is the author of numerous collections of poetry as well as the novel *The Red Menace*. He has received the Friends of Literature Poetry Prize, a Best American Short Stories Award, a Pushcart Prize, and various other awards. He taught for many years at the University of Illinois—Chicago.

Michael Basinski is a poet. After 33 years in the Poetry Collection of the University Libraries, he retired in 2017. As Curator Emeritus, he now spends each day fully in the realm of the poem. He is a UB grad.

Charles Bernstein is the author of *Near/Miss* (2018), *Pitch of Poetry* (University of Chicago, 2016), and Recalculating (2013), from the University of Chicago Press, and *All the Whiskey in Heaven: Selected Poems* (Farrar, Straus & Giroux, 2010). Bernstein is Donald T. Regan Professor of English and Comparative Literature at the University of Pennsylvania, where he is co-director of PennSound. At Buffalo, Bernstein was appointed the David Gray Professor of Poetry and Letters in 1990, and subsequently SUNY Distinguished Professor. Bernstein was a co-founder and director of the Poetics Program and the Electronic Poetry Center. He left Buffalo for Penn in 2003. Bernstein is a fellow of the American Academy of Arts and Sciences.

Michael Boughn is the author of *Cosmographia — A Post-Lucretian Faux Micro Epic* (Book Thug, 2011) and City — A Poem from the End of the World (Spuyten Duyvil, 2016). His most recent book is *Hermetic Divagations* (Swimmers Group, 2017), an homage to H.D. With Kent Johnson, he is co-editor of the online journal, Dispatches from the Poetry Wars.

Eun-Gwi Chung is Professor in the Department of English Literature and Culture at Hankuk University of Foreign Studies, Seoul, Korea. She got her Ph. D at State University of New York at Buffalo in 2005. She was the director of the Department of English Literature from 2013-2014 and the Editor-in-Chief of the prestigious scholarly journal in Korea, *In/Out: English Studies in Korea* from 2013-2015. She teaches English literature, poetry and translation, focusing on cultural poetics, multiethnic literature, translation theory and practice, world literature. Her publications include articles, translations, poems, and reviews, and several book chapters on poetics. She is the Daesan recipient of Korean literature translation, and the Korea Literature Translation Institute recipient of Korean poetry translation.

Penelope Highton Creeley was born in London, raised in New Zealand, studied at the University of Otago in Dunedin NZ, and at Cornell University in Ithaca NY. Married Robert Creeley in 1977, with whom she had 2 children, William and Hannah. Participated in community work in Buffalo, NY, and now lives in Buffalo and Maine.

Robert Creeley was the author of more than sixty books. He is widely recognized as one of the most influential American poets of the 20th century. He taught at the University at Buffalo from 1966 to 2003. He died in 2005.

Michael Davidson is Distinguished Professor Emeritus at the University of California, San Diego. He is the author of *The San Francisco Renaissance: Poetics and Community at Mid-Century* (Cambridge U Press, 1989), *Ghostlier Demarcations: Modern Poetry and the Material Word* (U of California Press, 1997), *Guys Like Us: Citing Masculinity in Cold War Poetics* (U of Chicago, 2003). and *Concerto for the Left Hand: Disability and the Defamiliar Body* (U of Michigan, 2008). His most recent critical book, *Outskirts of Form: Practicing Cultural Poetics* was published in 2011 by Wesleyan University Press. He is the editor of *The New Collected Poems of George Oppen* (New Directions, 2002). He is the author of six books of poetry, the most recent of which is *Bleed Through: New and Selected Poems* (Coffee House Press, 2013).

Carl Dennis is the author of thirteen books of poetry, including *Practical Gods, New and Selected Poems* (1974-2004), *Callings* (2010), and *Night School* (2017). A winner of the Pulitzer Prize and the Ruth Lilly Prize, he taught for many years in the English Department of the State University of New York, and in the Warren Wilson Writing Program in North Carolina. He lives in Buffalo, New York.

Geoffrey Gatza is an award-winning editor, publisher and poet. He is the driving force behind BlazeVOX, a small press located in Buffalo, NY and was named by the Huffington Post as one of the Top 200 Advocates for American Poetry. He is the author many books of poetry, including *Apollo, Secrets of my Prison House, Kenmore: Poem Unlimited* and *HouseCat Kung Fu: Strange Poems for Wild Children*. Most recently his work has appeared in *FENCE* and *Tarpaulin Sky*. His play on Marcel Duchamp was staged in an art installation in Philadelphia and performed in NYC.

Loss Pequeño Glazier is Professor Emeritus of Media Study (University at Buffalo) and Director, Electronic Poetry Center. He is author of the first book-length study on digital poiesis, *Digital Poetics: the Making of E-Poetries* (Alabama UP, 2002), *Anatman, Pumpkin Seed, Algorithm* (Salt, 2003), and *Small Press: An Annotated Guide* (Greenwood, 1992). Many of his oft-cited, acclaimed book-length digital literary projects such as *Bromeliads, Io Sono At Swoons, Territorio Libre, Four Tesselations*, and the transmedial *poésie concrète book, cordoniz* are available on his Web page. His forthcoming *Array Poetics* launches ecstatic colocations of the digital-literary-as-writing, plying code, variants, algorithmic soundings, the rapturous tangle of the "media mestizo" (vs. the "born digital's" cultural privilege).

Albert Glover is a poet, editor and publisher born in Boston 1942. He received his BA from McGill University in 1962, his PhD from SUNY at Buffalo in 1968 [dissertation *Charles Olson: Letters for Origin*, dir. John Clarke]. He taught at St. Lawrence University department of English from 1968 – 2005, and is currently Frank P. Piskor Professor of English emeritus. A complete bibliography of published work is available at author's page, Amazon.com. *A Curriculum of the Soul*, a collaborative text in twenty-eight books based on "A Plan for a Curriculum of the Soul" by Charles Olson is currently available from Spuyten Duyvil in two volumes.

Susan Howe's collection of poems *That This*, won the Bollingen Prize in 2011. In 2017 she received the Robert Frost award for distinguished lifetime achievement in American poetry. Her earlier critical study, *My Emily Dickinson*, was re-issued in 2007 with an introduction by Eliot Weinberger. Three CDs in collaboration with the musician/composer David Grubbs, *Thiefth and Souls of the Labadie Tract, Frolic Architecture, WOODSLIPPERCOUNTERCLATTER*, were released on the Blue Chopsticks label (2005; 2011). Her selected essays *The Quarry* was published in 2015 and a poetry collection *Debths* (2017) both from New Directions.

Bruce Jackson is SUNY Distinguished Professor and James Agee Professor of American Culture at UB. He is the author or editor of 36 books. In collaboration with Diane Christian he made five documentary films. His photographs have been widely published (*Aperture, New York Times, New Yorker*, etc.) and exhibited (Albright-Knox Art

Gallery, Center for Documentary Studies, Aperture Gallery, etc.). His field recordings led to a dozen disc and tape releases. One of them earned a Grammy nomination; another was the basis for a 2017 production by New York's famed Wooster Group. For his ethnographic and anti-death penalty work, the French government named him Chevalier in both the Ordre des Arts et des Lettres, and the Ordre national du Mérite.

Myung Mi Kim is James H. McNulty Chair of English and Director of the Poetics Program at the University at Buffalo, State University of New York. Kim is the author of *Penury, Commons, DURA, The Bounty*, and *Under Flag*, winner of The Multicultural Publisher's Exchange Award of Merit. Her fellowships and honors include awards from the Fund for Poetry, the Djerassi Resident Artists Program, Gertrude Stein Awards in Innovative North American Poetry, and the State University of New York Chancellor's Award for Excellence in Scholarship and Creative Activity.

James Maynard, a graduate of the Poetics Program, is Curator of the Poetry Collection of the University Libraries, University at Buffalo, The State University of New York. He has published widely on and edited or coedited a number of collections relating to the poet Robert Duncan, including *Ground Work: Before the War/In the Dark* (New Directions, 2006), *(Re:)Working the Ground: Essays on the Late Writings of Robert Duncan* (Palgrave Macmillan, 2011), and *Such Conjunctions: Robert Duncan, Jess, and Alberto de Lacerda* (BlazeVox Books, 2014). His edition of *Robert Duncan: Collected Essays and Other Prose* (University of California Press, 2014) received the Poetry Foundation's 2014 Pegasus Award for Poetry Criticism. A critical study *Robert Duncan and the Pragmatist Sublime* is due out in spring 2018 from the University of New Mexico Press and he is currently editing a volume of Duncan's uncollected prose.

Steve McCaffery is the author of over 40 books and chapbooks of poetry and criticism and his work has been translated into a dozen or so languages. A founding member of the sound poetry ensemble Four Horsemen, TRG (Toronto Research Group) and the College of Canadian "Pataphysics and long-time resident of Toronto, he is now David Gray Professor of Poetry and Letters at the University at Buffalo.

Peter Middleton writes on modern poetry, and on science and literature. He is the author of *Distant Reading* (Alabama UP) a collection of essays on poetry performance and poetics, and *Physics Envy* (Chicago UP) a book about American poetry and science in the second half of the twentieth century. His poetry is collected in *Aftermath* (Salt) and *Tell Me About It* (Barque). An essay on "unknowns" which started as a talk at Kelly Writers House is forthcoming in Chicago Review. A collection of essays on recent poetry is due to be published next year by University of New Mexico Press, and he is currently writing a book of creative non-fiction on the broad theme of codes, cryptography and communication. He teaches in the English department at the University of Southampton, UK.

Debora Ott is a conceptualist whose abiding passion is to build community through a shared appreciation of the creative process. She is the former Literature/Arts Education Program Manager at the Georgia Council for the Arts, the founder of Just Buffalo Literary Center http://www.justbuffalo.org/ and LitTAP http://www.littap.org/, and a member of the Steering Committee of LitNet http://litnet.org/. A dot connector, literary curator, creative consultant, and arts advocate and organizer, she designs and implements programs and networks that invite people in communities to value, access and engage in the arts.

Sean Pears is a graduate student in the Poetics Program. His writing and reviews have appeared in *The Emily Dickinson Journal, Jacket2, The Colorado Review, The Santa Fe Writers Project Quarterly*, and elsewhere. His dissertation focuses on nineteenth-century American literature. He runs the online audio-journal of poetry, *ythm*, at www.ythmjournal.org.

Evelyn Reilly has written three books that attempt to manifest a poetics of the Anthropocene: *Styrofoam* and *Apocalypso*, both published by Roof Books, and

Echolocation, forthcoming from Roof in 2018. Her poetry and essays have been published in many journals and anthologies, including *The Arcadia Project: Postmodernism and the Pastoral*; *The &NOW Awards2: The Best Innovative Writing; Omniverse*; *The Eco-language Reader*; and will be included in the forthcoming *Earth Bound: Compass Points for an Ecopoetics*, edited by Jonathan Skinner and *Big Energy Poets of the Anthropocene*, edited by Heidi Lynn Staples and Amy King. Reilly has taught at The Poetry Project at St. Mark's Church and the Summer Writing Program of Naropa University, and has been a curator of the Segue Reading Series in New York City.

Andrew Rippeon teaches American literature at Hamilton College, with a focus on poetry and poetics from the 19th century to the present. His research explores intersections between poetics and materiality (including sound, typography, and artists' books), and he is also the editor of a collection of letters and unpublished prose from Larry Eigner to Jonathan Williams. In addition to his teaching and research, he is also the founder and director of Hamilton College's letterpress laboratory, a collaborative space for the study of typography and material textuality, and the production of limited-edition prints and books.

Juliana Spahr's most recent book is *That Winter the Wolf Came* on Commune Editions, a press she co-edits with Joshua Clover and Jasper Bernes.

Stephanie Weisman received her MA in English/Creative Writing program from SUNY-Buffalo. Awarded an artist-in-residency from Just Buffalo/NYSCA for her Masters thesis poem, *Dancemasters*, she developed it into a solo performance. After moving to the Bay Area, she founded The Marsh, a breeding ground for new performance in 1989; where she serves as Artistic/Executive Director. In 2006, Weisman premiered her opera *Aphrodisia*, for a women's chorus, chamber ensemble, dancer and performer. In 2018, she will premiere her solo performance musical, *Breed and Rescue*. She is currently writing a memoir, *30 days/30 years*, 30 days to become a performer/30 years running The Marsh. She lives in Oakland with her husband, Richard and her 3 dogs, Trinity, Marsha and Junior.

Max Wickert immigrated from Germany in 1952. After graduate work at Yale, he served on the University at Buffalo's English Department faculty until his retirement in 2006. He is the author of three published collections of poetry and of three volumes of verse translation from the Italian of Torquato Tasso. With Hubert Kulterer, he co-translated Beat poet Tuli Kupferberg's *1000 Ways to Live Without Working* into German. As founding Director of the Outriders Poetry Project, he has edited twelve books by Buffalo area writers as well as two anthologies, *An Outriders Anthology* (2013) and *Four Buffalo Poets* (2016).

The Plonsker Series

Each year Lake Forest College Press / &NOW Books awards the Madeleine P. Plonsker Emerging Writers Residency Prize to a poet or fiction writer under the age of forty who has yet to publish a first book. The winning writer receives $10,000, three weeks in residency on the campus of Lake Forest College, and publication of his or her book by Lake Forest College Press / &NOW Books, with distribution by Northwestern University Press.

Past winners:

- JD Scott, *Moonflower, Nightshade, All the Hours of the Day* (fiction)
- Meg Whiteford, *Callbacks* (fiction)
- Jessica Savitz, *Hunting Is Painting* (poetry)
- Gretchen Henderson, *Galerie de Difformité* (fiction)
- Jose Perez Beduya, *Throng* (poetry)
- Elizabeth Gentry, *Housebound* (fiction)
- Cecilia K. Corrigan, *Titanic* (poetry)
- Matthew Nye, *Pike and Bloom* (fiction)
- Christopher Rey Pérez, *gauguin's notebook* (poetry)

For more information about the Plonsker Prize and how to apply, visit lakeforest.edu/plonksker